DELAWARE
WEDDINGS

DELAWARE WEDDINGS

THREE-IN-ONE COLLECTION

JENNIFER JOHNSON

BARBOUR
PUBLISHING

Our mission is to publish and distribute inspirational products offering exceptional value and biblical encouragement to the masses.

Member of the
Evangelical Christian
Publishers Association

Printed in the United States of America.

Dear Readers,

Once again, I am thrilled and humbled to have the privilege of writing this letter to you. Let me just start by saying, I love this series. I love it because it is so close to my heart. Each story deals with an unexpected pregnancy. The amazing thing about the God we serve is that He can and will take our unexpected, unplanned—even unwanted—pregnancies, and He will bring good from them. He'll bring GREAT from them. Praise God, He is always about reconciliation and restoration.

These contemporary stories, *Finding Home*, *For Better or Worse*, and *Gaining Love*, are set in our country's first state, Delaware. The stories focus on a family. Cam Reynolds, the hero in *Finding Home* and Kelly Coyle, the heroine in *For Better or Worse*, are siblings. Zoey Coyle is Kelly's oldest daughter. As a whole, the family is largely based on my own. In some ways, Kelly is forced to deal with her oldest daughter, just as my mother had to "cope" with me during my teen years. Additionally, Kelly, like me, is the mother of three daughters, who happen to be the same ages as mine. Adoption is also intertwined in these stories, and I am blessed to have two adopted sisters. Overall, my own family is woven throughout these stories. They were so much fun to write.

I hope you enjoy these books. I pray God uses them to touch your heart, and that they will encourage you to draw closer to our Lord and Savior, Jesus Christ. I would love for you to visit my Web site at www.jenniferjohnsonbooks.com. You can also e-mail me at jenwrites4god@bellsouth.net. God is so good!

Sincerely,
Jennifer Johnson

FINDING HOME

Dedication

This book is dedicated to my little sister, Tabitha Lydia Miles. Tabitha, you are a truly beautiful young lady, not only physically but also because of your deep love for Jesus. I pray that God blesses your life and that you always strive to live for Him. I love you.

Prologue

The unrelenting wails of the newborn filled the hospital delivery room. All other noise—beeps of monitors, instructions from the doctor, murmurs from nurses—seemed to stop. Sadie could only hear the cries of the infant. Before her mind could wrap around the truth of what had just happened, the doctor laid the squalling child on Sadie's chest.

Sadie looked at the babe, barely wiped off from having just made her entrance into the world. The tiny girl had a head full of dark brown hair, just like her mama.

But I'm not her mama.

In truth, Sadie had just delivered the baby, but she wouldn't be the child's mother. Brenda Reynolds would be her mom, and Cam Reynolds would be her dad.

Tears filled Sadie's eyes. The six- or seven-pound weight of the baby seemed more than her chest could bear. Sadie's legs shook with no hope of ever stopping. It was as if every emotion she'd ever known in her life had left her body with the delivery of the baby. Now her body remained little more than a cavity, raw and empty.

Touching the baby's soft head ever so slightly with her fingertips, a wave of emotion washed over her as quickly as it had evaporated only moments before. *I love you, baby girl.*

As if sensing Sadie's thoughts, the child quieted and looked up into Sadie's eyes. Her gaze seemed to say, "So you are my mommy." Sadie's heart broke and tears streamed down her cheeks. The moment ended and the tiny girl began another chorus of squalls.

"Would you like to kiss her before she goes?" The nurse's voice was soft, and Sadie noted the tenderness in the older woman's expression.

She nodded and pressed a soft kiss on the infant's head. "I love you, little girl," she whispered before lifting the bundle into the nurse's arms.

The nurse wrapped the baby—Sadie's baby—in a pink blanket and walked out of the room. Sadie knew Cam and Brenda waited outside the door. They waited for their baby, for her baby.

The emptiness, sheer, strong, and painful, overwhelmed her again. A sudden heaving of sobs filled her chest and spilled from a void that made no sense.

How could she feel so much in the midst of such emptiness? How could this be happening to her?

There are always consequences for actions.

The reminder wasn't condemnation, but rather a fact. Sadie had chosen to step outside of God's will, and natural consequences had taken place. Having left the safety of her parents' home for college, Sadie had fallen into the arms of her first real love. At least, Sadie thought it had been love. But when Sadie discovered she was pregnant, her boyfriend wanted out of the relationship, and her parents were devastated. At nineteen, Sadie knew she couldn't raise the baby. Her college church family guided her through the adoption process.

And now my baby is gone.

Sobs racked her body again. She knew God had forgiven her sin. She knew God was guiding her life once more. She knew God had led her to the right couple to adopt her baby girl.

So why do I feel so much pain?

Chapter 1

Five years later

Rain beat Sadie's windshield. The sky, dark and angry, fueled Sadie's mood. The father of one of her students had been undeservedly harsh because his son had not made the progress dear ol' Dad felt was appropriate. As an occupational therapist for their small county in North Carolina, Sadie had shown the man document after document detailing the marked improvements his young son had made since the car accident that had stolen much of the child's memory, including his academic memories. This father wanted his son to be "just like everyone else" and negated the wonderful strides the boy and his special education teacher had made. Paining Sadie further, he'd voiced his complaints in front of the child. Sadie wondered how much harder it would be to help the student improve when the new school year rolled around again.

Frustrated, Sadie parked the car in front of her small apartment. In less than a month, the lease would be up on the one-bedroom place she'd called home for the last two years. The weeks couldn't pass fast enough.

Sadie grabbed the umbrella from the backseat, stuck it out the driver's door, and popped it open. The wind caught it, flipping it inside out and rendering the umbrella useless. Letting out a disgruntled huff, Sadie stepped out of the car and straight into a puddle.

"That's just great," she muttered as she lifted her nearly new suede shoe out of the puddle. "Okay, this day can only get better."

She swiped a wet strand of hair away from her cheek and raced toward her mailbox. Five years and two weeks had passed. She knew that any day she would receive a package containing several pictures and a letter. Rain, sleet, hail, sunshine—nothing would keep her from checking the mail until that package arrived.

She opened the mailbox door. A large, white, duct-taped envelope rested beneath a pile of junk mail. Gingerly, she pulled it out and noted the Delaware address in the top left-hand corner. *It's here.* She tucked her treasure into her jacket, protecting it from the elements.

She raced to the front door and fumbled with her keys to unlock the door. Her heart raced in anticipation of opening the package. Once inside, she kicked off her shoes and placed the mail on the table. After racing into her bedroom, she slipped into a comfortable gown and a robe. She wanted to relish every picture, devour every word Brenda Reynolds wrote. Being garbed in wet clothes would only distract her.

With shaky hands, she grabbed her "Ellie" album from the bookshelf in her bedroom. How could she ever repay the Reynoldses for naming the baby after her? Five years before, Sadie Ellis had given birth to a baby girl, and her adoptive parents, Cam and Brenda Reynolds, named her Ellie in honor of the birth mother. What other adoptive parents would do that?

Unexpected tears filled her eyes as she thought of how God had blessed her baby with the perfect couple. To this day, this very moment, Sadie wished she had been able to keep her little girl. And yet Sadie knew then, as she still intellectually knew now, God had provided Cam and Brenda for Ellie.

Sadie cuddled up on her couch with the album and package. As she did every year, she looked at the album before she opened the new package. She wanted to reexperience Ellie's growth from year to year and then bask in the changes the new package would reveal.

The first year of Ellie's life, Sadie had been surprised at how much she looked like her biological father. But the next year, Ellie's appearance shifted to look more like Sadie. By the time she was four, Ellie's hair had grown just past her shoulders and her eyes had deepened to a dark brown, the same shade and almond shape as Sadie's.

Finally, it was time to open the mail. Inhaling deeply, Sadie peeled back the tape. Several pictures fell out. Sadie devoured each. One specific picture held Sadie's attention. Ellie sat on the floor with a group of children, probably at preschool, or maybe Sunday school. Ellie sat sideways toward the camera, her focus on a blond girl sitting beside her. Her dark hair fell well past her shoulders, a bit disheveled from a day of play. Long eyelashes framed dark eyes. Her cheeks were a bit pinker than they should have been, and Sadie wondered if Ellie had been wind-kissed only moments before. But her smile. Sadie couldn't take her eyes from the smile that lit Ellie's face. Her little girl was happy, and Sadie was so thankful.

After several minutes, Sadie picked up the single-page letter that had fallen from the package. *That's strange. Brenda usually writes several pages.* After opening the sheet, Sadie realized Brenda hadn't written at all. It was from Cam. She read it quickly.

Hello Sadie,
    Ellie has grown a lot this year. I guess you can see that from the pictures. She's a great kid. I wouldn't have known how to deal with Brenda's death had it not been for Ellie.

I know sometimes it can be hard for her without her mom. If you ever want to visit Ellie, that would be great. Not the norm for a regular adoption situation, but hey, who says what's normal? Just let me know.

Cam Reynolds

Sadie skimmed through the note again. "What?" She rested her hand on her chest. "Brenda is dead?"

She scooped up each letter from the previous years, scouring them for any hint as to what happened to Brenda. Had she been sick? Was she in an accident? What could have happened? Sadie couldn't find a hint of a reason.

Brenda must have died in an accident. But when? How long had she been gone? Why wouldn't Cam have told her? *Why would Cam have told me? I gave my baby to him. He doesn't have to tell me anything.*

Sudden, full realization weighed on her heart, and she picked up a picture of Ellie. She traced the child's face with her finger. Cam was the only parental figure in Ellie's life now. She remembered him to be a man who worked hard with his hands but didn't have a lot to say. He was a man who would probably be a super dad to a bouncing baby boy, but what would he be like raising a little girl on his own? Tears pooled in her eyes. Her baby didn't have a mother.

※

Cam rubbed his biceps before knocking on the babysitter's door. The days had been almost never-ending the last month, as he'd finished the remodeling of the older home he'd found for his sister and her daughters. Her husband, Tim, had passed away only two months before, and it hadn't been difficult to talk Kelly into moving herself and the girls back to Delaware. Finding a reasonably priced house with few renovations needed was another story.

Though Kelly and the girls had been out of Cam's home and into their own the last week, the house still had several small problems to keep him busy. His business renovations had taken a beating due to the time he'd spent at Kelly's. Thankfully, he would be able to focus on his work again beginning the next week.

"Daddy!" Ellie's squeals pierced through the screen door before he'd had a chance to actually knock.

"Come here, Ellie-Bellie." Cam pulled open the door then lifted Ellie up to his chest. She was a bit big to be held in this way, but she was his little girl; she'd be his *only* little girl, and as long as she would let him, he would hold her. With his free hand, he waved at his babysitter. "Thanks so much, Ann. We'll see you later."

The middle-aged woman smiled. "See you Monday, Ellie."

In only a few strides, he reached his truck and slipped Ellie into her seat belt.

He made his way around to the driver's side. "So how was your day?"

"Good. What's for dinner, Daddy?" Ellie looked out the window. "We made fish sticks for lunch at Ms. Ann's house. She let me push the sticks in a line. Trudy tried to mess up my rows of sticks, but Ms. Ann told her no. I told her no, too. It isn't nice to mess up people's stuff, is it, Daddy?"

Cam shook his head and inhaled a deep breath. *Oh boy, here we go.* He loved his daughter—adored her more than life itself—but when that child got to talking, a man's head could burst from the incessant chatter.

"And then when it was nap time, you know what that Trudy did? She took my blankie. She knows I have to have my blankie."

Cam nodded and looked at the seat next to Ellie, spying the shredded peach and green material. *Whew. She must have had it in her hand when I picked her up.* Once upon a time, a doll and lamb had been quilted into the piece of fabric, but it had been well over a year since the blanket even remotely resembled what it had once been. Ellie took it with her everywhere. He couldn't even count the times he'd had to drive back to Ann's house to retrieve Ellie's special blanket. With Ellie just turning five, maybe it was time she became less attached to the matted piece of material. But Cam didn't have the heart to take it from her, especially since Brenda had died only ten months ago.

Her death hadn't come as a surprise. He had watched Brenda's valiant battle with breast cancer for two years. He and Ellie, even at her sweet young age, had been prepared that Brenda might need to "go live with Jesus," as Ellie said. Whether they were prepared or not, her death had still been hard. His five-year-old toting a dilapidated old blanket around with her was the least of his concerns.

"And then when it came time for you to come get me, Trudy said. . ."

Cam pulled the truck into the driveway and put it in park. He took in the length of his yard. Already it needed mowed again. He loved spring. Normally, he welcomed the season and the opportunity to dig into the earth of his land. This year, he just didn't have time for yard work.

"Daddy, you never said what we're gonna eat for dinner. I'm hungry, Daddy." She unbuckled her own seat belt and jumped off her booster car seat.

Cam grinned as he grabbed her hand in his. "I think we'll make spaghetti."

"Mmm. I love sgabetti." Ellie's face shone with pleasure.

Yet another thing he hadn't been able to bring himself to correct her about. Ellie often mixed up the pronunciations of large words, but the mix-ups were simply so cute, he didn't have the heart to point them out. He escorted her into the house.

"I'll stir the sauce, and I want to put the sgabetti into the pan. Oh, but I have to go potty first, Daddy. Okay?"

Cam grinned as he laid the keys on the counter. He watched as Ellie rushed down the hall toward the bathroom. "Make sure you wash your hands, Ellie."

"I will, Daddy."

Cam walked into the pantry and took down a can of spaghetti sauce and a box of pasta. If Brenda were still alive, she would have made them homemade sauce, filled with meat, tomatoes, peppers, and onions. Brenda made the best spaghetti sauce around. It was a family favorite when his sister's family and his parents came to visit. Now he and Ellie simply dumped sauce from a can.

His little girl trotted back into the kitchen and pulled a chair up to the counter. After stepping up onto it, she grabbed the sauce, attempting to pop the lid. Pursing her lips, she twisted the lid unsuccessfully until her face turned red.

"Need some help?"

She handed him the can then swiped a chunk of hair away from her eyes. "I can't get it, Daddy."

He popped the lid, and within minutes, Cam and Ellie had fixed their supper. After listening to several more injustices that the infamous Trudy had bestowed upon Ellie, Cam and his daughter finished their supper and put the dishes in the dishwasher, and he gave Ellie a bath.

"Daddy, can Trudy spend the night tomorrow?"

Cam grinned. "We'll see, pun'kin."

Cam brushed Ellie's long dark hair. It was much easier to deal with if he worked out the kinks while it was wet. The girl ended up in tears when he tried to comb through tangles once it had dried. He couldn't begin to count the times her babysitter had to fix her hair after he got her to Ann's house.

Once finished, Ellie twirled around in her pink pajamas. "Do I look like a princess, Daddy?"

"The prettiest princess I've ever seen."

Ellie pushed her long strands of hair from her eyes. "Will you tell me a mommy story?"

Cam sucked in a deep breath. He knew she'd ask. She did nearly every night. Tonight he felt raw, raw to his very core. He missed Brenda. Missed her kiss when he walked in the door from work. Her soft touch when he'd had a long day. He'd taken over so many of the household chores during her sickness that he hadn't realized how much he still needed her presence until she was gone.

Cam closed his eyes and blew the air from his chest. "Well, one time, when you were just a tiny baby, I came home from work and Mommy was holding you real close and rocking you in the rocking chair. She was still wearing her pajamas, and so were you."

Cam tickled Ellie's belly, and she giggled. "Her hair was all messy. Dishes and clothes were all over the house. I was worried that you or Mommy were sick."

Ellie's eyes widened; then she frowned. "Mommy was sick, wasn't she?"

Pain sliced through Cam's heart. Ellie had witnessed sickness too much in her young life. He wished he could have protected her from it. "No, pun'kin. She had spent the whole day rocking you. She said she loved you so much she just couldn't put you down."

Ellie smiled. "I love Mommy, too. One day we'll see Mommy in heaven with Jesus."

"Yes, we will."

Ellie wrapped her arms around Cam's neck. "I love you, Daddy." She jumped beneath her covers and cuddled up with her blankie.

"I love you, too." Cam leaned down and kissed her forehead. Thankfully, unlike his sister's girls, Ellie loved bedtime.

Cam turned off her light then walked to his room. After getting ready for bed, he slipped between his king-sized covers and stared at the empty space beside him. *Ten months and four days. Lord, I miss her so much.*

❧

Sadie sipped the coffee she'd brewed herself. The grocery-store French vanilla flavoring proved nowhere near as good as the java she enjoyed from her favorite gourmet coffee shop. But she had spent her budgeted coffee allowance two days before and payday wasn't until tomorrow. Though not a miser, Sadie prided herself on being frugal with her income. Staying faithful to her budget allowed her to save a substantial amount of money to put into a savings account for a down payment on a house. *I'll be a home owner by the time I'm twenty-five.*

The reminder brought a smile to Sadie's lips. She took another sip, believing the taste to be better than she'd originally thought. Opening her laptop, she pictured the small two-bedroom house she'd viewed online. With its covered porch and neatly manicured lawn, Sadie had instantly fallen in love with the home. *If only I felt as content about living here in this county.*

She turned on the computer. *Lord, Paul learned to be content in all situations. Show me how. Is there a reason I don't like it here?*

Her discontent made no sense. She lived in one of the most beautiful places in the United States, on the edge of the Smoky Mountains in North Carolina. She attended a wonderful church with a booming singles' group. Sadie filled most of her weekends helping her closest friend with her toddler sons. She worked for a terrific school system and for one of the kindest Christian women she'd ever met. And yet something was missing.

She pulled up the realty Web site and selected the link to the small home. "Sold?" She blinked and peered at the four bright red letters covering the picture. "But it wasn't even under contract yesterday."

Sadie grabbed the phone and dialed the Realtor's number, sure that a mistake had been made. She listened, stunned, as the secretary explained that a client had purchased the home outright the day before.

Saddened to the core, Sadie called her friend Lisa. The phone rang a few times, was answered, and then crashed to the floor. Amazingly, it stayed connected and Sadie could hear the faint murmurs of "Hi. Hi. Hi." A smile bowed Sadie's lips. Without a doubt, one of the boys had answered the phone and was talking into the wrong end. Just as she started to hang up and try again, more rustling sounded over the line and Sadie heard a frantic "Hello?"

"Hey, Lisa. Sounds like the boys have you hopping."

A long sigh sounded. "Don't they always? But hey, I was going to call you later. Guess what?"

"What?"

"Our house sold. Looks like Rick and I will be making the move to Alabama."

Sadie's heart crashed to the bottom of her gut. "But your house has been on the market for two years. I didn't think you were even serious about moving anymore."

"We never stopped praying about it. You know that. Rick's dying to be closer to his family. And I'm still not kidding about you coming with us and getting a job there, and—"

Sadie interrupted her. "I'm not moving to Alabama."

A long sigh sounded again. "I know. And I'm going to miss you something awful."

Doom seemed to wrap itself around Sadie. First, she discovered Brenda had died. Next, her dream house sold out from under her. Now, her only close friend was moving hundreds of miles away. Raw emotion threatened to expose itself. She swallowed and said the first thing she could think of. "My house sold, too."

"Ah, Sadie. I'm sorry."

The genuine sympathy in her friend's tone brought tears to Sadie's eyes. "It's okay. God knows what. . ." She couldn't finish the sentence. She believed God, trusted Him with every fiber of her being. But right now she felt robbed. Gypped. And very much alone.

"Rick has to work tonight. Why don't you come over later? We'll watch a movie together."

"Okay. I'll call you later." A tear streamed down her cheek. Swiping it away, Sadie determined to hold herself together. A breakdown would only make her friend feel worse. "I've got to get to work. I'll call you later."

Before Lisa could respond, Sadie hung up the phone then grabbed a tissue out of its box. Dabbing her eyes, she inhaled several times to keep tears from ruining her makeup before the day even began. She imagined what her life would be like without Lisa. Sure, she participated in several of the singles' outings put together by the church. She'd even gone on a few dates with a couple of guys. But the only person in North Carolina she'd grown close to was Lisa. Probably because Lisa had helped Sadie get through the loss of Ellie to adoption, and then later allowed Sadie to be the godmother to her precious two-year-old twin boys. Sadie stared back at the screen of her laptop for several moments. The SOLD sign smacked across the picture of the house that Sadie had prayed so fervently for seemed to mock her. *What now, God?*

A sudden idea sped through her, lightening her heart faster than she would have believed. A frivolous thought, really. And yet the impression was so strong, and her curiosity so piqued, Sadie couldn't help but type the words into her favorite search engine. *When nothing is there, I'll know it's just a silly notion.*

Within seconds, the Web site popped up. Sadie selected the Job Vacancies link and scrolled down. *Surely not?* She stared at the opening for several minutes.

Blinking a couple of times, she took a long gulp of her coffee. She looked at the occupational therapist opening in the school district where Cam and Ellie lived. "God, is this merely a strange coincidence?"

She leaned back in her chair. Why had she even considered checking out the site to begin with? She had no business even dreaming of visiting Ellie, let alone living near her. She bit her bottom lip. And yet wasn't it Cam who suggested she visit? Maybe it would be okay to simply send in her application and résumé. Just to see what happened.

But he didn't say I should move near them.

She shook the thought away as her heart fluttered at the idea of seeing Ellie on a regular basis. She'd made poor choices before her pregnancy with Ellie, but since then she'd kept her head about her and sought God in decisions she had to make, both big and small. And in truth, she didn't believe in coincidences. She believed God's hand was in every circumstance of His children, even the hard ones.

"Maybe, God, this is from You?"

Chapter 2

Cam scratched at the day's growth of stubble on his jaw as he looked over his home renovation business's financial sheet for the month of April. The month had been a rough one, his expenses outweighing his income. Thankfully, he'd thrown himself into his work the first six months after Brenda's death, and his wallet could afford one bad month.

Now that Kelly and the girls are settled into their house, I'm going to have to focus on my business again. He put the sheet on his desk and picked up the stack of work requests. Honest pride filled him as he sifted through potential clients. God had always blessed his hard labor and given him a multitude of customers seeking his skills. Living just over thirty miles from historic Wilmington, Delaware, didn't hurt much either.

He glanced at the clock. Kelly would be expecting him for dinner in a little over an hour. Ellie had spent the day with her aunt and cousins. Kelly's girls were all older than Ellie, but they loved their little cousin and doted on Ellie every chance they could.

Until Kelly moved back to Delaware, Cam didn't realize how thankful he'd be to have her living near him. Their parents had retired to Florida several years before, so he and Ellie only saw them every four to six months. Brenda's parents lived in Nevada, and Ellie hadn't seen them since Brenda's death. They'd never been keen on the idea of the adoption, and aside from a Christmas and birthday package every year, they never contacted Cam about Ellie.

Having Kelly and the girls in Ellie's life gave her some female influences. Cam wished Kelly could spend more time with Ellie, but with her recovering from her husband's death, working full-time, and raising three daughters—a preteen and two teenagers—Kelly simply didn't have it in her to be a consistent mom figure to Ellie as well.

Don't dwell on things you can't change, Reynolds. He arranged the papers on his desk. Allowing Ellie to be feminine stayed at the forefront of his thoughts. She loved princesses and dolls and hair bows and all that other girlie stuff, and Cam feared he'd turn her into a rough-and-tumble tomboy without her mommy around to keep him balanced. He'd enrolled her in ballet classes that would start in a couple of weeks. *Ballet, for goodness' sake.* But he knew she would love it.

The front door of his office creaked open. He glanced at the clock—5:30.

He'd forgotten to lock the door. He walked to the front of the shop, looked at the customer, and stopped. He felt his jaw drop. His heart seemed to skip over itself. He couldn't believe who stood in his doorway.

✺

Sadie twisted the strap of her purse. The surprised expression on Cam's face relayed his disbelief that she would really take him up on his offer to see Ellie. In truth, she was scared out of her wits at the prospect of seeing the girl. She had no idea what the five-year-old would think of her, the woman who didn't want to be her mommy. But oh, how Sadie wished she could have been Ellie's mother. Day in and day out, she thought of what it would have been like to give the child her baths, to comb her hair, to kiss away boo-boos, to clean up her spilled juice. Sadie knew she couldn't even begin to imagine all the joys and trials she'd missed with her little girl.

And now here she stood, in small-town Delaware, hundreds of miles from the place she'd called home since graduating college. And staring at the man who was raising her daughter. Cam looked just the same as he had five years before. Brown hair, cut short. Short stubbles tracing his chin and jaw but not so long as to cover the deep dimple in his chin. Kind yet inquisitive hazel eyes. Yes, Cam was every bit as handsome as he'd been when Sadie gave birth to Ellie. If anything, he'd grown in girth, the muscles through his shirt appearing larger, stronger than she'd remembered.

She pushed a wayward strand of hair behind her ear. "Hello, Cam."

"Sadie?"

Though he said her name as a question, she knew it was more of a statement, a mixture of shock and disbelief. It was obvious she was the last person on earth he'd expected to see standing in his doorway. Lifting her purse strap up onto her shoulder, Sadie then pressed at the wrinkles in her pencil-straight black skirt. She'd come directly from an interview with the school superintendent. Well, directly was a relative term. In truth, she'd sat in her car in the parking lot for more than an hour trying to muster the courage to drive the route the Internet had given to Cam's place of business.

An inner battle raged over what Cam would think of her arrival in his town. Would he think she was nuts? *Am I nuts? What biological mother tracks down her five-year-old daughter?* She revisited the piercing of her heart, that moment when the nurse took her baby away. There were probably a lot of biological mothers who wanted to track down their children.

Praying every moment, she'd been able to follow the course and then walk into his office. *What will he think when he learns I accepted a position here in town?* She still couldn't decipher what she thought about it. Never in her wildest imagination would she have thought the superintendent would offer her the occupational therapist position immediately after the interview. It was the middle of May. He had an entire summer to interview candidates, and yet he'd hired Sadie instantly. *And who does that? I've never heard of a superintendent hiring a candidate on the spot. Surely that was from God.*

To her surprise, she'd accepted without a moment's thought. Now that more than an hour had passed, she wondered if she'd accepted too soon. *Maybe I should have prayed more about it. Have I really given this to God? Why did I even think to check that Web site? Lord, it's such a huge decision.* Uncertainty overwhelmed her.

The memory of Lisa's reaction to Sadie's interview slipped into her mind. Her friend had been elated, feeling the opening had to have come from God. At the time, Sadie had joined in her friend's excitement. And for some reason, though she felt anxious about the choice, Sadie also felt content with the decision.

It's kinda like I'm Ruth following Naomi to a land she'd never known. What was it Ruth said? Something like "Where you go, I'll go. Your people will be my people." Well, Lord, I'm not following my mother-in-law. I'm following my daughter. Give me the right words to say.

Sadie cleared her throat. "Thank you for the pictures of Ellie. I was so sorry to hear about Brenda." Unsure what to do with her hands, she allowed her index and middle fingers to trail the long satin ribbon at the waist of her fitted mint green cardigan. The bow came untied, and she quickly retied it.

Cam nodded but didn't reply. He still didn't seem to have registered that she stood in his office. *Maybe I should have called him before I showed up at his office door.*

Sadie swallowed the lump that formed in her throat. "How long has Brenda been gone? I mean. . .what happened? I mean. . ." Sadie stopped. She had no idea what to say to him. *God, help me here!*

"Ten months. Breast cancer."

Cam seemed to have found his tongue, but his shocked expression hadn't changed. Sadie frowned. "I'm sorry, Cam. I didn't know. It must have been so sudden."

"No. She fought for two years."

Two years? Sadie had no idea. Brenda had been sending pictures and long letters, and for two years she'd been battling breast cancer. Why hadn't she told her? Maybe Sadie could have done something to help. At the very least, she could have prayed for Brenda. *Maybe she was afraid I'd show up on her doorstep, as I'm here on Cam's now.*

She pushed back the fear and anxiety that crept into her body. Maybe she shouldn't have taken that job, shouldn't have even looked it up on the Internet in the first place. *God, what am I doing here?*

"What do you want, Sadie?" Cam's voice was monotone, his face without expression.

"To see Ellie." Before Sadie had time to think, the answer slipped from her lips. It was the longing of her heart. To deny it would be like denying her lungs of breath. Who would have imagined an unplanned child whom she'd seen for only a moment would impact her life in such a way? *I did carry her for nine months. I felt her first movements. Was first to hear her heart beating. I can't help but love her.*

Cam leaned against a desk and crossed his arms in front of his chest. He hadn't responded to her answer, and she still couldn't read his expression.

She shifted her weight from one foot to the other. "Your letter mentioned that maybe I could see Ellie. I've been thinking about it and praying about it, and. . .well, I'm not sure how this would work, but I really want to see her."

An unexpected tear slipped down her cheek. She sucked in her breath and wiped it from her cheek. Her heart's greatest yearning lived with this man. It felt as if all her hopes rested in his hands. *God is in control of my life and all that happens in it. Not Cam Reynolds.* The reminder boosted her confidence, and she stood straighter.

"I didn't really expect. . ." Cam stood to his full height, towering over her. His gaze softened, but questions and confusion still lingered behind his eyes. "I don't know if I'm ready. . .or if Ellie would be ready. I need time to think. I'm sure you came a long way, but. . ."

"It's okay. Don't worry about the drive. . ." Once again feeling a bit irrational at the expedient decision to move to Delaware, she stopped herself before mentioning it. She grabbed a pen and paper from her purse and wrote down her number. "This is my cell number. You can call me anytime." She shoved the paper in his hand. Looking up, she stared into his eyes. Once again, she noted the kindness gazing back at her. It quickened her heart and boosted her confidence again. "I know my appearance must come as a shock to you, but I've been praying about this, Cam. Please, promise you will as well."

"I will."

She turned and walked out the door. A sudden peace squelched the anxiety that dominated her time in his office. God was the Alpha and the Omega, the First and the Last. He was the Beginning and the End. He guided Ruth into an alien land and blessed her with more than she ever would have imagined. He knew what would happen with Sadie and her little girl.

❧

Cam couldn't believe Sadie Ellis had been standing in the doorway of his office only fifteen minutes ago. The teen who had given birth to Ellie no longer looked anything like a teenager. Sadie, with her long dark hair and light green eyes, had grown into a woman. To his chagrin, he'd noticed how long her legs looked in the straight skirt. When she played with the ribbon on her sweater, he couldn't help but take in how trim her waist was. She was ten years his junior. In his mind, Sadie was little more than a girl.

But, wow, how the girl has grown.

He shook his head as he walked up the steps of Kelly's house. The noise he heard inside the walls would keep his mind from such thoughts. He opened the door and was instantly wrapped in a bear hug.

"Hi, Daddy. Aunt Kelly made lasagna. She let me help put garlic on the bread." She scrunched her nose. "Garlic stinks. Like garbage."

She pushed a chunk of hair behind her ear. Something he'd seen her biological mother do only minutes before. Again, he marveled at how much Ellie looked like Sadie. He thought of updating his gun collection before his little girl grew up. If she grew to be as beautiful as Sadie, he'd need to do all he could to keep the boys away.

He pinched her nose. "Garlic stinks, but it tastes good."

Ellie giggled and squirmed away from him. "That's what Aunt Kelly said."

"Ellie!" The voice of one of his nieces yelled from the back of the house. "If you want me to braid your hair, you've got to come here."

"Britty's going to fix my hair." Ellie smiled and raced away. "I'm coming."

Cam chuckled at Ellie's nickname for Kelly's middle daughter. The poor thirteen-year-old's name was Brittany, but since Ellie couldn't pronounce it when she was just a little thing, the whole family took to calling her Britty.

"Hey, Cam." Kelly walked into the living area. "Do you have the gasket for the kitchen sink? The dripping is driving me crazy."

Cam looked at his sister, only two years older than him. She exuded exhaustion and sadness. The sudden death of her husband had taken a toll on her. She and Tim had been married almost eighteen years, since the month after she graduated high school. He'd been with her through the birth of all three of their daughters, as well as supported her through college so that she could get her degree in teaching. When she was only thirty-six, a traffic accident had taken her lifelong sweetheart from her.

"I got it right here." He held up the gasket. "It'll only take a minute to fix." He smiled and sniffed the air. "Something smells awfully good."

A slow smile formed on her lips. "You fix my sink; then I'll feed you."

"Deal."

Cam headed to the sink. Within minutes, the drip was gone, and he and the family enjoyed a dinner of salad, homemade lasagna, and garlic bread. Having practically gorged himself on the home-cooked food, Cam sat back in his chair while Ellie played with Kelly's youngest daughter and the two oldest girls argued over which one would do dishes.

Kelly set a cup of coffee on the table in front of Cam. She settled into the seat beside him.

"Thanks." He took a drink of the strong black coffee. The argument ensued in the kitchen. He cocked one eyebrow. "You going to help those girls decide?"

"Not unless it goes to blows. And if it goes to blows, they're both in a world of trouble."

Cam chuckled at Kelly's response. Six months ago, Tim would have gone in and settled the dispute with no questions asked and no further arguments. The girls seemed to wear Kelly down.

"You want me to handle it?"

Kelly frowned. "No. They're fifteen and thirteen years old. They've always had to help, and now that Tim's gone, I want them to be even more responsible. They have to learn to work together."

Cam nodded and looked back at Ellie and his youngest niece. He couldn't get over how much Ellie looked like Sadie. *What would she think if I allowed her to meet Sadie?* He and Brenda had always been honest with Ellie that she had been adopted. His daughter had always beamed when they told her she had been chosen to be their little girl. A few times, she'd asked about the lady who'd given her birth. The most recent time had been when she'd seen a pregnant woman at the store. But they'd never talked much about Sadie.

"So, Cam, what's up?" Kelly's voice interrupted his thoughts.

He shrugged. "Nothing, I guess."

"Whatever." Kelly swatted the air. "I'm your big sister. I know when something's up."

Cam stared at his sister. As tired and frazzled as she'd become, she was still the caring, intuitive person she'd always been. "Sadie showed up at my office today."

Kelly furrowed her eyebrows. "Sadie? Who's Sadie?" Realization shone on her face. "You don't mean. . . ?" She gazed at Ellie then back at Cam.

Cam nodded. "The one and only. Ellie's birth mother."

"What did she want?"

"To see Ellie."

"Why?"

"I think it's my fault." Cam rubbed his jaw. "Brenda has always sent a letter and pictures to Sadie on Ellie's birthday. Well, of course, this year I sent them." He frowned, trying to remember exactly what he'd written. "I think I told her she could come see Ellie if she wanted. I didn't really mean anything by it. Don't even know why I wrote it. I put the whole envelope together really fast. I haven't had a lot of time lately." He stopped and looked at his sister's face. She twisted the earring in her right ear, a sign that Kelly was thinking.

"What did you tell her?"

"I'd have to think about it."

"Hmm." Kelly continued to twist the earring. "Wasn't Sadie a Christian?"

"Yeah. She seemed like a really good kid. Made a mistake in college. Her parents were less than happy about the situation, and she was kinda stuck on her own. Brenda loved the girl."

"Hmm."

"Mom!" A screech from the kitchen interrupted their conversation. "Brittany is being a jerk." Kelly's oldest daughter, Zoey, stomped into the dining area. "I did the dishes last night. Just because she vacuumed today doesn't mean I should have to do the dishes again."

Cam watched as irritation wrapped his sister's features. "What chores have you done today, Zoey?"

"Well. . ."

"Well? Nothing. That's what you've done. You've hidden yourself in your room watching movies and talking to your boyfriend on instant messaging. Brittany has picked up the house and played with Ellie. You have the dishes."

The fifteen-year-old redhead stamped her foot. "It's not fair. I did them yesterday."

"It is fair. Now get in the kitchen."

"Mom, you just—"

Kelly pointed her finger at the girl. "Zoey, if you argue with me, I'll take away your instant messaging."

Zoey clamped her lips shut and stomped back into the kitchen. Kelly slumped down into her chair and let out a long breath. "That girl is getting harder and harder to handle."

Cam put his hand on Kelly's. "She's fifteen, and she's just lost her father. It only makes sense that she's getting more difficult to manage."

"You're right, but I'm not sure how much more I can take. Tim was so good with the girls."

Cam squeezed Kelly's hand. "I will help you in any way. You name what I can do."

"You've already done so much, Cam. I'm thankful God gave me a good brother to help me get through this. Did I tell you Mom and Dad are going to take the girls for a few weeks in July?"

Cam smiled. "That will be great, sis. You'll get some time to rest, and they'll love visiting their grandparents in Florida."

"Yeah. That's what Mom said. I think they want Ellie to come, too."

Cam frowned. He didn't know if he was ready to allow Ellie to be away from him for two whole weeks. She'd probably love spending the time with her grandparents and her cousins, but what would he do without her?

Kelly lifted her mug to her lips and took a sip of her coffee. "About Sadie."

Cam's heart sped up. He'd forgotten they'd been talking about her before Zoey threw her fit. He looked at Ellie. Again she pushed a stray hair that had escaped her braids behind her ear, mimicking the gesture Sadie had made. It might be good to allow Ellie to meet Sadie. But what if Sadie decided she didn't want to see Ellie after only one or two visits? He wouldn't allow her to walk in and out of Ellie's life. The child had been through enough with the loss of her mom. And if she really wanted to see Ellie, why wouldn't she have contacted him months or even years before? *I wonder if she ever contacted Brenda.*

He pushed that thought away. Even if her desire to see Ellie was honorable, what had she been doing the last five years? For all Cam knew, she was married with more kids and wanted to steal his little girl out from under him. She could be an alcoholic, be married to a drug dealer, could have spent time in the penitentiary.

"I've been praying about this." Sadie's words slipped through Cam's mind. In his heart, he knew none of those things were true. Call it intuition or maybe the Holy Spirit, but Cam could tell by the way Sadie looked and how she talked that she was being genuine.

"I think you should let them meet." Kelly's words penetrated Cam's mind.

"You do? But what if Sadie doesn't hang around? I don't want Ellie's heart broken."

"Hmm. That's true." Kelly stood and picked up his empty cup. "Maybe you need to pray about it."

Those had been Sadie's words. She'd said she'd been praying about it. He'd told her that he'd pray about it, too. *Maybe I need to do just that.*

Chapter 3

In only three weeks' time, Sadie had found a cute one-bedroom apartment in small-town Delaware, packed up every belonging she owned, and moved herself hundreds of miles away from all she knew. Her parents hadn't thought much about the move, but they hadn't been overtly involved in Sadie's life. . . well, ever. The singles' group at church had given her a wonderful party that, in some odd way, seemed to confirm her decision to move. Leaving the kids and colleagues from the school system was harder than she'd imagined, and saying good-bye to Lisa's boys had nearly ripped her heart in two. And yet she'd left. Gone. *All for a little girl I'm not at all sure I'll be able to have a relationship with.*

The words of Ruth from the Old Testament flowed through her mind. *"Where you go I will go, and where you stay I will stay. Your people will be my people and your God my God."* Sadie knew she wasn't following her mother-in-law away from a pagan land as Ruth had, and yet she felt very much like a drifter without a goal. Her life's purpose had become the opportunity to have a relationship with the baby she'd held for only brief moments after delivery.

"Where do you want me to put the extra sheets—top shelf or middle shelf?" Lisa's voice sounded from the hall.

"Middle shelf. I'll use the top one for thicker blankets." Having Lisa at the apartment for the last two days had been an enormous help. Not only was her friend a great packer and unpacker, she also kept Sadie's mind from wandering to thoughts of why Cam hadn't called yet, or what Ellie would think if she saw Sadie, or if Ellie would hate her, or. . .

Organizing dishes in the top oak cabinet, Sadie squelched the fear of rejection that threatened to bring up the sugary, high-calorie breakfast of strong coffee and day-old donuts she'd eaten several hours before. *Now is not the time to worry about what Ellie will think of me. It's time to work. And maybe have a little faith.*

She sliced through the duct tape of another box. As she lifted out a pot and lid, she thought of Cam's expression the night she'd shown up at his office. He seemed more than shocked; something akin to horrified described the way he looked. Shoving the pot into the bottom cabinet, she pushed the remembrance away. She didn't need to worry about Cam's response to seeing her at this moment either. *Have a little faith, Sadie.*

She glanced at her watch. It was nearly lunchtime, and she was determined to finish unpacking the kitchen before she took a break. She noted the two additional large boxes marked KITCHEN that sat mockingly on the linoleum floor beside her. *I might work a little faster if I wasn't thinking about Cam and Ellie every five seconds.*

But she couldn't help it. Three weeks had passed and she still hadn't heard from Cam. She pulled her cell phone from the front pocket of her jean shorts to check for missed calls. *Maybe my phone malfunctioned and didn't ring the call through.*

None. The last call she'd received had been the dental appointment reminder. The one before that had been Rick in a panic because he couldn't find the new package of diapers Lisa had bought before helping Sadie move. *Help me with my faith, Lord.*

She sighed. Who was she kidding? She'd checked her phone a million or more times since she'd seen Cam. Each time, she told herself she wouldn't check; she'd wait for the ring. Then she'd check again ten minutes later.

If he didn't call by the time she'd completely unpacked—and since he hadn't returned the two, okay, three calls she'd made to him in the last week—then she'd have to pay him another visit. She knew he could deny allowing her to see Ellie. He had every legal right to keep them separated. She knew he probably feared Ellie experiencing more pain on top of Brenda's death. *He may be afraid I'll walk away again.*

The very notion felt like a punch in her stomach. It had nearly killed her giving Ellie away the first time. Now that she was twenty-four and had her degree and a stable job, not to mention a right relationship with the Lord, Sadie could never walk away from Ellie again.

She didn't regret the decision to allow Ellie to be adopted. It had been the right choice at the time, and Sadie's faith in the Lord had grown substantially as a result. *Which is why I must trust Him now.*

The thought nearly brought her to her knees. She placed the casserole dish in her hands on the stove. Gripping the edge of the countertop, she bowed her head. "Oh sweet Jesus, help me to trust in You as I wait for Cam's answer. You put everything in place for me to move here. I know Your hand is in this. I only need to trust You for timing."

✺

"Don't burn me, Daddy," Ellie squealed as she flinched away from the curling iron. The little urchin had found the gadget buried in the back of the bathroom cabinet and had begged him to fix her hair.

Cam blew out a breath as he pulled it away from her. "Ellie, if you flinch like that, it *will* burn you. Hold still."

He gripped her newly cut bangs between his fingers then smashed them with the curling iron. Ellie flinched again, causing him to burn his finger.

"Ouch!" He pulled his hand away, turned on the cold-water faucet, and stuck his finger beneath the cool stream. "Ellie, you have to hold still."

"Sorry, Daddy. You scare me. I can feel the hot on my forehead." She sniffed, and a tear slipped down her cheek.

He felt like an overgrown grump. It wasn't Ellie's fault he had no idea how to work the hair contraption. "It's okay, pun'kin. Why don't we leave the hair fixing to Aunt Kelly and the girls?"

He took in the curls flipping outward at the sides of her bangs. It would be okay—if one side wasn't resting a full inch higher than the other. Poor Ellie looked like someone had taken a hacksaw to her hair. He would never be able to fix them right. *Which is why I didn't want her to get bangs cut in the first place.*

"But my hair looks funny." Ellie puckered her bottom lip and gripped her blanket closer to her chest. "I'll sit still. I promise."

Cam held back the growl that formed in the back of his throat. Brenda would take care of this if she were still alive. Cam was the parent who wrestled with Ellie in the yard, taught her how to catch a ball, and drenched her with the water hose as they cleaned the truck. He didn't know any daddies who curled their daughters' hair.

But then, he didn't know any daddies raising their little girls alone. *Ah, Brenda, this is only one of the many ways I miss you.*

In the two years she'd battled cancer, several times he'd prayed, sought God, and even come to terms with the knowledge that he would miss Brenda's touch as a woman. He knew he'd miss her help as caretaker of their home and Ellie. But he hadn't been prepared for how hard it would be to teach Ellie about the feminine side of life. Let's face it, what did he know about being a girl?

Sure, Kelly was a part of Ellie's life. And through the summer, Kelly and the girls planned to spend a good amount of time with Ellie. But fall would come. And when it did, Kelly would be swamped with her girls and teaching. Cam had no choice but to do the "girly" things with Ellie.

With a snarl, he picked up the curling iron then grabbed a piece of her hair and quickly pulled it through the iron. Fifteen minutes later, her hairstyle wasn't great, but it was presentable. That was all he could give her.

"All done, Daddy." Ellie raced out of the bathroom. He heard the television turn on, and the theme song of one of her favorite cartoons pealed through the air.

Cam placed his finger under a stream of cold water once more. A large water blister had already formed, stinging more than he would have thought. *Who would have known fixing hair could be so dangerous?* He swallowed back an ironic chuckle that formed. He'd smashed every one of his fingers, torn off nails, and attained more cuts, scrapes, and bruises than he could count at his job; but a little bitty curling iron burn had him putting his finger under a stream of water. *Talk about stealing a man's testosterone. I need some manly activities in my life.*

He grunted like Tim Allen from one of his favorite old sitcoms, *Home Improvement.* Before the grunt ended, he heard the ranting and raving of his sister and her daughters as they bounded through the front door. He rubbed his temples with his fingertips. *Nothing like a house full of women to make a guy feel like a man.*

❧

Sadie checked the miles she'd driven against the miles left to Cam's house. According to the directions she'd printed off the Internet, she didn't have far to go. She and Lisa had finished unpacking her things the day before. They'd enjoyed a wonderful girl night of pizza, popcorn, and movies. Early this morning, Lisa left to head back to North Carolina. Afterward, Sadie spent the rest of the morning in prayer. Cam still hadn't called, but she could wait no longer. She had to do something. She didn't have to talk to Ellie, but maybe if she just drove by their house, just saw where Ellie lived. *He's going to think I'm a stalker.* She placed a hand on her chest. *I would think I was a stalker, but waiting on him is killing me.*

Peering out the windshield, she noted the serenity of nature around her. The land looked like grass-covered ocean waves, rolling high and low on each side. Large, lush trees covered much of the ground without cluttering it. Occasionally, she passed a large pond. Delaware was every bit as beautiful as the Smoky Mountains in North Carolina, just in a different way—a way she could easily get used to.

Just ahead, Sadie spotted a stone house with a room built onto the side. The exterior walls of the room were made of nothing but windows. At first glance, she thought the room was a patio; but as she drove closer, she noted the lattices in the windows. *Maybe it's a library.*

She recalled the home of one of her high school friends that had an elaborate library. Two walls were covered with bookshelves. The other two walls were windows opening the room to a glorious, mountainous view. The room had seemed to be the most amazing escape, and Sadie had thought she'd want a room just like it in her own home one day. *I haven't thought about Rachael in years. I wonder how she's doing.*

Sadie glanced at her mileage again. She was getting closer. Thoughts of high school girlfriends slipped from her mind. One of the next few houses should be Cam and Ellie's. Her heart began to beat faster beneath her chest. She took deep breaths in and out. What would Ellie think of her? If she was discovered, what would Cam think about her driving by his house? Would he think she had been watching them for days?

A man stood in the front yard of the first house on this street, holding a large shovel in his hands. He wore a T-shirt that he seemed to have outgrown many years before, a pair of dirt-covered denim shorts, and sandals. The muscles in his arms glistened in the sun. Sadie couldn't help but admire the strength those muscles implied. The man scooped mulch from the back of a truck and walked toward one of the many flower beds dispersed across the meticulously landscaped yard.

She drove closer and peered out the passenger window as she passed the house. The man turned his face slightly to the right. It was Cam.

Sadie swallowed the lump that had formed in her throat. *Cam Reynolds is hot!* She shook the thought away. She had not driven all the way out here, had not moved all the way from North Carolina, because Cam Reynolds was a good-looking man. Building a relationship with Ellie was her goal.

After pulling into the next house's driveway, she turned around and headed back toward Cam. Thankfully, several acres separated the houses, and Sadie had a few moments to settle her racing heart before she pulled into his driveway. *So much for just driving by.* She inwardly berated herself. *But it's his fault. He told me I could see Ellie in his letter; then he won't call me back!*

A cold sweat broke out over her body as she inched toward his house. Dizziness enveloped her, and she released long, slow breaths through her lips. She opened her water bottle and took a quick drink. *Calm down, Sadie. You can do this.*

Fear wrapped itself around her and tunneled throughout her body. She could only imagine what Ellie would think of her. What if she said she hated Sadie? And Cam. He hadn't called her. For all she knew, he would call the police, put out a restraining order, or do whatever he needed to do to keep her from Ellie.

What if Ellie hadn't been told she was adopted?

Sadie hadn't thought of that. Brenda had always told Sadie that she and Cam were honest with Ellie about her being adopted, but then again, Brenda hadn't told Sadie that she had cancer. Maybe Brenda lied about having told Ellie. If Sadie showed up on Cam's doorstep, she may crush all that her little girl had ever known to be true in her life.

Unexpected tears traced down her cheeks. *God, what do I do? I didn't think this through all the way. I should have waited for Cam's call. Oh God, I'm so sorry.*

Sadie brushed the tears away with her fingertips as she drove closer to Cam's house. Determined to head back to her apartment and wait for his call, she snuck one last peek at his house. She drove at little more than a crawl, but she couldn't stop herself. Maybe she would see a glimpse of Ellie. The child would just think a lady passed by in her car.

Cam turned around. Their gazes locked for a brief moment; then he motioned for her to come over. Swallowing the knot in her throat, she tapped the top of the steering wheel, begging God to guide her through this encounter with Cam and her daughter. Sucking in a deep breath, Sadie stepped out of the car.

"Hello, Cam." Her gaze strayed from his face to his sun-kissed biceps. His muscles bragged their hard work. Pushing a strand of hair behind her ear, she forced her gaze away.

A slight sigh escaped Cam's mouth, and she looked back into his eyes. She was always taken aback at the kindness behind his eyes. He threw the shovel into the back of his truck. "I think I need a break. Why don't you come on in, Sadie?"

"Is. . .is Ellie here?"

"No, she's not."

Sadness mixed with relief as Sadie followed Cam into his house. She took in the historic furnishings of the home, displayed in several hues of browns and greens. The house had a manly feel to it, but touches of lace and satin in the curtains and pillows tattled of a woman's touch. "Your home has such a peaceful feel to it."

The words slipped from her lips before she'd had a chance to think them through. He looked around the room as if he were seeing it for the first time in a long time. He gazed back at Sadie. "Thanks."

She followed him into the kitchen. He grabbed a towel out of the laundry basket that sat on the floor beside a door and wiped off the sweat from his forehead. He motioned for her to have a seat at a small table, and she obliged. Wordlessly, she watched as he washed his hands and then opened the refrigerator and pulled out a can of soda. "You want a drink?"

Thinking to decline, she licked her parched lips and thought better of it. "Sure."

He pulled out another drink and set it on the table in front of her. With complete ease, he slid into the chair across from her. He popped open his can and took a long swig. "I guess we need to talk."

Sadie nodded. She struggled to open her soda. Her nerves had gotten the better of her the last few weeks, and she'd bitten her fingernails well past the tips of her fingers. In one motion, Cam swiped her drink and popped the top. He handed it to her, and she took a slow sip.

He rubbed his stubble-clad jaw. "Where to start?"

"Does Ellie know she's adopted?" The question came out fast, and Sadie watched as Cam frowned.

"Yes. Why?"

Relief washed over Sadie. "I just. . .I. . ." She wrapped her fingers around the can, allowing its cold wetness to calm her nerves. "I so wanted to see her. Then when I passed your house, I had this sinking feeling. . .that maybe she didn't even know."

"Brenda told you from the beginning that we would tell her."

"Yes, but I didn't know about her cancer, and I just thought. . .I mean, I was afraid. . ."

"That she lied." Pain etched his face.

"I didn't mean it like that. I can only imagine how hard it would be to tell your child that you were unable to have one. I mean, on your own."

An expression wrapped his face that Sadie couldn't decipher. He scooped up his soda, taking a long gulp. "You have no idea. But that's not what we need to talk about."

"No." Sadie folded her hands on the table, willing herself to have courage. "Cam, I want the opportunity to have a relationship with Ellie."

He didn't respond, simply studied her for several moments. Finally, he nodded. "I know. But why?"

Why? Why! I've spent the last five years of my life mourning that child. That's why! "Cam, I love Ellie. I have loved her from the moment I knew I carried her in my womb. At nineteen, without support from my boyfriend and with minimal support from my parents, I couldn't keep her." She looked into Cam's eyes, begging him to believe she was telling the truth. "I know God provided you and Brenda for Ellie. You were such a great guy, and Brenda was such an amazing. . . God-fearing woman."

She looked down at the soft drink on the table and chased the condensation down the can with her fingertips. Her heart broke with the knowledge of Brenda's death. She couldn't imagine how Cam and Ellie felt. She gazed back into Cam's eyes. She could see how much he missed Brenda reflected in those hazel pools.

"I'm twenty-four now, Cam. I've spent the last five years of my life finishing school and then working with children in a school system in North Carolina. I've helped my dear friend with her twin boys the last two years. I cooked and cleaned while her husband worked double shifts and she was on bed rest. And I. . ." Sadie took a deep breath. Her nerves were getting the best of her. "Now I have a job here in Delaware. . . ."

"You have a job in Delaware?"

She smiled. "In this very county. I've already moved into a new apartment. I live here."

His eyes widened at her words, and she couldn't hold back a slight nervous giggle. "I've left everything I've known to be closer to Ellie. I kinda feel like Ruth following Naomi to her homeland." She swiped her hand through the air.

"Never mind the Ruth stuff. I just can't help but hope that God has given me an opportunity to get to know my little girl."

Silence weighed the room down thicker than a foggy morning in the Smokies. Sadie took a sip of the soda and forced it down her throat.

Cam traced the top of his can with his fingertip. The gesture made the can's top seem surprisingly small beneath his fingers. "What happens when you get married?"

Sadie blinked several times. Married? She didn't have a boyfriend, didn't even want one. Not yet anyway. The few guys she'd dated since Ellie's father had been wonderful, God-fearing men, but they just didn't seem to be right for Sadie. In truth, she'd kept herself so busy with work, odds-and-ends ministries at church, and helping Lisa that she hadn't thought much about it. Sure, she'd gone on practically every singles' outing at church, but the guys there had been more like buddies than anything. "Why would. . . That wouldn't change how I feel about Ellie."

Cam sat back in his chair. "What about when your husband's job has to move him somewhere else? What about when you have other kids?"

Sadie frowned. She hadn't really thought about what would happen if she got married and had children. It was true that one day she did want to marry. She did want children. It would be quite unusual to be Mom to children who lived with her and her husband and be Mom to Ellie who lived with Cam. "Honestly, Cam, I hadn't thought about that." She searched her mind and heart for what she was feeling. "But I can't imagine loving Ellie any less."

Without thinking, she touched her stomach. "She'd still be my firstborn child. Her kicks were the first ones I'd ever felt. Her cries were the first I'd ever heard. That will never change."

Cam stared at her. He didn't move a muscle, didn't even flinch. Sadie's heart sank as she feared he'd already decided not to allow her to be part of Ellie's life.

I am in control of the universe. Have faith in Me.

The Spirit's reminder lifted her heart. She could trust her heavenly Father. She would trust Him. Cam had all legal rights to Ellie, but God's will was in control of all the earth. He loved Ellie even more than Sadie did. If it was God's will for Sadie to have a relationship with her little girl, He would make it happen. "I trust you, Lord."

"What was that?"

Sadie gasped. She hadn't realized she'd said her prayer aloud. She shook her head. "Nothing. Just a little prayer."

Cam leaned forward, resting his elbows on the table. "Okay. Here's the deal. Let's start off slow."

Sadie's heart leaped within her, and she couldn't stop the quick, quiet clap of her hands. "Okay."

Cam's mouth bowed into a slow, hesitant grin. "How about you come to our church on Sunday? We'll take you to lunch afterward."

"That sounds great." Sadie stood and lifted her purse strap to her shoulder. "What church do you go to?"

"First Community." Cam stood and guided Sadie to the door. "But, Sadie, let's not tell Ellie who you are. Not just yet."

Sadie's heart plummeted. She wanted to wrap her arms around the little girl, smother her with kisses, and assure her that her biological mother had loved and prayed for her every day of her life. But Sadie allowed his words to sink into her spirit. She nodded. Maybe taking things slowly would be for the best.

Chapter 4

Cam brushed a piece of lint off his khaki pants. Sadie still hadn't arrived, and church would begin in less than fifteen minutes. He looked beside him at Ellie. She sat in the pew with one leg crossed beneath her and her attention focused on the coloring sheet in her lap, a picture of Jesus surrounded by a group of children. Her bangs looked a little crooked again this morning. The left side had a mind of its own. No matter how many times he smashed it with the curling iron, it always bounced up higher than the right on Ellie's forehead.

He glanced at his watch again. He'd chosen a pew farther back from where he and Ellie normally sat. Assuming Sadie would already be nervous about seeing Ellie, he didn't want to add to her anxiety by having to greet the entire congregation as she made her way to the front of the church. *If she doesn't hurry up, I'll have to introduce her to Ellie after the service.*

Thoughts of what the congregation would think of Sadie had already plagued him through the night. Ellie looked so much like her biological mother that people were bound to make assumptions. The church already knew Ellie had been adopted. He shifted in his seat. Long ago, he'd learned that a man shouldn't worry about things he had no control over, and what the congregation thought of Sadie was out of his hands.

At least Kelly and the girls are at home. It wasn't that he wanted his nieces to be sick; he just didn't want them to meet Sadie. Not yet anyway.

Stealing another peek at the door, he sucked in his breath. Sadie stood in the entrance. She greeted one of the deacons and took the offered bulletin from his hand. Her dark hair flowed long and silky past her right shoulder. She wore a frilly white blouse that accentuated her trim figure. Her green and white skirt flowed out from the middle of her knees. She looked like she'd just finished modeling for a catalog, and once again, Cam noted how much she'd grown up since Ellie's birth. He tore his gaze away from her. *What are you thinking, Reynolds? The girl is ten years younger than you.*

Clearing his throat and his head, he looked back at her. She saw him and smiled. Her gaze immediately fell beside him. He noted her gasp when she saw Ellie. Fear draped across her features, and she looked back up at him. Cam tried to calm her with a smile. He motioned her toward them. When she reached the pew, he took her hand in his. Ignoring how soft her skin felt, he greeted her.

"Hello, Sadie. It's good to see you this morning."

"Hello, Cam." Her voice sounded weak, and her hand shook slightly.

"Ellie?" His daughter looked up from her coloring, and Cam heard Sadie's slight gasp. "I'd like you to meet a. . .friend of mine. This is Sadie Ellis."

Ellie grinned. "Hi. Your name sounds like mine." She placed her hand over her mouth as she giggled.

Sadie leaned over. "Yes, it does." She touched Ellie's hand. "I'm new to this church. Can I sit with you?"

Ellie pushed her crayons and papers farther down the pew. "Yeah. But I go to children's church in minute." She looked up at Cam. "Daddy, can Ms. Ellie sit with you?"

Cam could feel Sadie relax as she grinned at Ellie. "My last name is Ellis, not Ellie. But why don't you call me Sadie."

"Okay, Sadie." Ellie scooted down the pew. "Can Sadie sit with us?"

Cam looked at Sadie. Delight topped the contentment that framed her expression. In an instant, he knew the choice had been right to allow Sadie the opportunity to see Ellie. "Of course she can sit with us."

Sadie settled in beside Ellie. She oohed and aahed over the coloring Ellie had already done. Sadie picked up one of the crayons and began to color with his daughter. Cam glanced around the packed sanctuary. With the church bursting at the seams and the pastor's extended family from New York visiting, no one seemed to notice the new woman sitting beside him. The music began and Ellie popped up from her seat. She grabbed Sadie's hand and helped her stand. Complete bliss filled the woman's expression.

After several songs of praise music, the children were dismissed to their church. Cam watched as Ellie hugged Sadie good-bye then flitted past him and down the aisle toward her teacher.

Sadie's soft hand wrapped around his own. Surprised, he turned toward her. Her face was mere inches from his. She mouthed the words "Thank you." Tears glistened in her light green eyes, displaying her happiness and vulnerability. A primal instinct within him that he thought had died with Brenda forged its way to the front. He wanted to grab her in his arms and kiss the tears away, to share her joy and soothe her fears.

Blinking the thought away, he nodded. She released his hand, and he felt overwhelmingly weak from the loss of her touch. With full effort, he focused on his preacher's moving lips. If only he could actually hear what the man said. The only noise he could decipher was the pulsing beat of his heart pounding in his eardrums.

❧

Sadie could hardly comprehend that she sat at a table directly across from her daughter. Church had ended half an hour before and Cam had taken them to one of Ellie's favorite restaurants. He'd promised Ellie she could play in the play area once she'd finished her lunch. While Cam got them some napkins and ketchup, Sadie studied the child.

Ellie took a big bite of her hamburger then washed it down with a large gulp of her soda. Sadie noted the hint of fatigue through the determination on Ellie's face. Without a doubt, the child would eat, play awhile, and then take a good long nap when she got home.

Oh, how Sadie wished she could cuddle up next to Ellie for a Sunday afternoon nap.

Ellie's resemblance to Sadie was uncanny. Her long dark hair with hints of waves and curls, her slightly upturned nose, even the shape of her eyes—nearly everything about Ellie looked like Sadie. The only difference was that Ellie's eyes were a rich brown, a shade lighter than Sadie's ex-boyfriend's had been, and Sadie's eyes were light green.

Ellie wore a yellow sundress with a large sunflower on the chest. Sadie loved the color on her. She remembered seeing the dress in one of the department stores in North Carolina. As Ellie grew, Sadie couldn't help but browse the children's department of the stores. Many times, she'd picked out clothes, believing Ellie would be such-and-such size. She would hold them as she walked through the store, enjoying the texture of the materials, considering which would be most comfortable to wear. Finally, when it was time for her to leave, she would put them back where they belonged on the rack. She longed to buy cute outfits for Ellie. The little sundress was one Sadie would have picked out. "I like your dress, Ellie."

Ellie wiped her mouth with the back of her hand. Sadie grabbed a napkin as Cam sat beside his daughter. "Don't wipe with your arm, Ellie," he reprimanded. "Use a napkin."

Ellie nodded and swallowed her bite of food. "Aunt Kelly got this for me." She hopped down and twirled in a circle. "It's a twirly dress."

"Yes, it's very pretty." Cam lifted her back on her chair. "But we don't need to twirl right now. We need to eat."

Sadie couldn't help but grin at Ellie's exaggerated pout. "Your daddy's right. You need to eat. But your dress is definitely pretty."

She shifted in her chair again. "Aunt Kelly got me another dress. It's red and has a ladybug on it."

"I bet it's pretty, too. Does your Aunt Kelly live around here?"

Cam wiped ketchup from Ellie's mouth. He crumpled the napkin and laid it on the table. "Yeah. Kelly's my sister. She and her three girls just moved here a few months ago."

"Uncle Tim went to see Mommy in heaven." Ellie took another drink then jumped off the chair. "Can I play now, Daddy?"

"Sure. Take off your shoes and put them in one of the slots. Sadie and I will be right here."

Sadie frowned at what Ellie had said. Had Cam's sister's husband passed away as well? Before she could think more about it, Ellie had slipped off her shoes and bounded inside the massive jungle gym.

"My sister's husband died this year." Cam's voice was low, just over a whisper.

"I'm sorry."

"It was a car accident." He leaned back in the chair. Sadie followed his gaze to the ball pit. Ellie waved at them, and they waved back. "It's been a hard year. A lot of loss."

Sadie didn't know what to say. She'd never really had to deal with death. Even though their relationship had been strained the last five years, both of her parents were still alive. She didn't have any siblings, and she'd grown up away from her grandparents. When her mother's dad and her father's parents passed away, she'd felt only some sadness. "I'm so sorry for all of you."

Cam looked at her. "Ellie misses Brenda, but she's dealt with her death better than I ever would have anticipated. Now she's watching her aunt and cousins grieve their husband and daddy. She doesn't need any more loss."

Sadie swallowed. A part of her felt offended that he would insinuate or, worse, believe that she would walk into Ellie's life and then turn around and walk back out. Sadie had every intention of being a mother to Ellie. She knew it sounded crazy, even in her own mind. How could a woman give up her baby and then five years later decide she wanted her back?

But Sadie did want her back.

She didn't want to take Ellie from Cam. Cam was Ellie's father, in nearly every sense of the word. He cared for Ellie, nurtured Ellie, loved her. It was obvious he'd been a terrific dad, and Sadie felt blessed that God had provided Cam and Brenda for Ellie.

But the situation had changed.

Sadie never would have taken Brenda from Ellie. If she had known, Sadie would have prayed tirelessly for Brenda's healing. Sadie cared for Brenda. She considered her somewhat of a friend, a sister in Christ. Sadie knew Brenda loved Ellie as if she'd been her biological mother.

But death had physically separated Ellie and Brenda. With a confidence of spirit that overwhelmed Sadie at times, she knew God wanted her to be in Delaware, near her little girl. "Cam, I promise you I will do nothing to hurt Ellie."

He nodded, but she noted the uncertainty that still lurked in his eyes. Sadie wished she could say something to put his mind at ease, but she knew he would need time to see that she wasn't going anywhere.

"Daddy, I. . ."

Sadie's heart dropped as Ellie limped toward their table, tears welling in her eyes. In a flash, Sadie hopped out of her chair and lifted Ellie into her arms. She pushed the wrappings away from the table, giving her a place to set Ellie down and check the damage to her leg. Sadie gingerly touched her foot and examined both sides of her ankle. "Let's see, sweetie. I don't see any. . ."

A slight chuckle sounded from Cam, and Sadie looked up to see Cam covering his mouth with his hand as Ellie's eyes widened. The child sniffed and gawked at Sadie. "I hurt my toe."

Sudden heat raced up Sadie's neck as she took in the barely visible scratch. The skin hadn't even broken. Knowing she'd overreacted, she clicked her tongue. "You're fine. Just a scratch."

Cam picked her up. "I'd say she's more tired than hurt."

"I'm not tired," Ellie whined, obviously deciding to go with the notion that she'd been maimed in some way. "I'm hurt."

"Okay." Cam smoothed her hair with his free hand. "Let's see if the hurt goes away after we take a nap."

"I don't want a nap."

Sadie cleaned up the wrappings off the table and threw them in the trash. She followed Cam and Ellie out the door and stopped at his truck. She'd driven herself, so this was apparently the end of the visit. She ran her fingers through the bottom of Ellie's hair. "I was glad to meet you, Ellie."

Ellie turned to face Sadie, her eyes puffy from crying. "I don't want a nap."

Sadie touched her cheek. "You know what, I'm probably going to take a nap, too."

Ellie looked at Cam. "Daddy, can Sadie take a nap with us?"

Ellie's innocent statement planted a picture in Sadie's mind, and she quickly shook it away. Looking at Cam, she thought he'd imagined the same thing. "I don't think so, pun'kin." His voice sounded scratchy, and he cleared his throat.

"I'd love to see you another time." Sadie tried to convey the urgency she felt to see Ellie again through her gaze.

Ellie perked up, grabbing Cam's jaw with her hands. "Can she go fishing with us, Daddy?"

Sadie grimaced, and Cam laughed. "I think that's a great idea, pun'kin." He cocked one eyebrow. "Will you go fishing with us this Thursday evening?"

Fishing was definitely not her forte. But Sadie would do anything to be close to Ellie. "Sure. Just tell me when and where."

"My house. Seven thirty."

"You got it." She patted Ellie's back. "I'll see you then." Sadie slipped into her car. Seeing Ellie had been bliss. She could hardly wait for Thursday to come. *As long as I don't have to touch a worm or a fish, I will be perfectly content.* She bit the inside of her lip. If that was what she had to do to see Ellie, she wouldn't complain.

Chapter 5

Cam dropped the handsaw to the ground then scratched the beard that had formed over the past four days. *I've got to get Sadie out of my mind.* He measured the wood with his tape measure. "I cut half an inch more than I should have."

He threw the tape measure into his toolbox. "It's all this daydreaming." He growled as he leaned back against the wall of his garage. *A man shouldn't spend his time thinking about silky brown hair; long legs; a trim waist; and eyes, so full of determination, gazing at him through green orbs.*

He pushed away from the wall. "What has gotten into you, Reynolds?"

"What *has* gotten into you, Cam?" Kelly's voice sounded from the front of the garage. She walked to his worktable. "Weren't you working on this two days ago?"

He folded his arms in front of his chest. "Yep."

"Did you say you cut this piece too short?"

"I did."

"As I recall, the last time my brother messed up his woodworking was when he was falling for a cute little blond by the name of Brenda."

Cam grunted. "What is that supposed to mean?"

"It means even when Brenda was sick, even after she died, you stayed focused on your work. If anything, your pieces turned out to be near perfection." Kelly sat on the stool. "So what's going on? Does it have to do with Sadie?"

"I don't know." Cam shrugged. "Just because the woman wants to step in and be a mother figure in Ellie's life?" His voice dripped with sarcasm as he waved his hands in front of his chest and shook his head. "No. That's not stressing me out in the slightest."

Kelly peered at him for several moments. He wondered if the temperature in the room rose several degrees. Kelly furrowed her eyebrows. "I don't think that's all of it."

"Whatever." Cam picked up another piece of wood. He measured the appropriate length and penciled a mark. He knew he was being abrupt with Kelly, but he wasn't ready to admit to himself the feelings he was experiencing, let alone talk about them with his sister.

"Ellie said she met a pretty lady named Sadie at church on Sunday." Kelly's voice took on a winsome tone. "She said Sadie liked her dress and that she colored a picture with her and that she was coming to the house to fish tonight."

Cam measured the wood again to double-check his mark was right. "Yeah, so?"

"I'm assuming Ellie doesn't know who Sadie is."

Cam peeked back at Kelly then picked up the handsaw. "No, she doesn't. I want them to see each other a few times first."

"Zoey thinks Sadie must be your girlfriend for you to be introducing her to Ellie."

"Humph." Panic welled within Cam. Zoey would be surprised to know just how much a part of Cam wished that to be true. Logically, it made no sense. And Cam had to keep telling himself to think logically. He scratched the top of his head then rubbed his jaw.

"Just as I feared."

He turned and looked at Kelly. "What are you talking about?"

"You scratched your head and then rubbed your jaw."

"So?"

"So. You always do that when you're trying to hide something."

"Trying to what?"

Kelly stood and walked to Cam. She rested her hand on his arm. "You're attracted to Sadie, aren't you?"

It was on the tip of his tongue to lie, but his spirit stopped him. He slumped back against the wall. "I guess I am."

Kelly nodded and walked out the garage door. "I'll be praying for you, little brother. Have fun tonight."

He stood back to his full height, rested the blade against the wood, and then second-guessed himself. Picking up the tape measure, he knew he would have to check the length one more time to ensure he'd marked correctly. All this girlie daydreaming was interfering with his and Ellie's livelihood.

Pray for me about tonight. She'd better be praying. Between his raging emotions and Sadie's amazing looks and adorable excitement with Ellie, he had no doubt he would need all the prayers he could get.

⌇

Sadie stared at Cam and Ellie's house. Her nerves were getting the best of her. Flattening the wrinkles from her new khaki shorts, she remembered the red hat she'd purchased to go with the ladybug sundress that Ellie's aunt had bought her.

One of the advantages of her new state was no sales tax, and Sadie had made full use of the perk over the last few days. Owning only dressy casual clothes, she'd had no idea what to wear on a fishing trip, and she was sure her grunge/bedtime clothes covered with stains and holes would not be appropriate. Venturing into the largest city in Delaware, Sadie had made her way to the Concord Mall. In

North Carolina, she'd had to drive over an hour to get to a shopping mall, so she intended to relish the ninety or so stores in the mall. With plans to buy something casual and cheap to wear, she found herself strolling through some of the children's stores selecting cute outfits for Ellie. With no sales tax, she would have been able to purchase more than she'd intended.

Of course, after she'd picked up a dress and two short outfits, Sadie had come to her senses and put them back. Ellie wouldn't know what to think of a nearly perfect stranger buying her a bunch of clothes. *I'm not sure Cam would have appreciated it either.*

Unable to keep herself from buying something for her daughter, Sadie selected an adorable fisherman's-style hat to match Ellie's dress. Then she'd made her way to the women's department to find her khaki shorts and T-shirt.

Exhaling a deep breath, Sadie scooped the hat out of the passenger's seat of her car and headed for the front door. She'd barely reached the step when Ellie bounded out onto the porch.

"Hey, Sadie."

The child's hair was fixed in two flat braids that rested over the front of her shoulders. She wore the sweetest red and white gingham shirt and little blue jean shorts. Sadie wanted to lift her little girl into her arms and squeeze her with the pent-up love she'd held back for so long. *Patience, Sadie. She has no idea who you are, and if she found out right now, it would probably scare her to death.*

Sadie leaned over and flipped a braid around Ellie's shoulder. "Hey, Ellie. You look like you're ready to go fishing."

Ellie nodded then grabbed Sadie's hand. She practically dragged Sadie into the house. "Daddy, Sadie's here. We can go now."

Cam walked out of the kitchen wiping his hands on a dishrag. "Perfect timing. I just finished cleaning up the kitchen."

Sadie held back a whistle. There was something over-the-top enticing about a man big as a Smoky Mountain bear with a full-grown beard and a masculine glint in his eye who was holding a dishrag having just finished the kitchen work. Cam Reynolds would be a better catch than any finned creature they might see at his pond.

What is wrong with me? Sadie shook the wayward thought from her mind. *I can't think about Cam that way. He's the father of my daughter.* She pursed her lips. *Okay, that didn't sound right. But he is ten years older than I am.*

She snuck another peek at him. He had squatted down in front of Ellie to tie her shoelaces. *What is ten years when a man looks like that?*

"Stop it," she muttered.

"What's that?" Cam looked up at her.

Heat flooded Sadie's cheeks and neck. She looked down at the hat in her hand. "Oh, Ellie. I almost forgot. I bought this for you."

Ellie skipped back over to Sadie. She took the hat from Sadie's hands, placed it on her head, and then looked at Cam. "Look, Daddy. Aren't I pretty?"

"You sure are."

"Am I as pretty as Sadie?"

Sadie sucked in her breath. What had beguiled the child to say that? She glanced at Cam, noting his beard didn't mask the red that spilled across his cheeks. "I would say you are."

Sadie cleared her throat. "Ellie, I got that hat to go with the red dress your aunt bought you."

"My ladybug dress?"

Sadie nodded. She snuck a peek at Cam, whose posture visibly relaxed with the change of subject. "Did you know the ladybug is your state bug?"

Ellie scrunched her nose. "Our state bug? What's a state bug?"

"It's the bug that represents Delaware."

"What's 'represents' mean, Daddy?"

Cam chuckled. "It kinda means it shows who we are."

Ellie shoved one of her braids into her mouth. Sadie thought to tell her not to eat her hair, but decided if Cam didn't mind, she shouldn't correct her child either. *Her* child—Sadie couldn't stop thinking of Ellie as her child. Biologically, she was. Now all Sadie could think about was living out being a mother to Ellie as well.

Ellie pulled her hair from her mouth. A frown still etched her face. "You mean I am a ladybug?"

Cam laughed out loud.

"But I don't want to be a bug, Daddy." Ellie reached up and grabbed Cam's hand. "I don't like bugs."

Sadie didn't know what to say. She regretted even mentioning the state bug thing. How did one explain a state bug to a child? *Ellie's right. Why in the world does a state need a bug as a mascot?*

"No, sweetie." Sadie searched her mind for an explanation a five-year-old would understand. "It's not that you're a bug. Each state has a bug, a flower, a flag—all kinds of things that represent who they are. For Delaware, the state bug just happens to be a ladybug. Probably, there are a lot of ladybugs living in Delaware. . . ."

Cam lifted Ellie over his right shoulder then turned to Sadie and smiled. The man could make her lose all sense of reality when he looked at her like that. "Don't worry, Sadie. Ellie here *is* a ladybug."

He held her with his right hand and tickled her belly with his left. Ellie folded over into uncontrollable giggles.

Sadie brushed a piece of hair away from her face. "Thanks for saving me."

"You're welcome." Cam put Ellie down and picked up a container that she assumed to be his tackle box. "So where'd you learn that ladybugs are our state bug?"

Sadie rolled her eyes. "My landlord. He knows everything about the state of Delaware and wants to be sure I know how fortunate I am to live here."

Cam's gaze softened. "No, *we're* fortunate you live here."

Sadie's heart felt as if it had melted beneath her lungs. He was glad to have her around. He was giving her the opportunity to get to know her daughter. *Sweet Jesus, You are too good to me. Thank You for softening his heart.*

⁓

With a bottle of lemon-flavored water in his hand, Cam settled onto the metal bench that he'd placed some fifteen feet from the pond. The cool June air rested on him with more comfort than a long, soothing sit in a hot tub after a day of hard manual labor. The sun had set a little more than an hour before, and Ellie had been sound asleep for about as long. Again, he was thankful the pond was so near the back of the house. He couldn't count the times he'd sat in this very spot, sometimes for several hours, after Ellie had gone to sleep. Sometimes he'd mourned Brenda's death. Other times he'd praised God for a blessing of some kind. This spot was the place he did most of his talking, and listening, to God.

The water lay still and peaceful with only an occasional fish popping up his head to snatch at a bug of some kind that had landed on the water. He grinned at the memory of the evening he and Ellie had spent with Sadie.

"Are we catching weakfish today? I've heard they're the Delaware state fish," Sadie had asked while she held the fishing rod he'd given her at an odd angle. He'd feared she would hook herself or one of them before the trip ended.

"Weakfish are saltwater fish," he'd responded.

"Oh." She'd lifted her eyebrows then furrowed them deep into a frown. She'd had no idea what he was talking about. Her confused expression made her even more attractive.

"A pond has freshwater in it."

She'd pushed her head back, her lips forming the cutest O he'd ever seen. "I see."

Cam laughed out loud. She didn't "see." It was apparent she didn't have a clue what he meant.

"Daddy, are we fish now, too?" Ellie'd grown as confused as Sadie.

Leaning back on the bench, Cam smiled at the memory. He took a drink of water then wiped his mouth with the back of his hand. He'd had more fun today than he'd had in years.

It pained him to think that way. He'd loved Brenda, had poured his heart, body, soul, and mind into their relationship. God commanded him to love Brenda as Christ loved the church, with a willingness to give his life for her. He'd heeded God's command, not only out of obedience, but also out of a true, deep desire. She had been all he'd ever wanted in a spouse.

Still, he couldn't deny the last two years of her life had been hard ones. The surgery, the chemo, the radiation had taken a toll on her physically and emotionally. Brenda had been a real trooper the entire time, and her good days were really good. But the bad days had been misery to endure.

Guilt stabbed him at the joy he'd felt fishing today. Sadie was very different from Brenda, in looks, in personality, but Cam found himself drawn to the younger woman.

He leaned forward, resting his elbows on his knees. It felt wrong to think of Sadie that way. He felt unfaithful to Brenda. In only a few weeks, it would be one year since her death. He'd never imagined he would find himself so drawn to another woman. Not only did he feel guilt, but part of him also felt selfish. He knew plenty of people who never found the right person to cherish for all their lives, and here he was contemplating a second.

He huffed. *What am I thinking? Contemplating a second? I barely know Sadie. My feelings are probably simply a man's natural reaction to a beautiful, sweet lady after his wife's been gone awhile. I'm not some young pup who can't think with his mind.*

He stood, stretching the kinks out of his arms and back. *Maybe I need a cold shower to get my mind in right order.*

Cam walked toward his pond. He bent down and picked up a rock, then skipped it across the water. He'd done it earlier in the day as well. Sadie's face had brightened when the pebble bounced several times on top of the water. For a gal who'd lived around the Smoky Mountains for several years, she didn't know very much about nature. Her unsuccessful efforts to skip a rock had made him laugh. Even now, the memory brought a smile to his lips.

He scratched his jaw to clear his mind. Even if he wasn't being unfaithful to Brenda, Sadie was too young for him. He was thirty-four, nearly thirty-five. Sadie was a full ten years younger than he was. An entire decade. Why, when he was a senior in high school, she would have only been in second grade. He snarled. The thought was disgusting.

But you're not in high school, are you? Nor is she in second grade.

He sighed at the inner nudging of his heart. In truth, ten years probably wasn't too much time since they were both adults. She'd experienced as many challenges in her life as he had in his. Of course, hers were different, but they were no less difficult. She'd graduated college; he'd never even attended. She'd had a child and given her up; he'd experienced the first five years of raising a child, but not a biological offspring.

Growling at where his thoughts were going, he shoved his hands in his pockets and stared into the night sky. Stars dotted the expanse, and as it had since he was a child, his gaze sought out the Big and Little Dippers. He thought of the third reason he didn't need to think of Sadie in such a way.

This reason had brought devastation to Brenda. As long as he lived, he would never forget the look in her eyes when they'd heard the news. She was committed to him, to their relationship, but her eyes tattled of a heart broken into a million pieces.

God, I could never do that to another woman. Never.

He turned and started back toward the house. *"For God is greater than our hearts, and he knows everything."* One of the many verses that Brenda had pasted around the house during her battle flooded his mind.

What do You mean, Lord?

A slight breeze brushed his face, and only the insects responded to his question. In his spirit, however, he knew. It had something to do with hurt and healing.

Chapter 6

Sadie slipped into one of the available seats around the oversized, oblong meeting table. In a little over a month, she would begin working every day in her small office, reviewing and preparing files for the various students for whom she would provide services. She'd guide the special education teachers throughout the county in proper physical or mental exercises that would benefit students who were delayed or injured in some way. She'd meet with parents, interview students, study their abilities, work to find their physical and mental boundaries, design activities to stretch them. She would celebrate with students, parents, and teachers as individual goals were met and exceeded. Though at times trying—she remembered the father she'd worked with the last school year—overall her job proved exceptionally satisfying.

Today, however, she'd have the opportunity to meet the principals, assistant principals, and counselors from each of the schools. Though she felt no small degree of trepidation, she'd looked forward to this day. Confident in her ability to get a good feel for a person quickly, she expected to leave with an idea of how to work and communicate effectively in each school.

Most of the chairs were already filled, and though she sat beside an older woman on her left and a middle-aged man on her right, neither opted to introduce themselves. Normally, Sadie would go ahead and do so herself, but already the atmosphere in the room had taken on a more professional, less friendly air than what she was accustomed to in North Carolina.

Don't worry. She inwardly discouraged the butterflies that had begun to flutter in her stomach. *By the end of this day, I will know everyone's name. The woman whose position I've acquired worked here for thirty years. I knew before I accepted the job I'd have big shoes to fill.*

Sadie forced a smile to her lips as she scanned the faces around the table. Most everyone was at least twenty years her senior. Of course, it made sense for principals and counselors to be the more experienced people in a school building, but she was used to working with at least assistant principals who were closer to her age.

Sadie found herself picking at her already-chewed nails. Again, she inwardly reprimanded herself for the atrocious habit. It made her hands appear a wreck, and it definitely wasn't sanitary.

More people had come in. Only one seat remained unfilled. She noted the superintendent had not arrived either. Just as she realized his absence, he walked in. A young man, much closer to Sadie's age, followed him and claimed the empty seat.

Relief flooded Sadie. At least one face seemed to be somewhat near her age range. She clasped her hands at the silliness of her unease. In North Carolina, her dearest mentor had been a woman at one of the elementary schools who'd been thirty years older than Sadie.

Maybe it's not their ages that have my stomach tied in knots. Though the superintendent had started to speak, Sadie looked around the table once more. It wasn't age difference; it was the way they held themselves, the expressions on their faces. They all appeared to be generally unhappy to be there.

Sadie let out a long, slow breath. She noticed the younger man who'd walked in with her new boss. He smiled at her, exposing straight, ultra-white teeth. *Wow. He could be in a teeth-whitening commercial.*

Sadie stopped herself from laughing out loud. She didn't have a single problem with people who whitened their teeth. One time she'd even bought some over-the-counter whitener, but it had made her teeth so sensitive she quit using the strips after only three days. Still, every time she saw someone with knock-you-down white teeth, she had this inner urge to tell them just how unnatural it looked.

Of course, some of her friends had coffee and tea stains lightened at the dentist's office, but apparently there were various shades of white from which a dentist could choose. Ultra-white would never be her choice.

Sadie clenched her hands together on top of the table. *What am I thinking? Whitened teeth? I need to pay attention to my boss.*

Determined to listen, she looked up at her superintendent. He pointed to a chart on the wall that showed the statistics of kids in the county with disabilities of various kinds. *It does seem odd that he didn't introduce me to these colleagues.*

She squelched the thought. Different people handled new employees differently. He would most likely introduce her to them when they had a break or at the end of the session.

She tried to focus anew on her boss's words. Her nerves were getting away with her, and she found herself scanning the faces around the table again. The young guy was already looking her direction. He lifted his eyebrows and slightly nodded.

Sadie acknowledged him with a grin. This time she noted his hair was a shade of brown, but not as dark as Cam's. His eyes, from across the table, appeared to be a light shade of blue, a very pretty color, but they didn't seem to portray the kindness that Cam's did. The man didn't even have a hint of a five o' clock shadow, unlike Cam, whose beard transformed him into a grizzly bear before the day ended. Of course, it was only the beginning of the day.

Why am I comparing him to Cam?

The realization sent her head spinning. The last thing she needed to do right now was fall for Cam Reynolds. Her goal was to spend as much time as she could with Ellie, eventually gain her trust, tell her the truth, and be the mother figure Ellie no longer had in her life. She did not need to start having feelings for a man who was still grieving his wife. For crying out loud, she was grieving his wife as well. In a different way, of course, but Sadie could honestly confess that she knew Ellie could not have been raised by a godlier, more loving, woman than Brenda.

God, I can't think about all this right now. Please help me focus on the superintendent. Picking up a pen, she looked back at her boss, determined to be able to relay everything he said, word for word.

After two days of never-ending meetings with her new colleagues and never-ending inner battles about Cam Reynolds, Sadie was glad for the reprieve of spending a day with Ellie. Of course, Cam joined them, so she still had to fight her unyielding attraction; but at least she didn't have to try to keep her mind focused on the words of her superintendent. Sadie had at least been able to make her acquaintance with the others. As she feared, most of her colleagues had shared a close relationship with the past occupational therapist. She knew it would take time to gain their trust, and she was confident God would help her do so.

Sadie held Ellie's hand as they walked toward the breathtakingly gorgeous and ostentatious Winterthur country estate. Her landlord had told her she would need to visit Brandywine Valley multiple times even to begin to get a glimpse of some of Delaware's rich heritage. "You won't find history anywhere else in the United States like you'll find in the country's first state," he'd boasted. Taking in only a portion of Winterthur's majesty, she believed him to be correct.

She drank in the pink, lavender, blue, and white flowers, clustered together in various places. She wasn't very good at remembering the names of flowers, but she did note the yellow and orange daylilies that proudly displayed their perfection with the other flowers. She felt as if she were part of a picture that a master artist had created. The only word she could conjure in her mind to describe it was *breathtaking*.

And the smells. Oh, she could wrap herself up in the array of fragrances around her. Her heart raced and she threw back her head for a long, luscious inhaling of the place. A woman could easily get caught up in the romance of it. Unintentionally, she looked at Cam, who had slipped Ellie's free hand in his own.

He is such a good dad. Sadie could easily picture him with a whole team of children racing around his feet. She wondered if his children would have the same cute dimple that he had in his chin. *Ah! I've got to stop thinking about him like that.*

Ellie's voice squeaked as they neared their destination, allowing Sadie to escape her thoughts. "We're almost to the Enchanted Woods!"

"Yes, we are." Still holding Ellie's hand, Sadie leaned over and gave her an Eskimo kiss. "You'll have to show me everything."

Sadie stood back up and smiled at Cam. She knew her elation probably showed through her eyes. The kindness that always radiated from him encouraged her to feel at ease with expressing her excitement.

With Sadie and Cam still holding her hands, Ellie began to swing her arms back and forth. "Oh yes, I will show you the stones you can walk on, the bird's nest, the troll's bridge. I'll show you the tree house. . . ."

"What about Harvey?" Cam asked.

Sadie watched as Ellie scrunched her nose. She let out a long breath. "I guess I'll show her Harvey, too."

Cam released a hearty laugh. "You're willing to share Harvey? You won't even let me touch Harvey."

Ellie pursed her lips and scowled up at her father. "Daddy, you are a boy. You're not allowed to hug Harvey."

"Hmm. I think I need to know who this Harvey is if I'm going to be hugging him." Sadie looked from Cam to Ellie.

Ellie puffed out her chest. "He's a frog."

Sadie felt her mouth drop open. "A what?"

Cam roared with laughter. "Yep. That's right, Sadie. Ellie loves to drag me over here so she can visit a frog."

Ellie stomped her foot. "You don't laugh at me and Sadie, Daddy."

Cam released Ellie's hand and lifted both of his in surrender. "Okay. Okay."

He peered into Sadie's eyes. Laughter still danced in them, and Sadie found herself willing to hug a nasty old frog for him. *Not him. For Ellie. I'd hug the frog for Ellie.*

"The frog is really a fountain that sits on a rock. He's enchanted, like the frog prince." Cam winked, and Sadie thought her feet would collapse beneath her. "You hug him for good luck."

"Not for luck, Daddy." She put her hand on her hip. "Because we love him."

"You're right, Ellie." Sadie mimicked her daughter by putting her hand on her hip and frowning at Cam. "There's no such thing as luck. Only God's workings."

"Touché." He lifted an imaginary hat off his head and bowed. "I completely agree."

Sadie's heart swelled. Yes, they did agree. Unlike Ellie's biological father, Cam had a relationship with God, a true love for the Lord. *And of course, now I know that is the most important thing I would ever look for in a mate.*

She pushed the thought away, and yet she couldn't deny the quickening of her pulse.

⁕

Cam snuck a peek at Sadie in the passenger seat as they drove out of Wilmington. Her head leaned against the window, her eyes closed. Unsure if she was actually asleep or simply resting, he didn't dare look at her for too long. *Better keep your eyes on the road anyway, Reynolds.*

He looked in the rearview mirror. Ellie was asleep in her child seat. It had been a wonderful day at Winterthur. He'd visited several times with Ellie over the last few years. Brenda had endured the trip one time, but the heat and enormity of the place had worn her out for several days after.

Today was a really good day. He remembered the bliss on Sadie's face as she and Ellie crossed the troll's bridge hand in hand. Ellie had been every bit as excited as Sadie. His heart had nearly lurched out of his chest when Sadie and Ellie sat across from each other at the Acorn Tearoom. Their resemblance was uncanny. Somehow, it seemed right for the two of them to be together.

"Good heavens." Sadie sat up. She rubbed her eyes then trailed her fingers through her hair. "I can't believe I fell asleep. The drive isn't even that far."

"Nope."

Sadie touched his arm. Pleasure coursed through his body. "How long was I out?" She turned in her seat and looked at Ellie. When she did, she released his arm, and he instantly missed the weight of her hand. "Guess I'm not the only one who's exhausted."

"Definitely not. We'll be back at my house in just a few minutes."

Sadie nodded then leaned her head back against the seat. "Thanks so much for including me, Cam."

"It was my pleasure."

She had no idea how much pleasure it was for him. She was vibrant and exciting. He'd never meet another woman who would love his daughter any more than Sadie. The truth of it sank into his gut, making him yearn for the freedom to care about her as more than Ellie's biological mother. He exhaled as he pulled into his driveway. He unbuckled his seat belt and looked back at Ellie. "I think that kid's down for the count." He dangled the keys in front of Sadie. "Would you mind opening the door for me?"

Sadie bit her bottom lip but didn't take the keys. She stared into his eyes for a moment. "Would you mind terribly if I carried her inside?"

Cam lifted his eyebrows. "No, but she is a bit heavy."

Love filled Sadie's eyes. "She won't be to me."

His heart raced at the intense expression on her face. She loved with fierceness, with passion. The knowledge of it scared him, and he looked away and nodded. He fumbled for the car's handle. Finding it, he pushed open the door. He willed his feet to steady as he made his way to the front door and unlocked it.

Within moments, Sadie was behind him with Ellie draped over her shoulder. He'd never witnessed a person so happy to carry the deadweight of a sleeping child. Opening the door for her, he nodded toward the end of the hall. "Last room on the right."

"Thank you, Cam." Sadie's voice was little more than a whisper and was filled with intensity and hope.

Cam followed her inside Ellie's bedroom. He opened the dresser and lifted a pink nightgown from inside it while Sadie laid Ellie on the bed. Cam watched as Sadie gently unbuckled Ellie's sandals then slipped them off her feet.

Ellie startled and her eyes opened, her gaze searching the room in panic. Sadie caressed his daughter's cheek. "Hush now, sweetie. You're okay. You're home. In your bed."

Ellie's small frame relaxed, and she nestled her cheek into Sadie's hand. Cam heard Sadie's light gasp. She turned and took the nightgown from his hand. Gingerly, she changed Ellie then tucked her into bed as if she'd done it every day of Ellie's life. Leaning over Ellie once more, Cam watched as Sadie barely kissed his daughter's forehead.

Sadie stood to her full height and gazed at his child for a moment. Then she covered her face with her hand as her chest heaved in a cry. Cam wrapped his arm around Sadie's shoulder. She fit perfectly. "Come on." He guided her out of the room, down the hall, and into the living area.

Sadie broke away from his grip. "I'm so sorry, Cam." She swiped unsuccessfully at the tears that streamed down her face. "I can't believe I got this upset. I'm so. . ." She covered her face again.

"Come here." He wrapped her small frame in his arms. Her sobs escalated. Her back heaved. All he could do was caress her soft hair. "It's okay."

"I'm so sorry, so. . ."

"Shh." He nestled her closer. "It's okay to cry."

For what seemed an eternity, Cam endured her tears without the ability to kiss them away. He endured the light scent of her hair without the ability to inhale his fill. He endured the softness of her skin without the ability to really touch.

Finally, she pulled away. Inhaling deeply, she wiped her face with the back of her hand. With a slight chuckle, she looked at the black that smeared the top of her fingers. "Well, I must look a fright."

"Not too bad." Cam didn't have the heart to tell her that black streaked across her forehead, nose, and cheeks. He couldn't tell her that her eyes were swollen and puffy and that her nose shone like Rudolph's at Christmas. Anyway, he thought she looked adorable.

"I'll try not to do this every time I see you."

Cam lifted his hand and willed his heart to slow to its regular pace. "Not a problem."

"When can I see Ellie again?"

Cam let out a long sigh and smacked his jaw. "I forgot to tell you."

Sadie furrowed her eyebrows. "Forgot to tell me what?"

"Ellie is going to stay with my parents in Florida for two weeks. We're leaving in two days."

Sadie's shoulders slumped. "You'll be gone, too?"

Cam's heart skipped at the idea that she would care if he would be gone as well. "I'm flying her down there, but I'm coming back."

"Oh." Sadie frowned.

Cam shifted his weight from one foot to the other. "I thought it might be for the best. The anniversary of Brenda's death is next Thursday. . . ."

Sadie looked up at him. True regret shadowed her face. "Cam, I'm sorry."

His emotions seemed heightened tonight, and he swallowed back a lump that formed in his throat. "Thanks. I wasn't sure when my parents offered, but then my sister, Kelly, and I figured it would do the kids good to get away during that time."

"I'd say you're right." Sadie wiped at her face once more. "Will you call me when she gets back?"

Cam nodded. "I will."

She turned and walked toward the door. Cam watched as Sadie made her way to her car. She looked at her reflection in the rearview mirror, and Cam watched as she gasped and quickly licked her fingers to wipe at the traces of makeup across her face.

He chuckled. Two weeks would be an awfully long time for him not to see Sadie.

Chapter 7

Four long days had passed since Sadie's trip to Winterthur with Cam and Ellie. She was amazed at all Delaware had to offer, as well as the natural beauty that filled the state. Contented warmth filled her when she thought of Ellie grabbing her hand and escorting her to Harvey. Allowing Sadie to hug the frog statue proved to be an enormous honor Ellie gave to Sadie.

Night and day, she'd been physically ill with the desire to see her little girl again. She'd tried to keep herself busy with the food pantry ministry at the church. She'd talked with Lisa on the phone a couple of times, but her friend was busy caring for the boys, unpacking, and visiting with Rick's family. Sadie had also enjoyed a nice lunch with one of the assistant principals. The woman talked nonstop about her youngest daughter getting ready to head to college in the fall, but at least the outing had filled part of one day. Despite all that, Sadie had watched the news and checked the Internet multiple times two days before—the day Cam and Ellie were scheduled to leave for Florida. No airline accidents had been reported that she could find. Everything in her wanted to call and confirm they'd arrived safely, but Sadie didn't want to push too hard or too fast. *Especially after I broke down on him the other night.*

She slumped at the remembrance of it. It had been a long time since she'd come so unglued. Not one to embarrass herself quickly or handle it well, Sadie had been horrified at her body's overwhelming response to tucking Ellie in bed. She'd missed so much.

And Cam. She inhaled deeply as the light musky scent of him washed over her anew. How perfectly she fit in his embrace. His chest and arms were strong around her. The caress of his hand against her hair had been so gentle. A shiver coursed through her, and she cleared her throat, demanding her mind to clear as well.

Determined to think of something else, she drove to the Concord Mall in hopes of finding a new devotional book. She found several, finally selecting one. Of course, she couldn't help but notice the devotionals dedicated to little girls. She lifted the bookstore bag higher onto her elbow. *I can just say it's a welcome-back gift to Ellie.*

Sadie approached the counter of the fast-food restaurant in the food court. She smiled at the teenager standing beside the register who appeared to have more metal in her mouth than she had teeth. Cringing at the frizzy, un-netted hair of the teenage cook, she focused on not thinking about whether or not the boy's hands were clean.

"What can I get you?" The girl tapped her fingers on the counter.

"I'll take a bacon cheeseburger, no onion, a medium fry, and a chocolate milk shake." She brushed away the notion that she was probably going to devour an entire day's worth of calories in one meal. *One fatty meal won't kill me.*

She paid the cashier, took her food and several packets of ketchup, and headed for one of the few empty tables she could find. She sat and closed her eyes for the briefest of moments. *Thank You, Lord, for this food. Please allow me to enjoy it, because it's probably apple slices and water for dinner tonight.* She might have to add a bit of peanut butter to the slices, and maybe have milk instead of water. A gal needed her nutrients after all.

Opening her eyes, she saw a familiar face sitting across from her. "I didn't want to disturb your prayer," Mr. Ultra-white Smile explained. He motioned around the food court. "You can see there're no empty tables." Sadie spied one off to her right. "I thought we could share lunch together. . .maybe get to know one another a bit before school starts."

Though it unnerved her that he'd watched her pray, Sadie agreed it would be great to get to know him before the school year started. "Sure." She extended her hand. "In case you forgot, I'm Sadie Ellis."

The man smiled, exposing the teeth that reminded her of small pieces of Chiclets gum. Truly, they were very nice, just so bright. He shook her hand. "Yes. I remembered your name. I'm Charles Mann."

"It's nice to meet you again." Sadie took a drink of her milk shake. "I don't remember which school you work at."

"I'm the assistant principal at the middle school." Charles took a bite from his fruit cup.

Sadie noticed the grilled chicken wrapped in a wheat tortilla and cup of fruit on his plate. His drink looked clear, probably water. The man probably thought her diet was atrocious. "Great. Is there anything special you could share with me? Any specific ways of doing things?"

Charles told her who the secretaries were and which ones handled different office duties. He shared the way the past occupational therapist had communicated with the school counselor and psychologist. He filled her in on a few students he knew she'd be working with. His information was invaluable, and Sadie listened attentively. By the time she'd finished her lunch, she knew she could go into the middle school with some ease.

She wadded up her cheeseburger wrapper, careful to keep from spilling any condiments on the plastic tray. "Thanks so much for all the information,

Charles. You've been very helpful."

"You're more than welcome." He paused, and she noticed he looked at her left hand for the fourth time since he'd sat down. Her female intuition knew what was about to happen, and she was not prepared to consider going on a date with one of her brand-new colleagues. He started to open his mouth again.

Sadie jumped up, scooping her tray into her hand. "Well, Charles, it was very nice having lunch with you, but I've got to go."

"Well, I. . ."

She looked at her watch. Truth truly was going to save her. "I really have to go. I have an appointment in half an hour."

"Okay. I'll see you."

She raced out to the parking lot. "Thank You, Lord, for hair appointments."

❧

Cam wrapped his fingers around the cool glass. Condensation wet his hands, bringing some relief from the warm Florida air. His mother had learned to make some really good sweet tea since she'd moved south, and he enjoyed as much of it as he could when he visited. He watched as his nieces and Ellie splashed around in his parents' pool. In a bit, he'd probably join them. His ears just weren't quite ready this early in the morning for the squealing of four girls.

The back door opened, and Kelly slipped into the seat beside him on the patio. "I told Mom and Dad about Sadie."

Cam nodded. It wasn't something he intended to keep from them. He'd struggled with missing her so much he'd simply opted out of talking about it.

"Mom's getting ready to join us outside."

"And Dad?"

Kelly swatted the air. "You know Dad. He doesn't have much to say about anything. He's going fishing."

Cam laughed. It was true. Norm Reynolds didn't get overly concerned with the intricate happenings in his children's lives. He cared about them. He wanted to see them happy. He just didn't need to know all the details.

"I'm a simple man," he'd proclaim and point to his chest every time Cam's mother got upset that Norm didn't want to listen to something she'd have to say. It wasn't that his dad didn't care. He had been a rock for Cam when Brenda died, but Cam knew Sadie showing up would be out of his dad's realm of possible discussion topics.

"Well, there you are." Cam's mother, Anita, slipped into the empty chair beside Kelly.

Cam grinned. His mother was going to ease herself toward the topic. But her *easing* often took so long they never actually had a chance to get to the topic.

Kelly leaned back in her chair. "Mom, I already told him I told you."

Cam chuckled. His family was so predictable. Dad bails. Mom eases. Kelly gets right to the point. *I wonder what I do.*

"Fine. Fine." His mother shifted in her chair. "I just didn't want to make the boy uncomfortable." She reached over and took Cam's hand. "You know you can talk to me about anything, don't you?"

"Yes, Mom. And I'll be happy to tell you what's going on. It's really quite simple. Sadie, Ellie's birth mother, finished college a few years ago. Now she's gotten a job in Delaware and wants to have a relationship with Ellie."

He didn't go into the fact that she'd purposely moved to Delaware after she found out about Brenda's death. And he most certainly wasn't going to tell her that the thought of her was keeping him up at night.

Kelly smacked the table and clicked her tongue in sarcasm. "See there, Mom. Nothing to it."

"Oh dear." His mother picked at the paper towel in her hand. "Why?"

Cam furrowed his eyebrows. "Why what?"

"Why does she want to do that? She gave Ellie up."

Cam searched his mind for the right response. His mother had no idea how hard it was for Sadie to allow Ellie to be adopted. He hadn't fully realized it himself until the other day when she cried in his arms.

Brenda and Sadie had often corresponded through e-mail and phone calls while Sadie was pregnant, and Brenda thought highly of Sadie. Once Ellie was born, they seemed to distance themselves from each other, but Brenda still felt so highly of Sadie that she was willing to keep her updated as Ellie grew. "Mom, Sadie was young when Ellie was born. She didn't have any help. She was very selective in choosing Brenda and me. I believe she's always loved Ellie."

"Well, yes. That may be so, but she did give her up. She can't just decide five years later she wants to be a mom."

Cam looked from his mother to Kelly. The last time he and his sister had talked about Sadie was that day in his garage. He wasn't exactly sure how Kelly felt about the situation either. "I don't think it's like that exactly. Sadie is a Christian, Mom. She was when she made a mistake in college. If you met her and talked to her, you would be able to see that her motives seem pure."

His mother straightened her shoulders. "That's a wonderful idea. I'd like to meet her when we fly the kids back to Delaware."

Panic punched him in the gut. The last thing he wanted was for his mom and dad to meet Sadie. Cam shook his head. "No, Mom. Ellie doesn't know who Sadie is yet. We're taking it slow."

His mom seemed to ponder his words. Cam looked at Kelly. He still couldn't decipher how she felt. Taking a long drink of his tea, he rested back against the seat.

"You know, Mom," Kelly began. She twisted the straw in her drink between her fingers. "It might be good for Ellie to get to know Sadie."

"But what if she decides to up and leave? Ellie's already dealt with the death of a good, caring mother."

"You're right." Cam scratched his jaw. "That was my biggest concern, too." His own word—*was*—smacked him in the face with full force. Ever since the other night when he'd held a sobbing Sadie in his arms, Cam knew in his spirit that Sadie wouldn't leave Ellie.

He grabbed his mother's hand in his own. "I've only seen Sadie and Ellie together a few times. The woman adores my little girl. She. . .loves her."

His mother looked over at the girls playing in the pool. She turned back toward Cam and sighed. "You're a great dad, Cam. And you've always been a great judge of character. I'll be praying for you." She grabbed his chin between her finger and thumb. "But what's this look in your eyes?"

"What?"

"Are you developing feelings for this woman?"

Cam's mouth dropped open. He scowled at his sister.

"Kelly!"

Her eyes widened and she lifted her hands in the air. "I didn't say anything."

"What?" his mother squawked. "You really do have feelings for the girl? I was teasing. Well, sort of anyway. I thought I saw a bit of something in your eyes," she blustered and stood to her feet. "I'm heading to my room right now. You're going to wear out my knees praying for you, son."

"Join the crowd, Mom. I've already got calluses on mine."

✀

Sadie hung up the phone. It was Father's Day, and though she'd sent a card, her spirit urged her to call her father. He'd grunted his thanks for the card then passed the phone over to her mother. The conversation was stilted, never venturing from work or the weather.

Our relationship was never great, Lord, but I wish it were better than this.

Once a year she saw her parents, who lived in the state of Washington. When she'd been offered an academic scholarship at the small college in North Carolina, it had been an easy decision to leave home. Sadie resented how her parents had thrown themselves into their work while she grew up. They claimed to be Christians, attending church every Sunday and Wednesday. Her mom served on several committees, as did her father. But somewhere there had always been a faulty connection when it came to expressing feelings.

Well, I sure fixed that my sophomore year of college. Nothing like your only daughter calling home to say she's pregnant and her boyfriend's run off. Sadie shook her head at her actions. She was smarter than that. She was more conscientious than that. *Lord, You were dwelling within my heart and I tainted Your temple with my foolishness.*

Tears pooled in her eyes. She walked into the bathroom, grabbed a tissue, and stared at her reflection. "You've forgiven me, Lord. I know that." She wiped the tears from her cheeks. "But the consequences remain."

Not Ellie. Oh, how she loved Ellie. How thankful she was that Ellie was fearfully and wonderfully made within her womb.

But she could never again get her virginity back. And her aloof relationship with her parents had grown more distant. The truth of it weighed her heart and spirit. Guilt always seemed to knock at her heart's door, begging for entry. Some days, shame would sneak up on her and she could barely see.

"For God is greater than our hearts, and he knows everything."

It seemed such a strange verse that always leaped into her mind when she struggled with her sin, and yet the years had shown her the verse fit perfectly within her spirit. Her heart was overburdened with the remembrance of the sin. Shame and guilt would always threaten. But God was greater than her heart—her feelings. He knew about her sin. He knew the outcome of mercy—the birth of Ellie—that resulted from her sin. He was stronger than her guilt, greater than her shame, and He knew everything.

Thank You, dear Jesus, for reminding me.

Chapter 8

Cam shoved the tickets to the DuPont Theatre into the front pocket of his jeans. He'd delivered a piece of restored furniture to one of his regular clients only an hour before. Mrs. Lawley had insisted he take the tickets she couldn't use. "Surely, there's some young lady at your church you could take to the musical? The DuPont always puts on a splendid performance."

Mrs. Lawley meant well, but he wasn't the slightest bit interested in going to see an all-student performance of *Less Miserable* or whatever she'd called the show. She'd said it was some famous musical, but he'd never heard of it. But then, he wasn't exactly current on musicals either.

Besides, it had been only one year, to the day, since Brenda's death. The last thing he wanted to think about was a musical or dating. *Mrs. Lawley doesn't realize she picked the worst day of the year to give those to me.*

From the passenger's seat, Cam grabbed the bouquet of flowers he'd bought to put in front of Brenda's tombstone. Deep emotion welled within him. He remembered Brenda's short blond hair, her light blue eyes. She had the sweetest dimple in her left cheek when she smiled.

His mind traveled back to their morning ritual before Brenda was sick. Cam would shower, dress for work, and then walk into the kitchen. Every day, Brenda would be sitting at the kitchen table, mug filled with hot tea in her hands, her gaze focused on a devotional. She'd look up at him and smile then turn her attention back to the book.

It was daily things like that Cam found he missed the most. He missed her strands of hair that had fallen in the bathroom sink, the robe she left lying on the closet floor, her slippers that stayed by the back door. They were all things that made life normal with Brenda, things that weren't found around the house now.

It is better that Ellie isn't here. I need to do this alone.

He stepped out of his truck, shut the door, and then leaned against it. It had been only a month since he and Ellie visited Brenda's grave, but today seemed harder. Not only was it the anniversary of her death; it was the first time he'd come alone.

Sadie would have come with me.

He looked at the heavens and whispered, "Why would I even think like that, Lord?" Taking a woman he was attracted to on a visit to his wife's grave was ludicrous. It was wrong.

One of the last memories with his wife began to replay in his mind. "Cam, I want you to promise me something," Brenda had said.

Cam held her hand tight. "I'll promise you anything, Brenda."

Tears welled in her eyes. "Promise me that if God gives you another woman to love, someone who would be a good mom to Ellie, you'll accept her."

"What?"

He remembered the fury that erupted within him. How could she even talk like that? God was going to heal Brenda. He would never be able to love another woman. No one else would ever have the opportunity to be Ellie's mother.

"You're young." Brenda had lifted her hand to his cheek. Even now, he could almost feel the softness, and weakness, of it. "And I know you will always love me."

Cam pushed the memory away. The idea had been ridiculous to him. He loved Brenda. He still loved Brenda. And he would never betray her.

You're not betraying her. There is no sin in your feelings for Sadie.

He pushed away from his truck. He would not think about Sadie Ellis today. Trudging toward Brenda's tombstone, he noted the smattering of flowers, wreaths, and trinkets adorning several of the graves. He wondered at the people who'd put them there, knowing they came from spouses, children, parents, friends of the people they'd lost. Death was so hard.

Finally, Cam reached Brenda's place of rest. A wreath rested on her grave. Cam frowned. It had been months since anyone but he and Ellie brought flowers here. Some of Brenda's friends from church had, on occasion, but not for a while. Her parents lived out of state and had seemed to want almost nothing to do with him or Ellie since Brenda's death. *Surely, they would contact me if they drove up.*

But it was the one-year anniversary; it would make sense for someone to bring a token of remembrance today. He looked around the wreath to see if a card or name tag was attached. He couldn't find anything.

Through his peripheral vision, he glimpsed a woman with long brown hair walking away from another grave. She looked familiar, and he turned to get a full look at her. *Sadie?*

Before he had time to consider his actions, Cam walked to her. Her back was still to him when he asked, "Sadie, what are you doing here?"

She turned, gasped, and covered her chest with her hand. "You startled me." She let out a breath and brushed a strand of hair back with her fingers. "I. . .well, I came to visit Brenda's grave. You'd said. . .well, you'd said she died on this date, and I guess I just wanted to say good-bye."

Shifting from one foot to the other, she looked down at her fingernails. She seemed to avoid making eye contact with him, and Cam gazed at the tombstone she had been looking at. "Do you know this person, too?"

"Oh no." She glanced up at him, made eye contact, and then looked away. "I just noticed his dates of birth and death. He was only a baby. I guess I was just thinking about his mother."

Cam studied Sadie.

"Look, I didn't mean to be here when you were here. I just. . .well, I didn't know about her death when it happened." She picked at one of her fingernails. "And I. . .well, I thought of her as a friend. But I don't want to impose. I'm sorry."

She turned away from him, but Cam grabbed her arm. "Hey, it's okay. A lot of people cared about Brenda."

The musical tickets seemed to poke into his leg. It was on the tip of his tongue to invite her to go with him. But he couldn't.

Not today.

Today, he had to focus on the wife he'd lost.

Sadie looked into Cam's eyes. He drank in the compassion he saw reflected there. "Thanks, Cam." She moved from his grip and walked away.

Cam turned and headed back to Brenda's grave. A war raged within him. His love for Brenda, his attraction to Sadie. Guilt at the feelings Sadie stirred, sorrow at the memories he carried for Brenda.

The leaves of the trees scattered around the cemetery and seemed to fold the land into their embrace. He spied an American holly tree and could almost hear Sadie's voice. "The American holly is Delaware's state tree." Ellie's response would be to scrunch her nose and wonder if she was no longer a bug or a fish but now a tree.

A quick grin bowed his lips at the thought. He peered down at Brenda's grave, and remorse swept through him. *How could I think like that today? What kind of man am I?*

"Why do you look for the living among the dead?"

Scratching his jaw, Cam frowned. "Why in the world would I think that?" The angels asked that question to the disciples when they couldn't find Jesus' body after the crucifixion and burial. *But Jesus was alive. He's our Savior. Brenda is in heaven with Christ. She's not going to rise from this grave.*

"Exactly. But Sadie is alive."

Cam shoved his hands in the pockets of his jeans. He shook his head. "No. I will not think like this. I love Brenda. I will always love Brenda."

"Remember your promise. And the one who asked you to make it."

Frustrated, Cam swiped his hand across his face. He squatted and touched Brenda's engraved name on the tombstone. He traced the words LOVING WIFE, ADORING MOTHER. He whispered, "I will always love you, Brenda. You made me promise to allow another woman into my heart. I thought it was crazy. How could I ever do that?"

He cupped his hand over his mouth and looked past the grave, past the cemetery. He spied a single red house sitting just beyond a clear blue pond. Landscaped trees and bushes lay peacefully in perfect position around the home. He looked back down at the tombstone. "And here I find myself falling for another woman."

He closed his eyes and lifted a silent plea to God for help. Looking back at her name, he sighed. "Thank you for your blessing, Brenda. I don't know if I could have ever overcome the shame of how I feel for Sadie."

"Shame is never from Me."

Knowing the Spirit's nudging was true, Cam stood and turned in the direction Sadie had gone. The corner of the tickets poked into his leg again. *If she hasn't left, I'll ask her.*

Cam quickly made his way past several graves and to the road that curved through the cemetery. Her car was there, and Sadie sat in the driver's seat. He picked up his pace. Her eyes were closed. He didn't want to scare her. "Hey." He announced his presence, and she looked over at him.

A slow smile bowed her lips. "Hi, Cam."

"Penny for your thoughts."

Sadie blew out her breath. "I was just asking God to comfort you. . .and Ellie. I don't know if she knows that today is the anniversary of Brenda's death, but just in case." Her hands clutched the steering wheel. "I know this is hard for her, too."

Cam adored her sweet, caring spirit. She seemed to understand how much Brenda meant to him and to Ellie, and she wasn't jealous of it. She wanted to carve her own place in Ellie's life without taking away from Brenda. His heart swelled. *Now's a good time to ask.*

He pulled the tickets out of his front pocket. "A client of mine gave me tickets to the DuPont Theatre."

He gripped them tighter in his hand. It had been years since he'd asked a woman on a date. *Is this really going to be a date?* His gut tightened, and his head started to thump. *Just ask her, Reynolds.*

"It's some musical put on by students. I was wondering if you'd like to go."

"As a date?"

Cam felt heat creep up his neck and cheeks. *She probably thinks I'm too old for her.* "I. . .well, we could always talk about when we'll tell Ellie."

Way to wimp out.

Sadie seemed to relax. "Sure. I would love to."

⊱⊰

I cannot believe I didn't even ask him which musical we're going to see. Sadie stepped into a black high-heeled sandal while she pushed the back of her diamond stud earring into place. She looked into the full-length mirror and twisted her hips, allowing the simple, knee-length black dress to flare. A black satin ribbon, tied in the front, gave the dress just enough pizzazz to make it appropriate for an evening out.

She'd debated on whether to wear her hair in a clip or allow it to hang free past her shoulders. The hairdresser had cut several layers into her long hair, and Sadie loved the way the first layer framed her chin, the second rested just below her shoulders, and the length of it finally ended at the middle of her chest. Since Cam had never seen her hair up, she'd decided to go ahead and use the clip. The choice accentuated the curve of her neck and shoulders.

I certainly look like a woman going on a date, not just spending a little time with the father of her daughter.

Rolling her eyes, she picked up her small black purse. "Every time I think that, it sounds so weird, even to my own ears."

Her doorbell rang. *There's Cam.*

She snuck one last peek in the mirror before she straightened her shoulders and headed to the front door. Sucking in her breath, she tried to plaster a how's-it-going-friend smile on her face. He'd made it perfectly clear he wasn't thinking of this as a date. The last thing she wanted to do was make him think she was hitting on him. She flung open the door. "Hi, Cam."

"Wow." His mouth popped open, and he stared at her.

Sadie could have responded the same way. Cam looked sensational in his dark khaki pants and pressed polo shirt. The deep green color of the shirt brought out the flecks of green in his hazel eyes. She took in his jaw and chin, shaved clean, and once again noticed his deep dimple. Without thinking, she poked it.

She sucked in her breath and pulled her hand back. Warm embarrassment washed over her. "I'm so sorry."

Cam laughed. "As scruffy as I usually look, you probably didn't know it was there."

Sadie shook her head. *What was I thinking?* "I can't believe I did that."

"Hey, it's nothing. Kids used to ask me all the time if someone poked my chin with a pencil." He offered her his elbow. "You ready?"

She nodded, slipping her hand into the crook of his arm. He smelled amazing. The light musky scent she remembered the night she'd cried in his embrace was stronger and fresher. If he'd belonged to her, she'd have leaned over, touched the side of his neck, and inhaled her fill of him. *But he isn't mine, and*

I would do good to remember that.

"You look beautiful, Sadie."

Cam's voice was so close she could almost feel the softness of it. If she turned and tilted her head just a bit, she could kiss him.

"Thank you," she whispered, determined to keep her focus ahead. After what seemed an eternity, they made it to the passenger side of his truck. He opened the door and she slipped inside; then he walked over and jumped into the driver's seat. "I never asked, but what musical are we going to see?"

Cam scrunched his nose much like Ellie did, bringing a smile to Sadie's face. *She must have picked that up from him.* "It's some weird French name, *Less Miserable.*"

"*Les Misérables?*" She bit the inside of her lip.

"Is that bad? I've never heard of it. 'Course, I don't check out musicals very often. We don't have to go."

"Oh no. No. It's a wonderful story. You may love it."

"But you don't?"

Sadie contemplated her answer. "It's not that I don't like it. It's an amazing musical, full of emotion."

Cam cocked one eyebrow.

"The last time I saw it, I cried through the whole thing." Sadie spit the words out as fast as she could.

Cam grinned. "So we need to stop and get some tissues?"

She shrugged her shoulders. "Maybe."

Cam's laughter filled the cab of the truck. He turned the ignition and pulled out of the parking space. "The last time you used my shirt as a tissue."

Sadie ducked her head. "Sorry 'bout that."

"I didn't mind."

❧

Cam couldn't pay attention to the musical. He really didn't care much about it to begin with, but having Sadie beside him, smelling like a flower garden and looking like she'd stepped down from heaven, all the while sniffling and wiping her nose with a tissue, was more than he could handle. He'd been raised to protect women, especially the lady he loved, and right now, she sat beside him drenching yet another tissue with tears. *I'm not sure how her tear ducts keep up with all the leaking.*

He bit back a laugh at his thought. Sadie was without a doubt one of the most emotional women he'd ever met. He'd never seen anything like it, but it did explain why Ellie seemed so prone to tears and dramatics.

A soft sniffle sounded beside him, and Cam could take it no more. He gently lifted his arm around her, squeezing her shoulder with his hand. To his surprise, Sadie nestled closer to him and rested her head against his shoulder.

His breath caught at the nearness of her. Her scent grew stronger around him, and it would only take a slight turn of his head to kiss her head. Her soft hair caressed his neck, sending his nerve endings into overdrive. *Comforting her may not have been the wisest of ideas, Reynolds.*

He swallowed back his desire to draw her closer to him, to tilt her head, take her face into his hands, and claim her lips against his own. *Lord, give me strength,* he inwardly begged, knowing it would take God's intervention to keep him from blurting out his feelings for her.

Again, he tried to focus on the musical. His awakened senses at Sadie's nearness had kept him from watching a large portion of it. He had no idea where the plot was going, and in truth, he didn't care. He only wished the thing would end so that he could release Sadie's shoulder and then get some fresh air.

Finally, the musical ended and Sadie looked up at him. She hadn't sat up and Cam found his lips mere inches from hers. "Thanks for holding me."

Her words were soft, her gaze filled with emotion—from the play, he forced himself to believe. And yet she seemed to search him as well.

"You're welcome." Cam's voice was rough and low. He swallowed back his desire to kiss her. Sadie seemed to hesitate before she moved away from him. Cam couldn't help but wonder if she yearned for a kiss as well.

Cam shook his head. He wasn't ready to think that way. Brenda may have given her blessing for him to find another wife, but Cam hadn't agreed. He never would have imagined himself with someone like Sadie, and he had no intention of imagining it now. *I'm just feeling weak because of the anniversary of Brenda's death. I don't really have feelings for Sadie.*

Cam stood and offered Sadie his arm. Her nails scratched gently against his skin, sending shivers up and down his arm. *Sure. You just keep telling yourself that, Reynolds.*

Chapter 9

Two weeks without Ellie had been hard on Cam. With her trip over and his parents back in Florida, Cam was glad to be tucking his little girl into her own bed again. He kissed the top of her head. She sat up and wrapped him in yet another hug. "I missed you, Daddy."

"I missed you, too, pun'kin."

Ellie released his neck and lay back on the bed. She nestled her special blanket close to her cheek. "I missed Sadie, too."

Cam nodded. "I bet she missed you as well."

"Daddy"—Ellie pulled the covers up to her chin—"is Sadie your girlfriend?"

Cam furrowed his eyebrows. "Why would you ask that?"

"Zoey said that she must be your girlfriend since you bring her with us to places. She said. . ." Ellie sat up, scrunched up her face, and twisted her shoulders back and forth. Her voice took on a sarcastic tone. " 'Ellie, why would Sadie want to be *your* friend?' "

Cam shook his head and ruffled her hair as she nestled back under the sheets. "Of course Sadie would want to be your friend."

"Zoey's a meanie."

"Hmm." Cam couldn't think of a good response. Zoey had changed so much since Tim's death. She looked for the bad in people and said so many things she shouldn't. The fifteen-year-old had his sister at her wit's end.

"So is Sadie your girlfriend?"

"No."

"Does she still want to be my friend?"

"Absolutely." Cam leaned over and kissed Ellie's head a second time. "Now go to sleep."

He reached for her pink lamp with the feather shade and turned off the light. Ruffling her hair one last time, he knew he had to call Sadie. It didn't surprise him that Kelly's girls would think that Sadie was his girlfriend. Why else would a woman just start hanging out with him and Ellie?

Walking out of the room, he asked God to give him and Sadie wisdom for how to tell Ellie the truth. After fishing her phone number out of his wallet, Cam picked up the phone and dialed her number. A ring sounded in his ear. *Oh God, what will she say when I tell her? How will I tell her?* If he were honest with the lot of them, he would announce to the whole family that he'd like nothing more than to make Sadie his girlfriend.

He growled as another ring sounded through the phone line. *You know better than to think that way, Reynolds.*

"Hello?" His heart stirred at the sound of her voice. It had been a week since their date to the musical. Neither of them would come out and say it was a real date, but for Cam it had been nothing less. "Hi, Sadie. How have you been?"

"I'm good." She hesitated. Cam detected the uncertainty and hope in her voice. "Is Ellie home?"

"She is." Cam tried to keep his tone light. He wasn't sure if Sadie was ready to fess up to her true identity. He wasn't sure he was ready, but he didn't see they had any other choice. "I need to talk to you about that."

"Okay." Her voice sounded meek, almost scared.

"Well, when I put her to bed, she told me that—"

"Oh, Cam, please don't say I can't see Ellie anymore." Her words came out fast, choppy, and filled to the brim with emotion. He could picture her eyes pooling with tears.

Cam frowned. "No. I wasn't going to say that. God's given me peace about you being in Ellie's life." He furrowed his eyebrows as he sought for the right words. "I think you're good for Ellie. She needs you."

I'm finding I need you, too. He shook his head at the thought. Focused. He had to stay focused.

"Thank you, Cam. I love her so much. I love getting to see her." She paused, and Cam knew she wiped tears from her eyes. The woman cried at the drop of a hat, and he adored her for it.

"We're going to have to tell her the truth," Cam blurted out before she could make more assumptions. "I know we were going to talk about it the night of the musical, but. . ."

"Okay." Silence filtered through the phone. "Are we ready for that?"

Cam walked into the living area and spied Ellie's snack dishes on one of the end tables. He rested the phone between his shoulder and ear so he could pick up the glass and plate. "I don't think we have a choice." He made his way back to the kitchen, rinsed the dishes, and placed them in the dishwasher. "Kelly's kids think you're my girlfriend."

"What?"

"Kelly's oldest told Ellie that you must be my girlfriend or why else would you be hanging around."

Sadie didn't respond for several moments. Part of Cam just wanted to tell her that he was all right with that assumption. If she didn't have a problem with the ten-year age difference, then he was ready to make it truth. If he hadn't seen her at the cemetery and then taken her to the DuPont Theatre, he didn't think he would have made it without seeing her the full two weeks Ellie was gone.

"Okay. When?" Uncertainty sounded from Sadie's voice.

Cam scratched his chin. "Tomorrow's a Saturday. If you're available, how 'bout we take her to the Brandywine Zoo tomorrow? We can tell her then."

"Okay. I'll be at your house at ten." She paused again. "Cam, can we tell her before we go? I want to be able to answer any of her questions. She has to know how much I loved her."

Cam smiled into the phone. There was no way Ellie, or anyone, could doubt Sadie's love for his daughter. "Sounds great. And, Sadie, don't worry. Ellie knows you love her. She loves you."

⁂

Praise music blared through the car's radio as Sadie drove the road to Cam's house the next morning. Sadie had not slept a single moment since her phone conversation with Cam. She'd tossed and turned, lifted the covers higher under her chin, pushed them off, turned on the fan, turned off the fan. She'd read scripture, which helped some, but she could not hand her fear of Ellie's reaction completely over to God. What if her child never wanted to see her again?

Peeking in the rearview mirror, Sadie noted how puffy her eyes looked from her restless night. She glanced back at the road, screamed, and swerved, barely missing a squirrel. Placing one hand on her chest, she blew out several breaths. Every fiber of her body, inside and out, seemed to shake uncontrollably.

"Calm down, child. Doesn't My Word say 'the truth will set you free'?"

"Yes, Lord. I have to trust You. She needs to know the truth."

Sadie pulled into Cam's driveway, parked, then walked to the front door. Before she had a chance to knock, Cam opened the door and wrapped her in a bear hug. Momentarily taken aback, Sadie stood still with her arms stiff at her sides. Cam whispered, "It'll be okay."

Tension that seemed to have locked her joints and muscles released at his words and touch, and Sadie found herself wrapping her arms around Cam. He felt strong and secure. A wave of knowing she could face anything with him overwhelmed her. *How can I be falling for this man?*

She didn't know why. She simply knew she was. This embrace, so similar to the last one they'd shared, was Cam's way of calming her. This time she wasn't overwrought with sobs and sadness at the things she'd missed. This time her senses were very much awake and alive and sensitive to every inch of him embracing her. His breath warmed her scalp, and she feared she'd melt at the heat of it.

His hand cupped the back of her head. His lips brushed against her forehead. Then he moved his mouth down toward her ear and whispered, "I'll be right here."

He pulled from their embrace but kept one hand on her arm. She looked up into his eyes. *Wow! What this man does to me! I want so much to tell him how I feel. Why? Why can't I tell him?*

"Sadie!" Ellie's squeals of delight interrupted Sadie's thoughts. Ellie raced toward Sadie, and Sadie lifted her daughter off the ground and spun her around.

"I missed you so much." Sadie gave her little girl an Eskimo kiss.

"I missed you, too." She twirled a lock of Sadie's hair between her fingers. "Daddy says we're going to the zoo today. I'm going to show you the alligators."

"I can't wait." Sadie, still holding Ellie, walked into the living room and sat on the couch. "Your daddy and I want to talk to you first."

"But I'm ready." Ellie stuck out her bottom lip. "Daddy's already fixed my hair." She lifted her foot. "And I put on my sandals."

Sadie bit back a grin. She didn't know how she'd ever manage disciplining Ellie. Even her whining was so cute. *One day soon, I'll have no choice.* "I know, honey, but this is important."

Cam sat on the chair across from them. He leaned forward, clasping his hands between his legs. "Ellie, remember how I told you that Mommy and I picked you out special, just for us?"

Ellie nodded.

"Remember we told you that you were adopted?"

Ellie nodded again before scrunching her nose. "I can't remember what *adopted* means."

Sadie trailed the length of Ellie's hair with her fingers. She fought back the urge to squeeze her tighter into her lap for fear the child might leap away when she found out who Sadie really was.

Cam continued. "*Adopted* means that a different man and woman gave birth to you, but your mommy and I raised you."

"I don't get it."

Sadie smiled at Ellie's response. "How about this. Ellie, do you know anybody whose mommy had a baby?"

Ellie smiled. "Trudy's mommy had a baby."

"Did her tummy get really big?"

Ellie nodded. "Yep. That was the baby inside her belly. Trudy said the baby had to grow up a lot before he could be born."

Sadie nodded. "That's right. You had to grow up in somebody's belly."

"Yep. I grew up in Mommy's belly."

Sadie swallowed. Now was the time to tell her. "Well, actually. . ." Sadie gazed into Ellie's eyes, so innocent, so trustworthy. "You grew up in my belly."

Ellie scrunched her nose and frowned. Sadie compared a strand of Ellie's hair to hers.

"See how our hair looks alike?" She poked Ellie's nose. "And you have my nose?"

"But. . ." Ellie blinked several times. "Trudy's mommy is the baby's mommy. You're not my mommy."

Sadie's heart clenched. An expression that Sadie recognized from five years before covered Ellie's face. It was the same look of confusion and wonder that Ellie had when the doctor laid her on Sadie's chest before taking her to Cam and Brenda. *I am your mommy, Ellie. I am, just like Brenda was.*

Cam picked up the family picture that sat on the end table beside him. "Ellie, this is your mommy. Brenda was your mommy, because she adopted you." He touched Sadie's arm. "Sadie is the mommy who gave birth to you. She carried you in her tummy."

Ellie studied Sadie for several painstaking moments. Sadie wished she could plunge into Ellie's mind and discover all the thoughts and feelings that were going on inside. She wanted the opportunity to ensure every fiber of Ellie's being that she had always loved the little girl. Always.

Suddenly, Ellie's eyes widened and she touched Sadie's cheek. "Can I call you 'Mommy,' too?"

❧

A few hours later, Cam followed Sadie and Ellie as they walked hand in hand toward the lions' cage at the zoo. He was still in shock that Ellie wanted to call Sadie "Mommy." He'd expected her to handle it well. Even though she didn't fully understand adoption, he and Brenda had always told Ellie she was adopted.

At the same time, he hadn't expected her to replace Brenda in her mind so quickly. *Maybe* replace *isn't the right word.* He raked his fingers through his hair. *What is the right word?*

He watched as Sadie picked up Ellie and placed the child on her hip. Ellie was too old to be held, but he was guilty of the same gesture. Ellie'd had to deal with so much in her life that Cam often found himself babying her. Sadie would want to baby her because she'd never had the opportunity before now.

Brenda had been so sick for almost half of Ellie's life. Ellie had often been taken to a friend's, a church member's, or the babysitter's house when Brenda wasn't well. Everyone doted on his little daughter. As a result, she loved to go places and visit people. *Maybe that's why she's so quick to call Sadie "Mommy."*

And Sadie would be a good mommy for Ellie. There was no denying it. He watched as Sadie pointed to one of the monkeys in the far right corner picking bugs from its head and eating them. Ellie's laugh filled the air.

Though part of him felt sadness for Ellie's quick acceptance of Sadie, the other part of him praised God for it. With Cam's feelings growing each passing day, it made the possibility of dating Sadie much easier to consider.

He'd felt such peace at the cemetery about being able to let Brenda go. Maybe this was God's sign that Ellie would be ready, too.

He smiled at the thought of it. Walking up behind them, he touched Ellie's hand. "Are you ready for some lunch?"

Ellie nodded. "Uh-huh. I'm starving."

Sadie put Ellie down and grabbed her hand. "Well, then let's go eat."

"Okay, Mommy." Ellie reached up with her free hand and grabbed Cam's. "Let's go, Daddy."

Cam peered over at Sadie. Her bottom lip quivered, and he knew each time Ellie said the endearment, Sadie nearly came unglued.

They made their way to the nearest food vendor. After ordering hamburgers and fries, the three sat at an open table. While Cam opened a ketchup packet for Ellie, Sadie wiped his daughter's hands with a wet wipe.

"Your daughter is beautiful." An elderly woman stopped beside their table.

Cam and Sadie looked up and then at each other. Cam watched as Sadie's eyes widened in surprise. He winked then looked up at the woman. "Thank you."

"She's as pretty as your wife."

He glanced at Sadie, whose face and neck burned red. "Well, she's not my—"

The woman continued, "My own children were about five years apart. I had three boys." She looked from Cam to Sadie. "Are you planning to have more children?"

Sadie dropped the wet wipe in a glob of ketchup. "Oh my." She picked it up and tried to wrap the clean part around the soiled.

"We haven't really talked about it." Cam wasn't really lying. Yes, he knew the woman believed them to be married, but they *hadn't* talked about more children.

Sadie's mouth dropped open, and her cheeks blazed.

"Wouldn't you like a little brother or sister?" The woman bent down and pinched Ellie's cheek.

Ellie looked up for the first time. She turned to look at Cam and then Sadie. "I can have a baby brother or sister?"

"Well—" Cam touched Ellie's hand. *Okay, now the conversation is getting out of control.*

"I want a baby brother like Trudy has. Then I can feed him and change his diaper. . . ."

A man called from several tables over. The elderly woman waved then peered back down at them. "I'd better be going. My husband has our food." She pinched Ellie's cheek one more time. "You are a little cutie. Bye, now."

"Bye," Cam and Sadie both mumbled over Ellie's chattering. She was still going on about the many things she could do with a baby brother.

Cam peeked over at Sadie, who looked as if she would pass out at any moment. "That was interesting." He dropped several fries in ketchup then shoved them in his mouth.

"To say the least." Sadie took a sip of her soft drink.

"Mommy?" Ellie sat on her knees in her seat to get her face closer to Sadie's. "Do you want to have a baby brother?"

Sadie swallowed. She gazed over Ellie's head and into Cam's eyes. "Only God knows how many children someone will have."

"But do you want one?" Ellie implored.

Sadie's gaze never left his. Her light green eyes seemed to probe him with questions and desires. Cam found himself crushing the napkin in his hand from the intensity of it. "Yes. I want as many babies as God will give me."

She smiled, and Cam knew to the depth of his being that Sadie returned his feelings for her. Her answer was meant for him.

And now that he knew it, he had to let her go.

Chapter 10

The month of July and the first part of August passed too quickly for Sadie. She'd taken every opportunity she could to spend time with Ellie. They'd swum at the pool, played at the park, eaten lunch at every fast-food restaurant they could find. Sadie couldn't get enough of spending time with her little girl. She longed to ask Cam if Ellie could spend the night with her sometime, but she hadn't quite gotten up the nerve.

Besides, something has changed about Cam. For a while, Sadie had been convinced that Cam had feelings for her. Though taken aback at the attraction she felt for Cam, over time she'd warmed to the notion and started to hope that God would allow something to flourish.

Sadie carried a box of file folders, papers, and personal items into the small office the school board had given her at the county's central office. After dropping the box on the desk, she smacked her hands together then wiped them on her shorts. She swiped the small beads of sweat that had formed on her forehead with the back of her hand.

But boy, was I wrong about Cam having feelings for me. Sure, he'd been nice to her, allowing her to see Ellie pretty much when she wanted. He still went with them on a few of the excursions. But *nice* was the only word she could use to describe Cam. He didn't hug her. He didn't look at her. He didn't talk except when necessary.

Sadie had no idea what had happened. *Surely, he felt something those times he hugged me.* Shivers raced up and down Sadie's spine as she reminisced the times. She still felt something from them. Her attraction to Cam hadn't diminished a bit.

She remembered the time Ellie had fallen and badly scraped her knee at the pool. Sadie had raced to the concession stand for an adhesive bandage and ointment. When she returned, Cam held a whimpering Ellie in his lap, rocking her back and forth. He took the first-aid material from her and within moments had bandaged the wound and carried her to the concession stand for a Popsicle. The man loved Ellie with all that was in him.

Sadie wanted that for herself as well.

I need to get back to work. All this stewing about Cam isn't going to change the way he feels about me.

Sadie opened the file cabinet and thumbed through the names of the students she would be working with. The woman before her had been meticulous in her filing method. Everything was in order and color-coded with all documentation completed. "It's no wonder they all loved her. I love her myself."

"Well, hello there." Sadie looked up to find Charles Mann, the middle school assistant principal, leaning against the door frame, his smile brightening her room. He crossed his arms in front of his chest. "So are you ready to start?"

"I sure am." Sadie shuffled two of the files on her desk. She liked Charles just fine. He seemed to be a great guy, but she simply wasn't interested. However, each time she saw him, she couldn't help but think the feeling wasn't mutual.

"How long have you been here today?"

Sadie looked at her watch and gasped at the late hour. "Almost eight hours! It's nearly four o'clock." She thought of the peanut butter crackers and soft drink she'd swallowed down several hours before. *That's why I'm getting so hungry.*

Charles chuckled. "You've put in a long day. Why don't you let me take you to dinner?"

"I'm sorry. I can't. I have kindergarten orientation tonight."

Charles frowned. "They require you to go to kindergarten orientation?"

Sadie chuckled. "No."

She watched as he looked at her ring finger then back up at her face. "Do you have a child in kindergarten?"

"Well, I..."

Charles's cell phone rang. He looked at the number. "I'm sorry. I have to take this. I'll talk to you later."

Sadie sighed in relief as he walked down the hall. She realized again how difficult it would be to explain her relationship with Cam and Ellie to other people. She'd been so worried about Ellie's response to her that she hadn't considered others. Many of the people at church now knew and for the most part had accepted her. She'd become so involved with the children's ministry, the food pantry, and Sunday school that many of the parishioners had been able to get acquainted with her as a person as well as her as Ellie's biological mom. The memory of telling Kelly and her girls permeated her mind. Kelly already knew and seemed happy for Sadie to be a part of Ellie's life. It had been wonderful to meet her.

But her girls, especially her oldest daughter, were another story. The youngest one's expression only showed her disbelief and uncertainty. The middle daughter was quiet, retreating to her room. But the oldest was quite vocal. She hadn't held back her thoughts on the situation. "It's not right for her to come here," the girl had argued with Cam. "She gave Ellie up. She didn't want her.

How could you do that to Aunt Brenda?"

Though Kelly had reprimanded and grounded the girl and made her apologize, Sadie was haunted by the teenager's words. She wondered how many people would feel as Kelly's daughter did. *They just probably won't be as vocal to my face.*

With anxiety about the kindergarten orientation mounting within her, Sadie placed the folders back in the file cabinet. She locked her door and headed out into the parking lot. In a little over an hour, she was going to meet Cam and Ellie at a restaurant for dinner before they headed to the school. She needed to talk to Cam in private before that. After pulling her cell phone from her purse, she dialed his number. His answering machine picked up. "Cam, I hope you check this. I'm going to come over before we head to the restaurant. We need to talk."

⤳

"What could she possibly need to talk about?" Cam mumbled as he lathered his face with shaving cream. He hadn't shaved in a few days, and he knew this was going to hurt. He could thank his father for his hairy genes.

"Daddy, I put on my dress that Mommy bought me," Ellie called from the other room.

Cam moved the razor down his jaw then rinsed it in the sink. "Okay, pun'kin." The girl wore that dress every day she could. This weekend, Cam planned to ask Sadie to go with them to buy school clothes. If Ellie thought Sadie picked them out, he knew Ellie would want to wear them.

After finishing his shave, he patted his face with a warm towel. He heard the front door open, and Sadie's voice filtered through to his bathroom. He glanced at the clock on his bedroom dresser. *She's an hour early.*

Inwardly, he groaned. It had been hard enough trying to avoid looking at her when they had lots of activity planned. Having her in his house for a full hour of talking would unravel him. His attraction intensified with each moment they spent together. But he couldn't have her.

The ten-year age difference he'd been worried about in the beginning was nothing. He'd even come to accept Brenda's blessing to allow a new wife, and Sadie would fit perfectly into his and Brenda's hopes for a mother for Ellie. But having more children. . . There was no getting past the difficulty *that* caused.

He tossed the towel in the hamper and walked into the living room. Sadie sat on the couch with Ellie sitting on the floor between her legs. Sadie was fixing Ellie's hair in some sort of fancy knots down the back of her head. Sadie looked up at him and smiled. "Hey."

Cam's heart thumped beneath his chest. He wanted this woman. She looked right sitting on his couch, fixing their daughter's hair. *Our daughter.* What an irony that Ellie truly was the daughter of both of them.

Sadie twisted the ponytail holder in Ellie's hair. "Now go get a ribbon from your box that matches the dress."

"Okay, Mommy." Ellie skipped out of the room.

Sadie leaned forward. "We need to talk while she's gone."

"Okay."

"What are we going to tell her teacher?"

"About?"

She pointed at herself and then at him. "About us."

Cam's pulse quickened, and he slowly sat in the chair across from Sadie. She had no idea how much he wanted an "us" between them. Not only was Sadie one of the most beautiful women he'd ever known; she was a wonderful mother with a sweet, giving nature, and she loved the Lord. She was perfect for him. But he could never be perfect for her. He gripped the arm of his chair. "What about us?"

Sadie shook her head. "Really, I guess I mean *me*. What are we going to tell her teacher about me?"

"That you're her mom."

"What about you?"

"I'm her dad."

"But what if she asks if we're divorced? Is this going to be hard for Ellie? I wanted to be in Ellie's life so badly." Sadie wrung her hands. "I never thought about what other people would think or say. Remember your niece's reaction."

Cam frowned at the memory of Zoey's complete disrespect. In truth, he hadn't thought much about the reaction of other people until then either, but he didn't think a teacher would behave as badly as Zoey. And why would they have to tell her anyway? "Sadie, I really don't think a teacher's going to come out and ask if we're divorced." He nodded. "I know she'll probably assume it, but is it necessary to tell her the whole situation?"

"I don't know." Sadie raked her hand through her hair. "Is it?"

"No, I don't think so." Cam looked out the french doors that led to the backyard. He watched several ducks swimming leisurely on his pond. He looked back at Sadie. "If you're uncomfortable, you don't have to go tonight."

Sadie's lip puckered, much like Ellie's did when she was upset. The expression tugged at Cam's heart. "But I want to go."

"You know what? We don't have to tell her anything. You're Ellie's emergency contact number. For all she'll know, you're Ellie's aunt or cousin."

"I don't know."

Sadie's worried expression drew him. He wanted to slip onto the couch beside her, wrap her in a hug, and assure her all would be fine. But he didn't. He couldn't risk his emotions growing any stronger. *Who am I kidding? They couldn't possibly get any stronger. I know I love this woman.*

"I could just tell the truth." Sadie's voice was low. "Jesus told us 'the truth will set you free,' and it did when we told Ellie."

Cam shrugged. "I really don't think it will even come up."

❧

The kindergarten room was everything Sadie would have expected. The names of the students were printed in perfect handwriting on multicolored kites taped to the front door. A huge "welcome tree," filled with colorful leaves and birds, greeted them as they walked through the door. Small red tables with two yellow and two blue chairs each were placed strategically around the room. One corner contained a "reading" carpet. Another corner was designated for crafts. Six computer desks were lined up against one wall. Bright numbers and letters filled the walls, even hung from the ceiling. It was a beginning-of-education dream, and Sadie could hardly wait for Ellie to experience all of it.

A tall young woman walked up, her thin hand extended to them. Blond tendrils escaped the clip that held back her long hair. Her eyes, the bluest Sadie had ever seen, shone with warmth and excitement, and Sadie couldn't help but wonder if it was her first year of teaching. "Hi. I'm Miss Montgomery." She shook Cam's hand and then Sadie's. She leaned down and took Ellie's hand in her grasp. "Welcome to your classroom. What's your name?"

Ellie lowered her chin and clamped her lips together. She grabbed Sadie's hand, gripping it with all her strength. It was the first time Sadie had ever seen Ellie respond bashfully.

"It's okay if you're nervous, sweetie. We all get nervous sometimes," Miss Montgomery crooned. She touched the ladybug on Ellie's dress. "I like ladybugs. Did you know they're the state bug?"

Sadie bit her lip. She heard Cam bite back a grunt. Ellie glanced up at Cam. "Why does everyone think we're bugs, Daddy?"

Cam howled, and Sadie couldn't hold back her chuckle. Confusion crossed the teacher's expression. Sadie put her hand on Miss Montgomery's shoulder. "I'm sorry. We've been learning about the state's symbols, and Ellie hasn't quite gotten to the point where she understands the concept."

Miss Montgomery smiled. "So your name is Ellie. You must be Ellie Reynolds. Did you see your name on the front door?" When Ellie shook her head, the teacher grabbed her hand. "Let's see if we can find it."

Sadie watched as Ellie and her teacher sought out and found Ellie's name. Miss Montgomery took time to show Ellie where her seat and cubby would be, as well as some of the daily activities she could expect. The whole time, the teacher made sure Cam and Sadie understood all that was expected. *There's no way this woman could be a first-year teacher. She intrinsically knows so much.*

"Ellie, why don't you color that sheet of paper sitting on your desk while I talk with your mom and dad? It will be your first kindergarten assignment," Miss Montgomery said.

"Okay." Ellie's face split with a smile. "I'll stay in the lines, too."

"That's wonderful." The teacher turned toward Cam and Sadie. "Were you able to complete the information packet I sent to you?"

"Yes." Cam handed her the packet.

She pointed toward the small chairs at an available table. "I know they're small, but if you'd like to have a seat, I'll make sure I have all the information I need." She opened the packet and skimmed the papers. She looked at Sadie. "You're Sadie Ellis?"

Sadie swallowed hard. She twisted her purse strap between her fingers. *She wonders why my last name is different. She's going to ask. Lord, what will I say to her?* "Yes."

"Are you our new occupational therapist?"

Sadie exhaled a long breath. "Yes."

"It's so nice to meet you. I hope you like it here."

Sadie's nerves started to settle. "I think I will. Thank you."

Miss Montgomery looked back at the papers, then back up at Cam and Sadie. "You're listed as her emergency contact number, but I like for that person to be someone who isn't in the home."

"I'm not in the home."

"Oh, I'm sorry." Miss Montgomery pointed to the paper. "I see here you have a different address. You must be divorced."

"No. Not divorced. We were never married."

Miss Montgomery's eyebrows furrowed into a straight line.

"I mean. . .we. . ." Sadie felt heat rush up her neck and cheeks.

The teacher shook her head. "It's okay. You don't have to explain."

"No, but I don't want you to think. . ." Sadie's heart sped. Panic pulsed through her veins. "Cam's her adopted dad. I'm her biological mom. You see, I was young when I found out I was pregnant, and then Cam's wife died, and I felt God was giving me the chance to see my daughter. . . ."

Beneath the table, Cam grabbed Sadie's hand and squeezed it. The warmth of his touch calmed her slightly, and she took a breath.

Miss Montgomery shook her head. "It's okay. Really. You didn't have to explain."

Sadie nodded. Embarrassment swelled within her, and she moved numbly through the rest of the meeting. Her mind reeled with worry. What if this young woman thought poorly of Ellie because of Sadie? Surely, she wouldn't. No one could fault Ellie. What if she talked with other teachers? Would they think negatively of their new occupational therapist? Bile rose in her throat. That was a real possibility.

Chapter 11

Mommy, this one is itchy." Cam watched as Ellie scrunched her nose and scratched at the back of the blue jean shorts. Sadie pulled the tag away from Ellie's skin and then buttoned the front. She slipped a hot pink shirt over Ellie's head. "I don't like it. It scratches my back." Ellie squirmed away from Sadie's grasp.

Cam bit back a chuckle. He rarely took Ellie shopping for this very reason. She whined. She complained. She got tired. It was easier to simply order stuff off the Internet and hope it would fit. Of course, they had been in the mall for three hours, and even the best of five-year-old shoppers would be getting tuckered out.

With the patience of an experienced mother, Sadie twirled Ellie to face her. "It only scratches because we can't take the tags off." She let out an exaggerated gasp as she turned Ellie toward the mirror. "Look at how pretty you are."

"I don't like it." Ellie puckered her lips.

"Hmm." Sadie cupped her chin with her thumb and finger. "I'll tell you what. As soon as we find one more outfit for you, we'll walk over to the pavilion and get some lunch. Would you like that?"

Ellie's eyes lit up. "I like this one." She started to unbutton the blue jeans. "Can we go eat now?"

"We sure can." Sadie helped her out of the new clothes and into the ones Ellie had worn to the store.

Cam scooped up the various shirts, pants, and dresses they'd selected and headed toward the register. "You know you're pretty good at this?"

"Pretty good at what?" Sadie pushed a strand of hair behind her ear—something about that always stirred Cam. Maybe it was the contour of her neck, or the slight, sweet whiff of her hair, or maybe he just wanted to be able to feel the softness of the lock.

Forcing his thoughts back, he laid the clothes on the counter then pulled out his wallet. "Taking Ellie shopping. You're very patient."

Sadie shrugged. "She's just a little girl, and we've been gone a long time. I know she's got to be tired—I'm exhausted."

Cam smiled as he paid for the clothes. Scooping up the bag with one hand, he grabbed Ellie's hand with the other. Sadie grabbed Ellie's free hand. They headed to the pavilion and—within minutes—sat at a table enjoying hamburgers, fries, and soft drinks.

Ellie seemed rejuvenated by the fatty meal and sugar rush. She talked incessantly about school and her new teacher. Sadie smiled and nodded, but Cam could see the hint of distress in her gaze. She'd gotten extremely nervous when they met Ellie's kindergarten teacher. Cam wondered if rumors were already flying about Sadie, the newcomer who'd given up a baby. People from all occupations could be cruel when it came to spreading gossip. Miss Montgomery seemed to be a wonderful woman, but he couldn't help but wonder if, and how, she would share the information Sadie gave.

"Well, hi, you guys."

Cam looked over to see Kelly and her youngest daughter standing beside their table.

"Hi, Aunt Kelly." Ellie jumped out of her seat and wrapped her arms around Kelly's waist. "I got new school clothes today."

Kelly looked at the bags on the floor. "It sure looks like it." She turned to Sadie. "Are you ready to start school?"

Sadie's distressed expression deepened, and Cam knew Sadie forced herself to smile. "I think so."

"Well, if you need anything, even if it's just someone to talk to, I'd be glad to listen. Remember, I'm at the high school. Junior and senior language arts."

Sadie tapped the side of her face. "That's right. I forgot you were a teacher." Her smile relaxed. "I appreciate the offer. I may have to take you up on that."

"You're the new girl, and some people can be. . .tough."

Cam noted the hesitancy in Kelly's voice. He wondered if rumors were already flying. Kelly looked at him, blinked, and then slightly nodded her head. Yep, the rumors were making their rounds. He'd given Kelly a heads-up about the kindergarten orientation, and Kelly was silently letting him know that Sadie would have a long haul ahead of her. Kelly looked back at Sadie. "I'm not just saying it." She patted Sadie's shoulder. "If you need someone to talk to, I'd love for you to give me a call."

Cam loved his sister. Despite all that was going on in her life, she remained a sweet, sensitive soul. Pride for her flooded him. She would be a good friend for Sadie, and Cam feared Sadie would desperately need one.

Kelly bent down in front of Ellie. "Hey, we're heading over to the movie theater to watch the new cartoon movie. Remember, the one you told me about? Would you like to go with us?"

Ellie raced over to Cam and squeezed his arm with both hands. "Daddy, can I go? Please, please, please."

"I don't see why not." He looked at Sadie. "Do you mind?"

She shook her head.

Kelly grabbed Ellie's hand. "All right then. I'll take you home after the movie." She turned toward Sadie again. "I've wanted to see the comedy that just came out Friday."

"Me, too." Sadie pressed her hand to her chest. "It looks like it will be hilarious."

"Mom, we're going to be late." Kelly's youngest pulled at her sleeve.

"Okay. I'll see you."

Cam watched as Kelly and the girls made their way toward the mall's theater. Sadie's expression dropped the moment they left, and Cam knew she worried about the start of school. An idea formed in his mind. "I've been wanting to see that comedy. Why don't you and I go?"

"Now?"

"Sure. Our movie will be over about the same time as theirs. It'll save Kelly a drive to my house."

Cam could tell she mulled over the idea as she bit the inside of her lip. Finally, she grinned. "Sounds like fun."

"Great." Cam stood and picked up the shopping bags with one hand. Without thinking, he grabbed Sadie's hand. She tensed and Cam started to pull away; then she relaxed and folded her hand around his. Pleasure shot through him at her simple, soft touch. Danger horns sounded mercilessly in his mind, but he couldn't remove his hand. He knew his touch calmed her, and he hated seeing the worry behind her gaze. After all, though he fought it with all that was in him, he knew he loved her. *Knowing it doesn't mean I have to act on it.*

※

Sadie hadn't felt this nervous since the day she'd told Ellie she was her biological mother. *That went fine. I just need to trust God that my first day of school will also go well.*

She sucked in a long breath and took one last glimpse in her full-length mirror. Her knee-length taupe skirt and bright pink blouse were professional yet fashionable. Having decided to pull her hair back in a clip and wear a bit more makeup than usual, Sadie knew she appeared older than her twenty-four years. *Between stepping in after a wonderful thirty-year veteran occupational therapist and the possibility of the whole school system knowing I gave up my baby for adoption, I'm going to need all the help I can get at looking like a professional.*

"Stop worrying. Remember, I am greater than your heart. I know everything."

Sadie released a long breath. God did know everything. He knew her exaggerated fears and worries. He knew how others would respond to her. The church members had been kind, and she knew the children she taught at church would be students in the various schools. Besides, she belonged to God. He would show her how to get through whatever lay ahead.

The story of Ruth flooded her thoughts again. How many times since deciding to move to Delaware had Sadie read the woman's story in the Old Testament? Too many times to count. Even at this moment, Sadie could hear Ruth telling Naomi that she would follow her mother-in-law anywhere, that Ruth would worship Naomi's God. *God, I know the situation is different, but I feel like Ruth. . . . I will go wherever You send me.*

Since Ellie's conception, God had shown Himself consistently faithful. He'd been there for her before that as well, when she was a girl and a teen, in good times and bad. Sadie simply hadn't acknowledged and allowed His lead with such certainty as she had since her pregnancy with Ellie.

Thank You for the reminder, Lord. I can do this through Your strength. Sadie grabbed her car keys and her purse and headed out the door.

The September morning sun was bright, and yet the air was slightly nippy. Her drive was pleasant, and she listened to her favorite praise music, allowing her soul to be rejuvenated with worship. Today, she would visit each school and meet a few of the teachers and students she would be working with. She knew introductions would probably take a few days, but she wanted to be sure she showed up at each school just the same.

After arriving at the central office, she stepped out of her car. The cool breeze felt wonderful on her cheeks, sending a soothing balm through her anxious body. *No one is going to be worried about me. I simply need to do my job and all will be fine.* She walked into the building. Anxiety started to mount again, and she was thankful she'd only eaten a container of yogurt for breakfast.

"Good morning, Sadie." The secretary at the front desk greeted her with a warm smile.

"Good morning."

She stood and lifted a good-sized office plant from the desk behind her. "This is a welcoming gift from our office. We know you'll like it here."

The beating of her heart slowed, and Sadie felt her nerves calm. She took the plant. "Thanks so much. I know I will."

She walked back to her office. Making room on the corner of her desk for the plant, she scolded herself for being so worried. She placed her purse in a desk drawer then took out the first grouping of files for the students she planned to try to meet, if only to say hello, before the day ended.

"How's it going?" The superintendent stuck his head in the door.

She smiled at the older man. "So far, so good. Thanks for the plant."

"Well, we're glad to have you." He waved then walked down the hall.

Feeling more settled, Sadie sat at her desk and turned on her computer. The bottom right-hand corner showed the time. Cam would be taking Ellie into the kindergarten room about now. Sadie yearned to go with him but wasn't sure if it would be overstepping her bounds. And Cam hadn't offered.

She envisioned Ellie, long hair swept up in a ponytail, wearing her new pink shirt and blue jean shorts. *No, I bet she wanted to wear one of her new dresses today.* It hurt that Sadie had no idea what her daughter was wearing for her first day of school. She didn't foresee Ellie crying and wanting Cam to stay with her, but one never knew what a five-year-old would do on her first day. *I want to see Ellie in the mornings. At lunch, I'll simply call Cam's cell phone and ask him. I won't know if I don't ask.*

Sadie finished the work she needed to do on the computer then grabbed her files and headed to the first elementary school. She was able to meet each of the students and teachers on her list before heading to the high school. Making her way up the stairs, she found Kelly's room—the last one on the right. She peeked in the door's window. Kelly saw her and made her way to the door.

"How's your first day going?" Kelly smiled.

"It's been great. My jittery nerves are all but gone."

"That's wonderful." Kelly's smile deepened, and Sadie noted the slight element of surprise in Kelly's tone. "Remember, if you need anything, give me a call."

"Of course." Sadie waved and walked toward the stairs. She hadn't exaggerated. Everyone had been friendly and helpful, and as lunch approached, Sadie felt more confident and comfortable about her new job. *I was just being overly sensitive this morning.*

She made her way out of the school and to her car. Once she arrived at the fast-food drive-through, Sadie flipped open her cell phone and called Cam. He answered on the first ring. "Are you busy?" Sadie asked.

"I'm working on an armoire, but I can take a quick break. How's your first day going?"

"Really well." Sadie heard the relief that sounded in her own voice.

"I'm so glad." She could tell his words were genuine, and she remembered the feel of his strong hand in hers when they walked to the movie.

"I was wondering, though, if I could come over in the mornings and maybe fix Ellie's hair before school. I really missed her this morning." *And I've missed you, too.* Sadie couldn't add that—though everything in her wanted to. She couldn't stop thinking about him.

"That sounds like a great idea. She'd love it."

Sadie got off the phone, paid and picked up her food, then drove toward Ellie's school. *The day is going much better than I ever would have anticipated, Lord. Ellie's school is next on my list. I'll have to sneak a peek into her room.*

Sadie swallowed her food before turning into the school's parking lot. After parking her car, she reapplied her lipstick and slipped a mint into her mouth.

She walked into the school and introduced herself to the secretary. The woman told her in which rooms she'd find the students she'd be working with, and Sadie made her way down the halls. Again, the teachers and students were friendly, and Sadie had already fallen in love with her job.

Trying to be discreet, Sadie peeked through the door of Ellie's classroom. The teacher sat on the carpet with a book in her hand. The students sat all around her. Miss Montgomery's expressions changed vividly as she read the book. Sadie could only see the back of Ellie's head, but by her nodding, Sadie knew Ellie was enthralled. As Sadie had guessed, her hair was in a ponytail and she wore one of her new dresses.

"May I help you?"

Sadie jumped and turned at the woman's voice. "I was just taking a peek in the room." Sadie smiled and offered her hand. "I'm Sadie Ellis, the new occupational therapist."

The woman's features softened as she took Sadie's hand. "Oh, it's nice to meet you. I'm one of the kindergarten teachers, Mrs. Black." She tapped her finger with her lip. "It seems I've heard something about you. Good, I'm sure."

Sadie's heart jumped. Why would she have heard anything about Sadie? Unless it was about Ellie. *I don't need to jump to conclusions. I may have a student in her class.*

"Well, it was nice to meet you." Sadie waved as she made her way down the hall. She stopped by the restroom then made her way back to the office.

"Yep, she's the one," Sadie heard a woman's voice say before she turned a corner. "Can you imagine giving your baby up for adoption?"

Sadie stopped. She knew they were talking about her.

"And then trying to be in the kid's life later. Sounds crazy to me," another woman responded. If Sadie was right, it sounded like Mrs. Black.

"I'll tell you, I couldn't do it," the first woman replied.

Tears welled in Sadie's eyes. She'd been foolish to think people wouldn't talk about her. Deciding to skip saying good-bye in the office, Sadie made her way back to her car. It took every ounce of composure she had to keep from bursting into tears before she made it out of the parking lot. *I'm such a fool.*

"I still know everything, Sadie, and I'm here for you."

"Oh God." Sadie swiped the tears that began to cascade down her cheeks. "I do need You. I felt such peace about coming here. I love Ellie. I love her so much. Was I wrong?"

Doesn't scripture say, "In this world you will have trouble"?

"But You, God, have overcome the world." She sniffed as she summarized the rest of the verse. "Thank You for the reminder, Lord. It has been a good day. Help me keep my mind on You and not worry about what others say."

Sadie wiped the mascara smears from beneath her eyes before she headed into her office. She let out a long breath as she sat at her desk. Checking the clock, she knew the schools had already dismissed and her day would be over in a matter of thirty minutes. Trying not to think about the women at Ellie's school, Sadie organized her files and planned her schedule for the following day.

"Knock. Knock." A familiar voice sounded just outside her door. Sadie gazed up into the kind eyes of Cam's sister, Kelly. She folded her arms in front of her chest and leaned against Sadie's door frame. "You've made it through your first day. I just thought I'd stop by and check on you before I head out to get the girls."

An unexpected wave of raw emotion overwhelmed Sadie, and tears streamed down her cheeks. Kelly stepped inside and closed the door. She pulled several tissues out of her purse and handed them to Sadie. "So the day didn't go so well?" Kelly sat in the chair in front of Sadie's desk.

Sadie shook her head. "Actually, overall the day was wonderful. Almost everyone was extremely kind and helpful."

"Almost?" Kelly's eyebrows lifted in question.

Sadie blew out a long breath. "Yeah. Almost." She wiped her nose with a tissue. "I overheard a couple of ladies at Ellie's school talking about me, and about how they couldn't believe I would try to be in Ellie's life after I gave her up." Sadie's voice cracked, and she wiped her eyes again. "I never should have said anything to Ellie's teacher. Cam told me not to say—"

Kelly touched Sadie's hand. "Amanda Montgomery is a wonderful Christian woman. I doubt the ugliness came from her."

Sadie felt consumed with embarrassment. She'd known many a wonderful Christian to show less-than-Christlike behavior. "How do you know? What if she takes my sin out on Ellie?"

Kelly shook her head. "No. I don't think so. Besides, you can stop by her room anytime and check to see how things are going."

Sadie took a deep breath, pondering Kelly's words and remembering the Spirit's nudging. "You're right." She wiped her eyes one last time. "You know, God overcame the world. He can take care of this."

Kelly stood and wrapped her arms around Sadie's shoulders. "You're absolutely right. If God can see Cam and I both through the deaths of our spouses, he will take care of Ellie's kindergarten year. . .and your first year here."

Sadie felt humbled by the comparison of loss that Kelly and her brother had experienced to the momentary embarrassment Sadie faced. She had no right to feel as she did. "You're right, Kelly." She pulled away from Kelly's embrace. "So how was your day? What can I do to help you?"

Chapter 12

Cam opened and closed his fist. His hand still ached from holding Sadie's hand several days before at the mall. Everything he touched reminded him, either by comparison or by contrast, of the softness of her skin. *This is nuts.* He tossed Ellie's sundress into the washing machine. *I was married for years, and here I'm acting like a lovesick middle school boy over that woman.* He growled as he poured laundry detergent over the load of clothes.

He glanced at the clock. It was still early, but he assumed Sadie would show up at any time to get Ellie ready for school. *Why did I agree to this? The woman already haunts me at night. Now, after a good whiff of her in the morning, I'll think about her all day, too.*

He scratched at his jaw. He hadn't showered or shaved this morning. His old basketball shorts that he wore to bed still hung from his waist. He picked at one of the many holes splattering his T-shirt. *I should have gotten ready before now. Having her come over here has messed up my whole morning.*

Cam made his way to Ellie's room. She lay curled in a ball under her covers, holding her blanket over her cheek. He pushed a tendril of hair away from her face. She looked like an angel, so much like her mother. A vision of Sadie sleeping filtered into his mind, and he shook the thought away. Cam gently tugged at the covers. "Wake up, pun'kin."

"Humph." Ellie grunted and gripped the comforter tighter.

The doorbell rang, and Cam took a deep breath as he made his way to the front of the house. *Lord, help me through this.* He opened the door and inwardly growled. Sadie looked adorable in a green shirt and polka-dotted skirt. She wore a matching headband in her hair and a few small pieces of gold jewelry. The whole getup made the green in her eyes shine, and if he was right, it appeared she had some gorgeous flecks of gold complementing that green. Her lips glistened with some kind of pink gloss, and it took every ounce of strength within him not to press those lips against his. In her hand was her infamous oversized cup of French vanilla, extra-cream java. Holding his snarl at bay, Cam opened the door wide. "Come on in."

"Is she up yet?" Her voice carried a higher lilt than usual, and Cam knew she hoped to be the one to wake Ellie.

"Nope."

"Great." Sadie whisked past him. The smell of her coffee mingled with the light scent of her perfume. Even her scent drove him to insanity.

Cam shut the door and padded his way to his bedroom. As it turned out, he was glad he hadn't gotten ready for work. It would give him something to do besides watching Sadie's every move while she got Ellie ready for school. "If you don't mind, I'll dress for work while you get Ellie ready."

"Sounds good," Sadie called from Ellie's room.

Cam could hear muffled sounds of laughter from his daughter before he started the shower. He turned the temperature a bit cooler than he normally liked. *Anything to keep my mind off that woman.*

It didn't take Cam much time to shower, shave, and dress. Within moments, he walked back into the kitchen. Ellie sat at the table with a bowl of cereal in front of her. Sadie stood behind Ellie's chair, once again tying her hair in long knots. French braids, Sadie had told him they were called.

"Hi, Daddy."

"Good morning, pun'kin." Cam patted her nose with his index finger.

"Mommy picked out my dress." She turned in her chair to show him what she was wearing.

"Hold still, Ellie, or I'll have to start over." Sadie's voice was kind but firm. Her maternal instincts were strong, and Cam couldn't deny what a terrific mother she'd already proven to be.

"Okay, Mommy."

"So where's my breakfast?" Cam teased.

Sadie blushed and shrugged her shoulders. "I didn't know what you liked, but I left the cereal on the counter."

"I'm just teasing you." Cam walked over to the counter and poured cereal into a bowl. Her blushes were entirely too cute. He needed to avoid unnecessary interaction with Sadie.

"All done." Sadie's voice filled the room. "You look awfully pretty."

"I'm going to go see." Ellie jumped out of her chair and raced to the bathroom.

Sadie grabbed her coffee off the table and took a drink. She looked at Cam. "She is so much fun."

"Humph." Cam took a bite of his cereal. "She's not usually this happy in the morning."

Sadie lifted one eyebrow and cocked her head. "Maybe someone else is a bit of a grouch in the morning."

Her tone and gaze were teasing and entirely too tempting. Cam looked away. "I don't know about that."

"Well, it seems to me. . ."

Blocking out the sweetness of her voice, Cam took a long swig of his coffee, strong and black, with none of the fanciness of Sadie's.

"I'm ready, Daddy." Ellie stood before him, already wearing her backpack.

Cam smiled at his daughter. *Saved by the kid.* The attraction he felt for Sadie was ridiculous, but he could not succumb to it. Even if she were attracted to him, he would never be able to give her all she wanted. *She deserves more.*

"Let me get your lunch out of the refrigerator." Cam grabbed her lunch box then turned toward Ellie.

Sadie bent down and gave his daughter a hug. She tickled Ellie's chin. "You have a good day."

Ellie giggled, and Sadie stood then wiped the wrinkles from her skirt. She pushed her hair back behind her shoulder. "I wanted to ask you something, Cam."

"Okay." Cam swallowed the knot in his throat. The look in Sadie's eyes was serious. He watched as she started to wring her hands together.

"I was wondering. . ." She shifted her weight from one foot to the other. "If you might want to get together. . ." She shrugged her shoulders. "For lunch, maybe."

"To talk about Ellie?"

"Or maybe just talk."

Cam's heart sank. Everything in him wanted to get together for lunch. He wanted to talk about her, what she yearned for in life, what her passions were. He'd gathered several of her heart's desires from the time they'd spent together with Ellie, but he couldn't deny he wanted his own time with her.

But he couldn't. He wouldn't do that to her. "I don't think so."

Sadie's gaze moved to the floor. He saw pink race up her neck and ino her cheeks. "Okay. I just thought since we had a good time at the movies. . ." She brushed her hand across her cheek, probably trying to push hair that wasn't there from her eyes. A habit, he presumed. "I'd better be going. Bye, Ellie." She bent down for one last hug then swept out the door.

I am such a fool. She has no idea how much I want to spend time with her. I just can't.

Why don't you tell her why?

Heat washed over his body. The reason was humiliating. It had taken him years to feel like a full man after he'd learned the truth. He still struggled with it at times. No, the last thing he wanted to do was tell her the truth.

⁓

Oh dear God, I'm so humiliated. Sadie looked in her rearview mirror for the thousandth time. Though she'd driven all the way to work, her cheeks still shone bright pink after the conversation with Cam. She leaned back against the headrest. "Why did I ask him that? Girls are supposed to let the guys ask them out."

I wasn't really asking him out, she argued with herself. *I just thought we'd go to lunch and maybe see what happens.*

She looked at her reflection again and tried to convince herself aloud. "After all, he held my hand as we walked to the movie. Isn't that kind of dropping hints at a girl? Guys don't just hold hands with friends, do they?"

Shaking her head, she grabbed her purse out of the passenger's seat and opened the door. "This is ridiculous. I can't believe I'm arguing with myself over this."

She greeted the secretary with a forced smile and walked back to her office. After turning on her computer, she sifted through several files on her desk. *I will not think about him. It's my first week of school and I still have students to meet.* She transferred the files to her shoulder bag then pulled her lip gloss and compact from her purse. After applying the light pink shade, she smacked her lips together and scooped up her purse and bag. "First stop is the middle school."

The middle school had been built on a hill just several hundred yards away from the central office. If it hadn't been Sadie's first week, she would have simply hiked the hill and enjoyed the fresh air and exercise. Not wanting to walk in with disheveled hair and clothes and inhaling deep breaths from the foot excursion, she'd opted to go ahead and drive her car. *Once I feel more settled, I'll enjoy the walk.* She pursed her lips. *Today I could use a good brisk walk.*

She huffed at the memory of Cam's rejection as she waited for the middle school secretary to electronically unlock the door to allow her inside. So much more security was needed since she'd been in middle school herself, just over a decade before. When the door clicked, Sadie plastered a smile on her lips, praying that it at least appeared genuine. She extended her hand to the secretary. "Hello. I'm Sadie Ellis, the new occupational therapist."

Before the woman had a chance to respond, a familiar voice sounded from the hall behind her office space. "Well, hello, Sadie." Charles Mann appeared, his smile as bright as she remembered. "This is Evelyn." He pointed to the secretary, and she nodded. "Come on back and I'll introduce you to a few more people."

Sadie felt herself relax at Charles's genuine welcome. "Okay." She looked at Evelyn. "It was nice to meet you."

The woman nodded, and Sadie followed Charles through several rooms attached to the back of the office. As he introduced her to people, Sadie repeated their names several times in her mind, hoping to remember them on a future day.

"Here's my office." He gestured toward a door. "Come on in and we'll talk a minute."

Sadie smiled. It was nice that he wanted to talk to her. His interest soothed her pride a bit after Cam's cool rejection that morning. Walking inside, she took in the historical decor filling his office. "You must have been a social studies teacher before you were a principal."

"How'd you guess?" His gaze swept through his office. "I especially love Revolutionary War memorabilia. Delaware has a lot of interesting places where I can find more information." He cocked his head. "Maybe I can take you with me sometime."

Sadie's pulse raced. She wasn't really interested in Charles in that way. He seemed like a great guy—nice looking, kind personality, and he obviously liked kids or he wouldn't be a principal. *Why shouldn't I be interested in him?* She contemplated the thought, knowing her lack of interest stemmed from how she felt about Cam. *Well, I might as well forget that.* She stood straighter and lifted her chin. "That might be fun."

Charles's eyebrows rose. "So how is school going so far?"

"Good." She patted her bag. "I'm here to meet a few of my students."

Charles nodded. He studied her for several moments, and Sadie could tell he mulled something over in his mind. He leaned against his desk before he spoke. "I guess you had reason to go to kindergarten orientation after all."

So the gossip has even spread to the middle school. Ah, well, soon enough something more interesting will come along to talk about. Sadie pushed her bag higher on her shoulder. She had no idea where this was going. Really, he had no right to question her past. "Yeah, I did."

Charles smiled, and his gaze softened. "The rumor mill, you know. I'm sure you know all about that."

Ha. Boy, did she ever. News spread fast when she'd gotten pregnant and then was dumped by her boyfriend. Not everyone at her college church had been thrilled with the idea of helping out the "sinner." Many believed she'd made her bed and should now lie in it.

It shouldn't surprise her that people were quick to judge, and yet that was one of the blessings God had given her during that difficult time. She'd been judged and humbled to the place that she always wanted to lend mercy to those who'd messed up. Even now, hard as it was, she knew those who spoke ill of her had hurts of their own they were avoiding.

"Yes, I know."

"Not everyone thinks badly."

Sadie studied Charles's expression. The kindness mixed with concern on his face filled her with gratitude and reminded her that he was right. The truth was just the truth. Some people yearned to dwell on the bad. Others focused on how God had redeemed. In that moment, Sadie knew Charles tended to take the latter view, and her respect for him grew. "You're right about that."

"I wonder." Charles folded his arms in front of his chest. "Is your little girl as pretty as you?"

Sadie laughed. "She definitely looks like me."

"Then she's definitely beautiful." Charles unfolded his arms and gripped the side of his desk. "I was wondering if you might be free for dinner on Friday."

Sadie debated her response. Her feelings for Cam couldn't just be turned off in a moment, and she didn't want to lead Charles on. And yet she might have considered Charles a great catch if she'd never met Cam. *Quit overanalyzing. It's just one date.* Sadie smiled. "I would love to."

"Great. I'll pick you up at six."

"Six it is." Light on her feet, Sadie glided out of the office. *A date will be fun.* Her mind whirled with thoughts of what to wear, then shifted to Ellie and Cam. With each step she took, her legs grew heavier. It just didn't feel right.

Chapter 13

Sadie gazed out the passenger's window of Charles's car. Though fall would be upon them in less than a month's time, the sun bathed the rolling hills in glorious beauty. Various shades of green painted the ground and trees and were accented by a splattering of white, pink, and purple wildflowers. Despite the air-conditioned car, Sadie could feel the warmth of the day outside. As they passed a pond set in a valley of sorts and surrounded by trees, she longed for Charles to stop the car and allow her to slip off her shoes and dip her feet in the water.

The week had passed faster than Sadie could have imagined. She'd been in a whirlwind at work, meeting students and colleagues, updating files, taking notes. She'd gone home late and exhausted each night. Outside of getting ready for school in the morning and attending church on Wednesday night, Sadie'd had only a few phone conversations with Ellie. She'd had virtually no contact with Cam. It surprised her how much she missed him.

I've got to stop thinking about Cam. He made it clear he's not interested. She glanced at Charles and forced herself to grin. *Besides, I'm on a date with another guy.*

"You like pizza?" Charles's voice was smooth and light.

"Love it." *Yes, let's talk. I need to keep my mind off the brown-haired, hazel-eyed, never-ending five o'clock shadow on his firm, square jaw. . . . Ugh! I've got to stop it.*

"Great." Charles's voice interrupted her wayward thoughts. "I'm taking you to one of my favorite restaurants."

Sadie studied Charles's profile. She'd figured him to be a guy who would want to fine-dine her, impress her with his eloquence. She took in his casual outfit of a red polo and jeans then glanced down at the soft yellow material of her sundress. A small, delicate floral pattern trimmed the neck, straps, and waist, making her look and feel very feminine; but it was definitely one of her fancier sundresses. *I think I've misjudged him a bit. He seems to be more of a down-to-earth kind of guy. More like Cam.*

She balled her fists and crossed her arms in front of her chest. *Sadie Ellis, you are not thinking about Cam Reynolds anymore today.*

"So tell me about yourself." Charles's voice saved her from reprimanding herself further.

Sadie shrugged. "There's really not much to tell. You know where I work. You know I have a daughter. What would you like to know?"

"Do you go to church?"

"Yes. I've been attending with my daughter."

"So you're a Christian?"

Sadie looked at Charles. He gazed back at her, his expression hopeful. "Yes."

"I knew it. That's great." Charles smacked the top of the steering wheel. He looked at the road then peeked back at Sadie. He let out a loud laugh. "Don't be offended by my asking. I found myself in a relationship several years ago with a gal who didn't share my faith. It ended poorly. I like to be sure on a first date now."

Sadie furrowed her eyebrows. She studied Charles's face. His sincerity and openness were intriguing. "I understand perfectly. I'm glad you asked."

Sadie looked out the windshield. The trees and grass grew sparse as they neared Wilmington, the "corporate capital of America," as the city was known. She preferred the quiet country setting of their town but couldn't deny her growing excitement at what Charles had planned. "So tell me about this pizza. What kind do you like?"

"My favorite is plain ol' pepperoni, thick crust, smothered in cheese. I tell them to pile it on." Charles licked his lips dramatically. "Mmm-mmm. A large Coke on the side. It's got to be a dish we'll eat in heaven."

Sadie chuckled at his enthusiasm. "It sounds fattening."

Charles put his hand around Sadie's wrist, connecting his thumb to his middle finger. "You're a scrawny little thing. A little fattening won't hurt you."

Sadie laughed. "Did you just call me scrawny?"

"Oh, come on, now. You're a beanpole. A skinny-mini as my sister would say. A regular Olive Oyl from those old Popeye cartoons."

Sadie howled. Charles certainly did not fit the hole in which she had pegged him. He was a character—a guy who could take her mind off her troubles. The big brother she'd never had. "Oh, I'll show you Olive Oyl. I'll eat you under the table."

He parked the car and swiped the keys out of the ignition. "Bring it on."

Before he had time to open her door, Sadie jumped out of the car. She hefted her purse higher on her shoulder and practically raced him to the front door of the restaurant. The Italian aroma permeated the air, even outside, and Sadie pressed her stomach to keep it from growling. She was starving, so Charles was in trouble. She'd make herself sick before she'd allow him to eat more food than her.

Charles opened the door for her. The room was huge, the walls painted a coffee brown. Italian cartoon chefs and cooking utensils adorned the walls. Red vinyl booths and chairs filled the room. A jukebox, playing old rock-and-roll music, sat against the far wall. "What a fun place."

"I told you it was great." Charles addressed the hostess. "Table for two."

The woman nodded and picked up two menus. "Right this way."

Sadie continued to gaze around the room as she followed Charles and the hostess. The atmosphere was endearing, and the smells tantalizing. She wondered what other music the jukebox contained. There were a few oldies she would love to hear.

Her chest tightened when she spied a small girl sitting with her back to Sadie at a table across the room. The lighting was dim, but Sadie could tell the child had long brown hair, swept into a ponytail. She appeared to be Ellie's age. *That would be impossible. I mean, what are the chances?*

Sadie looked at the person who sat across from the girl. Her gaze locked with the eyes of that person. *It can't be.*

❧

Cam sat stone still. *It can't be.* He blinked several times to clear his vision, and yet there she still stood in front of a booth across the room from him.

With another man.

Fury he hadn't known in years shot through him. His heart raced, and he clenched his fists. He took several deep breaths. Sadie was attracted to him— Cam—not this other guy. He knew she was. She was the mother of his daughter. She belonged to him.

Cam closed his eyes. *What am I? Some kind of Neanderthal?*

"Look, Daddy." Ellie held up the child's menu coloring page. "I colored in the lines."

Cam looked at the purple smiling Italian man holding the green pizza. "Good job."

Ellie wrinkled her nose. "Yeah, but the colors are all wrong." She held up the two crayons in her hand. "They only gave me purple and green. Do you think Mommy will like it anyway?"

Cam nodded, realizing he had to do everything in his power to keep Ellie from seeing Sadie. *Wouldn't that be great?* "I'm sure she'll love it."

Cam looked back toward the kitchen area then glanced at his watch. It had been fifteen minutes since they'd placed their order. Surely, their pizza would arrive soon. He tapped his fingertips against the table and scanned the room, trying to avoid Sadie and her date's booth. *Of course they'd be sitting directly in my line of vision.*

He couldn't help but peek at them. The man was a good-looking guy, Cam presumed. Brown hair. Average height. Closer to Sadie's age. Really white teeth. They nearly blinded Cam when the guy smiled at the waitress as he placed the order.

Cam looked at Sadie. Their gazes met again; then she looked away. She shifted in her seat, and Cam knew she was uncomfortable with him and Ellie being there. *Good. Let her squirm. She doesn't need to be dating anyway. She's a mother, after all.*

Cam growled at himself. He had no right to think like that. Sadie had invited him to lunch, and he'd turned her down. In his gut, he knew it was him, not her, who kept a possible relationship at bay. *Why does it have to be this way?*

"Like you said, it's your choice. You could tell her the truth."

Cam pounded the top of the table with his fist. "It's not that easy."

"I know it, Daddy." Ellie pointed to her picture. "See, I got out of the lines right here on his hat. It's hard to stay in the lines."

Thankful she was oblivious to his inner turmoil, Cam allowed himself to chuckle at his daughter. He tweaked her nose with his thumb and finger. "You're doing a great job." She giggled, and Cam noticed that Sadie looked over at them.

"Here ya go." The server arrived with their pizza, saving him from further agony caused by thoughts of Sadie.

"Thank you," Ellie chimed to the woman then shifted in her seat until she sat on her knees. "Can I get my piece?"

"Be careful. It's hot."

"I will." Ellie struggled with the spatula and the dripping cheese until she finally maneuvered a piece onto her plate. She blew on it several times then touched it with the tip of her finger before taking a small bite. "Mmm. This is good, Daddy."

Cam placed a piece on his plate, focusing his attention on his daughter and the food. He tried to listen to Ellie's chatter, tried to think only of filling his stomach. The pizza was usually his favorite. Tonight, it had no taste. Cam sighed a breath of relief when Ellie took a last bite, leaned back in her chair, and put her hand over her tummy—her way of telling him she was stuffed. He assumed she would be unstuffed by the time they passed the nearest ice-cream shop. That was fine with him. They'd made it through the entire dinner and Ellie hadn't seen Sadie. The quicker they got out of there, the better.

He peeked at her booth. The man said something then threw back his head in laughter. Sadie laughed as well then patted the side of her mouth with a napkin. Cam snarled. The scene made his stomach churn.

"Can I play something on the jukebox now, Daddy?"

"No—" Cam reached for Ellie's arm as she turned around to face the juke-box, but he was too late.

"Mommy!" Ellie's squeal ripped through the room. Cam groaned as his child jumped out of her seat and raced to the other side of the restaurant.

"Hi, Ellie."

Cam watched, stuck to his seat, as Sadie slipped out of the booth and wrapped her arms around his daughter. *I wonder if I can get away with staying here.*

"Daddy, look—it's Mommy." She patted Sadie's shoulder then motioned for Cam to come join her. "Come here."

"Just a minute." Cam pulled his wallet out of his pocket and laid the money for their dinner and the tip on the table. Slowly, he stood and made his way over to the booth.

"So you must be Ellie," the man said. "You are every bit as beautiful as your mother."

Cam scowled.

Sadie looked up at Cam, her expression as haunted as he felt. "Cam and Ellie, this is Charles Mann. Charles, this is Cam and Ellie."

"It's a pleasure to meet you." Charles didn't seem to detect the tension as he extended his hand, a blinding smile splitting his lips.

"Sure." Cam shook the man's hand. He knew his mother would be appalled to see his lack of manners. He should be nicer, but he couldn't. The man was on a date with the woman he loved, and there was nothing he could do about it.

Tell the truth. See what happens.

He shoved the idea out of his mind. Their relationship was doomed to failure. She was the birth mother of his adopted daughter. She was ten years his junior. The attraction was ludicrous. His teen years had long passed him by, and it was time he remembered that. He didn't need a replacement for Brenda. As if anyone could replace her. Sadie was already taking on the maternal role in Ellie's life. He didn't have to be included in that. It wasn't like there weren't tons of kids out there whose mom and dad didn't live together.

But you want her in your life. "He who finds a wife finds what is good and receives favor from the Lord."

Cam gritted his teeth against his spirit. He grabbed Ellie's hand in his. "You two have fun. We'd better be going."

"But, Daddy, I want to stay with Mommy. Can't we stay just a little longer?"

"No, Ellie." Cam nodded to Charles then forced himself to smile at Sadie. The hurt in her eyes pulled at his heart. How could she be hurt? She was the one ripping his heart from his chest.

"But, Daddy. . ."

"No." He gripped her hand tighter and guided them toward the door.

"Why not?"

"Because Mommy's on a date."

"What's a date?"

Cam sighed. "It's when a boy and girl who like each other go out to dinner and maybe to a movie."

"You and Mommy should go on a date. You like each other."

From the mouths of babes. "Honey, I just don't think that's possible."

"Why?"

Because I'm a stubborn, overgrown mule. He shook his head. It wasn't because he was stubborn. He just couldn't face the look on her face, the look that Brenda'd had, the look that he would never be able to erase from his mind if he told her the truth.

Chapter 14

"*You and Mommy should go on a date.*" Ellie's words echoed in Sadie's mind. She took another small bite of pizza. The cheese nearly gagged her. Or maybe it wasn't the cheese. Maybe it was the fact that seeing Cam had tied her insides into so many knots that her stomach didn't have room for anything more.

She looked at Charles. He'd quieted substantially since Cam and Ellie left. She watched as he swallowed a bite of pizza then took a drink of his Coke. He seemed to be avoiding eye contact with her. He wiped his mouth then cleared his throat. "So what movie would you like to see?"

Sadie twisted the napkin in her hand. "Charles, I don't think I can do this."

"Yeah. I didn't think so." Charles pushed his plate away and leaned back in the booth. "So you like this guy."

It wasn't a question. It was more a statement of fact, and Sadie pursed her lips. It seemed highly inappropriate to discuss her feelings for a guy when she was on a first date with another man.

Charles leaned forward, resting his elbows on the table. "It's okay. You can tell me. I admit I asked you out because I'm interested, but it's not like we've dated forever. We can be friends."

Sadie smiled at Charles. He would make a great friend. Hadn't she already thought of him as the brother she'd never had? And with so much happening in such a short time, Sadie had to admit she could use an extra friend or two. She smacked her hands onto the table in surrender. "I'm crazy about him." She shook her head. "It's totally nuts. The guy is my daughter's father, for crying out loud." She twisted in her seat. "Every time I think that, it seems preposterous, but saying it out loud. . ." She threw her hands up in exasperation.

Charles laughed. "I've got a hunch the feeling's mutual."

Sadie shook her head. "No. He's made it clear he's not interested."

"Hmm. I find that hard to believe."

"Seriously." Sadie picked at the crust of her pizza. "I wanted to go out to lunch with him, and he turned me down flat."

Charles scratched the side of his head. "I bet there's more to it than that. Have you told him how you feel?"

"Not in words, but. . ."

"Then you gotta tell him in words." Charles motioned for the waitress. "I'll take you home so you can pray about this."

"But our movie?"

"I can take you to the movie." He gazed into her eyes. "If that's what you want."

Sadie sighed. She felt physically ill from seeing Cam, and a drummer was beginning a light tapping in her head. "No. You're right. I think I'll call it a night."

Charles paid the bill then led her to his car. Sadie slipped inside and leaned against the headrest as the drummer's rhythm grew louder and more consistent. Wishing she'd brought aspirin with her, Sadie was thankful Charles didn't talk as he drove her home. Before she knew it, the car stopped.

"You're home." Charles's voice was soft.

Sadie opened her eyes and forced herself to sit up. Guilt mingled with the incessant pounding in her head. "Thanks, Charles. I'm sorry this date didn't exactly go—"

Charles lifted his hand. "Hey, it's okay. I've always been the girl's-best-friend kind of guy." Sadie noted a twinge of frustration in his voice. He winked. "I'll be praying for you."

"Thanks." Sadie slipped out of the car, walked to her front door, and went inside. She could hear him driving off as she shut the door. She kicked off her sandals and padded to the kitchen. After finding the pain reliever, she grabbed a bottle of water from the refrigerator and took the medicine.

She made her way into her bedroom, took off her dress, and put on a pair of pajama pants and matching T-shirt. The drumming had escalated from pounding to a roar. Her stomach knotted, and she knew her chances of revisiting the pizza she'd eaten had seriously increased. Plopping onto the bed, she covered her eyes with a pillow. "God, help my head, and calm my stomach."

Sadie closed her eyes and slowed her breathing. She was no stranger to headaches, especially those brought on by stress. She knew if she calmed herself, the medicine would kick in, and she would feel better. She sucked in a long breath. *Just breathe in and out, nice and slow.*

❧

Sadie woke with a start. She sat up and looked around the room, blinking repeatedly to get her eyes to focus. Her bedroom light was on and she could tell it was still dark outside. She glanced at her alarm clock. It read just after nine. She frowned and rubbed her temples with her fingertips. "What day is it?"

Her date with Charles washed through her mind. Cam's pained expression when their eyes locked planted itself in her brain. "Oh yeah." Sadie fell back onto the bed. Her first real date in Delaware had been a doozy. *After all, how many girls get to go out with a great guy they don't like only to run into the man they love? Oh yeah, with their daughter.* She groaned. Her life was a complete mess.

"God, I need some help."

"*I'm always here for you.*" Her spirit prodded her. She grinned and leaned over to pick up her Bible off the end table. Planning to open to the concordance to seek verses that might soothe her heart and thoughts, the book opened to a page with a sticky note she'd written before moving to Delaware. She read the verse aloud. " 'For God is greater than our hearts, and he knows everything.' First John 3:20."

She looked up at the ceiling. "God, You know everything. And You are greater than my heart. Take away these feelings I have for Cam."

Maybe the feelings aren't wrong. Maybe the fear is.

Sadie frowned at the thought. She knew the heart was deceitful above all things. She couldn't trust her feelings. She had to base her actions on what she *knew* was right in scripture. *Is it wrong that I love Cam? Does it go against God's Word? Or is it the fear in my heart that God is greater than?*

The thought gave Sadie pause. She brushed a strand of hair away from her face. Charles's encouragement to tell Cam how she felt flooded her mind.

"I do love him, God."

"*Tell him.*"

"But what if he rejects me?"

"*I know everything.*"

"Okay, what's the worst that could happen?" A vision of him smacking his leg bent over in raucous laughter drifted into her mind. *Okay, maybe I won't think that way.* Sadie's body trembled with excitement and trepidation. She slipped on a pair of sandals, grabbed her purse, and bolted out the door to her car.

Ellie would be in bed by now, so she would be able to talk with Cam alone. As she shifted her car into drive, she noticed she still wore her blue and white star pajamas. She smacked her forehead. "I didn't even get dressed."

With a sigh of determination, she shook her head. "It doesn't matter. If I don't do this now, I'll chicken out later."

❧

After flipping through channel after channel, Cam turned off the television. He grabbed his empty cereal bowl from the end table and made his way toward the kitchen. The last thing he wanted to watch was some reality show where a guy had to choose a potential wife from a group of beautiful women. Nor did he want to be entertained by sitcoms portraying a guy with the girl of his dreams, only to have her reject him in some cruel, inhumane way. Even the football game was showing a special report on one of the NFL's quarterbacks and how he and his wife met and married. He shoved the bowl and spoon into the dishwasher. *I need some fresh air.*

Cam made his way to Ellie's room. He stepped inside the door. As usual, Ellie was curled in a ball under her comforter, her special blanket nestled against her face. Her long eyelashes fanned her cheek in sweet, restful sleep. Leaning over, he brushed a light kiss on her forehead then tiptoed out of the room, partially closing the door behind him.

He walked out the back door and gingerly closed it behind him. If Ellie did wake up, she would be able to see him at the pond. He jammed his hands in his jeans pockets and watched his step along the short trail. How many nights had he spent sitting on the bench in front of these calm waters? The spot was his safe haven, his place to allow God to refresh his body and spirit. He looked at his bench. Someone was there.

Balling his fists, he stomped toward the stranger. No one would threaten the safety of his daughter. If this person planned to scope out a way to get into his home, the intruder would have to go through him first.

As Cam drew closer, the moonlight shone brighter on the person's form. *It's a woman.* Cam unclenched his fists. *Who in the world would be out here at this time of night? And what would she want?*

Kelly's girls were still too young to have traveled to his house alone, and the woman didn't have the same shape as Kelly. She turned her face to look at something to her left. Cam stopped as he drank in the profile.

Sadie.

Unsure what to do, Cam stood watching her for several moments. She was oblivious to his presence, and he could tell by the movement of her hands and head that she was having a conversation with herself, or maybe with God. It was late, but it wasn't *that* late. Cam wondered why she wasn't still on her date. And she wasn't wearing the same gorgeous dress she'd been wearing at the pizza place. Cam had felt a jealousy he'd never known in his life when he saw her all dressed up for another man.

What is she doing here?

Cam took a step closer. A twig snapped beneath his feet, and Sadie jumped up then turned around. She placed her hand over her chest and took several deep breaths. "Oh, Cam, you scared the life out of me."

Cam took in the blue T-shirt with a large white star on the front and the oversized blue pajama pants covered in matching smaller white stars. Her hair was tossed up into some sort of knot with strands of hair sticking out at all angles. *And this is how she gets dressed for me.* He bit back a smile at the thought. Actually, she looked amazing—like a woman he could wrap his arms around and not mess up. He scratched his jaw, already in desperate need of a shave. "Well, I didn't exactly expect to see you out here. Aren't you supposed to be on a date?"

"I was, but Charles took me home after we ate." Sadie clasped her hands in front of her and rocked back and forth on the balls of her feet.

Cam nodded. "Okay."

Cam waited for her to say something else, but Sadie just stood there staring at the tree beside her. Cam looked at the pond, then up at the moon, and finally back at Sadie. He had no idea what she wanted and no clue what to say. He didn't want to know if her date went well, didn't want to know if she liked the guy. Quite frankly, at that moment, he didn't really care if she wanted to see or talk about Ellie. He needed time to lick his wounds, the cuts that would never be able to heal from his inability to make her his own.

"Cam, we need to talk."

Finally, she speaks. Cam raised his eyebrows and pursed his lips. If he had a dime for every time that woman had said those words—but right now, he was not interested in talking.

"Please, Cam."

He looked into her pleading eyes. He could barely see the green in the dimness of the moonlight, but he could tell they implored him to give what she asked. The woman's eyes were his nemesis, and he knew better than to look into them. He smacked his hand to his thigh. "Fine."

She lifted one side of her mouth into somewhat of a grin. "You're not going to make this easy, are you?"

Easy? What was he making or not making easy? The woman he loved walked into a pizza parlor—looking irresistibly amazing and smelling unbelievably edible—with another man. Right in front of him. She had no idea how *hard* she'd been on him.

"I know I'm ten years younger than you." Sadie clasped her hands together.

Keep scraping the wound, woman.

She stepped closer to him. She bit her bottom lip, and he could tell she was breathing heavier. "And I know Brenda was your wife, and that you loved her." She grabbed his hand, caressing his palm with her thumb. "You have to know how much I cared for Brenda."

Cam held his breath. Her hand, so soft against his, sent electricity coursing through his veins. Every fiber within him wanted to scoop her into his arms.

She reached up her free hand, tracing her fingertips across the stubble along his jaw. Allowing her gaze to penetrate his, she turned her head up slightly. "I've fallen for you, Cam. I believe I love—"

All sense of restraint washed out of his body. He cupped her cheeks in his hands and lowered his lips to hers. She welcomed the kiss, and Cam felt his head swirl with desire. He loved this woman. He wanted this woman. Knowing he couldn't act on his feelings, he pulled away. Taking deep breaths, he peered into her eyes, filled with love and passion. She touched her bottom lip, her eyes begging him for an answer. "Please tell me you feel the same way?"

He brushed an escaped tendril of hair away from her cheek. "You have no idea how I feel."

"I love you, Cam."

Guilt, remorse, truth swept through him. He dropped his hand from her cheek. "I'm sorry, Sadie."

"Why, Cam?" Sadie grabbed his hand in hers. "Why are you sorry? You do have feelings for me. I see it in your eyes. I felt it in your kiss."

Cam swallowed hard. Humiliation filled his heart. He didn't want to tell her. He didn't want to see the look in her eyes. Couldn't stand the mixture of sadness and pity that would cover her beautiful face.

But he had to tell her. He couldn't just let her believe she meant nothing to him. "Sadie." Her gaze begged for a reason. He could see the fear of rejection in her beautiful green eyes. *I won't look at her face. Then I won't see the expression.* He pulled his hand away as he lifted his face toward the sky and stared at the moon. "I can't have children. Brenda and I adopted because of me, not her. I won't do that to another woman."

Chapter 15

Sadie's whole body had felt numb for two days. She'd opened up to Cam, even told him she loved him, and his response was to say he couldn't have children. He hadn't told her he loved her as well. Part of her believed he did. She touched her lips. His kiss, the look in his eyes—they spoke of true, deep affection. But what if his inability to have kids was just his way of saying he didn't want to have feelings for her?

And how do I feel about him not being able to have kids? Sure, Sadie had already been given the opportunity to carry a child in her womb, but she'd never experienced first smiles, first steps, first times to the potty. She wanted to be a mother more than she wanted to be an occupational therapist. Her deepest desire was to be a wife and mom. Could she be happy being the mother of only Ellie?

She rolled over in her bed, rubbing her temples with her fingertips. "Oh, I don't want to think about this anymore." She peered at the alarm clock beside her bed. "Well, I've definitely missed church." She forced herself to sit up. It was just as well. She didn't feel ready to see Cam again.

I'm going to have to get over it pretty soon. I'm not going to disappoint Ellie by missing getting her ready for school tomorrow morning. Forcing her legs over the side of the bed, she knew she at least needed to get ready and make her way to the store. She'd been out of laundry detergent for three days. Her clothes would be walking themselves to the washing machine if she didn't do something about them.

After showering, fixing her hair and makeup, and eating some breakfast, Sadie grabbed her Bible. She hated that she'd missed church and wanted to be sure she got some Bible study in her before leaving the house. Having just finished a women's Bible study a few days before, Sadie was unsure what to read. She didn't want to begin reading through the Bible because she already knew of another study she planned to pick up at the bookstore the following day.

She flipped through the pages. "Hmm, God. What can I read in a day?" The Psalms were always worshipful and uplifting, but she kind of felt like a story. Esther was one of her favorite books of the Bible, but she definitely wasn't in a "queen" mood. "God, I sound ridiculous. Your entire Word is breathed by You. You can speak to me in any chapter in any book. Show me, Lord."

The pages seemed to open to the book of Ruth. Perfect. Ruth had been on her heart for weeks. She started to read about Naomi and Elimelech and their two boys. She read about their move to the pagan land of Moab. By the end of chapter 1, all the men in Naomi's family had died, and she and her daughter-in-law Ruth were heading back to Naomi's homeland of Bethlehem. The story was so familiar to Sadie that she found herself speed-reading through the verses.

Then she reached chapter 3. Her reading slowed as she put herself into the character of Ruth. Naomi essentially asked Ruth to throw herself at the feet of Boaz, her kinsman-redeemer. In complete humility and vulnerability, Ruth obeyed by lying at his uncovered feet on the threshing floor. When he awoke, Ruth asked him to marry her. Actually, she said to spread the corner of his garment over her, but that was essentially a proposal from her.

Sadie thought of her admission of love to Cam two nights before. His response had been completely different from Boaz's. Boaz raced to the town gate to claim Ruth as his bride before the day ended. Cam had rejected Sadie.

"Did he really reject you?"

It sure felt like a rejection. Her lips tingled as the memory of his kiss swept through her. The kiss hadn't felt like rejection at all. *God, please just show me what I'm supposed to do.*

Sadie closed her Bible and held it to her chest for a moment. She loved God's Word and knew every bit of it spoke truth. Today, she'd felt led to look at Ruth. God would show her why. She stood and slipped on her sandals. After grabbing her purse off the chair, she walked out to her car. *I'm watching for what you want to show me, Lord.*

Dark clouds hung low in the sky, and Sadie knew at any moment rain would burst forth from them. The temperature had begun to drop. It would be no time at all before she'd have to start wearing fall clothes. She could hardly believe she'd been in Delaware that long. Already Ellie was halfway through being five years old.

As Sadie pulled into the grocery store parking lot, rain began to pelt her windshield. *I guess it's time to put an umbrella in the car.* She opened the door, covered her head with her purse, and raced inside. The store's air conditioner hit her with cold air, and Sadie shivered as she selected a grocery cart. She nodded and smiled at one of the cashiers as she walked to the fruit and vegetable section. *I should have made a list,* Sadie scolded herself as she selected a few apples, dropped them in a bag, then placed them in the cart.

She meandered down the bread aisle, picking up a loaf of wheat bread and a bag of bagels. She tapped her lip with her fingertip. *What did I come for to begin with?* She snapped her fingers. *Laundry detergent.*

Sadie made her way to the detergent aisle. A blond-haired woman stood in front of the brand Sadie liked. Sadie noticed a car seat clipped to the lady's cart. Taking a quick peek at the baby, Sadie couldn't help but smile at the beautiful Asian child.

"I'm sorry." The woman maneuvered her cart so that Sadie could get by.

"You're fine." She pointed to the child. "Your baby is adorable."

"Thanks." The woman adjusted the blanket around the baby's legs. "We've only had her a couple weeks."

Sadie frowned. The child wasn't old, but it was apparent she was more than just a couple of weeks.

"We adopted her," the woman continued. "She's our second daughter from China."

Sadie's heart skipped as she smiled at the woman and her baby. "Well, she sure is beautiful."

"Thanks." The woman pushed the cart down the aisle.

Sadie grabbed a container of her favorite detergent and placed it in her cart. She chuckled to herself. How could she, of all people, not have thought of adoption? She didn't physically have to carry a baby. God provided children in various ways—birth, foster care, adoption. She loved Cam. She loved Ellie. Future children would be in God's hands.

Her chest grew heavy with excitement. She'd simply tell Cam she didn't care that he couldn't have biological children. Then he could. . .

God, he never said he cared for me. Granted, I didn't uncover his feet and lie down in front of them, but Cam surely didn't act as if he'd go running to the town gate to claim me either.

The heaviness in her heart shifted from excitement to weariness. *But I do love him, Lord. What should I do?*

⌇

"Someone is a bit on the grumpy side today." Kelly picked up their dirty lunch dishes, stacking them on top of each other.

Cam pushed away from the table and stood. He grabbed a few dishes and followed Kelly into the kitchen. "Don't worry about these. I'll get them later."

Kelly swatted the air. "Hogwash. My girls and I just devoured all the lunch meat and cheese in your fridge. The least I can do is stick these in the dishwasher."

Cam nodded. "Okay. Thanks." He snapped the lids on the mustard and mayonnaise and stuck them back in the refrigerator.

"So what gives?"

Cam looked back at his sister. In only a moment's time, she already had all the plates in the dishwasher and a few of the glasses. He shrugged. "Nothing gives."

"Humph. Don't give me that." Kelly wiped a splash of water off her cheek with her shoulder. "You forget who you're talking to. I know when something is up. I was there for your diaper changings."

Cam grunted. "Oh yeah. You were two. I'm sure Mom had you changing all my diapers."

She lifted her index fingers. "I didn't say I changed them. I said I was there."

Cam rolled his eyes. "Like I said. Nothing."

"I noticed Sadie wasn't at church this morning." She placed the last two glasses in the dishwasher then wiped her hands on a towel. Turning toward Cam, she added, "I'm surprised she's not here right now."

Cam blew out a long breath. He had known this was coming. Though he had no desire to discuss the relationship, or lack thereof, with Kelly, he knew it was inevitable. "Where are the girls?"

Kelly dropped the towel on the counter. "Outside at the pond. Fishing."

"In the afternoon?"

"My girls don't care about the best time of day to fish. They just like to do it when they can." Kelly sat down at the table then patted the chair beside her. "Now quit stalling and tell me what happened."

Cam plopped into the chair. "Well, Sadie told me she loves me."

"That's great. You love her. It's as plain as the nose on your face."

Cam raked his fingers through his hair then smacked the table. "It's not great."

"Okay, so she's a little younger than you, and I admit this is not your normal situation with her being Ellie's birth mother and all, but you said yourself that Brenda loved Sadie, that they'd corresponded through the whole pregnancy and then after Ellie was born. . . ."

Cam glared at his sister. "It's not that and you know it."

"What then, Cam?"

"She wants children." Cam spit the words through gritted teeth. He'd had to admit his shortcoming so many times in the last few days he felt physically ill over it. *God, I thought I'd given this to You, but it's beyond humiliating.*

"Did you tell her?"

"Yes."

"What did she say?"

"Nothing."

"What do you mean 'nothing'?"

Cam pushed away from the table. "I mean she didn't say anything. She just left." Through with the conversation, Cam trudged into the living room. He stood beside the back door watching the girls at the pond.

"I think you need to talk to her some more, Cam." Kelly moved from the

111

table. He could feel her presence just mere feet from him.

"What's there to talk about?" He turned and smacked his hand against his leg. "I won't do that to her, Kelly. You didn't see the devastation on Brenda's face when we learned we could never have our own kids." He shook his head to keep from remembering the pain in her eyes.

That stupid accident. The memory of his bike wreck when he'd been only ten years old flooded his mind. The doctor couldn't say for sure it had caused Cam's sterility, but the doctor had seen it happen before. It was the only possible cause Cam could think of that he couldn't have children.

"This is different. Sadie knows the truth beforehand. You need to talk with her. If she's told you she loves you—"

"I won't marry—"

"Whoa. Marry?" Kelly lifted her hand. "Cam, if you are considering marriage with Sadie, then you owe it to the both of you to at least discuss this." She grabbed the doorknob. "I'm going to check on the girls. You need to do some praying."

Cam scowled as he watched Kelly walk toward the pond. She didn't understand. She couldn't. Brenda's mother had a terrible time conceiving. They'd just assumed their fertility problems stemmed from her. Brenda had gone through several tests and treatments, some more uncomfortable than others. Month after month, he watched her heart break when the pregnancy test came back negative. *God, I can't do that to Sadie. She's young. She could have several children.*

"This is different. Sadie knows the truth beforehand." Kelly's words popped into his mind. It was a different situation. Sadie could make a conscious decision to love him despite everything. But he could also choose not to do that to her.

The back door opened, and Ellie walked inside. She held her stomach, her face pale as powder. "I don't feel so good, Daddy."

"Are you going to throw up?" Cam no sooner asked the question than Ellie vomited all over the floor. "Okay then." Cam scooped Ellie into his arms and raced to the bathroom. The nauseating smell burned his nostrils before he'd had the chance to hold his breath.

Ellie's little body shook as tears welled in her eyes. "I still don't feel good." Her stomach heaved just as Cam got her in front of the commode.

Cam held her hair with one hand and patted her back with the other. *Nothing like a little upchuck to keep a guy's mind off his troubles.*

Chapter 16

Cam looked at the clock above the kitchen table. *Two o'clock in the morning, and I feel like I'm dying.* Cam had washed four loads of laundry and scrubbed the living room floor and the bathroom floor, and now he had to scrub Ellie's mattress. The poor child had thrown up no less than six times since that afternoon. And never in the same place twice.

He sighed. The smell of detergent, bleach, and vomit made his stomach churn. Hopefully, Ellie would feel better soon. She was running only a low-grade fever, and Cam presumed she'd caught some kind of stomach bug. *Well, she did start school last week. All kinds of new germs to grow immune to.*

"Daddy." Ellie's soft whimper sounded from his room. He'd laid her in his bed, a clean bucket on the floor beside her. This time he'd wised up and put a tarp beneath the covers. If she missed the bucket, which she tended to do, and threw up in his bed, she'd only soil the blankets, not the mattress as well.

"Coming, pun'kin." Cam walked into his room. He leaned over and gently rubbed her forehead. "What is it? Do you need a little sip of water?"

Ellie shook her head. "I want Mommy."

Cam's heart clenched. "Pun'kin, Mommy's not here."

Tears formed in Ellie's eyes. "Please, Daddy. I want Mommy."

"Ellie."

The tears spilled down her pale cheeks as her little chest heaved up and down. "Mommy." Her bottom lip puckered weakly, and Cam could tell she wasn't simply demanding her way. She genuinely wanted Sadie to comfort her while she was sick. "Please, Daddy. Mommy."

Cam bent down and kissed her forehead. "Okay. I'll call her."

✧

Sadie rushed to Cam's doorstep. She'd had limited exposure to sick children, but Cam had told her that Ellie wanted her, and nothing would stop Sadie from seeing her little girl. After only one knock, Cam opened the door and Sadie flew past him toward Ellie's bedroom.

"It's okay, sweetie." She looked at the bed, void of sheets, comforter, and most important, Ellie. She turned back to Cam, who still stood by the front door. "Where is she?"

He grinned. "In my room, across the hall."

She waved her hands in front of her nose. "It smells atrocious in here. That bleach smell is so strong I want to throw up myself. Maybe you could open a window."

"Sure."

A twinge of anxiety washed over Sadie as she walked into Cam's room. She felt something akin to an unauthorized trespasser as she took in the sage green walls accented with cream Victorian curtains. A large, dark armoire sat pristinely across from the oversized sleigh bed. The comforter, a light sage and cream color dotted with small embroidered roses, spoke nothing of Cam, only Brenda.

"Mommy?" Ellie's soft voice broke through Sadie's thoughts.

She rushed to her daughter's side. Caressing Ellie's forehead and cheek with the back of her hand, Sadie whispered, "It's okay, sweetie. I'm here."

"Mommy's here." Ellie nestled her cheek between her special blanket and Sadie's hand. She closed her eyes and let out a contented sigh.

Sadie looked back at the doorway. Cam leaned against the frame, and again anxiety swept through her. The man she loved bored through her with his gaze. *Maybe he feels I don't belong here in his and Brenda's room, too.*

"Thanks for coming, Sadie." Cam's voice was steady, but she could hear the exhaustion in his tone. She noted the bags beneath his eyes and wondered if today wasn't the first all-nighter he'd pulled. She knew she hadn't slept more than an hour or two since the other night.

"You look pretty tired, Cam." She maneuvered her body so that the blood could pump back to her hand again. "Why don't you lie down, and I'll take it from here?"

"No. You have to work in the morning. You don't need to stay long."

She shook her head. "I already called in."

His eyebrows furrowed in a straight line. "You what?"

"We have a number we can call in the night if we have to call in sick. I already called. I'll stay with Ellie tomorrow."

"But school just started last week."

"Cam, I'm her mother." Sadie stopped and bit the inside of her lip. She looked down at the sleeping girl. "I had to give her away, but now that God's given me the chance to be with her. . ." She looked back up at Cam, her gaze begging him to understand. "Please, I want to be her mother."

Cam started to say something; then he pursed his lips and nodded. "Okay then. I'm going to make a pallet on the living room floor."

Sadie watched Cam leave then turned her attention back to Ellie. The girl's hair was matted against her forehead, but Sadie was thankful she wasn't warm to the touch. Gingerly removing her hand from Ellie's grip, Sadie arranged the covers around her daughter. In what seemed only minutes, Ellie woke up feeling sick again. Sadie was ready with a bucket and washcloth and was able to keep the mess to a minimum.

Two more times, Ellie awakened sick. By five o'clock, Sadie was about to fall asleep sitting straight up. She placed her hand on Ellie's cheek. Still no fever, and it had been over an hour since she'd vomited. *Maybe I can lie down for a minute.*

Sadie contemplated slipping into bed beside Ellie, but she didn't want to risk jarring the child's stomach. She peeked in Ellie's room. Her bedsheets weren't on the bed, and Sadie didn't want to go on a search-and-find mission to discover where Cam kept them.

The silence of the house suddenly wrapped itself around her. Realization dawned that Cam slept only one room away. *I'm sure he's as gorgeous asleep as he is awake.* Despite still struggling with his rejection, Sadie tiptoed into the living room. *I'll just take a quick peek.*

She felt a slight breeze as she walked into the living room and noticed he'd opened a window just as she'd suggested. Her gaze moved to Cam. He lay on his back with his arms up and his fingers intertwined behind his head. The man looked as if he'd settled onto the floor to take in a football game on the television, not to sleep. A light blanket covered him from his chest to the bottom of his feet. His expression was peaceful, and Sadie found herself wishing she could bend down and gently kiss his lips.

The story of Ruth slipped into her mind, and she gasped. Cam stirred, and she covered her mouth with her hand. *Oh no, no, no, no. I am not going to go lying down at that man's feet.*

Sadie's heart raced, and she covered her chest with her hand. Cam looked so perfect sleeping. He was all she wanted in a husband—a Christian who loved his Lord dearly, a man who loved her daughter and took such good care of her, a true protector and provider. He even looked like the kind of guy Sadie had always been attracted to. *He makes the checklist I made up as a young girl.* She inwardly chuckled at the lists she and her friends used to compile for potential boyfriends.

"Go and uncover his feet and lie down." Naomi's words to Ruth filtered through her mind. Sadie shook her head. There was no way on the planet she would do what Ruth had done. Rustling blankets was no longer a sign of endearment, and it most definitely didn't stand for a wedding proposal in their day and time. *Like I'd propose to him anyway.*

The idea was ludicrous. Besides, there was no town gate for Cam to go running off to so that he could claim her as his own. She hadn't married another man—a relative of his, no less—and she didn't need a kinsman-redeemer. *The connection I feel with Ruth is crazy.*

She crossed her arms in front of her chest. Cam probably wouldn't even know what she was doing. What were the chances he was well versed on the book of Ruth? *And besides, I do have my pride.*

"Pride goes before destruction."

Sadie uncrossed her arms and raked her hand through her hair. She took several deep breaths then let her hands fall at her sides. *What have I got to lose? I love the man. God, I believe You brought me to Delaware for more reasons than I'd ever originally imagined. I'm going to trust You to help me through the humiliation if Cam laughs in my face.*

❧

Something jolted Cam awake. He blinked his eyes then wiped them with the back of his hands. Looking at his watch, he noted it was only six in the morning. A slight breeze blew through the window, and Cam curled his toes at its coolness. *No wonder. I pulled the covers off my feet.*

Cam sat up and grabbed the bottom of the blanket. *What in the world?* Sadie was lying at his feet. Her eyes were closed and her breathing seemed even. One of his throw cushions was wadded underneath her cheek. He scoffed at her sleeping on the floor without even so much as a blanket beneath her. *Why wouldn't she at least sleep on the couch? It's too small for me, but she would have fit.*

Cam jerked off his blanket with the intention of lifting her onto the couch when he saw his Bible sitting above Sadie's head. *I keep it on the table. What's it doing over here?* He leaned over and noticed it was opened to the book of Ruth.

Ruth? He scratched his jaw. His Sunday school class had studied Ruth only a few months ago. *Wasn't she the gal who married Boaz? The one who. . .*

Cam gasped. He scooped the Bible into his hands and skimmed the book. Finally getting to chapter 3, he read how Naomi sent Ruth to offer herself to Boaz by uncovering his feet and lying at them.

Cam's heart beat so hard and fast he thought it would burst through his chest. The action was like a marriage proposal. It was Ruth's way of saying she was willing to be Boaz's wife. Boaz, the man several years Ruth's senior.

He drank in the slight flush on Sadie's cheeks and the sweet peace that radiated from her expression of rest. Sadie knew he couldn't have children, and yet she wanted him. She was choosing him as her kinsman-redeemer. He closed his eyes, lifting his face heavenward. *I swore I'd never allow another woman to go through what Brenda had to go through.*

"I have a plan for you and for Sadie. I know what you need."

Cam opened his eyes and gazed at Sadie. Tendrils of her long dark hair cascaded down her cheeks and neck. Her long eyelashes brushed against her ivory cheeks. She was an older version of Ellie, even in her sleep. Cam leaned forward and pushed a strand of hair away from Sadie's face. Sadie's lashes fluttered; then

116

her eyes popped open and she bolted upright. "Is Ellie okay?"

"Ellie's fine. She's still asleep." Cam took Sadie's hand in his. "So you want me to be your kinsman-redeemer?"

A blush swept across Sadie's face, and she looked down at the floor. "Well, I—I mean. . ."

Cam pulled Sadie into his arms. His heart beat strong and loud beneath his chest, and he was sure Sadie could hear it. "I love you, Sadie."

Sadie fell into his embrace, wrapping her arms around him. A sigh escaped her lips. "I love you, too."

"You love me even though I can't have children?"

Sadie lifted her face. Cam drank in the love from her gaze. "We can always adopt."

Epilogue

Eight months later

S adie tied the cream-colored satin bow around Ellie's waist then turned her around and checked the front of the dress. She tweaked her daughter's nose. "I've never seen a prettier flower girl."

Ellie straightened her shoulders and pushed Sadie's hand away. "Mommy, I am six years old now. I'm too big to get my nose pinched."

"No matter how old you get, you'll always be my little girl." Sadie tickled Ellie's neck, making her squirm and giggle.

"Okay, girls. Let's not get all messed up before the wedding." Sadie's mom tapped Sadie's shoulder. "Stand up straight and let me make sure the buttons are all latched."

Sadie stood to her full height. She was glad her parents had flown to Delaware for the wedding. Cam had surprised Sadie by arranging for the three of them to visit her parents at Christmas. To her surprise, her parents really warmed to Cam and Ellie. She prayed her own relationship with them would mend completely one day as well.

Cam had contacted Brenda's parents about their upcoming wedding also. Though they'd only corresponded with Ellie through gifts at Christmas and birthdays, Sadie wanted them to know she wouldn't stand in the way of their forming a relationship with Ellie. It broke Sadie's heart that Ellie hadn't received a birthday present from them this year. Even more heartbreaking was that Ellie didn't even realize to miss it.

"Bend down." Her mother's voice interrupted her thoughts. "You have a flower coming loose from your hair."

Sadie looked at her mother's reflection in the mirror. Her mother was still as beautiful as she'd always been. Her hair still long, dark, and thick. Her skin still smooth and clear. Sadie hoped she would be as beautiful two and a half decades from now. Raw emotion filled Sadie's heart. She yearned for a closer relationship with this woman. "Mom, thank you for coming."

"It's your wedding. Of course we would come."

"I know. It's just. . ."

Her mom lightly wrapped her arms around Sadie's shoulders. "I love you."

"I love you, too, Mom." Her heart swelled with thankfulness at this quick answer to prayer and the hope it raised in her.

"Mommy." Ellie grabbed Sadie's hand and tugged. "It's almost time. I saw Daddy go to the front of the church. Miss Montgomery is here, too."

Sadie's heart swelled at the mention of Ellie's kindergarten teacher. Though Sadie had once thought the woman had been responsible for spreading rumors about Sadie, she soon learned Ellie's teacher had been one of her many colleagues who enjoyed basking in God's forgiveness and redemption. The fact that Miss Montgomery was smart enough to snag up Charles Mann only made her all the more wonderful in Sadie's eyes. Sadie had never known a more contented man as the middle school assistant principal now that he had the kindergarten teacher at his side. If Sadie's guess was right, their wedding would be the next in the small community.

"Okay then." Sadie snapped from her reverie, stood, and then walked to the door. She and Cam had planned a very small wedding. Only his family, her parents, and a very few select friends would be in attendance. They had no bridesmaids or groomsmen—only Cam, Sadie, and Ellie. Sadie had never even considered a wedding after she gave birth to Ellie. Now she needed the ceremony to be intimate and only between them. She wanted to drink in the promise she and Cam would make together in the presence of God, their families and friends, and their daughter.

Her dad stood in the hall waiting for her. "You ready?" He offered his arm and winked. "You look beautiful."

Sadie felt a blush creep up her cheeks. The long, simple cream-colored dress she'd chosen fit her perfectly. The all-satin, spaghetti strap design stopped at the floor in the front with a small train in the back. It seemed to have been made especially for her. Opting not to wear a veil, instead Sadie had her hairdresser weave baby's breath and small cream roses through her hair. She couldn't wait to see Cam's face when she and her father walked through the door.

Ellie grabbed Sadie's elbow. "When's it my turn, Mommy?"

"Well, you are first." Sadie straightened the bow on Ellie's flower basket. "When the right song begins, I'll tell you to go."

Ellie twisted back and forth, allowing her skirt to flare. "We look pretty."

"You both sure do." Sadie's dad winked.

The music began, and Sadie felt her pulse race. She could hardly wait to become Mrs. Cam Reynolds. After letting out a quick breath, she nudged Ellie. "That's your song, sweetie."

༄

The doors swung open and Cam inhaled a deep breath. He'd been waiting forever for this day to arrive. His precious daughter stepped onto the white carpet. She smiled brightly at him as she dropped one petal after another onto the floor.

He glanced at his family. His mom and dad beamed at Ellie. Kelly and her girls sat beside them, and even her oldest daughter, surprisingly, seemed happy to be there.

He noticed Charles Mann and his girlfriend sitting behind them. The sight of him almost made Cam laugh out loud. In truth, Cam should be thankful to the guy. If Charles hadn't asked Sadie out to pizza, they might still be dancing around their true feelings for each other.

Ellie finally reached the front and turned to stand beside him. He put his hand on her shoulder as the "Wedding March" sounded from the piano. "Wait till you see how pretty Mommy looks," Sadie whispered up at him.

He squeezed her shoulder. He couldn't wait. Thankfully, they'd scheduled their wedding for early in the day. He didn't know what he would have done if he'd had to wait until evening.

And then he saw her.

Her long hair was swept up on the top of her head with flowers adorning the sides. Several wisps of hair draped her neck, and he wished he could be one of them so that he could touch her softness. *Soon enough,* he thought, trying to persuade his beating heart. *She'll be all yours, soon enough.*

He drank in her dress. The spaghetti straps, though modest, exposed her shoulders and nape of her neck; and the material, so silky and shiny, draped her curves perfectly, sending Cam's mind in a tailspin.

His gaze moved up to her eyes, so full of love and hope. She and her father reached him, and he took her hands in his. "I love you," he whispered.

"Me, too," she whispered back.

In only a few minutes, Cam recited his vows. He listened intently as Sadie promised to love him, honor him, and cherish him through everything: sickness and health, riches and poverty. He devoured her sweet, sincere gaze as she spoke the words, knowing she meant them to the core of her being. Finally, he was able to kiss his bride. Her lips were soft and sweet, and once again he yearned for their time alone. He broke away, touching her cheek with the back of his hand. "Sadie Reynolds, I'm glad you found your way home."

FOR BETTER
OR WORSE

Dedication

This book is dedicated to my mother, Susan Miles. I am thankful for her love for God and desire to always be in the center of His will. Mom, I will always be thankful that you were such a good mom during my "Zoey" years.

Chapter 1

Kelly Coyle gazed around the room at the collection of family members who'd come to celebrate her day. Her mother, though in her midsixties and battling arthritis, still dyed her hair a dark brown, wore makeup to perfection, clothes that would look trendy on a thirty-year-old, and acted every bit as spry as Kelly ever could. Her father, with his salt-and-pepper hair and the most amazing, strike-you-down blue eyes she'd ever seen, sat on the carpet beside her mother's chair. Kelly's young niece, Ellie, had both of them immersed in a dog and cat puzzle the second grader had brought with her.

Kelly's sister-in-law's laughter sounded from the kitchen. Kelly knew her brother, Cam, was in there with her. There was no telling what shenanigans the two of them planned to pull for Kelly's thirty-eighth birthday.

Kelly's gaze turned to her three daughters. Somehow they had ended up sitting on the couch in stair-step order. Zoey, seventeen, her firstborn, sat with her legs crossed, elbow planted into the armrest and her chin plopped into the palm of her hand. Her appearance had undergone a marked transformation in the last three years—darker hair, darker makeup, darker clothes. Since Tim died, everything about Zoey had darkened.

Tall, thin, athletic, always-trying-to-please, fifteen-year-old Brittany sat in the middle of the couch. The middle child. Brittany second-guessed herself regarding every decision she made. She proved quick to follow others, and there were times Kelly grew more concerned about her follow-the-leader mentality than Zoey's rebellious attitude.

Candy sat cross-legged beside Brittany. Even though she was eleven and going into middle school in a few short weeks, Candy could not sit still. She was energetic, busy, and always into everyone else's business. She had to be the center of everything and everyone knew it. But her heart glowed as genuine as her body was active, and many a day God had used her youngest to give Kelly the motivation to keep going after Tim's death.

"Penny for your thoughts."

Kelly looked up at the man who'd whispered in her ear. Harold Smith, her knight in shining armor. In reality, he was more like the heating guy carrying the wrench, but he'd still saved the day. And after that he'd continued to bless her life. So many people struggle to find a godly love once, and yet God had blessed her twice. She smiled up at his expectant gaze. "I was thinking about how good God has been to me. What a blessing my family is."

"I agree." Harold leaned closer, gently pressing his lips against hers. It was cliché, something she could hear her high schoolers say or write in their short stories for her junior/senior language arts class, but the truth was that electricity still shot through her veins when that man's lips touched hers.

Harold stood to his full height, and Kelly caught a glimpse of Zoey's contemptuous expression. Kelly released a slow sigh. Tim had been gone for three years, and Kelly hadn't started dating Harold until almost a year ago. She'd dated no one else, but Kelly knew Zoey's bitterness wasn't directed at Harold. The teen had never gotten past Tim's car accident. She'd never made peace with God. Kelly picked up her glass from the end table and took a slow drink. Every day Kelly prayed Zoey would embrace God's peace.

Candy jumped off the couch, breaking Kelly's reverie. She walked to Kelly and put one arm around her shoulder then twirled a lock of her own hair around the thumb and index finger of her free hand. "Do you feel like an old lady now, Mommy?"

Kelly gulped her soft drink in an attempt not to spew it all over the floor. She wiped her mouth with a napkin as laughter burst from her gut. A chorus of guffaws sounded from the family. "Thirty-eight isn't that old."

Candy's cheeks flushed as the preteen furrowed her brows in embarrassment. It was apparent she didn't understand the response of the adults. Candy stammered, "But Sara's mom is only thirty-four, and Tabitha's mom is twenty-nine." She scrunched her nose. "I guess Tabitha's mom is the youngest mom in my class. But thirty-eight is the oldest. I don't know anybody else's mom who is that old."

Kelly wrapped her arms around her youngest child. "But I look good, right?"

"Huh?" Candy scrunched her nose.

Kelly released a laugh as she kissed the top of Candy's head. "You always make my day."

Harold grabbed Candy's hand, his lips tightly pinched in an obvious effort not to laugh. "Come on, you little flatterer, help me get your mom's cake."

Candy's face lit up. "All right." She pulled away from Kelly's embrace. "What's a flatterer, Harold? Why did everyone laugh at me? They're always laughing at me, and I don't know what I do that is so funny."

Kelly watched as the twosome made their way into the kitchen. Candy and Brittany had taken to Harold in only a matter of weeks. Zoey was a different story, but then she wasn't even fond of Kelly anymore. Harold looked back and winked, making her heart race. Three years ago, she would have never dreamed she would feel this way about another man.

When her husband and father of her three daughters died in a car accident, Kelly thought she'd never know happiness again. As time passed, God began to heal her pain and she was able to enjoy life—her family, her friends, her church, her students. Contentment was the appropriate word to describe what she felt before she met Harold. At peace with herself and her situation.

Then her heater quit working.

The memory brought a smile to her lips. Her brother, Cam, had taken care of all their repair needs after Tim died. Electrical problems. Plumbing issues Whatever needed fixed, Cam did it. But last November, Cam, his wife, Sadie, and their daughter, Ellie, had taken a short trip to visit her parents in Washington. When Kelly's heater gurgled its last, Kelly believed she and the girls would tough it out until Cam returned. Until the temperature in the house plunged to fifty degrees. Kelly had no choice but to call the heating guy.

Harold Smith was the first to answer the phone. When the tall, dark-haired, blue-eyed man walked through her door, Kelly's heart went to pitter-pattering, her knees turned to jelly, and giggles she hadn't heard since junior high spewed from her lips. The man didn't even have to cast a line; she was already hooked.

Cam nudged her shoulder, breaking her reverie. "How's it feel to be so old, grandma?"

Kelly glanced at her seventeen-year-old, Zoey, and her fifteen-year-old, Brittany. "I think I've got a few years before anyone will be calling me that."

Zoey rolled her eyes and peered out the front window. Brittany shifted in her chair, crossing her leg. "Really, Uncle Cam, I don't even have a boyfriend. Don't even want a boyfriend. They're all too short for me anyway."

"There's gotta be some six-footers at the high school." Cam continued to tease her. "I bet Zoey could hook you up with one of her friends."

"Yuk. Zoey's friends are weird."

Malice slipped from Zoey's lips. "At least I have friends. I'm not some six-foot freak of nature that boys have to wear stilts to even come close to looking at eye to eye. I'm not—"

"That is enough." Frustration welled inside of Kelly. "We are not going to start—"

"Okay now." Kelly's mom clapped her hands then stood and grabbed Brittany's hand. "Why don't you show me that new soccer medal since your grandpa and I didn't get to go to your last tournament."

Kelly noted the pooling of tears in her middle daughter's eyes as she led her grandmother to the bedroom. Focusing her attention back on her oldest daughter, Kelly pinched her lips together. Zoey's body was tense and rigid. She stared at Kelly, as if to dare her mother to say something to her. *I don't even recognize this child, Lord. I expect some squabbling between the girls, but this hatred that Zoey seems to feel—I don't know what to do with her.*

"Time for cake," Harold hollered as he and Candy burst through the kitchen door.

"Grandma." Kelly heard Brittany's voice from the hall. "Come on. Cake."

Candy's eyes gleamed with excitement as the twosome walked toward Kelly with the pastry that seemed to be covered with entirely too much fire for a woman who still felt like she was in her midtwenties. "You'll love this cake, Mom." Candy's face flushed as she covered her mouth with her hand, as if trying to hold back a secret.

Kelly peered into Harold's mischievous gaze. There was no telling what he'd had the baker put on her cake—a tombstone, a cemetery. It had to be something pretty silly for Candy to get so tickled.

He lowered the cake in front of her. Kelly gasped. It was not what she expected at all. She drank in the bright red cursive icing that read, WILL YOU MARRY ME?

⁂

Harold watched as Kelly's deep blue eyes widened in surprise. She lifted one hand to her lips. He almost chuckled out loud at the outlandish sparkling mess of flowers or something that covered her hot pink fingernails. He'd always thought nail stuff was silly, and here he was. . .in love with a woman who was the queen of the gaudy stuff.

Harold nodded at Cam. Kelly's brother stood and took the cake from Harold's grasp. Harold lifted the half-carat marquise diamond ring from the icing and wiped off the band. Kneeling on one knee, he took Kelly's left hand in his. The light from the living room window seemed to cast a glow around her shoulder-length brown hair, making her look prettier than any angel he'd ever seen in pictures. This woman was entirely too girly, way too smart, too beautiful, too perfect for an old, get-your-hands-dirty, blue-collar guy like him. But the love that radiated from her tear-filled gaze nearly took his breath away, and he couldn't help but practically yell out a praise to the heavens. He swallowed and whispered, "I love you, Kelly."

She nodded her head ever so slightly. "I love you, too."

Her admission calmed his nerves, and Harold took a deep breath. Never in his forty years of existence did he think he'd be doing this. He was a hermit at heart, a huge fan of Oscar the Grouch on *Sesame Street*. Harold always connected with the green muppet's penchant to be a recluse, to do as he wanted, make a mess if he wanted, and to be left alone unless he wanted to make an appearance.

And as for women. . .as a boy, Harold might as well have been a card-holding member of the Little Rascals' Women Hater's Club. When he was a teen, he'd avoided the female species like grease avoids water. As a young man, he'd thrown himself into his work. Something about women—maybe it was that they cried for no reason, got all bent out of shape for no cause, or fussed over the most ridiculous things—made him want to stay away from the whole lot of the female population.

Or possibly it was that they whined over what their hair looked like and sprayed the poor mass with sticky stuff until the ends stood stiff and straight on the top of their heads. And why did they want war paint on their faces? If God had wanted their eyelids to be purple and green, he would have made them that way.

Sure, Harold had to admit they smelled awful good when a guy got home after a long day of working around sweaty guys and broken toilets or busted heaters. Still, did women really need all those bottles and cases he saw in the store to help them smell that way? It seemed a little ridiculous, if not quite a bit pricey.

Then he met Kelly.

The woman he'd driven to that local fingernail place more times than he could count over the last year. The woman who got her hair trimmed and colored more often than he did laundry. The woman whose war paint made her eyes sparkle and her mouth irresistible.

And everything changed.

Now he was willing not only to marry a girl, but take on three more of them. Teenagers and a preteen to boot. The irony of it welled up within him. *You have quite a sense of humor, Lord.*

He gazed back at the woman he longed to cherish for the rest of his life. He yearned to hold her, comfort her, protect her as only as husband could. Ever so gently, he caressed her knuckles with his thumb. "I've waited forty years for you. Will you be my wife?"

Without hesitation, she leaped out of her seat and wrapped her arms around his neck, making him lose his balance and fall to the floor on his back. Lifting herself off him, she sat up on her knees beside his body. "Sorry 'bout that."

A mischievous grin formed on her lips as he rose to a sitting position. He touched her cheek with the back of his hand. "I'm assuming that means yes."

She giggled, wrapped her arms around him, knocking him off balance again. His back hit the hard wood with a *thud*, but he hadn't felt a thing. Kelly Coyle was going to be his wife.

Chapter 2

Kelly stuck the identification label she'd made for the new set of class novels on the inside flap of one of the books then handed it to Zoey to place on the bookshelf. "It's going to be kinda weird having your old mom for a teacher, huh?"

Zoey shrugged. She arranged a few books on the shelf, never turning toward Kelly.

Only seven years had passed since Kelly had finished her college degree. At the age of ten, Zoey's pride at her mom's accomplishment had been apparent. Despite having struggled in school, Zoey, from that point on, made every effort to earn good grades. Zoey had been successful, too. . .until Tim died. Since that time, Kelly's oldest child had spiraled more and more out of control.

Knowing that she had to keep trying, Kelly added, "I'm looking forward to having you in class. Language arts has always been your favorite subject, just as it is mine. We'll be able to share—"

"Do you really have to keep going with this song and dance?" Zoey peered at Kelly. Though they'd spent the better part of three hours working in Kelly's classroom preparing for the new school year to begin in only a few weeks, this was the first time today her daughter had so much as glanced at Kelly.

Kelly placed her hands on her hips, irritation welling in her gut. She'd spent the entire morning tiptoeing on pins and needles, searching for some way to connect with her oldest girl. "What is that supposed to mean?"

Zoey twirled her hand through the air. "This whole mother/daughter bonding stuff. I don't want to be here. You know I don't want to help you put your room together." Her tone dripped with sarcasm. "What? Are you hoping I'll tell you all my thoughts and feelings and that will make everything all better? That we'll be one, great big, happy family again." She spread out her arms, a snarl forming on her lips. "News flash, Kelly Coyle. Dad is dead. Things will never be all better."

"You will not take that tone with me." Kelly stomped toward her daughter. Though Zoey had grown a few inches taller than her mother, Kelly peered up at her child, demanding the respect she had not only earned, but as her mother innately deserved. "Every one of us lost your dad three years ago. We've all hurt—"

Zoey rolled her eyes then took a few steps back. "Yeah, some of us more than others."

"What is that supposed to mean?"

"It means"—Zoey grabbed her purse and walked toward the door—"I'm not going wedding dress shopping today. I'll catch you later."

"Zoey Coyle, you come back here." Kelly followed her daughter outside. Noting Zoey's car parked beside her own, Kelly cringed. She'd forgotten Zoey had met her at the school. "You're not leaving. You are grounded."

Zoey ignored her and kept walking. Before Kelly could reach her daughter, Zoey opened the car door, slid inside, and drove off. Kelly stared after her, the shock of her daughter's outright rebellion seeping through her skin. Zoey's defiance had hit an all-time high. Without a doubt, Zoey would be grounded. Kelly would take away the keys, the cell phone, the television, and whatever other privilege she could think of. But Zoey's problem wasn't one that could be fixed with punishment or discipline. Zoey's was a heart problem. *God she needs You so desperately, and I need to know how to be a good mom to her. Help me know what to do.*

※

Harold gripped the cell phone tighter. "Do you want me to go search for her?"

Kelly's exhausted voice mingled with tears of despair. "No. She's going to be grounded when she gets home, but I'm going to wait until she gets there. I just needed to vent."

Harold bit back a reply. He didn't want to hurt Kelly's feelings, and he didn't want Rudy, who sat in the truck's cab beside him, to see his frustration at the child. From what he'd seen of Zoey, she didn't need the opportunity to do as she pleased until she got home. She needed to be disciplined—and now. If he had his say, the girl wouldn't be wearing black makeup and baggy black clothes. Her hair wouldn't be dyed black and tied up in knots all over the place. The child's appearance screamed she had problems.

Truth be told, Harold was a little embarrassed when they went places together as a soon-to-be family. He'd never tell Kelly that. He loved that woman with all his heart. And the other two girls, Brittany and Candy, well, they were as sweet and as normal as could be. Sure, the two younger girls fought and picked and cried and whined at each other over the slightest things, like which of them would sit in the front seat of the car or who had to do dishes which days, but they didn't look at their mother with contempt as Zoey did.

Harold sighed. He loved the teen. God had given him a paternal love for Kelly's girls that he would have never dreamed possible before he met Kelly; however, there were moments he found himself struggling to like Zoey.

Not that he hadn't tried to connect with his soon-to-be oldest daughter.

He'd taken her to the movies, just him and her two sisters. He'd taken all three girls out to eat, played card games with the three and sometimes just Zoey. He'd picked her and her sisters up after school several times before she started driving. He even joined some group called Facebook on the Internet and tried to become her "friend." She denied his request. Nothing worked. She was cold, calculated, and downright disrespectful, and Harold had just about had it with her.

Now, he gets a call from Kelly, riddled with raw emotion, that Zoey had left the school in a huff and refused to go wedding dress shopping with her mother. The girl seemed to take pleasure in hurting Kelly. Harold cleared his throat. "I don't like it when she hurts you. Why don't I go find her?"

"No. Don't. I want this to be a good day. Brittany, Candy, and I will have a good time." She sniffed, and Harold knew she'd wiped her nose with a tissue. "You're still coming for lasagna, right? I'll have it ready by six."

"I wouldn't miss your lasagna for the world."

Her light chuckle sounded over the line. "I love you, Harold."

"I love you, Kelly. I'll see you tonight." He ended the call and slid his phone back into the case at his waist. Letting out a long sigh, he gripped the steering wheel.

"That girl's still giving her mom fits, huh?"

"Yep."

"Sorry to hear that. You know I raised two girls myself. It's not easy."

Harold looked at his most trusted worker. "How did you get through it?"

"I watched a lot of ball games and drank a lot of beer."

Rudy chuckled, and Harold simply stared out the windshield. Another reason he was glad he'd bit back any replies. Harold needed to be a witness to his friend. *God, help me live for You in the midst of this turmoil with Zoey. Help me be a good husband to Kelly, father to her daughters, and witness to those around me.*

The truth of his short prayer weighed on his heart. He would become the only living father Zoey would have from this point. He'd have to let God change his heart toward her.

❧

"I've been waiting all day for this." Fifteen-year-old Brittany slid into the front seat of Kelly's car.

"Who said you got to sit in front?" Candy stamped her foot and placed her hands on her hips.

"I got here first." Brittany stuck her tongue out at Candy.

"Mom, it's my turn!" Candy wailed.

Kelly raised her hand. "Enough." She pointed to the backseat. "Candy, you sit in the back. You can sit in the front on the way home."

"But—"

"No buts."

"Fine," Candy groaned as she slid into the back. "Where's Zoey?"

Kelly forced a smile. She refused to let the younger girls' squabble and Zoey's earlier actions take the joy out of the shopping trip. "Not coming."

"Oh no. What happened?" Candy growled from the backseat.

Kelly turned around in her seat. "Zoey doesn't want to come, and you know what, Candy, we're not going to worry about it." She looked at her middle daughter. "I pray for Zoey and her pain every day, but for now, the three of us are going to have a good time."

Brittany buckled her seat belt. "Finally."

"Where are we going to eat?" Candy asked.

Kelly smiled. Her youngest thought of little else but from where she'd receive her next meal. "Let's go to the boutique first."

Brittany let out a long breath. She twisted her purse strap between her fingers. "I can hardly wait to get there. I've been looking up dresses on the Internet this morning. There's just so much to choose from."

Not only was Brittany the most interested in sports, she was also a hopeless romantic. During the summer months, her sisters had to beg Brittany to stop watching one bride show after another. Candy, the dance queen of the family, knew the lyrics of nearly every song and the words of every movie she'd ever watched, but she was not overly interested in romance—which Kelly decided was a good thing since the girl was only eleven.

Kelly pulled into a parking space in front of the boutique Sadie, her sister-in-law, had suggested. The place was not at all what Kelly had envisioned, simply a small, office-style space in a strip mall of sorts. The store's name was posted in small, anything-but-ostentatious letters above the door. If Sadie hadn't suggested the place, Kelly would never have given it a second look. Kelly shifted the car into park.

"This is where we're going?" Brittany wrinkled her nose and pointed toward the plain door with such small lettering Kelly had no idea if it fronted a boutique or not.

"I guess so. Let's not judge a book by its cover."

Kelly and the girls stepped out of the car then walked into the boutique. Three-hundred-sixty-degree mirrors filled the back wall. Two ornately draped fitting rooms bookended each side of the mirrors. Rich paint and wallpaper covered the remaining walls, but Kelly couldn't help noticing the almost-bare racks.

Candy tugged her arm. "I'm not so sure about—"

"Can I help you, ladies?" A man—who had to have only moments before hopped off a Harley-Davidson motorcycle—stepped out from one of the fitting rooms. His long, wiry, sandy-brown hair was tied back in a ponytail. His beard, a much redder color, was also tied in a ponytail at the base of his chin. His skin bore a coarse texture from years in the sun or acne or the combination of both. His black T-shirt and black pants had seen better days, but the black leather vest he wore appeared to be in good shape.

"Mom." Candy grabbed Kelly's hand, and Kelly felt Brittany take a step back.

Kelly lifted her chin. The man looked rough, but that didn't mean he was a bad guy. She didn't want her girls to prejudge the man, just as she didn't want to judge the shop. *Just as I don't want people to think I'm a bad mom when they see Zoey.* The inward admission pained her. Daily, she teetered between feeling like a failure and inwardly defending herself as a mother. Shaking the thoughts away, she smiled at the man. "I was looking for a boutique. I'm trying to find a wedding dress. . ."

"Yeah. I bought this place a couple months back. The man said he was losing money, but I've sure had a lot of women trying to buy dresses." He waved his hand around the room. "What you see is what's left. It's all half off."

"Maybe we should just go," Brittany whispered.

Kelly turned toward her daughter and smiled. "Half off? Honey, I think we're going to look around." Extending her hand, she took a few steps toward the motorcycle guy. "I'm Kelly Coyle. Nice to meet you."

He grinned and shook her hand. He looked past her. "Jim Lucas. Nice to meet you. Are these your kids?"

"Yes. This is my second wedding. Their father died three years ago. . . ."

"Sorry to hear that. My wife died about five years ago from cancer. If it hadn't been for the Lord. . ." He shook his head and took a deep breath.

"I understand completely." Kelly looked back at her girls, who had already begun to inch their way toward her.

Jim winked at the girls. "There's peppermint on the counter, if you want some. I'm going to keep working in the back. Let me know if you need anything."

Kelly turned toward her daughters. She shrugged. "See. You never know."

Candy cocked her eyebrow. "You don't exactly feel that way about Zoey's friends."

Kelly lifted her finger. "Ah, but you forget. I'm a high school teacher. I already know the kids Zoey hangs out with. We didn't know him."

"I guess that's true."

"Oh, Mom, look at this dress." Brittany's voice sounded from the other side of the room. "It's a Mon Cheri."

Kelly made her way over to her middle daughter. Her mouth dropped. "You're kidding?"

"Who's Mon Cherry?" asked Candy.

Kelly shrugged her shoulders. "I don't know, but I've got to agree with Brittany. This dress is beautiful." She fiddled with the bodice of the gown. "Doesn't this thing have a size somewhere on it?"

Brittany pulled it off the rack and held it up to Kelly. "I don't know, but it looks close."

Excitement streamed through Kelly's veins. "Let's try it." She gently lifted the dress from Brittany's grasp and headed toward the empty fitting room. "Jim," she yelled, "is it okay if I use this fitting room?"

"Sure. Just ignore the mess." His voice sounded from somewhere in the back of the store. Kelly quickly took off her T-shirt and jean shorts then slipped into the dress. Thankfully, the dress zipped as well as having hook and eye buttons that covered the zipper. It was a tad big, but Kelly could hardly wait to see it in the 360-degree mirror.

She stepped outside of the fitting room. Both girls gasped. Candy covered her mouth with her hand. Kelly bit the inside of her lip and scrunched her nose. "Is that good? Is that a good gasp?"

"Turn around and look, Mom." Brittany turned Kelly toward the mirror.

Kelly closed her eyes. How would she feel seeing herself in a wedding gown? She had loved Tim completely when he was alive. Would seeing herself in this make her feel as if she'd somehow tainted his memory? She thought of Harold and how good and sweet he was to her and the girls. She knew Tim would have liked Harold. He would approve.

She opened her eyes and took in the straight, floor-length, ivory gown with off-the-shoulder lace sleeves. Delicate lace covered the soft silk material. The straight-line neck was adorned with dainty, floral, V-shaped beading. The same beading styled the waist and floor of the gown giving it a romantic and whimsical appearance. The gown was not too young looking, nor did it look like a dress to be worn by a mother. . .and Kelly didn't want to look like a mother on her wedding day, she wanted to look like a bride. Harold's bride.

"You look so pretty, Mom," Candy said.

"It's beautiful," Brittany agreed.

Tears pooled in Kelly's eyes. It was the first dress she'd tried on. "It's perfect. It couldn't be more perfect."

⁕⌁

Having just left the travel agency, Harold hopped into the cab of his truck and placed the Hawaii brochure and receipt on the front seat beside him. The honeymoon cost him a good deal more than he'd anticipated, but once Cam told him that Kelly had always dreamed of going to Hawaii, Harold knew he'd have to do whatever it took to get her there.

A slow smile bowed his lips. He and Cam had already discussed not telling Kelly where they would be going after the wedding. Cam's wife, Sadie, would pack her bags. His heartbeat sped up in anticipation. Harold could hardly wait to see the look on Kelly's face when she learned their destination. He latched his seat belt then glanced into his rearview mirror. "I've waited forty years for Kelly, surely I can make it another three months."

He turned the ignition and headed toward the shop. He'd left his right-hand man, Rudy, in charge of making sure the shop was clean and the trucks readied for the next day. It shouldn't have taken too long, as August tended to be a slower month in the heating, cooling, and plumbing business. It was the months that were the onset of hot or cold weather that usually had Harold and his men working more hours than the day possessed.

Which made a December wedding a bit nerve-racking for him. Oftentimes a good snow or two blanketed Delaware's countryside on or before Christmas, and Harold couldn't stand the thought of leaving his men one guy short while he was lying around on a beach in Hawaii.

"Don't think about it," he growled to himself as he parked the truck in front of the shop. "Cam promised to step in if it got bad while we're gone."

Harold got out and looked around the lot. Rudy's car was gone, a sign that the shop had been properly shut down and was ready for the next day. He made his way to the front door when a car pulled up the drive. He turned and smiled. Cam stepped out. "So, did you do it?"

Harold lifted the brochure and receipt in his right hand. "Got her right here."

"Let's see." Cam took the papers from Harold's grasp and fanned through them. "Man, Sadie will be so jealous. You know I'm going to have to plan a trip to the Islands now, don't you?"

"Sounds like that would break your heart?"

Cam grinned. "Not in the slightest." He rubbed his jaw. "But that's not why I'm here."

Harold folded his arms in front of his chest. "What's up?"

"Sadie's wanting the four of us to get together for dinner tomorrow night. She's already talked to Kelly."

Harold frowned. "That's all? What's the serious look for?"

"She wants to talk wedding colors and flowers and tuxes."

"Oh." Harold snarled. "I guess that goes with the territory."

Cam nodded. "Yep."

"And all I have to do is say yes to everything, right?"

"Yep."

Harold cocked one eyebrow. "You've gotten pretty good at this?"

"Yep."

Harold laughed out loud. "I'll be sure to heed your advice." He lifted the papers in the air. "I'm going to go lock these up and head over to Kelly's house. She's making lasagna."

Cam patted Harold's shoulder. "Have fun, my soon-to-be brother."

Harold chuckled as he made his way into his shop, stowed the papers in his wall vault, and went back to the truck. Cam proved to be a great perk to having fallen in love with Kelly. Not only did Harold find a woman he wanted to marry, but she came with a brother who'd become a good friend.

He glanced at the clock radio. Kelly was expecting him in half an hour. She'd gone dress shopping today, so Harold had already mentally prepared himself to listen to stories about lace and pearls and whatnot. He turned the ignition, noting his permanently stained fingernails, dry, calloused hands, and thick, hairy forearms. He was the beast marrying his beauty. What Beauty saw in him, he'd never know, but he sure thanked God for whatever it was.

Deciding he'd better stop for some gas, Harold pulled into an older, run-down gas station off Main Street. It was the usual hangout of some of the more shifty characters of their small town—a place he wouldn't want Kelly to frequent. But the owner was a man who God had laid on Harold's heart several years before, and Harold believed one day he would get Bill to come to church.

Harold finished pumping the gas then walked inside to pay. "Hey, Bill, how's it going?"

The balding, white-haired man hopped off the stool and shimmied toward the counter. His weathered skin hung beneath his eyes and jaws. "Not too good." Bill's voice scratched from years of smoking. "Couple kids have been coming in and out all day. I'm pretty sure they're stealing stuff, but I ain't caught them yet."

"I'm sorry to hear that. Have you called the police?"

Bill shook his head and growled. "What am I gonna tell them? I ain't actually seen the kids. . ." He peered past Harold, out the store's window. "Here they come again."

Harold turned, and he felt as if his heart stopped in his chest. Zoey was walking toward the gas station. She was with a man whose shaggy hair stuck out beneath a well-worn cap. He wore dark clothes, even baggier than Zoey's, and Harold noted his several-days'-growth beard. More importantly, Harold noticed he appeared to be older, much older than any of the boys he'd seen in high school.

Without a second glance back to Bill, Harold marched out the door and straight to Zoey. Surprise registered on her face for an instant before she masked the expression with anger. "What's up, pop?" Zoey exaggerated the less-than-sentimental term of endearment.

"What are you doing here, Zoey?" Harold suppressed every ounce of fury that begged to be unleashed on the teenager.

"Getting a drink. Last I heard, that wasn't a crime."

Harold grabbed her arm. "I think you're going to go home with me now."

Zoey jerked away and scowled at him. "I will not."

"Hey, dude, what gives?" The man Zoey was with took a step toward Harold. "Zoey and I aren't doin' nothing wrong. You need to back off."

"I need to back off?" Fury raced through Harold's veins. His fists clenched and he shoved them into his front pockets to keep from punching the young man in the face. "Do you know how old she is? Seventeen. That's right. This girl is still in high school."

The man smirked and crossed his arms in front of his chest. "Last I heard the age of consent was sixteen. She's plenty—"

Hot anger exploded inside Harold at the man's words. His fists came out of his pockets faster than he could control them. He grabbed the guy's grimy shirt in both fists, forcing his face mere inches from Harold's. "Now, you listen to me." The words spit from Harold's lips, splattering the man's face. "This seventeen-year-old is off-limits for you, buddy. If I so much as see you within fifty feet of this girl, I'll. . ."

"Stop it, Harold." Zoey pushed his arm, but Harold was too enraged to move or respond. "I'll go with you. Just stop it."

Fear laced the young man's eyes, and Harold felt his anger start to simmer. The work of the Holy Spirit, no doubt. Twenty years before, Harold would have sent the guy to the hospital. Squinting his eyes, he held the man tight for just a moment more. "I mean what I said."

"Fine, Harold. You mean it. Let him go." Zoey pushed his arm again.

This time he released the young man and turned toward Zoey. "Go, get in the truck."

"My car is here. I'll just drive."

Harold shook his head. He didn't trust Zoey. She seemed to have mellowed from when he first approached them, and her tone had settled substantially, but he still didn't want to take the chance that she'd run off again. "No. Your mom and I will get your car later."

Zoey let out a long breath. "Fine." She turned toward the man. "Jamie, give me my keys."

Shock coursed through Harold. "You let this guy have your keys? He's been driving your car?"

"You're mad. I get it." Zoey took the keys from Jamie's hands then started toward Harold's truck. "Can we just go home?"

Harold glared back at Jamie one last time. "I think you need to be heading on home now."

Jamie lifted his hands in surrender. "Fine. I'm gone." He turned and slithered back down the street.

Harold took several long breaths and rubbed the back of his neck with his hand. The age-of-consent comment Jamie made raced through Harold's mind repeatedly. What had Zoey been doing with that guy? Why was she so rebellious? Yes, she'd lost her father, but her family had been overwhelmingly supportive, and he'd tried, how he'd tried, to be good to her, her mother, and her sisters.

Before walking to the truck, he peered up at the clear, blue sky. The day couldn't be more beautiful—sun shining, slight breeze blowing. *Thank You, Lord, for stopping me before I pounded that boy. Give me wisdom with Zoey.*

Harold walked to his truck and slid into the cab. "Empty your pockets."

"Excuse me?"

Harold peered at Zoey. "You heard me. Empty your pockets."

Zoey's face turned scarlet as she pulled a few candy bars and a package of gum from her side pant pockets. Harold reached into his back pocket and pulled out his wallet. He pulled out a twenty-dollar bill. Grabbing her hand, he shoved it into her palm. She looked up at him and he locked onto her gaze. "I don't know how much you two stole, but you're going to take that candy and this money in there to Bill, and you're going to apologize. Hopefully, he won't press charges."

Shame wrapped Zoey's features, and for the first time, Harold witnessed a twinge of regret at what she'd done. A tear started to slip down her cheek, but she wiped it away in one swipe. "Fine. Give me just a minute, then you can take me home, pop."

The sarcasm and hatred were back, but Harold had seen a glimmer of hope. It twisted his heart in a way he hadn't expected. As much as she drove him to near insanity, the twist proved he cared for Zoey more than he realized. He wanted to see her straighten up, not just for her family, but for herself. *God, heal this little girl. Continue to work in my heart toward her, too.*

Chapter 3

Kelly popped the last bite of cracker into her mouth. The first few weeks of a new school year always sent her stomach into a tailspin. She loved teaching, but the getting-to-know a new batch of teenagers, the settling into a routine, and the always-new requirements by the state and administration never failed to take a toll on her nerves. *It's why I'm able to stay a pretty good weight. One month of the year I live on crackers.* She chuckled to herself as she unlocked her classroom door, walked to her desk, and dropped her school tote and lunch bag on the floor beside the file cabinet.

Thankfully, it was Friday. She'd made it through the first three weeks of school, as well as having Zoey as a student, without a hitch. She noticed the three pictures of the bridesmaid dresses she'd narrowed her choice to sitting on top of a pile of ungraded essays on her desk. Adding planning her own wedding to everything else she needed to get done only enhanced her stomach's inner turmoil. She plopped into her rolling chair, making sure not to rest her elbow on the broken left arm of the chair.

She picked up the three pictures. Her daughters would be her bridesmaids, or three maids of honor, as they chose to be called. Zoey didn't even want to go to the wedding, let alone be in it, but Kelly and her younger daughters deliberately ignored Zoey's pessimism and included the seventeen-year-old when they could.

Kelly clung to the slight change she'd noticed in Zoey after the night a few weeks before when Harold brought Zoey home for dinner. She never got a complete answer from Harold or Zoey about what happened that night, but she and Harold had gone to get Zoey's car at a gas station. Normally, Kelly would have demanded Zoey tell her what was going on, but something had changed in her daughter. It was small, almost unnoticeable, but it was enough that Kelly knew the Holy Spirit was instructing her to trust Harold.

She glanced at the pictures again. Two of them Brittany and Candy simply loved. The third dress her two younger girls didn't like, but it was the one Kelly knew Zoey would be most willing to wear. All of the dresses were practical, ones the girls could wear to church or to an occasion that called to be more dressed up. One of the dresses that Candy liked seemed just a bit old for her. It was appropriate for Brittany and Zoey, but. . .

Kelly cupped her hand over her mouth. "Oh my, why didn't I think of this before?" Favoring the right side, Kelly leaned back in her chair. "They're all in the same family of the deep emerald I'm using as my primary wedding color." She shook her head and laughed out loud. "And, they'd never be willing to wear the same dress after the wedding. I'll just have each girl wear a different dress all in the same color."

Still chuckling, Kelly turned toward her computer and booted it up. The students would be coming down the hall in five minutes or less. She clicked her e-mail to skim as many as she could before then. *To think I've been stressing over that for several days.*

She took a sip of her coffee, allowing the heavenly scent of hazelnut to wrap around her. It wasn't until after she started teaching seven years before that Kelly fell in love with the warm, caffeine-laden drink. Now, she couldn't start the day without it.

The first e-mail was from Harold. A smile bowed her lips. Each morning her man sent her an "I love you, and have a good day" e-mail. As she did every day, Kelly responded with the same message.

Before she could check any other messages, her students started to filter into the room. Extraordinarily tall and thin Logan Huff made his way through the door first, as he did every morning. "Hey, Ms. C."

"Hi, Logan. How has your morning been?"

"Good."

Logan made his way toward Kelly's desk. Most of the students congregated in the hall, spending every second they could with their friends before they were stuck in the classroom for over an hour. Not Logan. Instead, he spent his last few minutes talking with Kelly.

"I really enjoyed the reading last night," Logan went on. He pulled out a paper, and Kelly noticed Zoey walk in, place her books on her desk, and look toward Kelly and Logan. The boy continued, "I even made a few notes for our class discussion."

Zoey rolled her eyes then made a gagging motion. Kelly suppressed a smile. Zoey's action didn't contain the hatred it once had; it was done more in jest. Plus, Kelly loved to see that each day Zoey's makeup became a bit lighter and she wore a few actual colors of clothing on occasion.

The bell rang, and Kelly stood and walked around her desk. "I look forward to your comments, Logan. Now, go ahead and take your seat." She walked to the front of the room as the students made their way to their desks. "Good morning, everyone. Get out your warm-up sheets."

❧

Harold slid the keys out of the ignition, opened the truck door, and slipped out. Excitement coursed through him as he made his way up the sidewalk toward

Kelly's door. He'd been planning this Saturday excursion since before school started. Between starting back to school, the girls, and the wedding, Kelly had been stretched to the max. *This date will take things off her mind.* He smiled as the door opened before he had a chance to knock.

Kelly stood in the door, biting her bottom lip. "That smile looks quite mischievous. Should I be scared?"

Harold took in her long-sleeved T-shirt, jeans, and tennis shoes. Most of her hair was swept up in a ponytail, except the strands that weren't long enough, and her face appeared free of makeup. He whistled and winked at her. "You are adorable."

Kelly huffed, crossing her arms in front of her chest. "Are we going hiking? We better be doing something outside. You said to look natural, but if we end up at a nice restaurant, I'm gonna—"

Before she could finish, Harold wrapped his arms around her capturing her lips against his own. He could never get enough of the sweet scent of her perfume and softness of her lips. Pulling her closer to him, he deepened the kiss and she curled her fingers around his neck. The light scratch of her fingernails sent shivers racing down his spine, and Harold forced himself to pull away. "A little over two months until you're mine," he growled, then planted one last kiss on her forehead.

"That's too long," Kelly whined as her fingers traced a path through the back of his hair.

Harold took a step away from her and exhaled a long breath. "Woman, you are dangerous. Get your purse, and let's go."

Kelly giggled as she escaped back into the house, then reappeared seconds later with her purse strap over her shoulder. She shut the door and followed Harold to the car. "Can I get a hint?"

Harold opened the passenger's door for her then made his way to the driver's side. "Nope." He buckled his seat belt and started the truck. Kelly intently looked at her surroundings as Harold made his way toward Highway 1 South.

"How far are we driving?" Kelly quipped without looking his direction.

"It'll take us around an hour." Harold shook his head. The woman couldn't stand surprises. He assumed it was the teacher and the mother in her. She had to have everything planned to the last second, and she had to know what was going on.

"We're going to Dover, aren't we?"

Harold grabbed Kelly's hand, raised it to his lips, and kissed her knuckles. "I want you to sit back and enjoy our date."

"Okay. Okay."

Harold bit his bottom lip. He hated to say it, but he had to get Kelly's mind off their day's excursion. Mentally preparing himself for the onslaught of words, he planted a smile on his face. "Why don't you tell me where we are with the wedding plans?"

Kelly's face brightened. "Okay. Well, I picked out the dresses for the girls. I decided to let each wear a different. . ."

Harold listened as Kelly talked about dresses, ribbons, flowers, and other stuff he really didn't care much about. What he did enjoy was watching the happiness and excitement in Kelly's tone and expressions. He'd do whatever it took to make the woman he loved happy.

"You and the guys will need to get fitted for your tuxes in the next couple weeks."

Tuxes? He'd forgotten all about the fact that he'd have to wear a monkey suit. There had been only a select few times in his life that he'd worn a sports jacket and tie, never a full-blown tux. He was a jeans and T-shirt kind of guy, and the idea of someone taking a tape measure to him seemed weird. "You're going to go with us, right?"

Kelly clicked her tongue. "Nope. You, Cam, and your work buddies are going to go by yourselves. I don't want to see what you're wearing until our wedding day. Just make sure you don't get pink."

Horror smashed Harold in the gut. "They come in pink!"

Kelly laughed. "I'm kidding. Just pick black and white."

"Black and white, I can do that. I think." Harold turned toward his destination. Anticipation gurgled within him. He couldn't wait to see Kelly's expression. "It's just up ahead."

Kelly peered through the windshield. Harold peeked and noticed her eyebrows furrowed into a line. "I don't see a hiking trail or anything like that."

"I never said we were going hiking." He pointed toward the mammoth structure in front of them.

"The Dover International Speedway?" Kelly looked at Harold. "We've been together a year, and I never knew you liked to watch NASCAR."

Harold shrugged his shoulders. "I don't watch NASCAR."

Her frown deepened. "But?"

Harold grinned. "We're not watching. We're driving."

❧

Overwhelmed, Kelly followed Harold toward the Dover International Speedway, known as the "Monster Mile." She'd never been to a racetrack before and as they approached the main entrance the humongous monster statue mesmerized her. "Wow." She peered at the structure. The monster was a huge, gray, stonelike creature that burst through the top of a circular structure containing plaques of two hundred Dover Speedway winners. With his left hand gripping the top of the structure, the monster's right hand held a red and white racecar high into the air.

"It's something else, isn't it?" Harold pointed at its face. "His red eyes glow at night, making him even more fierce looking."

Kelly giggled. "His teeth kinda remind me of the abominable snowman in *Rudolph*."

Harold laughed. "Yeah. I can see that, but I don't think that's what they were going for." He grabbed her hand then pointed at the car in the monster's grip. "Come on. I can't wait to take a spin in one of those babies."

Kelly experienced a rush of stimulation overload. The place was huge, holding well over 100,000 spectators and the track itself was a mile long. Everywhere she turned she saw massive metal and concrete structuring and fences that seemed forever tall around the track. The bright-colored signs displaying various products were splattered all over the walls. Not to mention all the men and women clad in red shirts or a blue bodysuit of sorts.

While Harold took care of getting them set up, Kelly drank in the families who were taking pictures beside and inside the various cars. A person had to be eighteen to drive, but there were still plenty of young boys and girls rooting on their older siblings, parents, and even some grandparents.

Before Kelly knew it, she and Harold were in a "special van orientation" driving around the racetrack. She listened intently and thrilled when the time came for her final instructions with an in-car driving counselor. She was about to "ride and meet the Monster."

"So, do you think you'll like it?" Harold asked as he slipped one foot into the protective suit.

"Truthfully"—Kelly picked up her silver helmet with the yellow and red Monster Racing logo on the front—"I can't remember the last time I've had such an adrenaline rush. I can't wait."

Harold grabbed her close and planted a quick but firm kiss on her lips. "That's what I wanted to hear."

Kelly peered up at her man. The blue bodysuit mixed with the late morning sun gave his oceanlike eyes a brilliant glow. She touched his clean-shaven face. "You know, I've snagged myself quite a good-looking man."

"You don't look so bad yourself, Ms. Coyle, in that protective body gear. In fact, I'd say you look pretty enough to kiss again."

Kelly smiled as she allowed him one more kiss. Within moments, she slipped into the car. She rode as a passenger for four laps, studying how the instructor drove the vehicle as well as the course. Soon it was her turn to drive herself.

Trepidation raced through her as she considered driving the mammoth track in a speeding car...all by herself. She looked at her driving instructor. "How many laps do I drive by myself?"

"Ten."

Kelly's heart thrummed in time with the engines. "Okay."

"You're going to do fine. Remember, you don't have to go super fast. Just go at a pace you feel comfortable."

Kelly looked at the bright yellow stockcar that in only a matter of minutes she would be driving. When had she ever had an opportunity like this? To essentially let her hair down and let the wind rush over her. She'd always been a planner, a detail kind of girl. Not spontaneous. Not a daredevil. And yet her adrenaline pumped at the idea of throwing away her inhibitions and driving as fast as she could around this track. Determined to conquer her queasiness, Kelly nodded at the man. "It's going to be great."

She maneuvered her way through the window and into the driver's seat. Tubing covered nearly every crevice of the inside of the car. She couldn't imagine how someone as big as Harold would fit into one of these cars; she felt like a sardine being shoved into its tiny tin.

When it was time, she started the engine and followed the instructor's car out onto the track. Harold drove behind her in a three-car "follow the leader" formation. The car rattled so hard, which the instructor had promised was normal, that Kelly felt her insides would be tossed into wrong positions. *It's a good thing I ate a light breakfast.*

The first lap around was not too fast but more thrilling than Kelly expected. She followed the instructor without a hitch and even enjoyed the jolt to a higher speed as they started the second lap. The whiz of her own car and the changing of the gears sent tingles of excitement through her, and Kelly found herself focusing on nothing more than the joy of the ride.

Too soon her trip was over, and Kelly found herself scooting out of the car's window. "How was it?" asked one of the workers.

"A blast!" Kelly pulled the helmet off her head and fluffed her fingers through her hair.

"That was awesome!" Harold approached her from behind. Kelly turned. He'd already taken off his helmet and unzipped his suit. "I was hot as a July day in Bermuda, but that was so cool."

Kelly giggled at Harold's animation. He reminded her of one of her high school students instead of a forty-year-old business owner, but she understood his enthusiasm completely. "I agree. We need to do this again."

"You mean it?" Harold raised his eyebrows in surprise. "I wasn't sure what you would think. Did you know we got up to ninety miles per hour?"

Kelly nodded. "I don't think I've ever driven over seventy-five."

Harold stripped off his suit then wiped small beads of sweat from his brow.

"I don't know about you, but I'm starving."

"I think my insides remained intact." Kelly slipped her arms through the suit. "I think I could handle grabbing a bite to eat."

"All right, let's turn this stuff in and hit the road."

Kelly enjoyed the animation dancing in Harold's eyes. Tim had been a wonderful husband and father, but he'd never surprised her as Harold had. Tim would have never even considered taking his always-have-to-have-a-plan-and-be-safe-about-it wife to go NASCAR driving. Harold brought out the spontaneity in her. He brought out a need for adventure, and he wanted to have fun with her. She loved that about Harold.

God, You've been too good to me. You've given me a man who wants me to try new things, who wants me to have fun with him. Thank You, Lord. Help me to hand my cares over to You.

Harold returned and grabbed her hand in his. "You want to walk over to The Deli? It's just a little sandwich place that's right here at the speedway."

"Sounds good to me." Kelly squeezed his hand then leaned closer to him. "Thanks for this. I would have never guessed. . ."

"Well, I wasn't sure what you'd think, but I bet it took your mind off school, Zoey, and the wedding for a little while."

"Definitely." Kelly took a deep breath. "It was nice not to think about anything, to just have fun with you."

"Just being near you is fun to me."

Kelly thought of the three girls at home, probably this very moment arguing over who could watch which show and at what time. "You have no idea how fun your life is getting ready to be."

Harold stopped and turned Kelly to face him. "I don't deny it. You're a handful."

Kelly gasped and frowned.

Harold touched her cheek. "Let me finish. I knew when I started dating you that you came with three girls in tow. It was almost like God was playing a trick on me."

"Now wait a min—"

Harold put his finger over her lips. "But I love you. I love Zoey. I love Brittany. I love Candy. Somehow all four of you have wrapped me around your little fingers. And they're going to stress us out, but we're still going to have fun together."

Kelly kissed the tip of Harold's finger. "I love you, Harold."

"I love you, too." With her hand firm within his, he started walking toward the deli. "Besides, things will settle down after the wedding. You'll see."

Chapter 4

I feel like someone has shoved me into a shoe box and shut the lid." Harold shrugged then tried to lift his arms above his shoulders.

"No. It fits nicely." The saleslady adjusted the collar of the tux. "I suggest this vest to set you apart from your groomsmen in an ever-so-subtle way."

Harold looked at the piece of white material. It just looked like something else he'd have to squeeze his frame into, but it didn't matter to him. He just wanted everything to look nice for Kelly.

After slipping off the jacket, he put on the vest, buttoned it, then put the jacket back on. He looked in the mirror. He had to admit once he had a haircut and a good shave, the getup would look nice.

Turning toward Cam and his work buddies, Rudy and Walt, he stretched out his arms. "Well, guys, what do you think?"

"Not too shabby." Cam buttoned the second button on his jacket. "It's just a shame you don't look as good as me."

"Or me." Rudy wiggled his eyebrows as he sucked in his oversized stomach.

"No, I've got you all beat." Walt hefted the three-inches-too-short pants higher onto his stick-thin waist.

Guffaws sounded from all four men.

"Don't worry." The saleswoman smiled. "Everything will fit perfectly when you come back to pick up your tuxes. I think you all look handsome."

"All right then. Let's get out of these monkey suits and head over to Cam's for the big game," Harold said as he started to unbutton the vest.

"Now that sounds good," Walt said as he walked back into the fitting room.

"You can't get me out of this thing fast enough," Rudy added.

Once he'd dressed back into his comfortable blue jeans and T-shirt, Harold handed the items back to the saleswoman. "I'll take care of the paperwork if you all want to head on over to Cam's."

"Okay, see you there."

Harold watched as Cam, Rudy, and Walt walked out of the shop. The past several years Harold had been praying for Rudy's and Walt's salvation. Since Harold started dating Kelly, Cam had joined Harold in that prayer, and Harold had noted a softening in his workers, especially Rudy. Having decided weeks before that he would foot the bill for the guys' tuxes, he paid for the rentals then headed out the door.

He needed gas, and it had been awhile since he'd paid Bill a visit. In fact, he hadn't been back to the gas station since he'd encountered Zoey there two months ago. He knew he should have talked with Bill, and he probably should have been checking to make sure Zoey wasn't still frequenting the place, but one thing after another had kept Harold from being able to get over there.

"Well, now's as good a time as any." He hopped into his truck. He needed to pick up a few bags of chips, maybe a two-liter or two to take to Cam's house anyway. The guys had made it a regular Monday night event to watch that week's football game on Cam's wide-screen TV. Cam's wife and daughter would spend the evening at Kelly's doing one thing or another for the wedding.

Harold pulled into Bill's gas station. He pumped his gas then went inside. Bill sat behind the counter, coffee in one hand and the local newspaper in the other. Harold scooped up two bags of chips and a soft drink. "Hey, Bill. How's it going?"

A smile formed on Bill's wrinkled face, exposing the large gap between his front teeth. "How ya been, Harold? I haven't seen you in a while."

Harold nodded. "Yeah. I've been busy." Harold scratched his jaw, trying to think of the best way to ask about Zoey.

"Ain't seen that girl in here, either," Bill added as he totaled Harold's purchases.

Harold let out a breath as relief filled him. "I was going to ask you about that. So, she hasn't been around?"

Bill clicked his tongue. "Now, I didn't say she hadn't been around. Just not here." He placed the chips in a plastic bag. "I've seen her car driving up and down the street."

Harold's heart sank. "I was hoping—"

"She's still hanging around with some no-good characters, too."

"Thanks for telling me, Bill." Harold pulled out his wallet to pay, when he remembered he had a few business cards. He pulled one out and handed it to Bill. "Will you do me a favor?"

"Sure."

"The next time you see Zoey's car, will you give me a call?"

"I sure will." Bill shoved the card into his right front pocket. "Kids these days. Always up to no good."

"She sure has had me on my knees in prayer, that's for sure."

Bill huffed and swatted the air. "Like that will do any good."

Harold grabbed his bags. "It does me good. See ya later, Bill."

Harold made his way back to the truck. Bill was another one that Harold had been praying for years over. Now, he had the man keeping an eye out for his soon-to-be, wayward, Christian daughter. *Lord, what am I getting myself into?*

❧

Thanksgiving had finally arrived. The holiday felt especially sweet this year, and Kelly looked forward to Christmas and the few days after Christmas with such anticipation she could hardly contain herself. Kelly stopped cutting up slices of celery and wiped her hands on a towel. She opened the kitchen drawer she'd cleaned out and renamed "the wedding plans" drawer, pulled out a clear bag, and handed it to her mother. "This is the ribbon I've decided to go with for the bouquets."

"This is beautiful."

As her mother touched the soft fabric, Kelly's heart warmed with overwhelming thankfulness for her family and fiancé. She felt undeservedly blessed. "I'm glad you and Dad could come to Delaware for Thanksgiving. I can hardly wait to go dress shopping for you tomorrow."

Her mom shook her head. "I cannot believe I let you talk me into going to the mall on Black Friday."

"We'll have fun and you know it."

Her mom winked. "You'll have to go easy on me." She pointed toward the manila folder in the wedding drawer. "What's in that?"

Kelly handed it to her mom. "Pictures of the girls' dresses. Remember, I e-mailed them to you."

Her mother nodded. "Yes. They were very pretty."

Zoey walked into the kitchen. "So, are you going to finish the potato salad or talk about the wedding all day? Some of us are hungry, you know."

Noting the shocked expression on her mother's face, Kelly bit back her desire to yell at her daughter for such disrespect. Instead, Kelly forced a smile and grabbed several cans from the cabinet. "Why don't you help your grandmother and me? You make the green bean casserole."

Zoey snarled. "I don't know how."

"Why, Zoey Coyle," Kelly's mom responded. "You loved making the green bean casserole. Your daddy always said you made it the best of all of us."

"Well, he's not here now, is he?" Zoey retorted. She wrapped her arms in front of her chest.

Kelly's heart broke that her daughter still hurt so deeply over Tim's death, and she empathized with the teen's pain. But Zoey needed to stop making everyone else's lives miserable. Kelly shoved the cans into Zoey's folded arms. "Make the casserole."

Zoey glared at Kelly. "I don't remember how."

"Follow the directions on the fried onion can. It tells exactly how to do it." She turned and grabbed a glass pan from the cabinet. "We'll cook it in this."

"Fine." Zoey walked to the table and placed the ingredients on top of it.

The three finished Thanksgiving dinner in near silence. Occasionally, her mother would try to talk about school or their Thanksgiving menu, but Zoey would only mumble her replies.

"We're here." Kelly's sister-in-law's voice echoed through the house.

"Grandma! Grandpa!" Ellie, her young niece ran through the living room and into the kitchen. She spied Kelly's mom and wrapped her arms around her. "Grandma! I missed you."

"I missed you, too, sweetie."

While Kelly's mom bent down to hug the young girl, her dad walked through the doorway from the den. "Did I hear a little munchkin calling my name?"

"Grandpa!" Ellie squealed. She raced over to him and he picked her up. She pushed out her bottom jaw and pulled down her bottom lip. "Look, I lost a tooth."

"Well, you did," Kelly's dad responded.

"She sure did, Dad," Cam walked through the kitchen, stopping long enough to deposit a couple of pies and give Kelly and Zoey a kiss on the forehead and his mom a hug. "Head on back into the den so she can tell you how she did it. You've got the game on, right?"

Sadie rolled her eyes at Cam's words, and Kelly noted how the arrival of her brother and his family had lightened the mood of her home. She gave her sister-in-law a big hug. "I'm so glad you're here."

"I bet. I brought two homemade pumpkin pies." She placed the pies on the counter beside the ones Cam had deposited. "And a homemade pecan pie and a sugar crème pie. I've never made the sugar crème from scratch, so I guess we'll find out soon enough if I did all right."

"I'd be glad you're here even if you didn't bring food." Kelly glanced over at Zoey, who was arranging fruit on a tray and hadn't even uttered a greeting to her uncle and family.

Sadie winked and mouthed, "Got it." She walked over to the table and sat in the chair beside Zoey. "How's it going, Zoey?"

Zoey shrugged. "All right, I guess. Mom's making me help."

"At seventeen, I'm surprised she doesn't have you cooking the whole thing."

Zoey smiled. Kelly awed at the way Sadie could soften Zoey. From everything Kelly could see, Sadie didn't say anything special or specific that would make Zoey respond so positively to her, and yet she did. Maybe it was because there was just a little under a decade between their ages. More than likely, it was simply Sadie's attitude. The woman never judged Zoey—no matter what she wore, no matter what she said. There were times Kelly wanted to wring her oldest daughter's neck, but Sadie's belief remained steadfast that Zoey would be all right.

"Grandma!" Ellie called from the den. "Come here and see the cheer Candy and I made up for the ball game."

Her mother handed the wooden spoon she'd been using to stir the gravy to Kelly. "Here you go." She wiped her hands on a towel. "Okay. I'm coming, sweetie."

Kelly turned down the heat on the gravy. "Harold had better hurry. The food is almost done."

"Are you kidding me? Harold is coming?" Zoey asked.

Anger welled in Kelly. "Of course, he's coming—"

"He's part of the family," Sadie interrupted Kelly. She placed her hand on Zoey's. "I really like Harold. He's been good to your mom."

Kelly took several deep breaths as Zoey sat back in her chair. "Fine."

The doorbell rang and Kelly went to open the door for Harold. She hoped Zoey would be nice for the holiday. Her daughter had shown moments of an improved attitude, but with the holidays approaching, Zoey seemed to have sunk back into her shell. Kelly opened the door. "Hey, handsome."

"And there's my beautiful, soon-to-be wife." Harold wrapped his arms around Kelly and kissed her softly on the lips.

She closed her eyes and allowed his warmth to soothe her. Any hint of frustration slipped out of her mind at the tenderness of his touch. He released her, and she opened her eyes. "I needed that."

Mischief shadowed his gaze. "Well, you need never ask. I'm always available."

She smiled as she led him into the den. "Harold's here."

As her family greeted him, Kelly set the table that was meant to seat eight, but they were going to squeeze in ten. *A problem I'm thankful to have.*

With so many at the table, Kelly decided to leave part of the food on the counter and place the dishes she felt sure the family would eat seconds of on the table. Once everyone had filled their plates to overflowing, Kelly's dad said grace and the group began to eat.

Several conversations filled the room at one time and Kelly nearly burst into tears of thanksgiving yet again. They had so much to be thankful to God for. Her parents were healthy. Just a little over a year before, Cam and Sadie had married and were wonderful parents to Ellie. Her daughters were healthy, and God had given her the most wonderful man in the world to love for the rest of her life. Tears pooled in her eyes and she wiped them away with her napkin.

"This green bean casserole is awesome," Harold said. He took another bite. "I'm not usually a green bean fan, but this stuff is good. Who made it?"

Zoey jumped out of her seat. She slammed her napkin onto the table. "Is that a joke?" She peered at Kelly. "Did you tell him to say that?" She looked back at Harold. "You are not my father!" She stomped down the hall and slammed her door.

"What did I say?" Harold looked around the table, and Kelly felt an overwhelming sadness for the man she loved. He didn't deserve all the problems he'd be getting when he married Kelly.

"I'm sorry, Harold." Kelly shook her head as the tears pooled in her eyes anew. She could hear Cam explaining that Tim had always complimented Zoey's green bean casserole, but Kelly couldn't take anymore. She excused herself and walked into the bathroom. If she loved Harold, she wouldn't force him to endure all this.

❧

Harold sat on the couch in the den watching the Thanksgiving football game. Cam and his dad took turns rooting on their team and jeering at the referees. He could hear the girls in the living room playing board games. Normally, he would sit back and enjoy the game, but to his knowledge, Zoey still hadn't come out of her room.

He knew Kelly checked on her. Sadie went back there and talked with her for a long while as well, but the teen still hadn't rejoined the family.

Part of him wanted to tell her to stop all this nonsense and enjoy time with the family, that he would be a good stepfather to her. The other part of him understood her completely. It was the part that remembered being fifteen when his dad brought home the woman who would replace his mom who'd died only a few months before. *For years, I struggled with accepting that woman. But she was so patient with me.* Harold had lost both of them within months of each other only five years ago. *It's funny how I miss her every bit as much as I miss Dad.*

Cam's growl at the ref snapped Harold out of his reverie. He took a long swig of his soft drink. Just sitting there, not really watching the game, but worrying over Zoey was getting the best of him. He pushed up from the couch. "Be back in a sec, guys."

Kelly's dad just kinda shooed him out, and Cam didn't even look up. Harold walked through the kitchen and down the hall toward Zoey's room. He hesitated a moment. What would he say to her? *I'll figure it out if she lets me come in.*

He knocked, expecting her to growl or yell for him to go away. Instead, a small voice answered. "Come on in."

He opened the door. Her eyebrows rose in surprise when she glanced up at him. Just as quickly, she looked down at the small pillow that sat in her lap. She picked at the fringe. In the year that he'd dated Kelly, almost every time he'd talked with Zoey she had a hard edge, an anger that aged her well past her seventeen years. Today, she looked like a wounded twelve-year-old girl, one who'd lost her greatest treasure and could never get it back. He knew at that instant the only thing he needed to do was show her that he'd be there for her.

"What do you want?" Her tone expressed no emotion, simply asked the question with no anger, no frustration, no hope.

Harold shrugged. "Can I sit there?" He pointed to the chair in front of her desk.

"Sure."

Being sure to leave the door wide open, Harold pulled the chair away from the desk and toward the door. The last thing he wanted to do was to make Zoey feel uncomfortable. He sat, leaning forward to rest his elbows on his knees. "I'm sorry, Zoey."

She shrugged one shoulder. "Mom and Sadie said you didn't know."

"I didn't."

"It was just—that was what Dad used to say. He'd go on and on about how good I made the green bean casserole, that I mixed it just long enough and cooked it at just the right temperature and for just the right amount of time."

Zoey paused, and Harold held his breath. She was talking to him, and he needed to listen.

"It was silly, really," she went on. "I knew he was exaggerating. Even as a little girl, I knew that. But I loved the attention. I loved that my dad was so proud of something I'd done."

She looked at Harold, brushing tears from her eyes. "You don't look anything like my dad, Harold. You don't act anything like him, either. Dad was a pencil pusher. He made good money working behind a desk. He was shorter and thinner than you and GQ good-looking."

Harold swallowed. He'd seen many pictures of Kelly's first husband. The man was a good-looking guy, and he did make three times the income Harold ever would. Just by looking at his picture, Harold could tell the man didn't mind being the center of attention. Harold tended to shy away from all that.

"I don't want another dad, Harold."

"I know that."

"But you want to be my dad?"

"Actually, yes I do."

"Why?"

Harold looked around the room, taking in the nearly all dark colors, fabrics, artwork, and furniture. Only a few light-colored things remained—the pillow she held in her hand, a family picture with their father in a white frame on the dresser, and a pink lamp that she'd probably had since she was born. "I guess because I love your mom and every part of your mom, including you and your sisters."

He leaned back in the chair, praying for God to give him the right words. "Did you know my mom died when I was fifteen?"

"Yeah. You mentioned it."

"Did you know my dad married my stepmom seven months later?"

Zoey scrunched her nose. "That is not cool."

"At the time, no, it was definitely not cool. But after I gave her some time, I found that she was a good mom. She couldn't replace my biological mom. Not really. But she was a good substitute. And I grew to love her. I want to be your, Brittany, and Candy's substitute. And I hope you'll grow to love me as well."

Zoey didn't say anything, and Harold knew that he didn't need to say anything else. He sat there for a little while, watching Zoey play with the fringe on her pillow. He didn't know what she was thinking, but her expression didn't appear hostile. He assumed she was trying to decide what to do with all that had happened in her life.

Finally, she looked up and pursed her lips in a half smile. "Thanks for telling me all that. I'll think about it."

Harold stood and put the chair back under her desk. "You want to come on out and join the family?"

"I will. I just need a minute more. You can leave the door open."

"Okay." Harold walked back into the den. Cam and his dad were so engrossed in the game he knew they didn't even know he'd left. *God, keep drawing that girl back to Yourself. Help me know how to be a good substitute.*

Chapter 5

Kelly laid her newly pressed slacks on the edge of the bed. She grabbed the sapphire V-neck sweater off the back of the wingback chair that sat adjacent to the dresser. Her gaze took in the Victorian decor of her bedroom, all mauves and sages, aged lace and porcelain. This room was her favorite in the whole house.

It was her sanctuary—the place where God restored her soul during her quiet times of prayer, Bible reading, and meditation. After a long day she could walk into this room and feel almost instant relaxation. God had held her through many a worry and fear in this room.

In only two weeks, she would share it with Harold.

How she longed for the day that Harold could hold her in his arms. The day they professed their promise to one another as man and wife before their family, friends, and their Lord. The amazing beauty of it all was that her wonderful fiancé had actually mentioned he couldn't wait to join her in this room—and that he didn't want her to change a thing.

Lord, how could he have known that I love this room as it is?

Harold had been so good. He was always good. Steady. Faithful. Reliable. Everything she needed in a husband. Everything the girls needed in a father figure, even if Zoey didn't realize it yet. Even after her daughter's temper tantrum at Thanksgiving, Harold loved Kelly. And he loved the girls. Each one of them.

Releasing a long sigh, Kelly walked into the adjoining bathroom with her sweater draped over her arm. Before she put the sweater over her head, she caught a glimpse of her reflection in the mirror.

At thirty-eight and the mother of three children, her body was definitely not that of a young woman. Normally, she paid little mind to the imperfections—but with the wedding only weeks away, insecurities she thought she'd put long behind her seemed to creep their way into her mind. Though not overweight, wrinkles, crinkles, and stretch marks had fashioned their way through Kelly's physique, and she cringed at the sight of them.

"Oh dear Lord, I want to be pleasing in Harold's sight."

A scripture that one of the older women from her Sunday school class said surfaced in her mind. Kelly had heard the verses many times before, but never in the context of marriage. Her wise friend knew Kelly would endure a time of uncertainty regarding her body. For that reason, Kelly had promised to tuck the verses away in her heart.

"Do you not know that your body is a temple of the Holy Spirit, who is in you, whom you have received from God? You are not your own; you were bought at a price. Therefore honor God with your body." She quoted the verses aloud.

Thinking about the verses in terms of marital intimacy seemed funny to Kelly. She'd quoted the verses many times to her daughters to encourage them to remain pure before marriage, but Kelly's seasoned friend's words were right. Once wedded, her body would be still be God's temple, but as a married woman.

Yes, Lord. Thank You, Jesus. Harold will be pleased with me, because my body is Your temple, and You've chosen us for each other.

Kelly slipped on the sweater then stepped into her pants. Within moments, she'd accessorized with a long silver chain necklace and matching earrings. She added a few spritzes of Harold's favorite perfume and stepped into her slight-heeled black shoes. She glanced at her reflection again. This time she smiled. "Not too shabby, future Mrs. Smith."

She glanced at her alarm clock. Harold should be there any moment. This was their last official date before the wedding. Harold was taking her to dinner and a movie; then they would stop by the mall to pick up a couple of Christmas presents.

The doorbell rang, and Kelly made her way to the door. The younger girls had gone to Cam and Sadie's house for the evening, and Zoey was working at her new part-time, fast-food job. She opened the door and before she could say hello, Harold had wrapped her into his arms and planted his lips on hers.

"You look beautiful tonight," Harold mumbled against her lips.

Kelly giggled and she gently pushed him away. "You haven't even had a chance to look at me."

His gaze never left her eyes. "I don't have to look at what you're wearing to know you look beautiful."

Her heart skipped a beat as she threw herself back into his arms. "Harold, I love you."

His fingers found their way to the base of her neck then up through her hair as he pressed his lips against hers again.

Kelly pushed away again and sucked in a long breath. She turned and grabbed her purse off the table and pushed him out of the doorway. "We've got to get out of here."

Harold furrowed his eyebrows. "Why?"

Kelly took long strides down the sidewalk and toward his truck. "Because the girls aren't home."

Realization etched across his face. "Yes, we do."

Kelly waited while he opened the passenger door for her. She slipped in then watched his large frame cross in front of the truck then into the seat beside her.

"This is going to be the longest two weeks of my life," Harold growled as he turned the ignition.

Kelly felt his frustration to her core. "Tell me about it." She picked at a piece of lint on her slacks, begging her mind to drift to something besides their wedding. In only a matter of moments, they'd left their small town and were heading toward Wilmington. "So, where are we going tonight?"

"It's a bit of a surprise." Harold placed his hand on her knee. "Would you mind if we didn't go see a movie tonight?"

Kelly felt a smile bowing her lips. She lifted her hand to one of her silver earrings and twisted it around her fingertips. "We're not going racecar driving, are we? I'm way overdressed for that."

Harold laughed and tapped the top of the steering wheel. "No racecar driving tonight."

Kelly lifted her eyebrows. "Are you sure? I'm willing to go home and change."

Harold laughed again. He peeked at her for just a moment, and the merriment in his eyes sent Kelly's nerves into a spiraling gyro. How she loved this man! "We had a lot of fun, didn't we?"

Kelly moved as close to him as she could without unbuckling her seat belt. "The best."

"Tonight won't be quite the adrenaline rush."

Mischief rippled through Kelly and she raised one eyebrow. "Just being with you is an adrenaline rush."

Harold howled. "That's right. But tonight, no movie. Okay?" He leaned over and kissed her forehead.

Kelly smiled, relishing the smell of his cologne on his neck. "That's fine with me. I love your surprises."

"It's settled then." He turned toward the mall. "We're going to pick up those last couple of presents you needed to get, then we'll head to dinner."

Kelly shrugged. "Okay." She opened her purse to find her lipstick and Zoey's cell phone fell out. "Ugh!" Kelly growled. "She stuck this in my purse at the store because she was wearing sweatpants. She must have forgotten..." She turned her body toward Harold. "I have no way to get in touch with her."

"Do you want to run it by her work?"

Kelly bit the inside of her lip. "Well, she works until eleven tonight, and you've planned the evening. When's the best time to take it to her?"

A Cheshire-cat smile formed on Harold's lips. "Since we're already in

Wilmington, we'll wait until we've finished our date to take it to her. I can have you over there by nine o'clock."

Kelly looked at her watch. It was four. She figured dinner and a movie would have had her home a bit later. She had no idea what Harold had planned, but she knew she would love it.

⌘

Harold touched the small of Kelly's back as they followed the guy, maître d', or whatever the fancy host person was called. Cam had told Harold the Hotel Dupont would knock Kelly out of her socks if she could stay there on her wedding night. So, before they headed out for Hawaii, they would spend their wedding night in this hotel.

He would have been just as content in a cardboard box on his wedding night, as long as Kelly was with him. But he'd learned one pretty big lesson in the year he'd dated Kelly—and her three daughters. Women were very different than men.

Kelly gasped as they walked into the dining room. *Wow. The place sure was something.* His soon-to-be brother-in-law wasn't lying. The most fancy, dark red curtains he'd ever seen hung over humongous windows. The room was paneled in thick, dark oak wood. Large chandeliers twinkled from the ceiling with matching chandelier-looking lighting between each window on the walls. The tables and chairs were the snazziest he'd ever seen with soft white tablecloths and cloth napkins and fancy flowers and lamps on the tables. Musicians played a light tune in the background. It was a bit overwhelming for a simple, plumbing-and-heating guy, but he had to admit the historical feel of it nearly knocked him out of the shiny, black dress shoes he'd bought for the wedding.

He sneaked a peek at Kelly. Her expression of complete awe and thrill filled his chest with happiness that he'd chosen to bring her here. Standing in this hotel, he may feel like a square pipe being shoved into a circular hole, but he'd be just fine if Kelly had a good time.

He pulled out her chair, and Kelly slid into it. "Harold, this is amazing." She touched the tip of one of the fancy-folded napkins. "I've always wanted to come here."

Harold sat in the chair across from her. He looked at the array of glasses and silverware and whatever else was sitting in front of him and realized he had no idea how he was supposed to eat at this place. He looked up and into Kelly's sparkling eyes. "Cam told me you would love this place."

"I do." Kelly traced her finger around the top of one of the glasses. "But do you have to pay to stay at the hotel to eat here? Probably not. I'm sure they set up reservations, don't they?" Kelly furrowed her eyebrows. "This has to be awfully expensive. Harold, you do too much. You're too—"

Harold lifted his hand to stop her. "Kelly, I'm forty years old. I own my own business, and I've been a bachelor all my life. I can afford this, and it was part of a. . ."

He hesitated. He'd planned to wait until dessert to tell her this was where they'd spend their first night as man and wife. He'd hoped to watch her have a wonderful meal and then surprise her about the plans. She still didn't know they would be going to Hawaii for their honeymoon, and he planned to keep it that way.

The worry that etched her brow urged him to share his plan early. "We're going to spend our wedding night here."

Kelly gasped again. This time her eyebrows lifted in surprise, and she covered her mouth with her hand. Harold noticed the tips of her fingernails were a bright red and she had candy canes painted on both of her ring fingernails. He almost chuckled aloud at the irony of the scruffy plumber with the dolled-up teacher.

He grabbed the hand that covered her mouth. Lifting her knuckles to his lips, he kissed them gently. "Since we'll be at our reception the night of the wedding and then we'll be leaving for our flight in the early afternoon the day after the wedding, we won't be able to enjoy one of the Dupont's famous dinners on the night we stay here. I didn't want to take that treat away from you, so I arranged for us to share our Hotel Dupont dinner today."

Kelly leaned closer to Harold. Her free hand reached up and touched the side of his jaw. Harold's skin seemed to burn at her touch, even more so as their wedding drew nearer. "You are so good, Harold Smith, so, so good. How I praise God for you."

Harold smiled at her compliment. It was he, the old, scruffy, nowhere-near-as-educated bachelor who felt humbled and awed that she would accept him.

Before he could respond, a waiter dressed in a getup that may have cost more than the coat and tie Harold was wearing approached their table. He and Kelly opted for soft drinks, and Harold tried to focus as the man rattled on about goat cheese and mushroom cappuccino and other things he'd never heard of that they would choose from to be their first plate. Harold tried to appear interested and able to understand what the guy was saying, but who had ever heard of mushroom cappuccino? It sounded gross.

His frustration must have been apparent as Kelly smiled at him when the man had finished. "Honey, if you'll try the chicken broth, medley of vegetables, and chicken meatballs, I'll try the field greens and tomato carpaccio, and canta-loupe-peppercorn emulsion and maybe we can taste a bit of each other's."

Harold wasn't sure he understood what Kelly was getting, but he knew the words chicken and meatballs were for him, and that sounded good enough. He looked up at the waiter. "I think she has a good plan."

"Wonderful."

Harold reached over to take Kelly's hand in his, but the man began to prattle on about second dishes. Oh boy. Again, Harold tried to figure out what the guy was talking about, but all he could do was focus on the small mole on the guy's neck. It was in the shape of a star. He'd never seen a mole look like that.

Kelly saved him again, ordering some fancy shrimp for his second dish. When the man went on to the third plate, Harold wondered how long this would take. But this time, he heard the words "black Angus," and Harold knew what that meant. A good steak. Now, the guy was talking Harold's language. What red-blooded American man didn't love a good steak?

The guy finally left and Harold leaned toward Kelly. "You know I have no idea what I'm eating—except the steak."

Kelly giggled. She took the napkin from the center of the plate and placed it gently in her lap. "You know I would have been just as happy at a regular old steak house, as long as you were with me."

Harold smiled at the sweet woman beside him. "I know. But I also know that you love that we're here right now. I want to make you happy. Next time we'll go to that regular old steak house."

"Deal."

≈

Kelly leaned back in the passenger seat. She enjoyed the dancing of the city's lights as Harold drove out of Wilmington and toward their hometown. The hotel dinner had been absolutely marvelous. The waiter was wonderful, the ambiance stunning. It had been a treat she'd remember forever. She peeked at her fiancé who silently studied the road. *God, You have been too good to me.*

Her cell phone vibrated in her purse. She glanced at the clock. Sadie would have dropped the younger girls off at the house around a half hour before. Kelly was surprised she hadn't received a phone call with them fussing before this. She pushed the talk button.

"Mom, Candy won't let me watch my show. She had the TV last. Now it's my turn," Brittany squealed.

Kelly sighed. No "Hi, Mom. How was your date?" Just instant fighting. She could hear Candy's voice in the background. "Mom, it's that law show. I hate that show. It scares me."

"You watch it all the time in Mom's room. You just don't want to watch it right now," Brittany retorted.

"Brittany." Kelly tried to get her middle daughter's attention. "Brittany." She tried a little louder.

Harold looked at her and grinned. Kelly rolled her eyes. "Brittany."

"Mom, tell her," Brittany squealed.

"Brittany, I'm not going to let either of you watch TV if you don't listen. Let me talk to Candy."

"Mom wants to talk to you." Brittany's voice sounded muffled, but Kelly could still make out the mocking in her tone.

"Mom," Candy whined into the phone.

"Listen, you can go in my room and watch TV."

"I don't want to sit in that old, stuffy wingback chair," Candy whined.

"Just cuddle up in my covers." Kelly brushed a hair from her face. "I'll be home in just a bit."

"Really?" Excitement sounded in Candy's voice. "I get to get in Mommy's bed." Candy's voice singsonged at Brittany, then the phone clicked off.

No good-byes. No "Did you have fun, Mom?" Just squabbles. It was the story of her life.

Harold laughed, and Kelly scowled at him. "Just you wait, Mr. Smith. You get to listen to this all the time, too, in just a few weeks."

"I'll be hiding out in my man room."

Kelly chuckled at the room in her house that Harold had started to fix up as his man room. He hadn't brought his leather recliner and TV over because he hadn't moved out of his house yet, but she knew they would be finding a home in her house only a few days, or maybe hours, after they returned from their honeymoon.

As she put her cell phone away, she remembered Zoey's. "Don't forget we have to take this to Zoey." She pulled out her daughter's phone and accidentally pushed the middle button turning it on. Curiosity crept through Kelly as she noticed her daughter had a new text message. It was from a boy, but Kelly didn't recognize the name.

"Would it be bad to check your daughter's text messages?" She looked at Harold sheepishly.

"I don't think so."

"I was just being silly asking. Of course I'll check her messages. It's my job as her mom to make sure she stays safe."

Kelly opened the text and read it. Her mouth fell open and her blood seemed to stop flowing. "Oh no."

"What?"

Kelly could hear the worry in Harold's tone, but she couldn't look at him. Her eyes couldn't seem to leave the phone's screen. "Oh no."

"What is it, Kelly?" Harold tried to reach for the phone, but Kelly held it tight.

"Get me to that fast-food joint. We've got to get there fast."

159

She looked at the time again. According to the message, Harold had about fifteen minutes to get to the hamburger place before Zoey left.

"What is it?" Harold's voice pleaded again.

Kelly looked at her fiancé. Worry etched his expression, and she hated that this wonderful man was being dragged through all the difficulties she was having trying to raise her children.

"Tell me, Kelly."

She tried to hold her tears back. Harold hadn't had the blessing of holding the girls as babies, of getting slobbery kisses on the cheek, of seeing them reach huge milestones like using the potty and reciting the ABC's. Instead he met her when they're at the stage of arguing, complaining, being selfish, and making poor choices. *God, how can I do this to him? Sure, there are rewards with the girls at this stage of life, but it seems to be more about saying no, explaining why I say no, and ending sibling fights.*

"This isn't fair to you, Harold. I'm like walking chaos." She turned her body toward him and placed her hand on her chest. "And I don't like drama. I've never liked drama, but now I live with drama every day. Some days I think I've gone cuckoo from the overwhelming surge of girl-drama that happens throughout the course of one of my days."

Her humor fell flat as she inwardly acknowledged her selfishness at being willing to involve Harold in her life. Dating him had been wonderful, but the closer they got to marriage, the more she realized she was asking too much of him.

She thought of the Christian counseling sessions they'd had. At their small community church, the pastor required six sessions of counseling for all engaged couples before he'd wed them before God and family. Her and Harold's sessions had been especially sweet to her because she had been able to hear how Harold felt about taking on a ready-made family of all girls.

"*I don't know a lot about women.*" Harold's words just a few weeks ago filled Kelly's mind. "*But I know I love this woman.*" He'd pointed to Kelly. "*And all the Coyle women.*" His smile and quick wink had warmed her heart. "*I don't know what it's like to be a biological father, but when I see one of Kelly's girls get hurt, I know I want to help them. When I see them smile over something they're proud of, I feel prouder. When I see a boy looking at them inappropriately, I want to punch him in the face.*"

The last statement brought a smile to her face even now. *In the last year, he had proven his love for them. But now with Zoey. . .* Her thought broke and she closed her eyes. What was her oldest child thinking? *God, what will it take to bring her back to a right standing with You? How can I help her?*

She'd tried everything every Christian counselor had ever suggested. The girl simply refused to allow herself to heal from her father's death. She wanted to blame God. And the child was old enough—seventeen and a senior in high school—that all Kelly could do was watch the girl's emotional upheaval.

But this I can do something about. Kelly gripped Zoey's cell phone tighter.

"Kelly, tell me what's going on." Harold's voice broke her thoughts.

"She's meeting a guy after work."

Harold nodded. "Okay. That's not so bad."

"No." Kelly shook her head. "The boy's intentions for that meeting are written in the text. And she told me she was getting off at eleven, but she's supposed to meet him at nine thirty."

Anger etched on Harold's features as his foot pressed more firmly against the gas pedal. By all accounts, he looked like a father on a mission to save his little girl. The picture warmed Kelly's heart but saddened her, as well. She knew Harold loved the girls, even though Zoey especially was at her most difficult. His life had been much simpler before Kelly came along.

The guilt of it weighed her, and then she thought of the confrontation she and Zoey would no doubt have in just a matter of minutes. She felt older. Tired.

She didn't feel like a two-week-away bride. Nor like a woman who had just spent a romantic dinner at one of the nicest places she'd ever been to.

She felt like an old, weary woman, who was in for yet another "battle of her life." *God, I feel like I'm losing.*

Chapter 6

It had been an uphill battle getting to this day, but they'd made it. Harold looked at the calendar on his cell phone. December 28. His wedding day. Battle or no battle, Kelly Coyle—soon-to-be Smith—was worth it.

Harold buttoned the last button on his white vest. The thing had some kind of pattern on it. He thought the woman had called it paisley. It made him nervous that Kelly hadn't gone with him to pick it out. He wanted this wedding to be all that Kelly dreamed. At least Cam had gone with him. Kelly's brother knew more about clothes than Harold did.

"You don't look half bad." His friend, Rudy, walked into the Sunday-school-room-turned-men's-dressing-room. Walt followed behind Rudy.

Harold grinned at his friends. The two had surprised him by attending the church's Christmas service. Walt had even brought his wife and children. They hadn't talked much about it since, but Harold knew it was a start. And he clung to God's promise that His Word never comes back void. No matter what, he'd continue to pray for his friends.

Rudy patted his round belly. "I think I look ten pounds thinner."

Normally, the pair reminded Harold of the villains from the movie *Home Alone*. Seeing them decked out in black tuxes made Harold smile. "I'd say that you two don't look too shabby."

"Maggie thinks I'm hot." Walt straightened his shoulders then wiggled his eyebrows.

Harold and Rudy burst out in laughter. Harold nudged the taller man's shoulder. "It's good your wife thinks you look good."

Cam walked into the room. He clasped his hands together. "Are you ready for this, big brother?"

Harold felt excitement race through his veins. "Ready to be your big brother? You bet."

❦

Kelly looked at her daughters. The girls' green dresses fit beautifully and complemented the frame and personality of each one. Candy's deep green silk taffeta dress hinted at the eleven-year-old's budding shape but still allowed her to look like a girl. Brittany's knee-length silk spaghetti-strap dress accented her long, slender features in beauty and innocence. And Zoey—as much as Kelly didn't like the darker hair color, she couldn't help but admit the mixture of dark hair, light skin, and emerald green made the teenager look stunningly beautiful. The dress they'd chosen for Zoey was fashionable, but still hid the curves of her oldest daughter.

Kelly shook her head. *It was only a few years ago that I didn't have to worry about their clothes revealing too much.* Her mind drifted to the night two weeks before when she and Harold had stopped Zoey from meeting a boy at his house. Kelly purposefully shook the thought away. Today was her wedding day. She wanted to focus on Harold, and the life they'd share together.

"I have a present for each of you." Kelly pulled three small boxes from her bag.

Candy clapped. "Oh, I can't wait. I love presents."

Brittany moved closer, eyeing the boxes, but Zoey stayed across the room from them. Kelly knew she wasn't thrilled with the wedding, but her oldest had been moping since Christmas Eve, and Kelly wished she'd snap out of it, just for today at least.

"Each of you is wearing a beautiful dress, individual, as it made especially for you." Kelly smiled at her girls. She and Tim had made beautiful children, and each of them held such wonderful, unique qualities to place at God's feet for service. "But I wanted you to have one thing that's the same. I hope you like them."

She handed boxes to Candy and Brittany, then walked over to Zoey and handed the last one to her. At the same time, the girls opened their gifts. Kelly watched as Brittany allowed the slight gold chain to drape her fingertips. The small diamond pendant hung from the chain.

"It's so dainty," Brittany said.

"So pretty," Candy added.

"I'm afraid I'll break it." Brittany said. "You know how I am."

Kelly laughed. Yes, she knew her middle daughter. The girl would lose her head if it were not attached to her body, and she was just as fortunate her feet were attached as often as she tripped over them. "You'll be fine. Here, let me put it on you."

Amid thank-yous from her younger girls, Kelly put the necklaces around Brittany's and then Candy's neck. She walked toward Zoey to help her with the necklace, but her oldest already had the necklace on. Kelly gazed at her daughters. They were so big, so grown up. The years had gone by too fast. After inhaling a deep breath, she glanced down at the sweatshirt and T-shirt and jeans she still wore. "Okay, one of you go get your grandma. We gotta get my dress on me. She was waiting for me to give you your presents before she came back in here."

Candy giggled. "I'll get her."

Kelly walked toward the garment bag protecting her wedding gown. She'd forced herself not to look at it for the past several weeks as she yearned for the day to arrive. She started to unzip the bag, but the zipper stuck. She zipped it back up just a bit to be sure the zipper was lined up right. She unzipped it again; this time a piece of the antique white fabric caught. Kelly gasped. "Oh no."

She tried to gently pull the fabric away from the zipper's teeth, but the metal seemed more determined to bite into her beautiful dress. Anxiety welled within her, and her hands started to shake. "No. No. No."

Tears pooled in her eyes as she tried not to tug on the zipper or the fabric too hard.

"Here, Mom, let me help." Zoey stood beside her. She nudged Kelly out of the way, then gently and quickly released her dress from captivity.

Kelly blew out a sigh of relief. "Thank you, Zo-bow." The nickname she'd called her oldest as a baby slipped from her lips. She grabbed her daughter in a quick hug.

"Mom, I need to talk to you."

Zoey's voice sounded urgent, but Kelly could only focus on pushing the plastic away from her dress. "Where's Brittany?"

"She's in the bathroom. I need to talk to you alone."

"Okay. Go ahead." With the dress now plastic-free, she allowed her fingers to trace the exquisite beading. She could hardly wait to get into this dress, for Harold to see her in it.

Kelly's mom walked through the door. "Let's get that dress on you. You're getting married in only half an hour."

Excited trepidation raced through her. Even though Kelly felt moments of guilt at allowing Harold to take on her crew of crazy women—well, lately, it had been her trying oldest daughter—still, she could hardly wait to meet Harold in front of that pulpit and say "I do."

"I guess I'll talk to you later." Zoey's voice sounded small and for the first time in a long time, a bit unsure.

Concern inched into Kelly's gut, but she pushed it away. "We'll talk during the reception. I promise."

❧

Harold tried to inconspicuously hush his groaning stomach as he stood beside the pulpit, waiting for his bride. He had no second thoughts about marrying Kelly, but standing in front of a mass of people, half of whom he didn't know, in a monkey suit, made his knees quake.

He never realized their church was so big and could hold so many people.

The pastor leaned toward him. "You look like a man about to get married."

"That bad, huh?" Harold pulled the fancy napkin from his coat pocket and wiped the beading sweat from his forehead.

The pastor chuckled quietly. "Second thoughts?"

Harold grimaced. "No. I just don't feel comfortable in front of all these people."

Cam must have overheard, because he nudged Harold's elbow. "You're doing fine."

The music started, and the church doors opened wide. Harold calmed as the attention of the guests diverted to the back of the church.

Candy walked ever-so-slowly down the aisle. Her face beamed and she held her shoulders almost too far back. He didn't know for sure what paternal feelings felt like, but he believed he experienced them for Kelly's girls. Everything in him wanted to wrap that eleven-year-old in a bear hug and tell her what a pretty young lady she was becoming. He could see she wore the delicate necklace he and Kelly had picked out for each of the girls. Kelly wanted their gift to be special, and he agreed the small necklaces were perfect.

Brittany walked down the aisle next. So tall and slender, the teen was a combination of model and basketball player. With her hair all knotted up with shiny stuff and flowers and that dark green dress fitting her shape a little too snuggly, if someone asked him, Harold knew he was feeling some paternal feelings because his gaze instantly scanned the room to detect any young guy who might be checking her out.

Brittany reached Candy at the front of the church, and Harold winked at both of them. Their cheeks were flushed, and he knew they were happy that he and their mom were getting married. He looked forward, and Zoey stood at the doors. *If only she could be happy for her mom and me, as well.*

With everything in him, Harold believed one day he and Zoey would be friends. He didn't know if she'd ever allow him to be a true father figure, but if she did, he'd take the role seriously and do the best he could by her. He couldn't believe how lovely she looked walking down the aisle toward her sisters. Her dress was every bit as pretty as her sisters and her hair was just as fixed up, but sadness filled her eyes. Harold hated that.

But she didn't appear angry. Maybe that was a step up. Harold prayed she hadn't been hard on Kelly while they were getting ready. Taking in the sweet expressions on the younger girls' faces and the fact that all three of them were wearing the small diamond necklace, Harold believed their afternoon had gone well.

Only one more girl to walk down the aisle, and he would see his bride.

"Here comes my little munchkin," Cam whispered beside Harold.

His daughter, Ellie, wore a shiny white dress and held a small basket that was decorated with dark green ribbons and small red flowers. She dropped white and red rose petals on the white carpet. The girl looked like a smaller version of her mother, Cam's wife.

Ellie finally took her place beside Zoey, and the church doors were shut again. The music changed, and the congregation stood. Harold had to swallow the knot in his throat. He could hardly wait to see Kelly.

The doors opened again, and his bride stood in the doorway. Her father stood beside her with her arm tucked into his. Unbidden tears welled in Harold's eyes. *God, what have I ever done to be given such a beautiful woman?*

Her dress was stunning. The church's dimmed lights seemed to make it glitter. He couldn't see her face, as a veil covered it. How he longed to see her face!

What did a man want in a wife? A woman who encouraged him. A woman who respected him. A woman who made him feel like more of a man. And if she was as beautiful as Kelly on top of all that, well. . .

Emotion threatened to overcome him. He wasn't a crying man. He was simple. A forty-year-old bachelor. A heating guy, the plumber. He was happy working with his hands and living alone, until he met Kelly Coyle. Then everything changed.

Finally, she and her father reached the end of the aisle. It was time for her dad to pull back the veil and give Harold her hand. Her father kissed her cheek; then she looked at Harold. Her eyes glistened with love, and Harold wanted to scoop her up and head out of the church with her. He wiped his palm against his pants before he took her hand in his.

The pastor began to speak of love and commitment. He read scripture from 1 Corinthians about the meaning of love. "Love is patient, love is kind." The words had been etched in Harold's heart years before through Bible study and listening to his pastor. In the last year, Harold had lived those words, not just heard them, not just read them. Now he knew them. And nothing would change his love for Kelly. Nothing.

"Do you take this woman in sickness and in health, for better or for worse. . ." the pastor's voice continued on.

Harold squeezed Kelly's palms. This woman worried too much about the "for better or for worse" part. She worried over what the stress of having three girls would do to him. He'd have to spend the rest of his life proving to her how much he loved her and the girls. . .for better and for worse.

When the pastor had stopped talking and it was Harold's turn to speak, he squeezed her palms again. "I do," he answered. His gaze urged her to believe he meant those two words to the core of his being. They were true, and they always would be.

✼

Kelly took in the reception hall decorated in dark green and deep red. She'd had the most beautiful Christmas wedding she'd ever seen. It wasn't overly expensive, nowhere near as ostentatious as a few weddings she'd been to over the years, but it was still the best she'd ever experienced.

Her girls seemed to be having a good time talking with one relative or another church member or another. Many of her colleagues from work had come to support her day, and Kelly was exhausted and overwhelmed by the many people who'd attended. More than she'd expected.

"It's time to cut the cake," Sadie announced over a microphone.

What would Kelly have done without her amazing sister-in-law? The woman had taken care of every loose end in addition to being in charge of the reception food.

"I want cake, Aunt Kelly." Her niece Ellie pulled at the bottom of Kelly's dress.

"Okay. Let Uncle Harold and me cut it first, then we'll get you some."

She smiled and skirted away toward her dad.

"Uncle Harold?" Harold lifted his eyebrows.

"That's who you are now."

He grinned and leaned forward and kissed her lips softly. "I like it."

"No more kissing. We want some cake!" Cam hollered, and Kelly watched as Harold's neck turned a bright red.

She picked up the knife and had Harold wrap his hand around hers. They cut two small slices together. She squinted at him. "Are you going to be nice?"

"Yes. I want you happy later," he whispered.

This time Kelly felt her cheeks warm as he eased a bite of cake into her mouth and she smashed the piece in his. Howls of laughter filled the room.

He wiped the smeared icing from his jaw with his fingertips. "What was that for?"

She shrugged. "I guess I'm not worried about you being happy later."

Harold grinned and dotted her nose with some of the icing on his finger. "No, you don't."

He moved closer to her. She tried to give him a mean look, but she knew laughter lit her eyes. "Harold."

"Okay." Sadie's voice halted his lunge at her. "Since the bride and groom have to be going, we're going to toss the bouquet and garter now, then eat cake afterward."

Kelly glanced at the clock at the back of the reception hall. It was getting late, and she didn't want to be tired for their trip, wherever they were going, tomorrow. All she knew was they had a long plane ride ahead of them. She looked at her sister-in-law and mouthed, "Thank you."

Sadie grinned and winked as she arranged the single girls in a spot on the floor. Each of Kelly's girls stood in the mix, though it was obvious Zoey was less than thrilled. She threw the bouquet and one of her fellow teachers caught it. Within moments, Harold had tossed the garter.

Harold grabbed her elbow. "Are you ready?"

Warm tingles shot through her at the look of longing in her new husband's eyes. "You bet."

"Mom, I need to talk to you."

Kelly broke eye contact with Harold and looked at the owner of the voice. "Zoey, I forgot. Harold, make sure everything is in the car."

"You know they've trashed it."

Kelly rolled her eyes. "I've seen it. Tell Rudy and Walt and that brother of mine that I said thanks."

Kelly turned back to Zoey. Her daughter's eyes were so sullen, so frightened. It was as if Kelly were looking at her more than a decade ago when her new puppy had died. Something was wrong with Zoey, and Kelly had been so wrapped up in the day she hadn't taken time to really listen. In only moments, she'd be leaving, but she would listen now. "What is it, Zoey?"

Tears fell from Zoey's eyes. It was sudden, as if a dam had burst and now the waters couldn't stop. Fear wrapped Kelly's heart. Sobs wrenched her daughter, and Kelly guided her to the back of the building, away from anyone who could hear them.

"What is it, Zoey? Tell me."

"Oh, Momma."

Momma? Zoey hadn't called her Momma since long before Tim died. A vision of her wearing her favorite orange and pink pajamas and swinging on her swing set in the backyard slipped through Kelly's mind. "What is it, Zoey?"

"I can't tell you." Her words jumbled together and her nose started to run. "You'll be mad at me. I don't know what to do."

Kelly pulled up a chair and sat Zoey down in it. The girl didn't fight her, and Kelly grabbed another and sat across from her daughter. "I might be mad at you, but you have to tell me."

Fear and confusion welled in Kelly's heart. What could it be? Had she stolen something? Was she taking drugs? Was she failing school? Was she—

"Mom, I don't know how this happened." Zoey looked into Kelly's eyes. Her daughter's eyes were bloodshot and swollen from crying. "I was being so careful."

Kelly closed her eyes. *Oh no. Oh, no, no, no, no, no.* "Zoey, what do you mean you were being so careful? Are you—"

"Mom, I'm pregnant."

Kelly's world crashed around her. Her heart thudded inside her chest as she tried to process what her daughter had just said. Memories of past students who'd gotten pregnant in high school flooded her mind. Most didn't graduate. Their lives were difficult. They weren't ready.

Sleepless nights, soiled diapers, hours of colic raced through Kelly's mind. The constant worry the first few months that the baby would die while sleeping. The moments of indescribable frustration because the baby wouldn't stop crying. Kelly peered at her daughter. *Zoey is not ready for this.*

She looked down at her wedding dress. This was the end to her perfect day. In moments, she was supposed to get in a car with the man she loved and spend her first night with him as husband and wife. Then she was to get up and go on a honeymoon, spend a full week away from her children. And this was her parting news.

She looked at her daughter, broken and devastated. Pity and sorrow enveloped Kelly. *She has no idea how this will change her life. God, will this be enough? Will she finally surrender?* Kelly shook her head. *A baby? How would they handle a baby?*

Zoey's crying escalated. "I'm sorry, Mom. I told Jamie. He doesn't care. I haven't seen him since I told him. I don't even know where he is."

Kelly sucked in a deep breath. She didn't even know who Jamie was. Dreams of Zoey's wedding, of her future, seemed to evaporate before Kelly's eyes. Kelly wrapped her arms around her child. God would see them through this. He'd seen her through so much in her life. This wasn't too much for them. "It's okay, Zoey."

"I know you're mad at me."

Mad? No. Disappointed? Well, yes. Overcome with sorrow? Absolutely. I'm desperately hurt for her. So hurt.

As her own pain threatened to take over her body, Kelly held Zoey tighter. "I'm not mad at you. I'm sorry for you that you'll have to go through this so young. But I'm not mad at you. I love you, and God can work *all* things together for His good."

Believe what you just said, Kelly, she inwardly encouraged herself. Taking a deep breath, she begged God to fill her with a peace beyond her understanding. Her thoughts calmed, and she knew God would see them through this, just as He'd seen them through Tim's death.

Zoey snuffed, and Kelly marveled that her daughter hadn't thrown a fit at the mention of God. "I am sorry, Mom."

Kelly placed her hands against Zoey's cheeks. "Listen to me, child. We'll get through this. We just have to trust God, and that doesn't mean it will be easy."

Zoey nodded.

"I think we're all set." Harold's voice boomed down the hall.

Kelly's mind raced. She couldn't leave now. She needed to call a doctor, find out about this Jamie, make sure everything was all right. "Harold, I don't think—"

"Try to have a good time, Mom." Zoey hugged Kelly, and Kelly relished her daughter's touch. Zoey whispered, "Don't say anything right now. Go on your honeymoon."

Kelly touched Zoey's arm, keeping her voice loud enough for Zoey alone to hear. "I don't think I can go now."

"Yes, you can. You need to. I've been okay for two months."

"Two months?"

Tears brimmed Zoey's eyes. "I just couldn't tell you. I was so embarrassed."

Kelly exhaled a long breath. She studied her daughter, then looked back at Harold.

"Please go, Mom." Zoey nudged her toward the door.

Inwardly torn, she knew they would need this vacation, as things would change drastically sooner than they'd all believe. Kelly nodded and looked back at Zoey. "It's going to be okay. Try not to worry." She kissed Zoey's forehead. "We'll talk when I get back."

Zoey nodded and left the room.

"Is everything all right?" Harold furrowed his brows.

She shook her head. She didn't want to do anything to make him worry during their trip. They'd have plenty to think about when they got home.

Chapter 7

Harold shoved the boogie board beneath his arm and walked farther out into the ocean. Hawaii was more beautiful than he would have ever imagined. He'd only been to the beaches in Delaware, but the water around this state was crystal clear. It reminded him of ice cubes, only hot. He didn't have the words to describe how pretty this place was.

He turned his head, peeking back at his bride of only five days. Kelly would have the words to describe this place—his wife, Mrs. Kelly Smith. He loved the thought of her being his wife. The past five days had been as close to heaven as he could ever imagine. The ocean. Kelly's soft dark hair. The palm trees. Kelly's soft skin. The warm air. Kelly's sweet whispers of love. He'd never been so happy.

With ocean water up to his waist, Harold turned and pushed the boogie board in front of him. The next good wave he could see coming, he'd jump, chest first, onto the board and ride in on the wave. Boogie boarding was nowhere near as strenuous as surfing, but for a guy who would probably never visit Hawaii again, unless it was for a second honeymoon with his bride, boogie boarding was good enough.

He looked back toward the beach. Kelly sat in a beach chair with a magazine in one hand and a water bottle in the other. She looked absolutely adorable in Brittany's oversized white sunglasses. Her middle daughter had left a note in the suitcase telling her mom she needed to look cool in Hawaii. The black-and-white polka-dot bathing suit Sadie packed looked awfully good on her as well.

Harold waved at her, and Kelly dropped the magazine and waved back. The smile she graced him with was full and beautiful, and Harold knew he was blessed.

A good wave pushed him from behind, and Harold turned, noting another one coming. He jumped onto the boogie board, allowing the water to push his oversized frame forward toward the beach.

What a rush! He pushed off the board once the wave had died. Cradling the board beneath his arm, he walked toward Kelly and his lounge chair. He'd been boarding for a while and needed a break. At the very least, he needed a drink of water. When he reached Kelly, he realized she was on the cell phone. Again.

He dropped the board and fell into the chair. After opening the cooler, he grabbed a water bottle, opened it, and took a long drink. Kelly had spent a lot of time on the phone since they'd gotten to Hawaii. She'd spent a lot of time on the phone before and after their flight and even at the Hotel Dupont in Wilmington.

Maybe that's normal for a mom. He'd expected her to talk with the girls once, twice, maybe even three times per day while they were gone. He knew she would enjoy the time with him, but he knew she'd miss the girls, and they would miss her. But it seemed she talked to them more like ten times a day. Literally. Like every two hours.

Harold stuck the bottle back in the cooler and leaned back in the chair. He folded his hands behind his head and exhaled a deep breath. The funny thing was most of the time she was on the phone with Zoey. It seemed like all of a sudden, since Kelly left Delaware for ten days, Zoey needed her mother almost every minute.

Maybe that's a good thing. Maybe the teen will be ready to straighten up. Maybe she'll turn back to God. In Harold's experience with the teenager, he'd never witnessed her living for the Lord. Kelly and Cam often talked about Zoey's zeal for the Lord and telling her friends about Christ before her father's death. But that had been three years ago. All Harold had known was sullenness, darkness, and rebellion.

And yet, he cared deeply for the girl. It seemed an odd thing to him. He wondered when he first started dating Kelly how he would handle her kids. It wasn't as if he had his own kids to have given him some experience. He didn't even have any brothers or sisters. He'd had zilch experience with people under the age of adulthood, well, except the ones he ran into on heating, cooling, or plumbing jobs. Then he was often pulling toy cars and miniature doll heads out of the toilet.

But when he met Kelly and he saw that his feelings for her were growing serious, he hit the carpet, asking God to show him how to be a good male influence on those girls, to show him how to love them. It had been a true miracle, in his eyes anyway, because Harold did love them as if he'd been their father all along.

Kelly hung up the phone and put it in a bright yellow bag that was covered in big pink flowers. She sighed ever so slightly, but Harold still heard it. He studied his new wife. "How's everything at home?"

She smiled at him, the bright, beautiful smile that drew him each time she did it. "It's good."

But he knew something was wrong. Her eyes held just a hint of worry behind them. They had since they'd left the reception. Since he'd returned from checking on the car while she talked with Zoey. She'd assured him that Zoey's tears that day were just the same old stuff, but he had the nudging feeling that wasn't the complete truth.

"You know I haven't talked to the girls but once a day since we left. Do you mind if I call them?"

Kelly shrugged. "Sure." She pulled the phone out of her bag and handed it to him. "They'd probably like that."

Harold turned on the phone and noticed that almost every call to and from Kelly's cell was with Zoey's phone. He pushed the HOME number and Candy picked up the line.

"Hey, Squirt."

"Harold!" she squealed. "Have you gotten me a souvenir yet?"

Harold laughed. He knew that would be Candy's first thought. "We've gotten you one thing, but we're going to get you something else when we go shopping later."

"I get two things!" Candy yelled. "Brittany, I get two souvenirs from Hawaii." Her voice took on a bragging lilt, and Harold couldn't help but laugh out loud. Brittany and Candy fought over everything, and when Kelly reminded them they'd be friends one day and the girls vehemently denied it, Kelly would roll her eyes and say she was praying against them.

Brittany's voice suddenly sang over the line. "Hey, Harold. Are you having fun?"

Harold could hear Candy whining in the background at her grandmother that Brittany had stolen the phone from her. "Your mom and I are having a blast. Hawaii is gorgeous." He turned and winked at Kelly. "But nowhere near as pretty as your mom."

"Ew, gross, Harold."

The voice changed on the line again. This time it was Candy again. "What did you say? What's gross?"

Harold laughed. "You'll have to ask your sister. Is Zoey there, too?"

"Yeah. Just a sec." Her voice muffled as she started yelling for Zoey.

A moment later Zoey's voice sounded over the line. "Hi, Harold."

"Hey. How's it going?"

"Fine."

Harold pinched his lips. Zoey sounded different. Less edgy. Less angry. Less confrontational. "So, what do you want from Hawaii?"

"You don't have to get me anything. I'm fine."

Kelly poked his arm and motioned for him to let her have the phone. "Well, your mom wants to talk with you. Tell the girls I said bye."

He handed the phone to Kelly. Part of him wanted to tell the girls he loved them, but it still felt funny to say it. Kelly had been the first woman he'd ever said the words to. He'd barely said them to his parents before they died. He just wasn't good with words and all that. He was a man of action. A man who showed the people he cared about how he felt through doing things for them.

But he'd also learned from Kelly that girls like to hear nice things, too. The girls' daddy had died. He was the only one they'd get to have here on earth. If they let him, he'd be the one to walk them down the aisle, to hand them over to a husband, as Kelly's dad had handed her over to him. He wanted to be a good father to them. *Lord, help me.*

Peace surrounded him. Now that he and Kelly were married, things would settle down. He'd have time to learn to be a good father figure. The girls were handfuls, but they were still young. Things would only get easier.

❧

How am I going to tell Harold about this? Kelly stared at her reflection in the mirror. She looked like a woman who'd spent the last several days sunning on the beach and enjoying time alone with her new husband. Her skin was sun-kissed, making her blue eyes sparkle along with the diamond stud earrings and diamond pendant necklace. The white sundress Sadie had packed for her was one of the prettiest Kelly had ever seen and complimented her shape in all the right places. Her sister-in-law was a fashion whiz, and Kelly determined she'd never again go shopping without her.

But looks can be deceiving. And she had no idea how Harold would respond when she told him the truth about Zoey. She, herself, still didn't know how to respond. It was true her daughter seemed broken, but Kelly couldn't tell if it was from repentance or from the fact that she got caught.

Kelly closed her eyes and gripped the edge of the sink with both hands. "Oh Jesus, I'm not ready for this." Kelly peered back at her reflection. "And Zoey really isn't ready."

She flopped onto the toilet seat cover. "And Harold isn't going to be ready." Leaning forward, she placed her elbows on her legs and rested her forehead in her hands. "I never should have married Harold. I was being so selfish."

Raising teenagers had proven to be the most difficult thing Kelly had ever experienced. When Tim died the challenges seemed to have tripled. She loved her girls, wouldn't change a moment with them. She wouldn't even change the different quirks that made each one a unique young lady. But life would be so much easier if all of them wanted to live their lives in obedience to God and to their mother.

"That would be a perfect world," she mumbled and then chuckled at herself. "I wasn't the easiest teenager for my mom and dad to live with, either."

She sobered and exhaled a deep breath. "But I was the biological child of both my mother and father. I've married a wonderful man and forced him into the chaos I'm living in."

Her heart broke at the coarseness of her thoughts. When had she become such a negative thinker? When had she lost her faith in God, her trust that He would take care of everything in their lives?

God, I haven't lost my faith in You. You are my anchor, my core, but I feel so desperately guilty, so selfish for forcing Harold into all this. I'm not worth all the frustration and confusion and—she lifted her hands then smacked them down at her sides—*just everything.*

And a baby? What would they ever do with a baby? Zoey wouldn't be able to go to college; she'd have to get a job. And who would watch the baby? And what kind of job could she possibly get? The thought of diapers and bottles and formula and all the things a baby needed swirled through Kelly's mind. Babies were expensive. Zoey would be completely dependent on Kelly and Harold for financial help. The whole thing was overwhelming—and unfair to Harold.

She knew Harold loved her. It was evident in the gentleness of his touch, in the way he helped her in every aspect of her life—from the mundane of changing the air filter to providing a new outfit for Brittany's school dance. She couldn't question he cared for her and the girls.

But what will he think when I tell him?

She stood and shrugged at herself in the mirror. "He has to know."

"Know what?"

Kelly gasped when the bathroom door opened and Harold stepped inside. Her hands started to tremble as tears pooled in her eyes.

He pointed to the floor. "I forgot my sandals in here."

Kelly's gaze traveled to his shoes then back to his eyes. She bit the inside of her lip as her hand found its way to the diamond stud earring. Twirling it around, Kelly's heartbeat raced.

"Tell me, Kelly. What's going on?"

"I'm sorry, Harold." She covered her face with her hands. "I'm so selfish."

He wrapped his arms around her, and Kelly felt safe in his embrace. Harold was strong, so strong, and she wanted to lean into him, allow him to be her strength through the time that lay ahead of her. But he shouldn't have to deal with a new baby. He was a forty-year-old man. He'd been a father for only five days. In less then nine months, he'd be a grandpa. The idea was absolutely preposterous.

He released his embrace, gripping her arms gently in his hands. "Tell me, Kelly. We're in this together."

Yes, they were in this together. If she'd loved her husband as much as she believed she did, she never would have dragged him into this. But he had to be told. Taking a deep breath, she peered into his eyes. "Zoey's pregnant."

❧

"Zoey's pregnant." Kelly's words from a few days before washed over him again.

He leaned back against the airline seat. The announcement had put quite the damper on the rest of their honeymoon. They'd gone through the motions, lying on the beach, eating Hawaiian cuisine, and trying to enjoy their time together.

But the announcement had changed things. Kelly emotionally pulled away from him. He didn't know how to explain it exactly, but he felt it in her gaze, in her touch, even in the way she talked to him.

She'd said that she was selfish, and he knew what she meant. They'd discussed it many times before during their premarital counseling and on several of their dates. She felt guilty dragging him into a house of crazy teenage women.

He didn't know how many times he'd told her that he loved them and that he wanted to be a part of their crazy house, but she simply wouldn't believe him. To him it was a matter of her not taking him at his word. And Harold lived by the integrity of his word. His business thrived because if he told someone he would do something, then he would do it. He didn't understand why Kelly didn't believe he meant what he said. He'd proved himself many times over to her.

And what would they do with a baby? He didn't think he'd even held one. Anytime he'd ever been around one it was screaming its head off.

He looked at Kelly in the seat beside him. Her head was tilted to one side, her mouth slightly open. She'd fallen asleep. He knew she was exhausted. She hadn't slept much since she told him.

She smelled like that purple lotion she was always putting on. He loved the smell of it. And she looked so cute, probably ten years younger than she was, with her just slightly burnt nose and cheeks. Everything in him wanted to take her hand in his, lift it to his lips, and kiss her knuckles. But he couldn't.

He looked forward, staring at the gray plastic tray attached to the back of the seat in front of him. He unlocked the tray and let it rest as a small table in front of him. He'd get a drink of ginger ale when the flight attendant came by. His stomach was a bit queasy. If he were honest with himself, he'd admit it wasn't from the plane ride, but from the fact the woman he loved didn't trust him.

Chapter 8

Nearly two weeks had passed since they'd returned from the honeymoon. Kelly had been overwhelmed with schoolwork. As one of the senior trip sponsors for the school, she'd been doubly overwhelmed planning the trip to South Carolina—the trip she'd hoped would bring her and Zoey together. Instead, Zoey wouldn't be going, and she and Zoey were together on some emotional level every night.

Jamie, the much older boyfriend that Kelly didn't know about, seemed to have left the state of Delaware. Though Zoey mourned about it all day, every day, Kelly couldn't help but be thankful the guy was gone. From the pictures she'd seen of him in Zoey's phone, the man did not appear to be the kind of son-in-law she hoped to have. *I know. I know. Appearances can be deceiving.* She inwardly scolded herself. *But I'm not sure I can take much more, and the guy has already proven to lack a good deal of integrity by getting his teenage girlfriend pregnant and then leaving the state.*

Kelly took a deep breath. The bitterness she felt for the man threatened to set in on a daily basis. She constantly took her feelings to the Lord and begged Him to help her feel His mercy.

"Are you ready, Mom?"

Kelly turned at the sound of her oldest daughter's voice. The child no longer wore the darkest makeup she could find. Her face was scrubbed clean and her hair pulled back in a ponytail instead of falling over her eyes. Her attire had changed dramatically, as well, and Kelly knew her oldest wasn't spending all her time with her old peers. Instead, she spent all her time with Kelly. Usually crying. Always moping.

"I sure am." Kelly forced herself to smile. Heading to the obstetrician for the first time, she and Zoey would learn how far along she was in the pregnancy and if everything appeared to be fine.

"I'll be in the car." Zoey walked out the door. Kelly grabbed her purse and followed behind her. Kelly had hoped the pregnancy would encourage Zoey to return back to God, and she had stopped "doing" the things she'd been doing before, but her heart was still hard. So hard. The truth of it wounded Kelly's spirit.

Visions of watching Zoey raise her grandchild in an ungodly environment plagued her thoughts. Watching her daughter slip into the front seat of the car, her expression sad and a bit sickly encouraged the worry to well in Kelly's heart.

"Trust in the Lord with all your heart and lean not on your own understanding." She paraphrased the proverb in her mind. She had to trust God in this. *Besides, after the appointment, we're going to tell the family tonight. All of them.*

The reminder that her entire family was coming for dinner that evening made her wrinkle her nose. She couldn't even imagine what everyone would think. Sadie would understand, as she'd experienced an unexpected pregnancy and gave up the baby for adoption. As circumstances would have it, years later Sadie married the adoptive father, Kelly's own brother Cam, almost two years after his wife died of cancer. *But what would the girls think? Candy and Brittany?*

She shook the thought away. *One thing at a time.* She pulled into the doctor's parking lot.

"Are they going to examine me?"

Kelly looked at Zoey. Fear wrapped her daughter's features. "Probably."

Zoey studied her hands. It reminded Kelly of Zoey's first day of kindergarten. It was Zoey's telltale sign of being nervous. Her oldest was just a child, and she was having a baby.

Kelly placed her hand on Zoey's. "It's going to be okay. I'll go in with you if you'd like."

To Kelly's surprise, Zoey nodded. "I can't do this alone, Mom."

Truer words had never been spoken, and it pained Kelly's heart that her daughter wouldn't have a loving husband by her side to go through the pregnancy and birth of this baby. She squeezed Zoey's hand. "I'll be here. But more importantly, God will be here. You're not alone."

Kelly expected her daughter to sigh or roll her eyes or make a smart-aleck comment at Kelly's mention of God. Instead, her daughter nodded, unbuckled her seat belt, and quietly slipped out of the car.

Hope welled in Kelly's heart. *Draw her back to You, Lord. Draw her back.*

❧

Harold had been in a sour mood all day. He'd snapped at Rudy for leaving a tool in the wrong spot when as it turned out Harold was the one who'd misplaced it. He'd apologized to his long-time employee, but he still felt miserable.

And he definitely didn't want to go home.

He passed by his old house. Technically, it was still his house. Having been a bachelor for so long, Harold had paid it off some ten years before. Kelly didn't owe anything on her, well their, house because she'd paid for it with an insurance settlement after Tim's death. The two of them didn't need money, so he'd leased his house to a young family in their church who needed it far more than he did.

They still paid him a little bit of rent, just enough to cover the insurance and taxes, and part of the agreement was they'd do the upkeep on the house. Harold noticed the shoveled sidewalk and driveway as well as some kind of wreath on the front door. It appeared they were doing as they promised.

Life had been so much simpler when he lived in that house. After a long day at work, he'd have gone home, changed out of his work clothes, heated up a TV dinner, and settled into his recliner for a night of basketball or football or whatever sport was playing.

Now he returned home to a most-of-the-time home-cooked meal, which beat out the TV dinner, but then on Mondays and Thursdays he took Candy to dance. On Tuesdays and Thursdays he also took Brittany to basketball conditioning practice, not to mention picking her up from regular basketball practice on Mondays, Tuesdays, Wednesdays, and Fridays. If Brittany had a game, everything changed, and if she had it the same night as church or Candy's dance practices, then it really threw everything off.

He had no idea how Kelly had done it as a single mother. He was the family chauffeur, and while he ran the girls to their various activities, Kelly did laundry, cooked dinner, cleaned the house, and all the other household activities that had to be done. The girls had chores, but they were often running so much they didn't have time to do them.

"*Welcome to the life of the modern-day family,*" Kelly had said to him a week after they'd gotten married. She'd been teasing, and he loved spending time with the girls, but his life had taken a real turn after they returned from the honeymoon.

He turned onto their street, noting that Cam and Sadie had already arrived. He blew out a breath. Zoey's appointment had been today. If everything was fine, they were going to tell the girls and Cam's family tonight. Ugh, he dreaded this. He pulled into the driveway and took his keys from the ignition. *Might as well get this over with.*

He walked into the house and spied Kelly in the kitchen. She looked so pretty in her light blue sweater. It was one of his favorites. After making his way to her, he couldn't resist placing his thumb beneath her chin and lifting her face so he could give her a kiss. He released her and she smiled up at him, her expression one he remembered from a month ago—before Zoey's news had turned their world upside down.

"How did everything go?"

"Everything is fine." She lightly nodded her head, and he knew she was letting him know they'd be sharing the news tonight.

"Okay." He nodded back. He'd been a dad for only a few weeks, and he'd be a grandpa in a matter of months, and both notions seemed outrageous to him. Yet, when he looked at Kelly, his heart stirred in a way it never had before, and he knew God had given her to him. He'd walk through whatever they had to walk through. She was his wife, and the two were one flesh in the eyes of his Lord and Savior.

He looked around the kitchen. "What can I do to help?"

"Well, Sadie is already setting the table. Zoey made a salad. You can get that out of the fridge."

He raised his eyebrows. "Zoey did?"

Kelly smiled. "Mmm-hmm." She looked at his clothes and frowned. "But before you touch any of this food, you need to change your clothes."

Harold grinned and kissed the tip of her nose. "I'll be back in a sec."

As he made his way to the bedroom, he noticed Cam in the backyard making a snowman with Brittany, Candy, and Ellie. "Where's Zoey?"

"In her bedroom. Getting ready," Kelly called from the kitchen.

Harold undressed and jumped into the shower. *How did a teenage girl get ready to tell her family she was pregnant?* He needed to find something else to think about. Finishing his shower, he got out and saw Kelly's bottle of purple lotion on the bathroom sink. He opened the cap and inhaled the soft, flowery fragrance. *Mmm.* He loved that smell. *I love it even more when it's on her.*

Smiling, he hurried and got dressed then headed into the kitchen and busied himself with the various things Kelly asked him to do. Soon, the family, all eight of them, sat at the table.

"I'm starving, Uncle Harold. Can we eat?" Ellie asked.

Harold couldn't get over the fact that the almost seven-year-old called him Uncle Harold. He loved the endearment and secretly wished the girls would one day want to call him Dad. It was probably a selfish wish. They'd had a dad, a really good one from everything he'd heard about Tim. He should just be thankful for the opportunity to be a father figure to them, and yet. . .

He pushed the thought aside. "Let me say blessing first, okay, Ellie?"

She nodded, and the family bowed their heads.

"Dear Lord, thank You for our food. Thank You for Kelly, Sadie, and Zoey preparing it."

Sitting beside him, Zoey stiffened at the mention of her name.

He went on. "Bless this food to the nourishment of our bodies. Bless our time together as a family."

His mind whirled as his usual prayer felt stilted and cold. His spirit stirred with feeling for this family, his family.

"God, thank You for my family, these people You've blessed me with. I love them, Lord."

Zoey shifted again at his left. Kelly grabbed his hand at his right and squeezed. Emotion threatened to overwhelm him, just as it had the day of the wedding.

"I love them all, sweet Lord. Amen."

"Amen," the family echoed, and Harold looked at Kelly. Her eyes brimmed with the hint of tears, and Harold couldn't help but smile at his sweet, sensitive wife. She'd cried more in the last month than she had in the year he'd known her, but he would help see her through. If she would let him.

Once they'd almost finished their meal of salad and Kelly's famous home-made lasagna, Kelly clasped her hands together. "Well, family, we have an announcement to make."

"You're pregnant!" Sadie exclaimed, looking from Kelly to Harold.

Harold burst out laughing. "No!" The idea was ludicrous. He couldn't even begin to imagine being a dad of teen girls, a grandpa, and a dad to a newborn all at the same time. He smacked his hand against the table and looked at Kelly. "Could you imagine?" He pointed from himself to her. "Me and you having a baby."

"Harold!" Kelly squealed. "I'm not sure how to take what you're implying. Are you saying I'm old?"

Harold frowned. His ire rose, as did his voice. "How could that possibly be about me saying you're old? Do you think we need a baby right now?"

Her face reddened. "No. I don't think we need a baby right now, but I don't like you implying I'm getting old, especially when. . ."

Tears welled in her eyes. Harold rolled his eyes. The waterworks. At that moment, he found himself sick of the waterworks. He knew he was being a jerk, but suddenly he didn't want to comfort his wife.

"I'm sorry," Sadie said. "I didn't mean—"

"It's not your fault," Zoey interrupted. "They're freaking out because it's my fault. I'm the one who's pregnant."

Kelly laid her head down on her desk. It had been a long evening at her house last night, with Sadie zipping Zoey off to another room, and she and Harold answering all of Brittany's and Candy's questions. Then there was a lot of silence. Stunned silence was the only thing she knew to call it.

The day at school had been equally trying. A fight broke out in the hall in front of her room. Kelly had never been more thankful to have a classroom beside the oversized male science teacher. Her computer quit working twice during her PowerPoint presentation and an array of other "little" things kept going wrong. Now, she rested her head on the paper she needed to sign to allow Zoey to be a homebound student for the rest of the year.

This wasn't what Kelly wanted for her daughter. Zoey would miss prom and basketball games and the senior trip. She didn't even want to walk at graduation.

A light knock sounded against the frame of her classroom door. She lifted her head and saw Cam walking toward her.

"Don't you look a sight?" He thumped her forehead with his middle finger.

"Ouch." She pushed his hand away and scowled at him. "What are you doing here?"

"Came to talk to you."

She leaned back in her chair. "Didn't we all do enough talking to last us a lifetime last night?"

Cam sat on the top of one of her student desks, clasping his hands in his lap. "Sadie's worried for Zoey."

"Me, too."

"We prayed over her a long time last night. Sadie mentioned she saw a bit of a change in her when she talked to her. For the good."

"I hope Sadie's right. Zoey needs God now more than ever."

"So do you."

Kelly sat up in her chair. She leaned over, placing her elbows across her desk. "I know. Clinging to Him is the only way we'll get through this."

"And Harold will help."

Kelly didn't respond. She reached for her earring, fiddling the coarse prongs between her fingertips, she twisted it forward and then back.

"I knew it." Cam smacked his hands together.

Kelly frowned. "What?"

"I wasn't sure if you were struggling with God or with Harold, but I knew it was one of them."

"What's that supposed to mean?"

"It means you've got to let your guard down. I could tell last night you were stiff as a two-by-four. That explains why you two got so mad over Sadie's question."

Kelly shook her head. "Oh, I hope we didn't hurt Sadie's feelings. It wasn't about—"

"She's fine, but you're not. You and Harold can help each other through this."

Kelly turned away from her brother. How could she explain the guilt she felt every time she looked at Harold? He'd become the "Coyle women chauffeur" man. The only perk he received from the situation was having one of them share his name. She loved Harold, or at least she thought she did, but wouldn't true love keep the one they love away from heartache and trauma?

She'd thrown him into a den of lionesses.

"Why are you pushing Harold away?"

Kelly faced her brother, spreading her arms wide. "Don't you see how selfish

I am? Zoey is due at the beginning of July. That's six months after our wedding. I found out she was pregnant at our reception. I had to fight through the worry every day of my honeymoon."

"That's why you should lean on your husband."

"No." Kelly shook her head. "Harold didn't sign up to be a husband, a father to three girls, and now a grandpa. He'd been a bachelor all his life, no siblings even. Don't you think my brood is a bit overwhelming for him? Why would he even want to be a part of it? I fell in love with him and didn't have the strength to let him live a peaceful life." She fell back into her chair. "I'm selfish."

Saying the words aloud heightened her despair. She'd had hinting moments before their wedding that she shouldn't force Harold into her drama, but he'd always been so kind, telling her how much he loved her and the girls.

"Big sister, I think you're nuts."

"What?" Kelly glared up at Cam.

"So, it's all your fault that Harold is forced to live in a house with four women. After all, he didn't know you had three girls the day he showed up at your house to fix your heater."

"Well, of course he knew—"

"And it wasn't him who asked you out on a date."

"He asked me, but—"

"And I suppose you were the one who asked him to marry you—I mean, as I remember we were at your house and he brought out a birthday cake and—"

"Cam, I know all that. But he didn't ask to be a grandpa."

Cam raised his eyebrows. "That's right, but you asked to be a grandma to your seventeen-year-old daughter's child?"

"Cam—"

"No, you listen. Kelly, you *are* being selfish."

Kelly's heart dropped at his words. She knew they were true, but that didn't make her feel any better.

Cam continued, "But not because you married him. It's because you aren't trusting him now."

Kelly grew defensive. "I trust Harold. I can't believe you would say that."

"Do you, Kelly? If you trusted him, you'd give him some of the burden."

"But they're not his kids, Cam. It's not fair—"

"I can't believe you would say that. To me, especially."

Kelly stepped out of her own spiraling gyro of misery and looked at her brother. Cam would never be able to have biological children. Ellie would be his only child, and she was adopted, unless he and Sadie chose to adopt more. She knew her brother loved Ellie more than his own life, but Cam had chosen to adopt Ellie.

Just as Harold chose to marry me with three girls attached.

She shook her head. That's where her thinking was slanted. He didn't choose to marry her with three girls attached. He chose to be their father. He loved them. She knew he loved them. How could she have been such an idiot, so full of pride? She'd held the man she loved, who loved her, at arm's length since their wedding day.

"Cam, you're right. And I'm sorry."

A smile bowed Cam's lips. "Wow, that admission was rather quick."

Kelly shook her head at his sudden silliness. "Will you do me a favor?"

"Sure."

"Can the girls stay with you and Sadie this Friday? Harold and I need some time alone. I've got some apologizing to do."

Chapter 9

Harold wiped the sweat from his brow. It was the end of January and Delaware was experiencing record cold temperatures, but he spent most of his days swiping off sweat. It seemed to be some kind of central air trend in his area that the units were shutting down. He, Rudy, and Walt had put in long hours, day after day, and yet the calls wouldn't stop coming.

It didn't matter that he didn't have time to go home. Life was easier this way. At home, Zoey clung to Kelly, Brittany had reverted into some kind of shell, and Candy was full of questions and concerns. And for some reason, she wanted to voice all of them to Harold. He thought of the conversation they'd had the night before.

"Will Zoey still live with us when she has the baby?" Candy asked as she sat next to Harold on the couch and leaned against his arm.

"Of course," Harold answered as he put his arm around the girl who was content to allow him to be a parental figure.

"Will the baby live here?"

Harold had always assumed the child would live with them. It would be hard; definitely more than he'd ever anticipated before marrying Kelly, but he assumed they'd take care of the child. "Well, yes."

"Will I get to hold the baby?" Her voice took on an excited lilt.

"Sure."

"And change her and feed her and—"

"I'd say you'll get to do plenty of that."

Candy's gaze dropped, and her tone changed. "The baby won't have a daddy. Zoey said she can't find her boyfriend."

Harold swallowed anew at the remembrance of the change in the discussion. "That's true, but I'll help with the baby, too."

"It's not the same."

Harold shook his head. The memory of the words tore his heart even now. He thought of the girls and how they'd been without their dad, Tim, for nearly four years. Four years was a long time, and they'd been very close to their dad.

He knew he probably shouldn't, but part of him, if he were honest, a big part of him, was jealous that he "wasn't the same" as having Tim in their lives. He could never take their father's place.

And yet he wanted to.

Having finally finished the last central air unit of the day, Harold dropped the last few tools into his toolbox. *God, I shouldn't be jealous of Tim. And I haven't been until just recently. Why, God? Why now?*

He knew the answer. Kelly wasn't the same since Zoey had told her about the pregnancy. He knew she wouldn't be. Wouldn't expect her to even pretend to be. What mother was happy when her seventeen-year-old daughter told her that she was pregnant? He had zero experience with babies, but he wasn't so dumb as to not understand that babies changed everything.

But it was the kind of change in Kelly that hurt him to the core of his being. It was as if she didn't want to lean on him for help. Didn't trust him enough to help. For a man who'd spent his entire adult life proving to people that he was a man of integrity, a man of honor, to have his wife not trust him, not be willing to allow him to help her in her time of need—well, it shattered his very existence.

How many times had he heard her almost-silent weeping against her pillow at night? He would try to draw her near to him, but the tears would stop and she would become rigid as a metal pipe. When he hugged or kissed her or even tried to hold her in his arms for only a moment, Kelly's gaze clouded and her body language screamed of a wall she'd built to keep him out.

So, he'd quit trying. They'd been married just a little over a month, and he'd spent the last two weeks focused on his work—even when he could have gone home.

Candy's words slithered into his mind again. *"It's not the same."* Would Kelly *have welcomed Tim's touch? Would she have allowed him to comfort her and soothe her through the anxiety and worry?*

Forgive me for thinking this way, Lord. The last thing Harold wanted to do was dishonor the memory of a man he didn't even know. But he didn't want to battle a ghost, either. He wanted Kelly to allow Harold to be her husband now, to love him and honor him, for better or for worse. She had to trust him with the worst.

But she didn't.

And for now, working long, hard hours over a heating unit or a plumbing system was much easier.

❧

Friday's finally here. Kelly slipped out from under the covers. Harold had left for work two hours before. She didn't know how the man could get up before five every day, but today she was thankful. He wouldn't know she'd taken a personal day from school to prepare a special evening with him.

After waking the girls up, she made a list of everything she wanted to get accomplished today. She'd drop the girls off at school, Zoey would spend the day with Cam, and Sadie would take the younger ones home with her afterward, so Kelly didn't have to worry about any problems with them. Then, Kelly would get her nails done, toenails, too, because she wanted to look extra special for Harold tonight. It made her laugh that her simple man loved her bright pink toenail polish, but paid no attention at all to her fingernails.

After that, she would go to the store, then maybe run by the department store to pick up something special to wear. When he returned home from work, Harold would be overwhelmed by a candlelit dinner and an evening for just the two of them.

Dear God, I can hardly wait. Please let tonight be wonderful. I haven't given Harold my whole heart lately. Forgive me, Lord.

"Mom," Zoey whined as she walked into Kelly's bedroom. "I don't feel good this morning."

"Go get some ginger ale and eat a cracker."

"I don't want to go to Cam's house today."

Kelly pursed her lips. Zoey's clinging had almost become unbearable, and though it was always tempting to give in to her girls when they didn't feel well, Kelly knew she and Harold needed this evening together. "Sorry, Zoey. You can rest at Cam's just as easily as you can rest here. But while you're resting, you have to do your schoolwork for today."

"Mom," Zoey whined and placed her hand over her stomach, "I really don't think I can do it. I feel so bad."

"You have to."

"But, I—"

"No buts. You're going to be a mom soon. You have to learn to keep going, even when you don't feel like it."

"Mom. . ."

Kelly looked her daughter in the eye. "I mean it."

Tears pooled in Zoey's eyes. "I never asked to get pregnant. Why does everything bad happen to me?"

"'For the wages of sin is death, but the gift of God is eternal life.' Zoey, I know you don't like when I preach to you, and I'm not. But the truth is you sinned. Now, you have consequences. Babies are a blessing, and we will love this baby, but you have to seek God's forgiveness. You need Him now more then ever."

Kelly expected Zoey to explode, to tell Kelly that she didn't want to hear about God and what He could do for her. Instead, Zoey was silent. Kelly couldn't tell if she thought about what Kelly had said or if she'd completely tuned Kelly out, but Zoey turned and walked out of the room. Once Kelly finished dressing and went into the living room, all three girls were ready. No one, including Zoey, had anything to say as they drove to school and then to Cam's.

After Zoey stepped out of the car, Kelly opened her cell phone and called Harold. His deep voice sounded over the line when he picked it up, and Kelly felt a twinge of excitement zing through her veins. "Hey, hun."

"Aren't you supposed to be at school?" His voice sounded confused, and she looked at the clock on the dash. *What was I thinking calling him right now? I should be getting ready to start first period.* So anxious about the evening, Kelly had just wanted to hear his voice, to be sure he was coming home for dinner.

"Uh. . .class is about to start." She grinned. She hadn't lied. She just hadn't said that she wasn't there. "I just wanted to be sure you would be home for dinner tonight."

"Yeah, I'll be home. Why? No one has practice tonight, do they?"

Kelly cringed at his question. Since they got married, Harold had become the practice-chauffeur king. He never seemed to mind, but again she wondered at the fairness of marrying him when she knew how hectic her life was day in and day out. *Stop it*, she inwardly fussed at herself. *Remember what Cam said. Harold knew about the chaos, and he still wanted to marry me. Just love him, and stop feeling so guilty.*

"No," she said. "No practices today. I was just planning to cook tonight and wanted to be sure you'd be able to get home."

"Yep, I'll be there. I'll see you tonight."

"I love you, Harold."

A moment of silence wrapped around her after she said those words. How long had it been since she'd told her new husband she loved him—a couple of weeks, maybe—and they'd only been married a little over a month. Her heart ached at her foolishness. *God, forgive me. Help me show Harold how much I love and appreciate him.*

"I love you, too, Kelly. So much." Harold's voice sounded somber and serious, and Kelly's heart pained at the tone. She clicked the phone off and gazed at herself in the rearview mirror. *Tonight will be special. No more pushing Harold away. No more feeling guilty for making his life crazy. I'm simply going to love him.*

Hours later, Kelly stomped the snow off her boots before she walked into the house. In addition to having her nails done, she'd also gotten her hair cut and colored. The style was quite flattering and a bit sassy, and she couldn't wait to see Harold that evening. She glanced at the clock. She waited five more minutes so she could call Harold without him wondering what she was doing. She clicked his number again. After only one ring, his deep voice resonated over the line, sending a thrill down her spine again.

"Hey. How has your day been?" she asked.

"Believe it or not, kinda slow."

She peered outside. The sun shone bright, glistening against the snow-covered ground. "I wouldn't think there would be any central heating units in the state left to fix. You've worked a lot lately."

Harold chuckled. "I think you're right."

"So, when will you be home?"

"I'd say five—five thirty."

Kelly looked at the clock again. That gave her two hours to prepare filet mignon, baked potatoes, fresh rolls, and whip up a salad.

"What's for dinner?" Harold's voice interrupted her thoughts.

"It's a surprise."

Harold laughed. "Okay. Just make sure Brittany doesn't eat it all before I get home."

Kelly smiled at the joke Harold and Brittany often bantered over. Her nearly six-foot-tall daughter, who was as big around as a twig, could eat every bit as much as Harold, and they loved to compete to see who could eat the most. "Don't worry about that. I'll see you tonight. I love you."

"Love you, too."

He clicked off and Kelly set to work. She took out the filets, seasoned them, and secured bacon around the steaks with toothpicks. She washed and scrubbed the potatoes and wrapped them in aluminum foil. With the meat and potatoes cooking in the oven, she mixed Harold's favorite ingredients for salad. She glanced at the clock again. *He'll be here in an hour.*

Finishing in the kitchen quickly, she picked up the fresh red roses she'd purchased, tore off the petals, and allowed them to fall in various places. She changed into the new outfit she'd purchased, then took the food from the oven. After setting the table with care, she glanced at the clock on the microwave. He would be home any minute. She lit the candles. *God, bless our evening together.*

≫∽

Harold trudged up the sidewalk toward the house. It was nine o'clock, and he was beat. Just before he was heading home for the night, a woman called. Her pipes had burst. Walt hadn't been able to stay to help, but Harold and Rudy spent the last four hours working at the woman's house. Kelly had called six times or more before he'd finally had the chance to answer and tell her what was going on. She sounded a little strange on the phone, but Harold figured Zoey was just driving Kelly crazy.

His favorite apple-cinnamon scent assaulted him as he opened the front door. The lights were off, but as he walked toward the kitchen, he saw the dining room table was set for two. Candles that looked to have been lit for hours, but were now dark, sat in the middle of the table. Rose petals covered the floor. Realization dawned on him and his heart dropped. *She planned a special evening for us.*

He strode into the kitchen, opened the refrigerator, and noted the filet mignon and baked potato wrapped in cellophane. Regret wrapped around him as he followed the rose petals down the hall. He should have answered her calls. He should have come home. They could have rigged the woman's pipes until the morning. He didn't have to fix them completely.

Standing in the bedroom door, he took in his beautiful wife curled up in the bed. She gripped a pillow at her chest. He could only see her profile, but he could tell her makeup had smeared down her cheek. *From crying, because I didn't come home.*

Slowly, he made his way toward the bed, then gently sat beside her. He leaned over and kissed her forehead. She jumped, her eyes widening in fear.

He stroked her hair. "I'm sorry, Kelly."

Her expression softened, and he was surprised to see she wasn't angry. "I'm sorry, too, Harold. I've been unfair to you."

"I should have come home."

Kelly smiled. She reached up and traced her fingers through his hair. "You're home now."

Contentment filled his heart. "I love you, Kelly."

She sat up. "I know you do, and from here on out, I'm going to let you."

The comment washed over him like a soothing balm. She trusted him. She would lean on him. He would be the husband he wanted to be, the one she needed him to be. And, he wouldn't let her down.

Chapter 10

A week passed since Kelly had let down her guard, and Harold enjoyed every moment of sensitivity. He hadn't realized just how emotional Kelly had become since finding out Zoey was pregnant. The woman cried at the drop of a hat, and her stomach often felt queasy. But now she allowed Harold to comfort her. At night she nestled into his arms and allowed him to pray over their family. They also spent time in the mornings sharing what God had shown them in His Word, and he'd grown to treasure the beginnings and endings of each day. Sure, he got to work thirty minutes later than he used to, but most people didn't head out before six a.m. The extra half hour wouldn't hurt the community or his business.

He walked up behind Kelly, wrapped his arms around her, and kissed the back of her head. "I had an idea this morning."

"Well, I have to be at work in forty-five minutes and I haven't fixed my hair."

She winked at him, and he chuckled. "I was thinking I'd take Zoey shopping today."

Kelly's eyes widened. "What?"

"She can do her homebound schoolwork when we get home. I'll probably only make it until after lunch anyway, but I'd like to take her to get some maternity clothes."

Kelly placed her hands on her hips. "You want to take Zoey to buy clothes—maternity clothes?" Her tone dripped with sarcasm and confusion.

"Well, of course I don't *want* to take her. I just think she needs—I don't know. She's still clinging to you a lot, and every time I pray, she remains heavy on my heart. I just think maybe I should. . .let her know I'll help her and the baby in any way I can."

Kelly stared at him for a moment, then tears welled in her eyes. *Oh boy, here come the waterworks again.* She wrapped her arms around Harold's neck. "I think that's a great idea. You're the best man"—she pressed her lips to his in a quick motion—"in the whole world."

Harold laughed and kissed her back. "Okay. Guess I need to tell Zoey."

"I'll tell her."

Kelly zipped out of the room. He could hear her and Zoey talking. Zoey didn't sound as excited, but he heard her consent to go. He put on his shoes and grabbed a quick breakfast. To his surprise, Zoey was ready to go.

"Where are we going?" Zoey asked as she buckled her seat belt.

"To the Concord Mall. Does that sound okay?"

Zoey nodded and looked out the windshield. The drive was a quiet one, and Harold was thankful when they finally made it to their destination. Silently, they walked into the mall. She looked up at him. "Where should we go?"

"You lead the way. I'm just here to pay for what you need." He laughed, trying to lighten the tension. She stared at him, but her expression wasn't hard as it once had been. Instead, it was a mixture of sadness and age. Zoey had changed so much since the pregnancy. She no longer argued. She helped out around the house without being asked. She'd allowed her hair to go back to her natural, auburn shade. But she still clung to her sadness. *Please, God, draw her back to Yourself.*

Harold followed Zoey to several stores. At the first one she picked up a few items without trying them on. The new clothes seemed to lighten her step a bit, and at the next store she asked if he minded if she tried on a few of the shirts before they bought them. Harold walked dutifully through each store, trying not to compare shopping to eating a metal pipe. He pulled out his debit card when it was needed then moved along behind Zoey.

"What do you think of this shirt?"

Harold hoped he masked the shock on his face when Zoey asked his opinion. He knew with each hour she loosened up a bit, making small comments, saying thank you at appropriate times. Now she was asking what he thought. He knew he'd never take the place of her father, but he wanted to make his own place in her life. *God, maybe I am making some progress with Zoey.* "It looks great. You should get two."

Zoey giggled, and for the first time in a long time, the smile reached her eyes. "I only need one." She placed her hand on her stomach. "I'm starving. Can we go eat after this?"

"Definitely." Harold looked at his watch. He thought he was going to have to eat his fist. Shopping was exhausting, and he'd worked off his measly bowl of cereal two hours ago.

He bought the items she'd selected, and they headed toward the food court. After ordering, picking up their food, and finding a table, Harold sat across from Zoey and nodded. "Wanna pray?"

"You can."

Harold bowed his head. "Lord, thank You for this day with Zoey. I've had a good time with her. Let this food nourish her and the baby. Amen."

Harold glanced up and noticed Zoey studied her food. "Thanks for taking me today, Harold," she mumbled without looking up.

"Not a problem." He motioned toward the food. "Now, feed that baby."

Zoey chuckled, picked up a fry, and stuck it in her mouth. "You know, Mom really loves you."

Harold took a slow bite of his sandwich. He hadn't expected Zoey to open up to him; he'd just wanted to let her know he was there for her. "I love your mom, too."

"She loved my dad, as well."

Harold swallowed slowly then wiped his mouth with a napkin. "I know she did. I think your dad must have been a really special guy."

"He was."

Zoey grew quiet as she took several bites of her sandwich. Harold tried not to watch as she chewed and took sips of her soft drink. He could tell in his spirit she had more to say. He wanted to encourage her, but no words would come to him. He wasn't good with words anyway. He'd always been more of a listener, and his experience with women was minimal at best. Though dating and marrying Kelly had changed that quite a bit.

"I've been so mad at God." Zoey's words were soft, and she still hadn't looked up from her tray. "I said really ugly things to Him when Daddy died. I told Him I hated Him."

Zoey looked up then, peering into Harold's eyes. Harold gripped his napkin between his fingers. *God, give me the right words to say.* "I know you don't hate God."

Tears pooled in Zoey's eyes, and she didn't bother to brush them away. Her gaze stayed focused on Harold's. "I don't. I don't hate God."

She looked back down at her food. She stuck a french fry in ketchup and twirled it around. "When I was doing stuff I shouldn't have been doing, I would come home at night and yell at God in my mind."

She dropped the fry and grabbed her straw and twirled it around. "I would tell Him that in Romans He said that nothing could separate me from His love."

"Romans 8:38–39." Harold said the scripture. He'd just read the verses only weeks before. They'd stuck with him because he'd thought of Zoey and how he wanted to make her see that God loved her so much.

The tears streamed down her cheeks. This time she brushed them away with her napkin. "Yes. That's right. I told Him He had to love me. He couldn't give up on me."

Harold reached over and squeezed her hand. "He hasn't given up on you, Zoey."

Zoey sniffed and looked up at the ceiling. "I don't want to yell at Him anymore."

"He'll forgive you."

"I know."

Harold waited as Zoey wiped her face with her napkin then started to eat her lunch again. His heart drummed in his chest. He knew something had changed within her. But what was he supposed to say to her? Nothing would come. No words. No great comment of wisdom. Some father figure he was. He took a drink then finished his lunch, praying for God to show him what he could say. Nothing. He wasn't hearing anything.

Harold and Zoey walked out to his truck. He placed her bags behind their seats. He started to hop into the cab when he felt Zoey beside him. Before he could say a word, she wrapped her arms around him. Stunned, Harold hesitantly returned her hug. "Thank you, Harold."

"You're welcome."

Harold patted her back then hopped into the truck. Zoey walked around to the passenger's side and jumped in as well. "God's forgiven me, Harold."

Harold smiled as he placed the key in the ignition. "Of course He has."

"I can feel His forgiveness, but it's not because I can feel it that I know He has. He says He has in His Word. If I confess my sins, He is faithful and just to forgive my sins and cleanse me from my unrighteousness." She shrugged. " 'Course, I said it in my own words."

"You know, I think you came pretty close to what the scripture actually says. Isn't that from First John?"

"Yep. Chapter one, verse 9. If I remember right, that book talks a whole lot about God's love."

Harold peered at his stepdaughter. "You know an awful lot about the Bible, young lady."

Zoey grumbled. "You would, too, if you grew up with my mom."

"Sounds like she's a pretty good mom."

"She is."

Without thinking, Harold reached over and ruffled Zoey's hair. He pulled his hand back, realizing she was too old for the gesture. Zoey laughed and punched his arm. Harold feigned pain. "I'm telling your mother."

Zoey's expression became serious. "Let me tell her about today."

"I wouldn't have it any other way." Harold stared out the windshield as they headed home. *She's finally beginning to heal. Thank You, Lord.*

❧

Kelly's stomach churned as she made her way into her classroom. She plopped into her chair and laid her head on her desk. Three of her students had been out with the flu in the last few days. She feared she'd caught the bug from them. *But I took my temperature this morning, and it was normal.*

She forced herself to lift her head and take a sip of the lemon-lime soda she'd purchased in the teacher's lounge. The lack of a fever meant nothing. She and all three of her girls were notorious for not running temperatures when they were sick. Taking slow, deep breaths, Kelly turned her rolling chair toward her computer and turned it on. She had a busy day today—team meeting with the principal during plan, a parent meeting over an at-risk-of-failing student after school. Plus she was starting *Hamlet* with her accelerated classes today. She didn't have time to be sick.

She took another quick sip of soda, then pulled a few saltine crackers out of her bag. She nibbled on a few, thankful her stomach seemed to settle just a bit. She had to get the students' warm-ups on the board before they started down the hallway. She forced herself to get up, walk to the board, and write down their daily prompt.

The bell rang, and Kelly heard the stampede of teenagers making their way down the hall. Her stomach rumbled again, and Kelly headed for the bathroom. She grabbed a paper towel and ran cool water over it. Trying not to mess up her makeup, she dabbed the towel against her neck and jaw. She let out a long breath. *I can do this. I can make it through the day.*

She walked out of the bathroom, down the hall, and into her room. The final bell hadn't rung, and students sat on top of desks and stood in clusters around the room. Someone had brought a cup of coffee to class, as she allowed them to have drinks until the final bell, but the smell sent her stomach into a whirl once again. Not to mention the various colognes and perfumes that mingled in the air. Normally, she didn't mind the smell, but today. . .

She scooped her soda off the desk and took a sip. *Once the day gets going, I'll be fine.* Trying not to push her stomach too far, she sat in her chair and opened the attendance page on her computer.

"Ms. Coyle—I mean, Smith," one of her students began. "I forgot my home-work at my dad's house, and I stayed at my mom's house last night."

Kelly looked at the tiny brunette. The girl never uttered a peep in class and was a straight-A student, but through her writing, Kelly had learned her parents' divorce had been a bitter one and it had taken a toll on the teen.

"And my mom wouldn't take me over to my dad's this morning, because. . ." She looked down. "Well, if I had my license, I could—"

Kelly shook her head. "Don't worry about it. You can bring it to me tomorrow."

The girl smiled, exposing dimples that made her look five years younger. "Thanks, Mrs. Smith."

As she walked away, the floral scent of her perfume wrapped itself around Kelly, turning her stomach. She bit into another cracker.

Logan, one of her sweetest and most talkative students approached her desk. "How's your morning going, Mrs. S.?"

The strong aroma of coffee smacked her in the face. She looked at his hand that carried the oversized cup of joe. The churning of her stomach whirled like a tornado. A hot flash washed over her body. Kelly grabbed her mouth and ran for the door. Bile rose in her mouth. She couldn't make it.

She spied the trash can beside her door. She gripped the sides as her body hurled.

"Gross," a feminine voice sounded behind her.

"That was awesome," another voice sounded.

"Mrs. S., are you okay?" Logan stood beside her. He'd placed his hand on her back. The boy meant well. He was such a sweet kid, but at the moment, she wished he'd take a few steps away from her.

"Here you go." Logan handed her a tissue.

Maybe she was glad to have him there after all. She took the tissue and wiped her mouth. "Thanks, Logan." She picked up the trash can and set it in the hall. "Will you call the office, please? We need a custodian, and I think I need a sub."

The principal sent her home before the sub arrived. He covered her class for her. She thanked God all the way home that she worked for such a wonderful man. The custodian had been so sweet to her, as well. Decked out in his plastic gloves, he wouldn't let Kelly help clean up her mess. She felt weak as a cooked spaghetti noodle and green as basil. The thought of Italian food sent her stomach to spinning again. *Lord, I don't want the flu.*

She pulled into her driveway and walked into the house. She just needed to sleep for a little bit. Without any overwhelming smells or noises or anything of that nature, she would be able to rest and then be ready to go the next day. She had to be ready the next day.

Using every ounce of energy she could muster, Kelly slipped out of her clothes and into a flannel nightgown. She crawled beneath the covers of her bed and curled up a pillow and pressed it gently against her stomach. She took slow, cleansing breaths and closed her eyes.

"Kelly, are you okay?"

Kelly startled at a coarse hand rubbing her cheek. She opened her eyes and saw the worried expression on Harold's face. "I think I have the flu."

"Oh, honey." He continued to stroke her face. "You don't feel warm."

"I know, but I never run a fever." She tried to sit up. Her stomach no longer felt queasy, and she realized she wanted something to eat. "What time is it?"

"One o'clock. Zoey's fixing some chicken noodle soup for you."

"That sounds wonderful." Embarrassment flooded her as she thought of her morning. "I threw up at school. In front of everyone."

Harold grinned. "I bet the kids loved that."

"I gave them something to talk about today, that's for sure."

Harold kissed her forehead. "I'm going to head in to work for a little while. You rest today."

"I will."

Kelly slipped out of bed and made her way to the bathroom. She felt so much better than she had this morning. She didn't even feel sick. Maybe it was just a quick bug. Kelly had found over the years that she seldom got as sick as her students. She figured her body had built a good immune system through working with so many teenagers.

Kelly walked into the kitchen and grabbed the bowl of soup Zoey had fixed for her. She sat at the small breakfast table. "Thanks."

"You're welcome." Zoey sat across from her. "How are you feeling?"

"I'll be fine. Just a bug, I'm sure. You better not get too close to me."

"I won't." Zoey grinned, and Kelly noted something had changed in her daughter. Her smile met her eyes for the first time since Tim died.

"How was your shopping trip with Harold?"

"Great. He bought me a lot of stuff."

"You want to show me?"

"Not right now. Mom. . ."

Kelly watched her oldest child. Zoey's light blue eyes shone with peace. Her hair, no longer a much-too-dark shade hung in auburn waves past her shoulders. The freckles that splattered her nose gave her a youthful look, but the swelling of her belly was proof that Zoey would grow up whether she was ready or not. But Zoey had grown up so much since Tim's death, even more since her pregnancy. Kelly knew the bitterness Zoey struggled with had been subsiding over the last few months. She'd prayed constantly for Zoey's reconciliation with God.

"Mom, I've made peace with God."

Bliss, pure and profound, poured over Kelly like a rush of water. She closed her eyes, allowing the answer to her heart's deepest prayer for the last three years to penetrate her soul. *Praise You, Jesus. Praise You.*

"I still don't know why God let Daddy die."

Kelly grabbed her daughter's hand. "I don't either, sweetie."

"But I know all things work together for good—"

"To those who love God." Kelly finished part of the scripture. "You've been reading Romans?"

Zoey shrugged. "I read through Romans a few weeks ago after my homework one day. Besides, you used to say that scripture all the time after Daddy died."

"I didn't know you were listening."

"I listen, even when you don't think I am."

Kelly studied her daughter. Contentment wrapped her features, and Kelly could hardly hold back her shouts of praise to the Lord. *Why hold it back?* "Praise the Lord!" she shouted.

Zoey jumped and placed her hand on her chest. "Mom, you scared the life out of me."

Kelly stood up and walked around the table. She embraced her oldest child, her firstborn. "Zoey, your life is back in you. And that is reason to shout."

Chapter 11

It had been over a week since Kelly had gotten sick at school, and she was still battling the virus. She'd never run a fever, but her stomach would settle for only a few hours a day, her body ached, and the fatigue was nearly debilitating. Daily, she barely made it in the door from school before she'd hit the couch.

Harold had been sweet, taking the girls where they needed to go, doing some of the laundry. And Zoey had been doing most of the cooking, but tonight they were planning a movie outing, and Kelly wanted to fix a nice lasagna dinner for the family. Willing herself to feel better, she dumped the hamburger into a skillet and let it start cooking. She quickly diced an onion and green pepper and mixed them in with the cooking meat. The smell, one she normally loved, filled her nostrils, and Kelly gagged.

This is ridiculous. I refuse to be sick any longer. Praying for strength she got out the tomato sauce, tomato paste, and various spices to make the sauce. She ignored her body's protests to the food and continued cooking until the lasagna was covered in aluminum foil and placed in the oven.

"Girls, you need to get ready," Kelly called through the house as she headed toward the bathroom. "We're leaving after dinner."

"Harold said we could go to my movie," Candy said as she walked into Kelly's room.

"I know."

"I can't wait to see Harold's face when it starts," Zoey called from the other room.

"Me, too," Brittany added.

Candy placed her hands on her hips. "All of my friends have gone to see it. It's supposed to be a good movie."

Kelly smiled. "I'm sure it is." She patted Candy's shoulder. "I think your sisters just find it humorous that Harold is going to watch a musical about high school students."

Kelly's stomach rumbled. The smell of frying hamburger meat mixed with onions and green peppers seemed to cling to her. "I'm going to take my bath," she said to Candy, determined not to show her family that she still felt sick. Besides the next day was Valentine's, and she knew Harold had a special dinner planned for the two of them. She had to feel better.

She started the hot water then pulled a towel and washrag from the cabinet. She slinked into the tub, hoping the water would soothe her nausea as it had the past several days. Lying all the way back, she closed her eyes and relished the warm water. Grabbing the timer beside the tub, she turned it to fifteen minutes. By then, she knew her stomach would be all right.

As she expected, the soak helped, and Kelly dressed and fixed up for dinner and a movie. She knew Harold had gotten home; she could hear him talking to the girls in the other room. She opened the bedroom door and saw Harold sitting beside Zoey at the table. They'd discovered that her simple man was quite adept at numbers, and he often helped the girls with their math, especially Zoey since she was homebound.

"I don't understand this part," Zoey said.

"Remember. You have to use this formula." Harold pointed to the book. "You punch it into the calculator like this."

Kelly leaned against the doorframe and watched her daughter pay attention to every word Harold said. The teen had done a full one-eighty since she'd recommitted herself to the Lord. Her belly had blossomed just a bit, and it would be only a matter of weeks before she'd have an ultrasound. Kelly prayed Zoey's faith would stay strong after the birth of the child. It had been difficult enough to have a baby at twenty with a husband. Zoey would only be eighteen without a father present at all.

"Harold, I need help when you're done with Zoey," Brittany said as she walked up beside them.

Harold grimaced, and Kelly remembered he'd said Brittany's Algebra II class was the hardest material for him to figure out. "I hope I can help you. I thought that boy was helping."

"Micah's a jerk," Brittany growled as she flopped into the chair beside Harold. "He kept calling me Amazon Girl today, even after I told him to stop."

Kelly watched as Harold patted her hand and said, "I think he's flirting with you."

"No he's not. He's a jerk."

No one had noticed Kelly yet, and she drank in the interaction between her husband and daughters. *God, Harold is such a blessing.*

"Hey, Harold." Candy skipped to the table and wrapped her arm around Harold's shoulder. "Mom says the movie starts at seven thirty. I can't wait."

"Me neither," Harold murmured, and Kelly almost burst into laughter. She knew the man would rather have his teeth pulled than see that movie. But he'd do it for Candy. Just as any dad would.

In due time, Harold would be the one who'd walk the girls down the aisle to their waiting fiancés. He would be the grandfather to their children. He'd be the one they'd turn to for advice or help. Like Zoey, she didn't understand why Tim died, and she'd never want to take away from his memory. *But thank You, God, for bringing Harold into our lives. He's such a blessing.*

"Penny for your thoughts."

Kelly looked at Harold. She'd been so engrossed in her prayer she hadn't realized he'd noticed her watching them. She strolled to the table and kissed the top of his head. "I was just thinking about how thankful I am to have you."

Zoey and Candy rolled their eyes, while Brittany made a gagging motion. Kelly pointed at Zoey's homework. "Especially since you can do math."

"That's true." Brittany nodded. "We definitely need you for the math. But that's it."

"Oh really." Harold jumped out of his chair and grabbed Brittany in a head-lock. She squealed as he rubbed her head with his knuckles. "Tell me I'm wonderful." He continued to rub her head. "Come on."

Candy giggled and tried to jump on Harold's back. Brittany squealed even louder. Kelly and Zoey bent over in laughter.

"Your sister's trying to help you, but she can't take me." He continued to rub Brittany's head. "Come on, Britt, tell Harold he's the bestest. Nobody's as good as Harold."

"Fine. You're the best," Brittany squealed.

"I can't hear you." Harold rubbed her head again.

"You're the best, you big meanie."

Harold let her go, and Brittany punched his arm. "Look at my hair."

"My turn," Candy yelled, and Harold wrapped her up in a headlock and rubbed her head.

The oven timer went off. Kelly wiped the tears of laughter from her eyes as she walked into the kitchen. "Okay, you bunch of monkeys, it's time to eat."

"Mmm, food." Harold let go of Candy and pounded his chest with his fists. "Monkey hungry."

Zoey shook her head, and Harold messed her hair a bit, as well. Again, Kelly praised God for her family.

❧

Harold nearly fell out of the chair when Kelly walked into the living room. His bride of less than two months stood before him wearing an all-black, silky dress. Two tiny straps touched her shoulders and held the fabric in place. The neck scooped down, but in a way that didn't show the world any of her chest. The skirt kind of flowed at the bottom, touching her knees when she walked. *Wow, she has great legs.*

He looked back at her face, noting the pleasure in her gaze. She liked that she had this kind of effect on him. He drank in her dark hair, piled up on the top of her head in a messy way that was so attractive. Little strands of hair rested on her neck, and he longed to switch places with one of those strands.

She touched the diamond necklace that rested perfectly in the center of her neck. He noticed her neck kind of glittered. In fact, her arms and legs even seemed to shine. But it wasn't just the glitter, Kelly looked fuller somehow. It was as if she were glowing in the most beautiful way.

"Honey," Harold stood up and kissed her cheek. "You are hot," he whispered in her ear.

He noted the redness trailing up her cheek, and he loved that she still thrilled at his attraction to her. Kelly twisted the bow at her waist. "I could hardly squeeze into this dress, and I just bought it two months ago."

"It sure looks awfully good."

Candy rushed into the room, and Harold backed away from his wife. Candy whistled. "Mom, you are hot!"

Brittany walked in, as well. Harold watched as her eyes widened. "No doubt, Mom." She turned to Harold and shrugged her shoulders. "Somebody's going to have to beat the guys off Mom tonight."

Harold laughed. The younger girls proved always dramatic, and always fun to be around. He winked at the two of them. "Don't worry. I'll take care of her."

"And I'll take care of them." Zoey stepped into the living room. She looked at her mom. "You look really pretty, Mom. It's like you're glowing."

Kelly touched her collarbone. The motion sent Harold's attraction into overdrive. "I did put on some of your glitter."

"You look wonderful." Harold looked at his watch. "And our reservation is in an hour. We need to get out of here."

"Okay. Have fun," Zoey said.

"Bye, Mom. Bye, Harold," commented Brittany and Candy.

As Harold guided his bride to the door, he could hear Brittany and Candy arguing over who got the TV first. He looked at Kelly and laughed at the worried expression on her face. "Don't worry about them. They'll be fine. I gave Zoey a TV schedule for the girls to follow."

Kelly's expression softened, and she kissed his lips. "You're a good dad to them."

"I want to be."

Harold opened the car door for Kelly. Since they were going on a nicer date, he'd parked the truck in the garage and they would go in Kelly's car. He walked over to the driver's seat and slipped inside. "You do look absolutely gorgeous." He winked. "I'd be willing to skip dinner."

Kelly giggled. "Oh no. You've been excited about these reservations for weeks. We are going to The Moro Restaurant."

"I don't even know if it's any good."

"They serve steak. Filets. You'll love it. And, I can't wait to try the baked chocolate mousse. I've heard it's absolutely divine." Kelly leaned closer to him and rested her cheek on his shoulder. "It's our first Valentine's Day as husband and wife."

"I know. I can hardly believe it." He glanced at Kelly. "What did you ever see in me?"

Kelly laughed. "Are you kidding me? There's not a day that goes by that I don't praise God for giving me a man who not only loves me, but loves my crazy brood, as well."

"They're my crazy brood now, too."

"Yes, they are."

Harold watched the road signs as they approached Wilmington. All week he'd looked forward to their evening together. He glanced at his wife. Her face looked pale. He noticed her breathing in through her nose and out her mouth. She wasn't feeling well again. She'd been doing this for two weeks. "Kelly, I think you need to go to the doctor."

She shook her head. "I'm fine." She looked at him and smiled, but he could tell the smile didn't reach her eyes. "Really, I feel fine."

Harold parked the car, then walked around to open the door for Kelly. He touched her hand. Clammy. "Kelly, I know you don't want to ruin our plans, but—"

"I'm fine."

They walked into the restaurant. Live jazz music mixed with the conversation of several couples enjoying their evening. Harold looked at the dark yellow and a-little-bit-of-orange-mixed-with-a-little-bit-of-pink walls. The color reminded him of a salmon fillet before it had been cooked. The lights and pictures were fancy, not as fancy as the Dupont Hotel, but still nothing like he'd have ever gone to if he weren't married to Kelly.

He loved the circle pattern the place had going. Several of the tables had a secluded feel to them as a large, circular molding extended about a foot from the ceiling around the table. A fancy chandelier hung from the middle. The architectural design of the place was quite interesting.

A guy, waiter, or whatever Kelly said they were called, showed them to their seats. He and Kelly settled into a booth, and the man handed them the menu for the day. The man walked away, and Harold took his wife's hands in his. He looked at her. Her color did not look good. "Kelly—"

"I'll be right back." Kelly covered her mouth and ran toward the restroom.

Harold sat back in the booth and let out a long breath. Something always seemed to happen to put a damper on their time together. *Zoey tells Kelly she's pregnant before our honeymoon. I mess up Kelly's surprise dinner. Now, she's sick. Is it always going to be like this, Lord?*

His cell phone vibrated in his pocket. The word HOME flashed on the screen. Trepidation washed over him as he pushed ON. "Hello."

"Harold. She's bleeding."

His heart started to race. "What?"

"It's Candy. She tripped over the rug. Hit her head. Zoey's hurling." Harold could hear screams and hacking sounds in the background. The television seemed to blare along with it.

"Slow down, Brittany. Have you put something on Candy's head?"

"Yes. A rag. But she's bleeding through it. I called Cam. He's coming."

Harold could hear her start to cry. "It's okay, Brittany. We're coming."

"Please hurry."

"Just hold the rag on Candy's head. Call me if Cam gets there first and has to take her to the hospital."

Harold raced toward the bathroom. He knocked on the door. "Kelly?"

Brittany, the most sensitive of the three, didn't handle crises well, and Harold knew the mixture of blood and vomit wouldn't be good for her to handle alone.

Kelly didn't answer, so Harold knocked one more time, then walked in. Someone was vomiting in the last stall. Thankfully, no one was in there but Kelly. "Kelly?"

"What are you doing, Harold? I'm fine."

"Candy hit her head. We've got to get home."

The door opened and an older lady walked in. She screamed when she saw Harold. He placed his hand on his chest. "Sorry, ma'am. We're leaving."

Kelly stepped out of the stall. Her face was puffy from vomiting, and some of her makeup smeared down her cheeks.

The woman frowned. She placed her hand on Kelly's and glared at Harold. "You don't have to go anywhere with him, young lady. I'll take you somewhere safe. He can find another woman to torment."

Harold rolled his eyes and looked at the ceiling. "Believe me, ma'am. I have enough women tormenting me right now."

Kelly walked to Harold. She looked at the woman. "It's okay, ma'am. He's my husband. He didn't hurt me. I've been sick."

Harold grabbed Kelly's hand and nodded to the older woman. The woman scowled at him but he ignored her. "Come on. We've got to go."

"What happened?"

"Candy must have fallen. Her head is bleeding a lot, and Zoey's throwing up."

Kelly covered her mouth with her hand. "Oh no."

"Cam's on his way to the house. They're going to call if she needs stitches or anything."

"Oh no."

Harold guided Kelly toward the car. She didn't move as fast as he would have expected. He could hear her taking deep breaths. Reaching the car, he pulled out his keys.

"Oh no," Kelly mumbled again. She turned away from him and vomited in the space beside their car.

Kelly was vomiting. Zoey was vomiting. Brittany was panicking. And Candy was bleeding. *So, this was life with a bunch of women?* Being a bachelor had definitely been easier. Not that he didn't love his girls. He loved each and every one of them. Whether they were happy, sad, laughing, crying, puking, bleeding. They were his girls, and he loved them.

Chapter 12

Kelly rested her elbows on the bar of the grocery cart. It had been a long day. Zoey had called several times asking about her schoolwork. Two more boys had gotten into a fight in her room. What is it with the boys and fighting this year? The nurse from Candy's school had called to let Kelly know she'd given her daughter pain reliever for her head. It was only four o'clock, and Kelly was ready to call it a night.

Willing herself to keep going, she stood to her full height and made her way toward the antibiotic cream. Candy's head wound three days before had resulted in a trip to the emergency room, but thankfully, only required three stitches and a regimen of cream application. Kelly frowned as she thought about the ugly bruise surrounding the cut above Candy's eyebrow. Harold had been the one tending the wound. It was true that when Tim was alive he took care of all the girls' cuts and scrapes, but since his death Kelly had played family nurse. But this time she simply couldn't handle it. Her stomach churned at the thought of it.

What is wrong with me? It's like I've become a full-blown wimp. These flu symptoms have been going on for too long.

Kelly stopped in front of the Band-Aids, bandages, medical tape, hydrocortisone cream, and more. How many days had she been suffering from the flu? *Okay, I was sick before our Valentine's date. . .actually, I was sick more than a week before that.*

She counted days on her fingers. "I've been fighting this for well over two weeks." She took in a long, slow breath. "This is ridiculous. I haven't run a fever or had any chills. I'm just so nauseated and tired."

Kelly grabbed the cream and dropped it into the cart. She continued down the aisle in search of cotton balls. Her gaze took in the display of pregnancy tests. A weight dropped in her stomach. *No.* She shook her head. *No way. That's not possible. I had my tubes tied five years ago.*

She pulled her pocket calendar out of her purse. *Surely, it isn't possible.* She checked each month.

November?

Fine.

December?

Fine.

January?

She searched the days of January. No marks appeared before her eyes. No proof of the days she'd had her menstrual cycle. She flipped the calendar back to December, then counted the weeks to when she should have marked days in January.

She closed her eyes, trying to remember what she was doing on the days in question. Nothing was coming to mind. Why couldn't she remember having her cycle?

Opening her eyes slowly, she stared at the pregnancy tests before her. *I skipped my period.*

Glancing around her to be sure no one watched, Kelly grabbed a box and tucked it under other items in the cart. I'm sure it's nothing, but if I go ahead and take the test it'll set my mind at ease.

No longer able to finish her grocery shopping, Kelly sped toward the checkout line. *If I were pregnant, I would be far enough along that I wouldn't have to wait until morning to take the test. I could take it now.* The very thought weakened Kelly's knees. Her heart raced as she got in line behind an older man with a few items.

"Hey, Mrs. Smith. I can get you over here."

Kelly looked up and saw one of her junior students motion her to his line. Empty line.

Kelly's heart plummeted. She glanced around to see if there was anyone— anyone—within the vicinity who could jump into his line. No one. She looked at the older man in front of her who had started talking to the cashier and had yet to place the first item on the conveyor.

"Come on, Mrs. Smith." She glanced at her student, Jerome. He motioned at her again.

Her feet felt as heavy as bricks as she slowly scooted toward his line, begging God to send someone to jump in front of her. What would he think when he saw the pregnancy test? *Oh, Lord, what do I do? Maybe, I should just take it back and. . . I know. . .*

She smiled at her student from her third period class. "Hello, Jerome." She pointed to her cart. "I forgot to pick up some toothpaste. Maybe I'll catch you in a minute." She maneuvered the cart around and headed back toward hygiene products.

There. I didn't lie. We do need toothpaste. I'll pick some up. Then I'll just wait until his lane is full, and then I'll get in someone else's line.

Kelly grabbed a tube of toothpaste, dumped it into the cart, and then watched the checkout lanes. In only a matter of moments, a woman, probably the manager, had walked over to Jerome, pulled out his money, and closed his line. Breathing a sigh of relief, Kelly slipped into line behind a young woman and a toddler.

Kelly smiled at the little tike and waved her hand. He turned his face, as if bashful, then smiled one of the sweetest smiles she'd seen in a while. Soon enough, she'd have a grandchild making those adorable faces. *And maybe another child.*

Bile rose in her throat at the idea of it. *What woman had a child months after her grandchild was born?* The thought was ludicrous. Preposterous.

While his mother stood at the front of the cart fumbling through her purse, the little guy leaned over and grabbed a candy bar from the shelf. Before Kelly could respond, he shoved the wrapper into his mouth.

Kelly scrunched her nose. "That's yucky." She grabbed the wrapper from the child's hands, hoping it wasn't too germ-ridden. His lips puckered, and his face wrapped in the most wounded expression she'd ever seen. Wails, louder than the tardy bell at school, expelled from the boy, and Kelly practically jumped out of her shoes.

"I'm sorry." She handed the candy bar to the child's mother, who now bore into Kelly with a menacing look. "He put this in his mouth. I'm sure it's not clean."

The woman didn't appear pleased with Kelly's decision to save the urchin from the threat of bacteria and virus as she took the candy bar from Kelly's grasp. She allowed the cashier to scan it, then pulled the chocolate from the wrapper and handed it to the boy. The child looked at Kelly as if she were the proverbial bully who'd taken away the child's sucker as he smashed the chocolate partly into his mouth, but mostly all over his face. Without a second glance, the woman finished paying and pushed the cart out of the aisle and toward the door.

The cashier, an older woman with white hair and a quick smile, winked at Kelly. "That guy was too little to eat chocolate."

Kelly's chin quivered as she forced a smile. Usually not that emotional, Kelly focused on taking the items out of the cart. She tried not to look into the woman's kind eyes as she rang up each item.

"Hmm. This one doesn't want to scan."

Kelly glanced up and saw the woman holding the pregnancy test. She moved it across the laser once. Twice. Three times.

"Do you know how much this costs?" She held the box up in front of Kelly, and Kelly felt sure her legs were going to fall out from underneath her.

Kelly shook her head and opened her mouth to tell the woman not to worry about it. That she didn't need it.

The woman leaned into the microphone next to her cash register. "Price check on aisle 12, I need a price check, please."

Kelly felt heat flash up her neck and through her cheeks. "It's okay." She tried not to beg the woman. "I'll just get one later."

"Well, hey again, Mrs. Smith."

Kelly closed her eyes at the sound of Jerome's voice behind her. Taking in a deep breath, she turned and smiled at her student. "Hello, Jerome."

The cashier shoved the box into Jerome's hand. "I need you to go find out how much this pregnancy test costs."

Kelly gripped the cart with all her strength, praying her legs didn't give out from beneath her.

"No problem." Jerome waltzed toward the pharmacy section and returned within moments. He quoted the price and handed it back to the older woman. "See you Monday, Mrs. Smith."

Kelly nodded as she pulled her debit card from her purse. She paid the bill then took the receipt from the cashier. The woman winked again. "You'll be a wonderful mother."

Kelly couldn't respond. She raced to her car, loaded the bags, then sped to her house. Shoving the pregnancy test into the bottom of her purse, she took a deep breath then marched into the house.

"Mom, I—" said Brittany.

"Don't forget—" said Zoey.

Kelly stalked past them. "Sorry, girls. Gotta go to the bathroom first."

Shutting and locking the door, Kelly swallowed the knot in her throat. She tried not to think about Jerome and what he thought or what he'd say. She tried not to envision a litany of teenagers scoffing at the pregnancy of their "old" English teacher. The one whose teen daughter was also pregnant. She dug into the bottom of her purse and pulled out the box. With trembling fingers, she opened the test and read the instructions. "Times have changed," Kelly mumbled, "I don't have to wait until the morning anyway."

After getting the test ready, she closed her eyes. "God. . ." What did she say to Him? She was too old to have another baby. Thirty-eight, for goodness' sake. She was going to be a grandma. And yet she was still a woman. And there was still this small, slight, microscopic piece of her that wanted for the result to be positive. To see what Harold's child would look like. To cuddle her own newborn once more.

"God," she started again. "You know."

She took the test. Staring at the result, tears welled in her eyes. How can a woman feel happy and sad, scared and excited? She gripped the side of the bathroom sink. Staring at her reflection, that of a thirty-eight-year-old mother of three daughters and soon-to-be grandma, her heart raced as if it were about to explode. "I'm pregnant."

After pushing the front door open, Harold tucked the dozen long-stemmed, red roses behind his back. He and Kelly hadn't been able to make up their Valentine's date, and though they'd spend this evening at Brittany's basketball game, he still wanted Kelly to know he longed for alone time with her. His bride of two months stood at the kitchen sink, her back to him. He sneaked up behind her and wrapped his free arm around her waist. She jumped and turned, but once recognition dawned in her gaze, Harold pressed his lips against hers.

"Harold," she whispered into his lips, and Harold longed to pull her closer.

Instead, he revealed the roses and handed them to Kelly. "We were never able to celebrate Valentine's Day properly." He kissed her forehead. "I love you, Kelly."

Kelly took the flowers from his hands and stared at them. Tears pooled in her eyes, and Harold brushed them away with his fingertips. She gazed up at him, and Harold expected her to thank him for the flowers, to declare she loved them, that he was wonderful for remembering red roses were her favorite. Instead, sadness lingered in her gaze. She seemed to hide herself behind a new wall that she built between them. But for what reason now?

They seemed to be settling into a routine as a family. Zoey, though still a pregnant teenager, had recommitted herself to God and seemed to be handling things well. Brittany and Candy thrived in school and in their activities. He couldn't think of a single reason for Kelly to shut him out. *Unless she just wishes she hadn't married me to begin with.*

He shook his head. He wouldn't allow his thoughts to go there. Quite frankly, it didn't matter if she did feel that way. He'd made a commitment before God, family, and friends. He vowed to love, honor, and cherish her in the good times and in the bad times, for better or for worse, and she'd simply have to learn to love him again. No turning back. The two were one flesh.

Unable to get a good grip on the frustration he felt, Harold strode down the hall. He looked in Candy's room. "Are you going to Brittany's game tonight?"

Candy looked up at him and frowned. He knew his tone was too terse. She hadn't done anything to upset him. "No. I have a project due tomorrow. I'm staying home with Zoey."

Harold should have asked her about it, but he still felt such aggravation toward Kelly that he simply nodded and made his way to Brittany's room. He knocked on the door. "It's time to go."

"Okay. I'll grab my stuff. You get Mom."

He strode into their bedroom and saw Kelly sitting on the bed. Red rims circled her eyes. "Harold. . ."

Harold didn't want to hear. He was tired of all the emotions, of all the crying and whimpering. Things didn't have to be as hard as his four women were always making them. He'd brought Kelly flowers. She had no reason to cry and shut him out. And he'd had enough of it. He pulled a few tissues out of the box and tossed them to Kelly. "Here." His voice was tense, angry, but he couldn't help it. "Clean up. We've got to go."

Without a backward glance, he stalked out to the car. In his anger, he'd forgotten his coat. He didn't need it. Frustration warmed him to his core. He started the car and waited for Kelly and Brittany to join him. Soon, they slipped into the car. The ride to the game was silent. Brittany seldom talked before she played, and Harold couldn't think of anything he could say to Kelly that would be in any way kind. Obviously, Kelly felt the same way.

Once at the game, Harold followed Kelly into the gym. They sat in their usual spot, midway up the stands on the right side. Harold smiled and nodded at the usual parents who joined them in their normal places as well. Within moments, the girls' team had emerged from the locker room to the shouts and cheers of the hometown fans.

Determined not to think about Kelly, Harold watched Brittany as she warmed up with her team. He felt such pride when his stepdaughter dribbled the ball from one hand to the other with ease. It was something she and he had practiced multiple times over in the driveway the past summer. Kelly's girls had become like his own children; he could only imagine how much more pride the biological dads of these girls felt.

"Hi, Ms. Smith," said a tall, African American boy scaling the steps beside them.

Harold looked at Kelly. Her face turned bright crimson as she merely nodded then peered down at her feet. Harold furrowed his eyebrows. That's not like Kelly. Normally, she smiles, waves, even strikes up conversations with her students. She'd always been the friendliest teacher he'd ever seen when she saw her students in public settings.

Maybe that kid's a troublemaker. Harold glanced up the stands at the boy. The guy looked familiar. If Harold's guess was right, he was the one who worked at their local grocery store. Harold studied the boy a moment longer. *Yeah. That's definitely the kid from the grocery. He's a great kid. Why would Kelly act so funny with him?*

Harold peered at his wife. Desperation traced her features. He couldn't fathom what was wrong with her. He touched her leg. She jumped. He frowned. "Kelly, what is wrong?"

"Nothing." The word came out loud and a note higher than she usually talked. "I've just got to go to the bathroom." She stood, and Harold watched as she walked down the steps then out of the gym.

Harold sighed. *God, I have no idea what is going on with her.* He propped his feet on the row in front him then leaned forward resting his elbows on his knees. He rested his chin on his fists. *I'm just going to focus on the game.*

He gazed up at the scoreboard. The game would start in less than two minutes. Brittany and her team had huddled around their coach by the bench. Harold couldn't help but chuckle at how much taller Brittany, a freshman, was than the rest of her teammates. Though still one of the weaker players, due to being thin and not fully matured, Brittany started as the center for the team. Brittany's dribbling skills warranted her a position as a guard, but the team's desperate need for a strong center won out, and Harold found himself trying to help his fifteen-year-old stepdaughter beef up in weight and strength.

With only seconds left on the clock before the game started, Kelly made her way back up the steps and sat beside Harold. Too frustrated to talk to her, Harold didn't ask if everything was all right. She wouldn't have told him anyway. The woman had spent more time shutting him out in the two months of their marriage than she'd spent opening up to him in the year they dated. This should be the most exciting time of their marriage, and yet Harold found himself growing more confused and flustered by his new wife.

Harold clapped while the other team was announced and stood and cheered when it was Brittany's team's turn. The teams lined up on the floor, and Harold howled when Brittany got the tip-off. He watched the game intently, no longer thinking about Kelly and her odd reactions of late.

"Hi, Mrs. Smith."

Harold looked over at the aisle. Two girls stood beside Kelly. The one talking smiled like a Cheshire cat. "Jerome told us he saw you at the grocery."

Kelly's face blanched, and she shifted in her seat. "Hello, girls." Kelly gripped her purse strap and twisted it. "I see Jerome at the store all the time."

Jerome. That's the boy's name from the store. Kelly's apprehension at talking to the girls stumped Harold. He peered back up the stands at the African American boy who'd spoken to Kelly earlier. He was standing, crossing his hand in front of him and shaking his head. He mouthed the word "no" repeatedly, and if Harold guessed right, it appeared Jerome was looking at the two girls talking to Kelly. Harold looked back at his wife.

"Yeah, but this was a couple of days ago." The girl's expression was arrogant and a bit bratty. "He said he had to help you with a price check."

The blond beside the girl giggled then shifted next to her friend.

"Jerome helps with price checks all the time." Kelly's voice had a fearful lilt to it. It almost sounded like panic.

"Yeah, but what did Mr. Smith think about this price check?"

The girl's tone was sarcastic and disrespectful, and Harold opened his mouth to tell her that it was time for her to go on back to her seat, when Kelly jumped up. "Excuse me, girls."

She pushed past the girls, nearly raced down the steps, and out of the gym door.

The girl looked at Harold and huffed. "I take it that means you don't know about her price check." The girl turned to her friend and shrugged. The blond giggled again and tugged on the mouthy girl to head back up the steps. He heard her mumble to her friend. "Poor guy."

Harold frowned. *What could possibly be going on with Kelly and some price check? And why would she let that teenage girl talk to her in such a disrespectful way?* In all the time he'd known Kelly he'd never seen her show a moment of weakness in front of one of her students, but tonight she practically ran out the door.

Harold looked up at the teenage girl. He had half a mind to stomp up those steps and tell that child she needed to find her teacher and apologize. He took a long breath. The girl didn't know him. He didn't know her. Kelly shouldn't have let her talk like that. It was almost as if she had something to hide from him. *But why is she always trying to hide things from me, God?*

Frustrated, Harold peered back down at the basketball court. He'd missed the last three baskets. He hadn't even heard the announcer say who'd made the shots. His phone buzzed. He pulled it out of his pocket and opened the text. It was from Kelly. She was going to stay in the car the rest of the game. She doesn't feel well, Harold grumbled at the last bit of her message.

Tonight, he was tired of her being sick. He was finished with her being secretive and trying to shut him out of her life. Tonight, he was going to watch his stepdaughter play basketball. If Kelly won't let me in on what's going on, she can just wait in the car.

He clapped as the buzzer sounded signifying the end of the first quarter. "God, I never thought I'd be saying this only two months in, but please, help my marriage."

Chapter 13

It was Monday, and Kelly still hadn't started her cycle, she'd taken two more pregnancy tests, and they still came back positive. *Thank You, Lord, that I won't have to face my students today, since they're out of school and we have professional development.* But then, Kelly would be missing that, as well. She'd have to make up the hours at a later date. Today, she was going to Zoey's ultrasound appointment. She peered at her reflection in the mirror and mumbled, "It's going to be a great day. I get to find out the sex of my grandchild and if they're doing okay." She clasped her hands in front of her chest. "And I get to make an appointment to find out about my baby."

Her expression sombered, and she plopped onto the toilet cover. "And I need to tell Harold."

Her stomach groaned with anxiety at the thought of what he would say. She'd had her tubes tied five years before, she never even considered worrying about getting pregnant. Besides, she was thirty-eight years old, not that she was too old, but when she was the mother of teenagers and about to be a grandmother—Kelly shook her head and sighed. This whole situation was ridiculously overwhelming.

She remembered the way he'd laughed when Sadie had mistakenly guessed that she and Harold were pregnant. He made it abundantly obvious that the last thing he wanted was for the two of them to have a child.

A knock sounded on the bathroom door. "Come on, Kelly. We don't want to be late."

Kelly groaned. And Harold was going with them to the appointment. Ever since he'd taken Zoey shopping for maternity clothes, Zoey wanted Harold to be a part of everything. Kelly couldn't believe he'd agreed to take the morning off to go to the ultrasound with them. Of course, she'd seen the look of shock and uncertainty that wrapped Harold's features when Zoey asked him to go. It was apparent he didn't feel exceptionally comfortable with the idea. But she also knew that Harold wouldn't say no.

It was one of the things she loved about him.

What's he going to say when he finds out he and I are going to have a baby? We'll be raising our child and grandchild at the same time, as if they were cousins. The very idea. . . Kelly stood and walked out of the bathroom. *Just don't* think about it right now. One thing at a time.

"Come on, Mom," Zoey hollered from the front of the house.

"I'm coming." Kelly opened Candy's door. Her youngest was still fast asleep, swaddled in a pile of covers. She gently shut the door, then headed toward Brittany's room. Kelly could barely get the door open from the clutter on the floor. This kid's going to clean her room today. She peered in at Brittany. She was asleep, as well. They'd probably be home before either girl awakened. Kelly shut the door, grabbed her coat, and slipped it on. She picked up her purse from the table and shut and locked the door.

As she walked down the sidewalk toward the car, she looked at Harold. His discomfort at going to Zoey's ultrasound was obvious, but she could tell he'd do whatever Zoey asked. She loved that about Harold. A vision of his expression when she told him she, too, was pregnant flashed through her mind. It wasn't pretty. She pushed it away. She could only imagine what he would think.

⁓

Harold wanted to crawl out of the doctor's room when Zoey lay on the bed and the nurse prepared her for the ultrasound. Standing close to Zoey's head, he focused on the blank screen that would soon show Zoey's baby. Why in the world would she want me here? Harold forced himself not to cringe. He couldn't recall a time he'd felt more uncomfortable.

But Zoey had changed so much since she'd recommitted herself to the Lord. He caught her reading her Bible all the time. She journaled constantly, and though he'd never read anything she wrote, he had a feeling she was often talking to God because her Bible always lay on top of her journal.

She also sought Harold out every day to talk to him about one thing or another. It had even been her idea for him to take her and her sisters to a movie the following weekend. "It'll be a father/daughter date." Her words ran through his mind. He'd nearly swallowed his tongue when she said that. He wanted so much for the girls to think of him as a father. Having never had children and knowing he never would, Harold found himself enjoying being a father to Kelly's girls.

"Okay, we're ready." The nurse's voice shook Harold from his thoughts.

He peered in amazement as the figure of a baby formed on the screen. The picture was so clear, so precise, it was almost like looking at a black-and-white photo of the child. The woman marked and clicked at various places, confirming the heart, the spine, the legs, that everything appeared as it should.

"Would you like to know the sex of the baby?" the nurse asked.

"Yes," Harold replied. His cheeks warmed as Kelly and Zoey chuckled at his excitement. He looked at their faces. "I mean, if you all want to."

"Sure," Zoey said.

"He's a boy," the nurse said.

A boy. Harold would have a blast playing with the little guy. He patted Zoey's shoulder. "He looks pretty strong."

Zoey chuckled. "Could I get two copies of the pictures you've taken? Someone else would like copies."

Harold frowned. Had Jamie come back to town? Was she seeing him and they didn't know it? His heart raced at the thought. Christian or not, Harold wasn't sure how he would respond if he ever saw Jamie again. The man had taken advantage of Zoey, and Harold wasn't sure he would be able to control his temper if he saw the guy.

Harold's thoughts must have gotten away from him because when he looked back at Zoey, the nurse had already left and Zoey was sitting on the edge of the patient bed. She gripped the photos in her hands. "I need to talk to you both."

Her tone was serious, and Harold looked from Zoey to Kelly. His wife hadn't said two words since they'd gotten to the doctor's office. She'd spoken with the receptionist for several minutes when they'd first arrived, but since then she'd been completely silent. Even throughout the entire ultrasound.

"I was going to wait until we got home." Zoey peered down at the pictures. "But I think I'll go ahead and tell you now."

If she said she was going to run off with that low-down, no-good fellow who got her pregnant Harold wouldn't be responsible for his actions. God, I know we're supposed to love everyone. We're supposed to forgive. But if Zoey is so foolish as to think that man would do right by her. . . Harold's blood boiled. His heart nearly beat out of his chest. His fists balled, and he knew that if it was within his power, no man would hurt his little girl.

And she was his little girl now.

He looked at his wife, whose face had blanched. Her hand rested at the nape of her neck. It trembled ever so slightly, and Harold knew she had no idea what Zoey was going to say. Though Kelly was as beautiful as ever, the last few months had taken a toll on her. Dark lines rested beneath her eyes, and Harold knew she hadn't slept well in a long while. She'd barely talked to him since the game on Friday night, and Harold had no idea what to do with her.

Just love her. That's all I can do.

"I've made a decision."

Harold looked back at Zoey. She peered up at her mother, then toward Harold. "I've been praying about it. Really seeking God's will. I've messed up, but God has forgiven me, and now I want to live for Him, to do what He wills."

Harold swallowed. His stepdaughter sounded so serious, so old. He believed that she'd sought God on whatever she was about to tell them. He'd watched her, and he knew she'd changed. He gazed at Kelly. She sat back down in the chair beside Zoey.

"What is it, Zoey?" Kelly's voice sounded tired.

"And I've already talked with Cam and Sadie about it. I think it's for the best."

Cam and Sadie? What did they have to do with any of this?

Zoey held up the pictures of her little boy. "I've decided to allow Cam and Sadie to adopt my son."

Harold let out a breath he hadn't realized he'd been holding in. The idea bounced back and forth through his mind. Cam and Sadie were wonderful parents, and they would adore Zoey's child. The more he thought about it, the more Harold realized the idea was a good one.

"I'm not ready to be a mom." Zoey looked at her mother. "Cam and Sadie could give my son everything he needed, and he'd have a big sister. And I would still be able to see him. . ."

"I don't know if you realize how hard giving up your baby would be." Kelly's tone was low and serious, her expression blank.

"You're right, Mom. I don't, but I love him enough to do what's right for him. I'll barely be eighteen when he's born."

"I was twenty when I had you."

Harold frowned. Allowing Cam and Sadie to adopt the child seemed to be the perfect solution. Zoey could go on to college. She could still see her son on a regular basis. And Kelly knew she'd been seeking God's will for her life. He frowned at Kelly. "It sounds like she's prayed a lot about this, Kelly."

Kelly stared up at Harold. "I'm not saying she shouldn't give her son up for adoption." She looked back at Zoey. "I just want to be sure she understands that either way, having a baby is a life-changing experience. Once you've become pregnant, there's no going back." She looked back up at Harold, and he wondered at the pleading expression on her face. "A pregnancy changes everything."

Zoey grabbed Kelly's hand. "I believe you, Mom. I feel this is what God wants. Will you pray with me about it?"

Kelly wrapped her arms around her daughter. "Of course I will."

Harold felt perplexed at Kelly's response. What was going on with his wife?

⌖

Kelly was thankful that for the last few days she hadn't felt quite as nauseated. She followed Harold and Zoey into the house. They'd just left Zoey's ultrasound appointment. Zoey and Harold had talked nonstop about her notion of giving Kelly's grandchild to Cam and Sadie. In the depths of Kelly's spirit, she knew Zoey was making the right choice. She'd support her daughter completely.

At the same time, it broke Kelly's heart to know that Zoey would experience heartache and trials no matter what she chose. Being a young mother herself when she had Zoey, she knew how overwhelming the physical care for a new baby would be. Kelly'd had the support of a loving husband when she'd had Zoey. But Kelly also knew that giving away a child would be equally as difficult. How many times had she and Sadie talked about Sadie's longings to be Ellie's mother? How would Zoey respond when her son called Sadie "Mom" or when Cam and Sadie had to discipline him or when he ran to them for help with a boo-boo. Either way, Zoey would experience pain and loss, and it broke Kelly's heart that her daughter would go through that.

"Hi, Mom," Candy squealed as they walked through the door. "Hey, Harold." She wrapped her arms around Harold in a hug.

"So, what's Zoey having?" Brittany asked.

"A boy," Zoey responded. "But I'm giving him up for adoption."

"You're what?" Candy's voice raised two octaves and she peered at her oldest sister.

"To Cam and Sadie," Zoey said seriously.

"Mom, did you know this?" Shock wrapped Brittany's expression.

Kelly couldn't handle this right now. She waved her hand. "Let me go to the bathroom, then we'll all talk."

Kelly practically raced past her daughters and into her bathroom. She shut the door, allowing her whole body to lean against it. She could hear Zoey and Harold talking to the girls about the baby. It was evident Harold supported Zoey's decision completely.

She couldn't blame him. The man was forty years old. He didn't have any siblings. He'd been thrown into a marriage of a bunch of nutty, hormonal women and learned on his honeymoon that his teenage stepdaughter was going to have a baby. He didn't want a baby in the house. His response had been overwhelmingly obvious of the fact.

"Adoption to Cam and Sadie probably is the best thing for Zoey's baby," her spirit nudged her. And Harold had never given Kelly any reason to think he wouldn't have been willing to keep Zoey's baby.

Being willing and wanting a child are two different things.

She growled as she flopped on the toilet cover. I started my day worrying right here.

She shook her head. Harold was going to completely freak out when he found out she was pregnant. She pulled her doctor's appointment slip from her purse. Because of her age and the fact that she'd had her tubes tied, the receptionist had made an appointment for her to see the doctor the following week.

One week. She would love to wait until after her appointment to tell

Harold about the pregnancy, but she thought of the students from school. By tomorrow morning, Brittany would probably hear rumors that her mom had bought a pregnancy test.

No. She couldn't wait the seven days. She'd have to tell Harold. She'd have to tell him tonight. The thought made Kelly's stomach churn. Her heart raced, her palms grew sweaty. How much could one man take? They hadn't even been married three months. The poor guy would probably go running and screaming from the house, vowing never to return.

A mental image filled her mind of her oversized, dark-haired husband flailing his arms through the air and racing from the house. She could see him in his light brown work shirt and stained darker brown pants. His big, clunky boots would leave massive prints in the snow. A smile bowed her lips. The image was too funny, and it lightened her mood.

God, You already know everything.

She shoved the appointment slip back into her purse and shrugged her shoulders. The truth was she was the mother of a seventeen-year-old pregnant daughter. She had a fifteen-year-old daughter who was a living, breathing, walking tornado, leaving traces of food, clothes, and dirt everywhere she went. She was the mother of an eleven-year-old whose body was beginning to blossom and who begged almost every day to shave her legs, wear makeup, and get a cell phone. And now, she was pregnant with her new husband's baby.

She lived a wacky life. It was the one God had given her. She was nervous about Harold's response, however she had no choice but to tell him. In the meantime, she'd change her attitude. *God, my life belongs to You. And if another baby is what You want. . .*

She shrugged her shoulders and opened the bathroom door. She could hear the girls talking over each other, and Harold's intermittent attempt to get in a word of his own. She sighed. *Then a baby is what we'll have.*

Chapter 14

Harold settled into bed. It had been a long day. He'd intended to go in to work after Zoey's ultrasound appointment, but when Zoey announced she'd be giving the baby to Cam and Sadie, his girls had needed him. They'd all done a lot of talking and praying. Thankfully, when he'd called Rudy to see how things were going at work, Rudy told him he and Walt had everything covered. *I'll just go in a bit earlier tomorrow.*

He turned toward his alarm clock and reset it for four thirty. After picking up his Bible, he turned to the book of Acts. He'd been reading through his Bible one chapter a night for several years. As much as he hated reading, he found his relationship with the Lord deepened just by reading a bit of scripture each night. *Even I can handle one chapter per night.*

Kelly walked out of the bathroom. She wore a long flannel nightgown that practically covered every inch of her body from her neck all the way down her arms and all the way down to her ankles. She padded on bare feet to the dresser, where she opened the top drawer, pulled out a pair of fluffy red socks, and quickly shoved them on her feet. He couldn't help but chuckle.

Kelly looked at him. Her face had been newly cleaned and was shiny from whatever lotion or cream she put on each night. She'd put some kind of band around her head to keep any hair from touching her face. "You know I freeze at night."

Harold patted the bed. "I think you look adorable."

She slipped into bed beside him and reached for a bottle of lotion on her end table. While she rubbed the flowery smelling stuff on her hands, Harold looked back at his Bible and started to read.

"Harold," Kelly whispered. "Do you love me?"

"You know I do," Harold mumbled and continued to focus on the words in front of him. He read about the Lord telling Ananias to go to Straight Street to look for a man named Saul. God's precise instructions always fascinated him. The Lord was specific, and Harold loved that about Him.

"Harold," Kelly whispered again. "You know I love you, too."

"Mmm-hmm." Harold continued to read about Ananias's fear about the harm Saul had already done to the Christians. Harold wondered if he would voice his concern to God as Ananias did. If Harold heard God's audible voice, he hoped he'd respond affirmatively right away. *But then sometimes I realize later He's right next to me trying to tell me something important, but I'm oblivious to His voice.*

"Harold," Kelly whispered again. "How much do you love me?"

"A whole bunch," Harold mumbled, as he continued to read the Lord's emphatic instruction to Ananias to do as God said. Ananias needed to listen to God and not doubt the men He chose to spread His Word. *Lord, I just don't think I would be so hardheaded. I think I would recognize that I needed to listen to You, to heed what You said.*

"Harold. . ."

"Hmm?" Harold continued to read. When Ananias placed his hands on Saul and spoke to him, scales fell from Saul's eyes. He immediately got up and was baptized. Saul didn't waste any time acknowledging God's prodding. *Well, he did spend three days blind, though, didn't he?*

"What if things changed?"

Harold looked at Kelly for the first time. What had she been talking to him about? He was trying to read his Bible, trying to unwind from a long day. What was all this concern about him loving her and her loving him? She knew he loved her. She'd been the one going bonkers on him lately. "What are you talking about, Kelly?"

She twisted a bit of the gown between her hands. "I just need to know that you love me."

"Of course I love you."

"No matter what."

He touched her chin. "No matter what." He looked back at his Bible.

"Even if things changed."

Harold looked at Kelly and frowned. "Can things change any more than they already have?"

She nodded. Fear traced her features. Maybe it wasn't fear, but more like hesitancy. But what could she be hesitant to tell him? He didn't believe there was a thing in the world Kelly could say that would surprise him. "When you married into my family, I should have warned you that things could always change—a lot."

He took her hands into his. "Not my love for you."

"That's good. . ." Kelly hesitated. She shut her mouth, then opened it again. " 'Cause. . ." She let out a long breath.

Concern worked its way through Harold's veins. What would Kelly possibly have to tell him that had her so nervous to just come out and say it? "Kelly?"

She pulled her hands away from his and covered her eyes. "I'm pregnant."

Harold stared at her. The words played once, twice, then a third time through his mind. "Did you say. . . ?"

She lowered her hands and pouted. "I said I'm pregnant."

"You're pregnant?" Harold felt his eyebrows raise, felt his mouth gape open. Excitement coursed through his body. He would be a father, a biological father, a father to a baby, then a kid, then a teenager. He'd get to go through all the steps and not just take the kid on once he'd gotten too smart for his own good. "You're pregnant!"

"I'm sorry." Kelly frowned and the pout deepened. "I never dreamed we'd have to take precautions. My tubes were tied, and I just can't—I can't believe it."

"You're pregnant!" Harold couldn't stop saying it. He was going to be a daddy. He was going to hold his own son in his arms. They would play catch together, go fishing together, and do all the things dads and sons did together. Never in his wildest imaginations did he ever dream he'd have the opportunity to have his own child. *God, what a blessing! What an unbelievable blessing!*

Harold pulled Kelly over to him, wrapping his arms around her. "Oh, Kelly."

"I'm sorry, Harold."

"Sorry?" Harold raked his fingers through her hair. "I can't remember the last time I've been so excited." He released her long enough to cup her cheeks in his hands. "I never thought I'd have my own child." He pressed his lips against hers. "You've given me the best gift."

"You're happy?" Kelly's voice sounded surprised.

Harold jumped out of bed. "I'm more than happy. Girls!" he yelled. "Girls!" Candy raced into the room. "What?" Brittany and Zoey followed behind her.

"Harold!" Kelly said. "I didn't expect you to tell them so quickly."

"Why not? It's the most wonderful news in the world." He turned toward his stepdaughters. "Your mom is pregnant."

❧

Harold's response had not been what she expected. But his excitement had eased her concerns and allowed her to consider what it would be like to have a baby in the home again—one that she and her husband would raise as their own child.

Candy and Brittany had been overjoyed, every bit as excited as Harold. Zoey had been more reserved. Kelly admitted the idea of the two of them being pregnant together seemed odd to her, as well. *Definitely isn't something I ever intended to happen.*

The next morning as she drove to the high school, Kelly thought about Harold placing his hands on her still-somewhat-flat stomach. He'd kissed her beside her belly button. "Good morning, baby." He patted her stomach, then stood and kissed her lips. "Eat right today. Make sure you don't let your students stress you out. Sit down every chance you can."

Kelly laughed at the memory. Harold would probably drive her crazy for the next several months. Her cell phone rang, and Kelly pulled it out of her purse and answered it. "Hello."

"Hey, Kelly." Sadie's voice sounded over the line. "I hear you have some big news."

"I'm guessing Zoey called you." Kelly couldn't help smiling into the phone. Sadie had been a terrific sister-in-law, and Kelly knew she'd been an encouragement to Zoey through the last several months.

"She did."

"Is she upset about me being pregnant, too?" Just saying the words aloud caused Kelly to scrunch her nose. She was relieved with Harold's excitement at the pregnancy, and she'd begun to allow herself to wrap her mind around being a mother of a newborn again, but it was still strange to be pregnant the same time as her daughter.

"Not upset," Sadie said. "Just a little weirded out."

Kelly laughed. "I'm a little weirded out, too."

"How do you feel about her news? About adoption, I mean."

"I was surprised, and I'm not at all opposed to it. I guess I just hadn't considered—"

"I just want you to know I never mentioned it to her. She came to Cam and me and asked us if we'd be willing to adopt the baby. We prayed about it for a while before we agreed. I don't want you to think—"

"You were trying to steal my grandbaby." Kelly laughed. "I know that, Sadie. In my heart, I know you and Cam are the best parents for her baby. It just hurts me that she's going to hurt. If she keeps the baby, she'll hurt. If she gives the baby to you, she'll hurt."

"You're absolutely right."

Kelly pulled into the school's parking lot. "Listen, I just pulled into work. I'll talk to you later, okay?"

"Okay."

Kelly clicked her phone off, grabbed her purse and lunch, and walked into the school. She opened her classroom, walked inside, and turned on her computer. Several messages showed in her inbox. She clicked the first one. It was one of her fellow language arts teachers asking her if she was pregnant. The next was from the curriculum teacher asking if there was anything she could do to help Kelly. Kelly didn't click the next. She shook her head. Boy, word sure travels fast. It's a good thing I talked to Harold last night. And I'm glad he went ahead and told the girls.

Kelly walked to the whiteboard and wrote her bell ringer for the day. Ironically, her junior class students were reading *The Scarlet Letter*. Though there was no sin involved in Kelly being pregnant, it still felt a little weird for her and her daughter to be pregnant at the same time. And Kelly still felt a little old.

The bell rang, and Kelly mentally prepared herself for the questions that were sure to come from student after student as the day progressed. She walked to her desk to be sure her worksheets were ready for the day. As expected, Logan was the first student in the room.

"Hey, Mrs. Smith." Logan dropped his books on the desk and walked toward Kelly.

"Hi, Logan. How was your three-day weekend?"

"It was good. My parents made us drive to Pennsylvania to visit my grandparents. Kind of boring, but it was okay."

"That's good." Kelly arranged the worksheets on her desk in order that she would need them.

"Can I ask you a question, Mrs. Smith?"

Oh boy, here it comes. "Sure. Go ahead."

"I heard you're pregnant. Is that true?"

Kelly let out a long breath. "Yep. It's true."

"Cool." Logan nodded. "My mom's having a baby next month."

"Really?" Kelly peered at Logan. "How old is your mother?" She shook her head. "I mean, it doesn't matter. . . ."

"It's okay. My mom's forty-three. She said the little guy was a bit of a surprise."

"Oh." Kelly's mind raced. She felt so old, so awkward having a baby at thirty-eight. Of course, Logan's mom wasn't having a baby the same time as her daughter.

"Yeah. It was a little weird because my older brother's already married with a kid. So his kid will be older than her uncle."

"Really?" Kelly drank in the information. Maybe she and Zoey weren't such an anomaly after all. The second bell rang and Kelly motioned toward Logan's seat. "It was nice talking to you, Logan, but we better start class."

Kelly walked toward the front of the room. *Thanks for that, God. I needed to know that someone else is going through close to the same thing as me.* She looked at her class, stopping at Logan. *Maybe I should call Logan's mom today, and tell her how much I enjoy having him in class.*

❧

Harold could hardly wait for the nurse to call them back to the room. He gripped Kelly's hand in his. He couldn't wait to find out her due date. Kelly said they might even be able to hear the baby's heartbeat. Harold had never heard a baby's heartbeat—well, except Zoey's baby, but this would be his baby.

He couldn't believe the emotions he felt over Kelly's pregnancy. He wanted to protect her, to make sure she ate properly, rested properly. He didn't want her to clean the bathrooms for fear the fumes would be too strong. Brittany had complained awhile about it, but he'd held firm that she, he, and Candy would take turns cleaning the bathrooms.

A young, light-haired woman opened the door leading to the examining rooms. "Kelly Smith."

Harold jumped up. He turned to Kelly, grabbed her hand, and helped her up. "Come on, hun."

Kelly giggled. "Harold, you're silly."

He nudged her forward, and they followed the woman back to the room where Zoey had her ultrasound. "I don't know if Marge called and told you, but the doctor wants you to have an ultrasound before he sees you." She looked at Kelly's chart. "It says here you had your tubes tied five years ago."

Kelly nodded, and Harold could feel she'd become nervous. Harold had no idea that an ultrasound would be a bad thing. *God, please let our baby be okay.*

The woman smiled. "Don't worry. It's just a precaution." She handed Kelly a half paper, half tissue blanket. "Go ahead and undress from the waist down. The ultrasound technician will be back in a minute."

Harold sat in an empty chair, while Kelly slipped out of her skirt and placed the blanket over her waist. He studied his wife. "Do you feel okay?"

"Yes, Harold. I'm sure everything is fine."

He could tell by the lilt in her voice that she was nervous. "You've never had an ultrasound this early before, have you?"

She shook her head.

Harold moved his chair closer to her. "Talk to me, Kelly. Be honest with me. You're scared."

She sighed. "I am scared. I'm older. I'm more tired than I've ever been."

"Is that normal?"

Kelly shrugged. "I don't know. Probably."

The nurse-technician-whatever she was called walked into the room. "Hello, Mr. and Mrs. Smith. How's Zoey doing?"

"Fine." Kelly's voice sounded weak. "It's a little funny to have me in here now, huh?"

"Don't worry about that." The woman patted Kelly's leg. "Babies are blessings."

Harold listened as the woman explained this ultrasound would be different than Zoey's because Kelly was so early in the pregnancy, but she assured them everything would be all right. Harold watched his wife for any signs of pain, but she seemed fine and he simply squeezed her hand to show her that he was supporting her.

Once again, the blank screen came alive with various shades of blacks and grays. Their baby didn't look the same as Zoey's had. Zoey's baby looked like a real baby, one a guy could hold. His baby's head was a lot bigger than the rest of his body. His arms and legs were there, but they seemed so scrawny.

Just as she had with Zoey, the technician clicked several places of the baby's image, measuring the head, the arms, the legs.

"Well, what do we have here?" the woman said.

"What?" Harold leaned closer to the screen. He couldn't see anything. He didn't know what he was looking for. He glanced at Kelly. She appeared confused and worried. He gently kissed her forehead.

"Hang on. Just a sec."

The woman moved the ultrasound instrument a little bit, and Kelly winced.

"What are you doing?" Harold demanded. He knew he sounded fiercer then he should, but the woman needed to spit out what was going on.

"Hang on." She touched Kelly's leg. "I know this is a bit uncomfortable, but I think—yep, there it is." She pointed to the screen. "Looky there."

"What?" Harold peered at the screen. He didn't know what he was looking at. Another round circle in Kelly's stomach. What was that? What was wrong?

Kelly gasped. "You're kidding."

The technician giggled. "Not kidding, Mrs. Smith. Do you know what that is?"

"What?" Harold wanted to scream at the two of them. What was wrong with his wife?

"Harold." Kelly grabbed his jaw and tugged at his face until he gazed into her eyes. Tears pooled in them once again, and Harold felt mad with anxiety.

"What is it, Kelly?"

"We're having twins."

"Twins!" Harold jumped out of his seat. "Two babies."

The technician looked at the screen. She started pushing buttons again, measuring the head, arms, and legs of his second child.

"Kelly!" Harold leaned over and kissed her forehead. "Two babies."

Tears streamed down her cheeks. "Harold, what will we do with two babies?" This time it wasn't fear that sounded in her voice. A slight giggle sounded behind her words.

"We're going to love them." Harold pumped his fist. "I'm having two babies. Two boys."

"Or girls," Kelly said.

Harold leaned toward the screen again. "Can you tell that yet?"

The technician laughed. "Not yet."

Harold gazed back at his wife. "Two babies, Kelly! We're having two babies!" He kissed her forehead, her nose, then finally her lips.

"Ahem." The technician cleared her throat.

Harold looked over at her, and the woman smiled. He gazed back at Kelly. "You've made me the happiest man alive."

Kelly laughed. "You say that until we're waist high in stinky diapers and dirty bottles."

"I'll say it then, too. I love you, Kelly Smith."

"I love you, too, Harold."

Epilogue

Kelly gazed around the room at the collection of family members who'd come to celebrate her day. It was like déjà vu. Her parents, in their mid sixties, still looked young and lively—and very much in love. Her father gazed at his wife and winked as he ran his hand through his salt-and-pepper hair, his striking blue eyes sparkling. She gave him a sweet smile in return. Despite battling arthritis, Kelly's mother wore her hair and makeup with perfection, and the spry woman was still as stylish and trendy as a woman in her thirties.

One year ago Kelly wasn't even engaged to Harold. Now, she was married—she twisted in her seat—pregnant, and about to pop, and her grandson sat nestled in her daughter's lap. Though Cam and Sadie were little Micah's legal mom and dad, when they visited they always allowed Zoey to take care of him. Soon, Kelly's oldest daughter would be living in Wilmington and going to college there.

The babies within her womb seemed to fight more fervently for space, and Kelly was anxious for the month to pass so that she could nestle her new children.

Harold and the girls had finished the babies' room just a week before. He'd been so protective that the only thing he allowed Kelly to do was pick out a theme. He wouldn't let her paint, hang curtains, nothing. She got to watch. She didn't complain. Carrying twins at thirty-eight, now thirty-nine, had not been the same as carrying a single child at the ages of twenty, twenty-two, and twenty-six.

Harold walked out of the kitchen. He placed his hands over Kelly's belly. "How are my guys doing?"

Kelly chuckled. "You do realize they could be girls."

Harold shrugged. "Okay, or girls."

"Do you wish we'd found out the sex of the babies?"

Harold kissed the top of her head. "Nah. I don't care either way."

"Is that why you put up a train set in their room?"

"Girls can like trains, too."

Kelly shook her head. She shuffled in her seat again. "These kiddos are killing me today."

Concern traced Harold's features, and Kelly noted the light gray wisps of hair he'd gotten in the year since they married. "You need to lie down?"

"No, I'll be fine."

Before Harold could say anything else, Brittany and Candy walked out of the kitchen holding Kelly's cake. The entire top of the pastry seemed to be on fire, and Kelly wondered how a woman her age would ever keep up with two active babies. *I'll be leaning on You big-time, Lord.*

This year she'd had a lot of practice at putting her full faith in her heavenly Father. It had been a time fraught with trials of every kind. She looked around the room at the family God had given her. Her gaze rested on her sweet husband. God had also filled her life with more blessings then Kelly could count.

"Time to blow out your candles," Candy said.

Kelly pushed her way to a standing position. "Happy birthday to you. . ." echoed through her home, and Kelly sang along with the family. Once the song was finished, Kelly closed her eyes, made a wish, then blew out the candles.

She opened her eyes and grabbed the bottom of her belly. "Uh-oh."

Harold jumped up and grabbed her shoulders. "Kelly, what is it?"

"My water just broke."

❧

Harold stood at Kelly's side as the doctors performed the emergency C-section on his wife. Initially, they'd wanted him to stay out, but Harold wouldn't have any part in it, and when Kelly also voiced her desire for him to stay with her, the doctor had finally relented.

He kissed the top of Kelly's forehead. "It's going to be okay."

"It's too early."

"Only five weeks early." Harold tried to sound confident.

Tears streamed down Kelly's temples. She was so scared, more scared than he'd ever seen her. He wanted so much to take her fear away, to do whatever he had to do to make sure that Kelly was safe and felt secure. Right now, all he could do was whisper words of comfort in her ear.

"Pray for me," she whimpered.

"Okay." Harold gently rested his forehead against Kelly's. "Please, dear Jesus, wrap Your arms around Kelly. Give her peace. Let our babies be okay. Bring them into the world strong and healthy. Let them thrive. Help us be good parents to them. You have given them to us. Be with Kelly, Lord. I love her."

He lifted his head and kissed her forehead again. She whimpered slightly then murmured, "Thank you, Harold."

Harold kept his gaze focused on his wife. He was too nervous to look at the doctor and nurses. There were so many in the room. He didn't look up, but he could feel the people who stood beside tiny baby beds, ready to whisk his children away if necessary.

A moment passed and he heard a baby cry. Excited, he looked at the doctor. The tiny red child squealed at the top of its lungs. "One girl."

Before Harold could fully focus or even respond, the doctor handed the child to a nurse, reached down, and pulled out his second child. This one was smaller, but the wails were just as strong. "A second girl," the doctor said.

Kelly's sobs of joy forced his attention back to her. He brushed her hair away from her face and looked back at his babies. "Kelly," he whispered against her ear.

Her laugh was hesitant and filled with emotion. "I told you we could have girls."

Worried for his wife, Harold stayed close to her side. He watched as the nurses wiped off his daughters, cleaned out their throats, and weighed them. He thought of flighty moods, the crazy hormones, the tantrums, the arguments, the hair spray and makeup, the outfit checks, and phone calls from boys. He thought of the gray hair that had formed since marrying Kelly. The proof that he loved and lived with a crew of women.

"You said for better or for worse."

Harold gazed at his wife, then looked back at his two daughters. He'd have five daughters now. When Zoey came home to visit, he'd live with six women. He turned back to Kelly. "Two daughters." He wiped the tears from her temples with the back of his thumbs. He thought of soft kisses, sweet hugs, and adoring gazes. *Daddy's girls.* He smiled. "I can't think of anything better than a home full of girls."

GAINING LOVE

Dedication

This book is dedicated to one of the sweetest women I know, my sister-in-law, Laura Miles. Laura, I am so thankful God placed you in my family. You are a wonderful Christian, wife to my brother, and mother to my precious niece and nephews. You are a treasure!

Chapter 1

I'm afraid you're going to have to lose weight."

Mark White cringed at the doctor's words. A decade before, when Mark was a high school football star, those would have been the last words uttered from a physician's lips. He glanced down at his soft center; it had once been firm and strong, sporting a much-coveted six-pack. His buddies often teased him about the excess weight when they got together for Monday night football or Boston Celtics basketball games, but he wasn't the only one who'd put on a few pounds since his late teens and early twenties. In good-natured fun, they all goaded each other now and then.

"Forty pounds would be ideal," continued the dark-haired, physically fit doctor who was probably fifteen years Mark's senior. "And I'm going to give you a prescription. Normally I allow my patients to attempt to alter their diet and exercise first. But your blood pressure is simply too high for me to feel comfortable with that."

Mark swallowed, concern creeping up his spine. When Mark was only a senior in high school, his father died at age forty-two from a stroke. The loss nearly devastated his mother as she cared for Mark's younger sister, who was battling leukemia. Pushing the mountain of memories to the back of his mind, Mark focused on the doctor. The man ripped the prescription off the pad.

"I'm going to start you at a small dose." He scribbled on yet another sheet. "You'll have to take a water pill, which will keep excess fluids away from the heart, but it will also make you urinate often. My suggestion would be to take it in the morning." He ripped that sheet off as well and handed it to Mark. "I want to see you in a month to be sure the medicine is working. Do you have any questions?"

Mark stared at the prescriptions. He hated medicine. His house had been burdened by bottle after bottle his last two years of high school. Blood pressure pills for Dad. Medicines for Maddy's leukemia. Anxiety tablets for Mom. To this day, Mark would hardly ever take a pain reliever for a headache. He normally just tried to squeeze in a quick nap. After all, it wasn't as if his social calendar bulged from abundant activity. Other than Monday night football with the guys and his men's Bible study on Thursday, mainly all Mark did was work, attend church, and spend time with his mom and Maddy.

Mark looked up at the doctor. "No. I don't have any questions."

"Okay then." The doctor extended his hand. "I'll see you in a month."

After accepting the handshake, Mark watched as the doctor walked out. Slipping off the patient bed, Mark looked at himself in the full-length mirror beside the doctor's chair. To see him in his dress slacks and shirt and tie, no one would believe Mark had forty pounds he needed to shed. He was a big guy, six foot five. He was an ex-football player who still sported the broad chest and shoulders as evidence.

But Mark knew he was soft. Too soft. His knees and ankles hurt when he tried to run, especially the left leg, which had been broken his last football season. He felt almost as strong as he'd been in high school, but he also winded easily. At times his heart seemed to beat faster, harder than it should.

At night, when he took off his banker's monkey suit and changed into a comfortable pair of long shorts and a T-shirt, Mark could see the extra weight. And he hated it.

With a sigh, he walked out of the room and to the front desk, where a young blond-haired woman took the sheet from his hand. With barely a glance, she smiled at him then looked at her computer screen. "Dr. Carr wants to see you back in a month."

Mark studied the receptionist as she scanned the available appointments. Not too many years ago, the woman probably would have giggled and flirted with him, and Mark would have sucked in the attention. *That was before I accepted Christ into my heart.*

And before I gained all this extra weight.

Mark inwardly chastised himself for such superficial thoughts, and yet the physical concern was not to be taken lightly. His father had packed on an extra hundred pounds in the last few years before he died. The doctor had warned him repeatedly that his blood pressure was out of control. Mark didn't want to die young as his father had. God had a plan for Mark's life, even if it never involved anything more than working at the bank and caring for his mom and sister. He wouldn't devastate them the way his father had.

"How about this day and time?" The receptionist handed him a reminder card.

"That will be fine." He took the card and turned to the door. Making his way to his car, he spied a fitness place. *First step: Join a gym.*

Mark drove to one of Wilmington's largest fitness facilities. *It shouldn't be too busy. Not yet anyway. With Thanksgiving in a few weeks and Christmas over a month away, people won't want to think about their waistlines until New Year's.* Walking inside, he couldn't help but notice that most of the people who appeared to be around his age—in their mid- to late twenties—seemed physically fit. The flabby ones were a decade or more older than him.

Out of the corner of his eye, Mark saw an obese man trying to bench press a weight that Mark would have snubbed his nose at when he was a teen.

"You can do it." A gorgeous redhead stood beside the man, encouraging him. "Come on. Just a little farther."

Mark watched the man's face redden as he held his breath, trying to get the weight to the bar. The woman lifted her hand over the bar, ready to help him if he couldn't push it all the way up.

She doesn't look strong enough to lift that weight, especially if the guy can't do it.

The crimson color of the guy's skin deepened until Mark feared a vein would burst in his head. The bar started to tilt, and before Mark could process what was happening, the tiny redhead lifted the bar up and set it in its place. The man sat up, straining for breath.

"You got five reps in." The pretty trainer patted his back. "You did good."

Mark looked at the bar. The guy couldn't have been benching more than 100 or 120 pounds, and he was a young guy. Probably younger than Mark. *The extra weight must make him soft.*

The thought of some young cutie having to lift a bar off him flashed through his mind, slamming his ego. God had changed Mark over the years, and he'd grown in leaps and bounds in the humility department. He glanced at the red-haired woman who couldn't weigh more than his left leg. If she had to spot him—actually lift a weight off him—well, a man had his pride.

Mark turned toward the door. He couldn't join this gym. He'd have to work out at home. Start running. Buy a bench. Check out exercises on the Internet. He'd talk to his buddies, Bruce and Chris. They might have a good idea of where he should start.

"May I help you, sir?"

Mark pivoted toward the voice behind him. The man, though probably a little older than Mark, appeared to be in terrific shape.

"Are you interested in joining our facility?" The man gestured around the expansive room.

"I was thinking about it, but I may just try going at it on my own." Mark started to turn back toward the door.

"At least let me give you a tour. Show you what we offer."

Mark turned back around and scanned what he could see of the place. A vision of telling his mom he would be taking blood pressure medicine shot through his mind. He looked back at the guy. "Okay. What do you offer?"

❧

Zoey Coyle set her shoulder bag on the table then dropped into the chair. Overwhelmingly whipped, she'd already led two personal training sessions and a water aerobics class. She looked at her watch. It was only noon. "Only five more hours," she grumbled as she pulled a turkey and lettuce sandwich on wheat bread and an apple from her bag.

One of the three credit card bills she'd received in the mail that morning stuck to the sandwich baggie. After pulling it off, she reached into the oversized purse and grabbed the other two. Putting the envelopes to the right of her lunch, she focused on retrieving her sandwich. She arranged the lettuce until it fit just right between the slices of bread then took a bite.

The sandwich had little taste already, but when her gaze kept wandering to the bills at her right, Zoey found it difficult to swallow. She rolled her eyes and scooped the bills into her hand. *Just get it over with. Stewing over it won't change how much you owe.*

Sliding her fingernail beneath the envelope's flap, she noted her acrylic nails were almost in need of a fill-in. Actually, with Christmas coming, she'd want to get red tips in celebration of the season. *I can't think of that right now. How much did I put on these cards this month?* Zoey tried to pinpoint in her mind her various shopping excursions. She hoped the totals wouldn't be as bad as the nudging feeling she had deep down in her chest.

She opened the first. The bill was higher than she'd expected, and it should have been the smallest one. Her heart fell. Before she could talk herself out of it, she opened the second and third. Staring at the totals, she reached for her sandwich and took a big bite. "Over a thousand," she mumbled.

Shaking her head, she shoved the envelopes back into the bottom of the bag. How had she gotten herself into so much credit card debt? She thought of the trip she'd made to the mall to buy a new pair of tennis shoes, but she couldn't resist the sale and bought a couple of pairs of casual shoes as well. Her mind then drifted to the trip she'd made to buy a winter coat, when she'd also bought a dress that caught her eye. She couldn't even remember all the cute outfits she'd bought for her precious Micah. And if Zoey bought something for Micah, she had to buy a little something for Ellie, too. Then she'd usually end up getting a gift for her little twin sisters.

She scooped up her bottle of water and took a long drink. There was no sense in reliving every shopping trip she'd made. It was time for action. She smacked the bottle down on the table. *If I work an extra day per week for the next two months, and only take five days off at Christmas break to visit Micah. . .*

The thought nearly ripped Zoey's heart in two. Since she'd started college, she'd spent every break staying with her mom, Harold, and her younger sisters. And she enjoyed seeing them, but it was Micah, her precious three-year-old, she treasured visiting the most.

At seventeen, Zoey had been rebellious toward God and her mother.

Eventually she'd ended up pregnant. God used that time to woo her back to Himself, but Zoey still faced consequences. One of them was she knew she couldn't care properly for her unborn child. She allowed her uncle Cam and his wife, Sadie, to adopt him.

The moment she handed her son to Sadie washed over her anew. It felt like she'd pried off a vital part of her body and given it willingly to someone else to nurture and love. She had to trust someone else with a piece of herself. She'd never felt such a connection with another human being as she'd felt with Micah. And yet she'd handed him over to her aunt Sadie. It had been the hardest choice she'd ever made.

Only five days. The mounting credit card debt was proof enough that Zoey wasn't ready to care for anyone in addition to herself. Because of her lack of restraint, she'd have to work extra hours to get rid of the balances before she graduated from college in May.

I need to learn to do better with my money, because my paycheck as a dietician won't be very much higher than it is now. The monthly inner scolding hadn't seemed to help her refrain from using her credit cards. Aside from cutting them up, the thought of which sent her heart fluttering and made her hands clammy, Zoey didn't know what to do to make herself stop completely.

"Zoey, how much longer is your lunch?"

Zoey startled at the voice of her manager behind her. She turned toward the man who was double her age but looked like he'd just stepped out of a body-builder magazine. "Uh, what time is it?" She glanced from him to her watch. "Wow!" She took a big bite of her sandwich. "Only ten minutes," she mumbled through her full mouth.

"Okay, good. I have a new client for you."

Zoey nodded. " 'Kay." She took an oversized bite of her apple. Having a new client would help her pay down some of her debt. *I know what I'll do to stop spending. I'll put my cards in my dresser. That way they're still available for an emergency, but I won't be able to use them when I run over to the Concord Mall.*

She took a long swig of her water, practically shoving her food down her throat. She took two more bites of her sandwich and another gulp of water.

Or maybe I could stick them in a bowl of water and freeze them. Didn't I see that on a movie one time? She stood and slipped her bag onto her shoulder. After throwing away her trash, she took another bite of apple then pitched it as well.

Of course, I'll still need to make myself stay away from Internet shopping. My credit card number just pops up right before my eyes for a few of my favorite places. Zoey growled as she walked into the employee locker room and put away her bag. Making her way back to the main fitness area two minutes before her lunchtime officially ended, Zoey scanned the room for her manager.

She found Zeke, noting the supertall man beside him—a good five inches over six feet. She couldn't see the guy's face yet, but his height alone suggested he had to be at least two times Zoey's weight. *Spotting him on a bench press should be a lot of fun, if not impossible.* Zoey smiled at the thought, but she did enjoy a challenge.

Chapter 2

Hi. I'm Zoey Coyle." The adorable redhead Mark had watched earlier stood before him with her hand extended. Before Mark had a chance to move, she looked at Zeke. "I'm assuming he's my new client."

Oh no. Mark closed his eyes. *A pretty, tiny woman?* What was this manager, Zeke, thinking? Mark was gargantuan compared to her. He opened his eyes. Her wrist bone looked about as thick as his pinky finger. Mark realized she still waited for his handshake, so he grabbed her hand gently in his. Her grip was firm for a gal who couldn't weigh an ounce over a hundred, but still. . .

"Zoey, this is Mark White."

Zeke patted his back as he spoke to the small woman, who, now that Mark looked at her more closely, appeared to be younger than Mark's little sister. *How many years could she possibly be out of high school?*

"It's a pleasure to meet you, Mr. White." His trainer widened her stance and placed her hands on her hips in a way that suggested authority. "Did Zeke explain what we'll do first?"

Okay, so the gal wasn't in high school. Much too authoritative for that, but she couldn't be too many years over twenty. Mark cleared his throat. "You'd like to ask me a few questions first."

"That's right." The woman nodded to her manager. "Thanks for introducing us, Zeke. I'll take it from here."

Mark watched as Zeke walked away, realizing he'd forgotten his trainer's name. So stunned by her dainty appearance, he hadn't paid close enough attention. *The fact that she has large, dark chocolate eyes and the creamiest skin I've ever seen—not to mention her thick, full lips and face shaped almost like a heart—that has nothing to do with it.*

Mark shook his head. What was he thinking? Forty pounds of excess weight. That was what he needed to focus on.

"If you'll follow me, I'll get the paperwork we need and we'll head to the conference room."

Without a response, Mark followed her past the front desk and into a small room with a table and chairs. Various athletic and physical fitness posters adorned the walls. He also noted a scale in the far corner.

She's going to weigh me. The realization humbled him. Maybe he wouldn't have cared so much if he hadn't been in such good shape when he was younger or if she weren't so attractive. Since when did a man care about what he weighed? *But I do.*

"Go ahead and have a seat." She pointed toward a chair and she sat in one across from it. "Okay, your name is Mark White. If you don't mind, I'd like to call you Mark, and of course, you may call me Zoey."

"That's fine." Mark rolled her name around in his mind. He had never met a Zoey, except his aunt's dog, but he wasn't sure the trainer would be happy to know that.

"Your age?"

"I'm twenty-seven."

Zoey scribbled on the paper. "Yeah? When's your birthday?"

"April twenty-first."

"Well, how cool is that. I'll be twenty-two on the twenty-seventh." She chewed the tip of her pen, her gaze focusing upward. Taking the pen from her mouth, she grinned. "You're exactly six years and six days older than me. Cool."

Mark lifted his eyebrows. The innocent expression on her face, as well as her bubbly and straightforward disposition, intrigued him. "That is interesting."

She looked back at the paper. "We'll get your weight after I finish asking all the other questions."

Mark squirmed. He didn't want her to get his weight. He would have preferred to keep track of it on his own, but he knew that would defeat the purpose of having a trainer. According to Zeke, Zoey was the best he had. Mark hoped so. He didn't want to be on high blood pressure medication for the rest of his life. When he got his weight down and his diet controlled, he planned to see if Dr. Carr would take him off the prescription.

"So what do you do for a living? Does your job keep you active?"

"I'm a bank loan officer, so no. I pretty much crunch numbers all day."

Zoey huffed. "Me, too, but not for my job. For my spending habits." She swatted the air with her hand. A nervous smile tilted her lips. "Sorry. I don't usually make so many silly comments. I mean, I'm not *bad* with money; I just need a little more discipline." She shook her head. "I have no idea why I just said—let's just go on to the next question."

Mark smiled. Zoey was as nervous as he was. He wondered if she felt uncomfortable with asking so many personal questions or if she could tell he was attracted to her. *Could that even be possible? A gorgeous woman like her—*

No way. That wasn't a possibility, so he might as well get the idea out of his head right now. Trying to relax, he folded his hands together on top of the table. "I could always help you with that if you wanted."

"It's just I graduate from college in May and I don't want any debt."

"What are you majoring in?"

"Dietetics."

Mark leaned back in the chair. "I'd say you and I could help each other quite a bit. Not only do I need a trainer; I need a better diet."

Zoey cocked her head, studying him. "Have you recently been diagnosed with a medical condition?"

Mark nodded. "High blood pressure." He patted his pants pocket. "I have two prescriptions to fill."

"Your doctor didn't want to try diet and exercise first?"

"Nope. It's too high."

Concern etched her brow. "But you're so young."

Mark exhaled a long breath. "I know. My dad died from a stroke when he was only forty-two. He battled high blood pressure and obesity. I don't want to follow in his footsteps."

"I'd say not." Zoey stood to her feet. "Stand up."

Taken aback, Mark did as she asked, and Zoey felt his wrists and arms, a determined look on her face. It warmed Mark that she would care so quickly for the medical well-being of one of her clients. He wanted to think she found him attractive but pushed the ridiculous notion aside. She probably had young, hulky men swarming her all the time.

"You're definitely a big-boned man." She kept hold of his hand as she walked to the scale. "Let's see what you weigh."

He stepped onto the scale, cringing at the high number he saw. Forcing himself to smile, he patted his belly. "Definitely a big boy."

Without a word, she turned him around to measure his height. She scribbled on her pad again then placed it on the table. Touching his bicep, she smiled. "We can do this. Six foot five. Two hundred eighty pounds. If you do as I say, we'll shed those extra forty to fifty pounds in four months or less."

Mark warmed at her soft touch. Whatever she said, he'd do it.

❧

What am I doing? Zoey quickly removed her hand from the man's arm. Something about Mark drew her. Sure, he was handsome enough with his dark blond hair and deep brown eyes. So deep brown that Zoey found herself wanting to study them to guess the thoughts behind those pools. And his scent—whatever cologne the man wore attracted her like a strawberry to angel food cake.

But his weight, his sheer size—Zoey was normally drawn to men closer to her height and on the smaller side. And yet she was attracted to this hulk of a man. Really attracted.

"Let's talk a bit more." She motioned for him to sit in the chair again. "Have you had any injuries that would keep you from using specific exercise equipment?"

"I broke my left leg my senior year in high school. It bothers me at times when I run." She noticed a blush creeping up his neck. "It may just be because of the extra weight."

Zoey wrote down the information then finished her questions. She knew many fitness centers simply allowed their clients to fill out the form and then give it to the trainer to skim before the session. Zoey loved that Zeke required the face-to-face interviews. She almost always got a feel for the route she'd want to take with her clients.

"Can you swim?"

"Yes."

She studied Mark. "How well?"

"I was a lifeguard during the summers when I was a teenager."

"Perfect." She picked up the stack of papers. "We're going to start with swimming laps." She shuffled his information to the front page. "It looks like Zeke has set you up for Mondays and Wednesdays at 5:30 and Fridays at 6:30." She looked at Mark. "Tomorrow is Friday. Are you starting tomorrow or Monday?"

"Tomorrow."

A smile bowed her lips, and Zoey found herself looking forward to seeing Mark the following day. "Don't forget your swimsuit."

Mark grimaced, and Zoey laughed louder than she intended. "Don't worry. It will be fun."

Mark studied her for several moments, and Zoey felt heat rushing up her cheeks. She wished she could read the thoughts behind those mysterious dark eyes. A slow smile spread his lips as his eyes shifted to contain a glimmer of mischief. "Yes, I think it will be."

When Mark walked out the door, Zoey placed her hands on her cheeks. She could feel the warmth. Racing to the far wall, she peeked into the small mirror that hung there. Yep, her white, almost translucent complexion sported a nice beet shade. *Why did I have to get so embarrassed?*

Sighing, she glanced down at her watch. She was teaching water aerobics in twenty minutes. Barely enough time to get to her locker, change into her suit, and head to the pool area. She placed Mark's papers into the file Zeke had given her. *I'll take these home. Go over my notes. I'll look up some good recipes for people with high blood pressure.*

Zoey's excitement swelled as she walked into the locker room. She loved helping people come up with healthy menus for their specific medical needs. She couldn't wait to finish school and hopefully get a job in a hospital or possibly a nursing home.

Opening her locker, Zoey spied a new text message on her cell phone. *It's from Brittany.* Her heart raced as she thought of her younger sister and the choices she'd been making lately. She opened the text. "Out with Neil. Don't wait up," she muttered.

Zoey's heart plunged as she pushed a response as quickly as her fingers would move. "Think, Brit. Think. Go home."

She shoved her phone into her bag and scooped out her swimsuit. *God, what can I do or say to get Brit to think clearly?*

Zoey recalled an incident only one week before when her sister was crying on her shoulder because of the ugly things her boyfriend had said in front of their friends. Zoey had witnessed his inappropriate comments toward other women right in front of Brittany. Zoey simply didn't understand why her sister would allow someone to treat her that way.

Zoey thought of the boy she'd been head over heels in love with during her senior year of high school. Dark-haired, mysterious, older—she had thought he was the most wonderful person in the world. No one could convince her otherwise.

God, I don't want Brittany to go through what I've gone through. I don't want her to make the same mistakes as me.

"Can a mother forget the baby at her breast and have no compassion on the child she has borne? Though she may forget, I will not forget you! See, I have engraved you on the palms of my hands. . . ." As the scripture from Isaiah sifted through her mind, she could feel the Spirit's nudging to remember that Brittany's name was engraved on His palms as well.

Zoey grabbed a towel from the locker room closet and made her way to the pool. She would trust God and encourage and love her sister every chance she could. And for now she'd focus on the women in her water aerobics class.

Chapter 3

Mark glanced down at his watch. *One thirty,* he inwardly growled. He was thirty minutes over his lunch break. Betty, the bank's manager, knew that Mark had a doctor visit and might be late, but he never intended to be a full half hour late. There was no telling what his colleague Kevin Fink would say. The man seemed to find pleasure in goading Mark every opportunity he had. *I can hear Kevin now.* He pushed open the front door of the bank.

"Did your watch malfunction, White?"

Mark turned toward Kevin's voice. His coworker leaned against the door frame of his office. *Just as I expected. The guy always has something to say.*

"Were you waiting for me, Kevin?" Mark could hear the irritation in his voice. He forced himself to smile at Kevin. No matter what it was, be it clients, paperwork, even ties and haircuts, Kevin liked to annoy him. Occasionally the younger man would mutter about Mark's faith. It was those comments that Mark believed were the source of the animosity. Kevin had a problem with him because he was a Christian. Mark tried to show God's love to the guy.

Most days.

"Must be nice to come strolling in to work whenever you want." Kevin chuckled and winked at the teller they'd hired a month ago.

Mark knew the man tried to sound as if he were teasing, but Mark knew better. Too many times Kevin had gone behind Mark's back to make it look as if he could do a better job. *Which is why I'm glad two of my stronger qualities are organization and documentation.*

Before Mark could respond, Betty Grimes approached him and put her hand on his arm. "How'd your appointment go, Mark?"

"Blood pressure's a little high." He patted his belly. "Gotta lose some weight."

The gray-haired woman peered up at him through thick, small-framed glasses. "You don't want to mess with that, Mark. Do what the doctor says. You're too young to end up on medication."

Mark nodded, deciding not to tell the woman who treated him like a nephew that he had already been given two prescriptions.

"You know what?" Kevin snapped his fingers, the tone of his voice too syrupy. "We should have a 'biggest loser' contest at the bank."

Betty patted Kevin on the back. "That's a terrific idea."

Kevin beamed, and Mark wanted to barf. The man would do anything to gain the boss's favor. *If he'd focus more on doing his job and less on how to avoid it, she might. . .*

"I've been wanting to lose some weight for years," Betty continued.

"Oh no." Kevin shook his head. "You don't need to lose any weight, Betty. You look great."

Mark looked from Kevin to the short bank manager. Betty needed to shed several pounds, and the truth was she'd put on more weight in the years that Mark had worked there. Betty knew it. Mark knew it. Kevin knew it. Mark would never consider being cruel about a person's weight, but he wouldn't lie, either. He studied Betty. "I know I'll physically feel better if I shed a few pounds."

Betty's eyes glimmered. "Me, too." She tapped her lips with her index finger, a sign she was mulling her thoughts around in her mind. "I'll get some sign-ups together, write up some goals and rules. Maybe even come up with a prize." She turned back toward her office. "This was a great idea."

"Glad I thought of it," Kevin yelled toward her. He looked at Mark, a scowl contorting his face. "Think I'll sign up, too."

Mark frowned as he sized up his much shorter colleague. The man couldn't have weighed much over 160. "You really don't need to lose any weight."

"A little weight loss never hurt anyone."

❧

Zoey dropped the bags of groceries onto the countertop. She glanced at the clock while pulling a container of sliced turkey and a fresh tomato from a bag. *It's barely past five. I'd hoped I would catch Brittany before she left.*

A sinking feeling weighed Zoey's gut. Neil was not a guy her sister needed to be hanging out with. He was all brawn and little brains. And absolutely no faith. Zoey remembered the time he'd grabbed her sister's arm a little too tightly when they'd been having an argument. Though Brittany swore Neil had never hurt her, Zoey feared one day he might.

Saying a silent prayer on her sister's behalf, Zoey walked to the slow cooker and lifted the lid. The aroma of roast beef and vegetables encouraged a growl from her stomach. She poked the tender meat with a fork. "Just the way I like it."

As she grabbed a plate out of the cabinet, the doorbell rang. "Who could that be?"

She walked to the front door and peeked through the peephole. A smile formed on her lips as she opened the door. "Harold? What are you doing here?"

Her stepfather wrapped her in a hug that nearly stole her breath away. "I had a job in Wilmington today, and since I haven't seen my oldest girls in a while, I thought I'd stop by for a visit." He released her and sucked in a deep breath. "Mmm. Smells like I'm just in time."

"In a while? We just saw you last week. Remember, I had last Saturday off, and—"

Harold shrugged. "That's a while to me."

Zoey laughed as she motioned him inside. "You always seem to pick the right time. It's almost as if a bird tells you—"

He straightened his shoulders and rubbed his belly. "Not a bird. A man just knows when there's good food to be eaten."

"That's funny. 'Cause I talked to Mom today and told her I had a roast in the Crock-Pot."

"What a coincidence. I talked to your mom today, too, and she told me you had a roast in the Crock-Pot."

Zoey laughed. "Head on into the kitchen. You know where the plates are."

She followed Harold into the kitchen. They fixed their plates then sat at the small table in the living/dining room. Her stepfather prayed over their food then stabbed his fork into a potato. "So where's Brittany?"

"Out with Neil."

Harold stopped chewing and let out a sigh. The wrinkles on his forehead smoothed as he contemplated Zoey's response.

Thankfulness filled Zoey's heart for the man who cared so much about her and her sisters. Four years ago she felt only animosity and anger toward the man who seemed to try to steal her daddy's place only a few years after his death. But Harold's character, patience, and love for the Lord, her mother, and them had shone through until Zoey couldn't help but fall in love with the man as a second father.

Zoey rolled her fork between her fingers. "I've been praying for her, trying to talk sense into her."

"We've been praying, too." Harold stabbed a piece of meat. "Wish I could pop some sense into her, but she's a young adult. She knows God. She knows what is right."

Zoey couldn't help but grin as she thought of her and Harold's first meetings. "I know you wanted to pop some sense into me."

Harold raised one eyebrow. "The first time I saw you?"

Zoey nodded.

"No. The first time I saw you, I wanted to wash the black out of your hair and scrub it off your face."

Zoey smiled, though a twinge of pain mingled with guilt swept over her at the memory of her last two years of high school. She'd rebelled against God and her mother after her father's death, delving into dark thoughts, dark hair, dark makeup, dark clothes, dark friends. . . *Thank You, God, for pulling me out of that.*

The quick praise made her think of Micah, the consequence of her sinful actions. Pregnancy her senior year of high school hadn't been easy. Giving her baby to her uncle and aunt to raise had been excruciating. And yet God had used what she believed to be a punishment, a consequence, as an indescribable blessing. Cam and Sadie received a son they never would have been able to have on their own biologically; Zoey received a reestablished relationship with her heavenly Father and the opportunity to be a part of her son's life.

Zoey wiped her mouth with a napkin. "So how are Micah and the girls?"

"Micah is great. Nice, quiet little man who adores Cam and does everything his daddy asks him to do. The twins. . ." Harold pointed to his fully grayed hair. "Well, do you see the top of my head? They've put the gray up there."

"I thought I did that."

"You got it going. Rebecca and Rachel finished it out."

Zoey giggled, picturing her adorable half sisters.

"I'm not kidding. Do you know what those two little rascals did the other day? They figured out that if one of them holds the lock to the back door gate and the other one pushes, then they can escape the backyard." Harold rubbed his temples. "Your poor mother was trying to do the dishes when she looked out the kitchen window and spied the girls trying to get into the car. She nearly had a heart attack."

"They are—active. That's for sure."

"Active?" Harold shook his head. "The preschool teachers are already making their rooms Smith-twins-proof."

Zoey leaned back in her chair and laughed, knowing that Harold's comment was completely true. "I can't wait to get home to see everyone."

"Christmas break's in less than a month, right?"

Zoey nodded. She didn't have the heart to admit she wouldn't be able to stay the full time.

"So how is school going?"

"Good."

"Any new guys in your life?"

A vision of Mark slipped into her mind. She didn't know why. The guy was nothing like the kind of men to whom she was normally attracted. *Do I even know who I'm attracted to? I went for the dark, older guys in high school, and I've gone out with a few men in college, some muscular, but most small and thin. Who am I attracted to?* As soon as the question popped into her mind, she thought of the many conversations she'd had with God about His will for her life. The man she wanted to be attracted to was whatever man God had for her.

She glanced over at Harold. "No. No guys for me. I'm still waiting on God's guidance on that."

Harold patted her hand. "Good girl." He stood, scooped up his plate and hers, and headed toward the kitchen.

"I can do the dishes, Harold."

He scowled at her. "Do you really think I'd just show up for dinner without at least helping out with the dishes?"

"No. You wouldn't." Zoey joined him. He handed her clean dishes from the dishwasher and she put them away.

Harold rinsed off a dirty dish and stuck it in the top tray. "Try to bring Brittany with you when you come home, okay?"

"I will."

❧

Mark struggled into the way-too-small khaki pants. Minutes before, he'd pulled the pair off a hanger in the closet without considering that he hadn't worn them in a few months. *I've already ironed them. I'm going to wear them.* He sucked in a deep breath and fastened the button. "Got it."

He allowed a slow exhale as he adjusted the knot of his tie. "They're a little tight." He dug his index finger beneath the waist of the pants, flattening the white undershirt and the button-down dress shirt. Peering in the mirror above his dresser, he smiled. "But I got them on."

Opening his dresser drawer, he pulled out a pair of black socks, sat on the edge of the bed, then lifted his right foot to his left knee. Before he could get the sock over his foot, the button popped off his waistband and hit the mirror with a loud smack.

"That's just great." Mark stood and pulled off the pants. After wadding them up and tossing them on the floor, he grabbed another pair out of the closet. With exaggerated effort, he yanked out the ironing board and popped it open. He turned on the iron then turned and stared into the mirror. He snarled at his reflection.

Men weren't supposed to care this much about their physique. Many sitcoms paraded overweight men, making them known for their laziness, lack of common sense, or both. Those men seemed to welcome their obesity, allowing it to be the punch line of many of the jokes. "But I don't want to be a joke."

Mark stared at his too-thick waist and spongy thighs. He touched his biceps, noting their softness beneath the sleeve. "Once upon a time, I was strong. Rock solid."

His mind wandered to some of the reality shows he'd seen advertised. A lot of the men, many older than his twenty-seven years, were in supreme condition. They looked good, felt good, probably got good reports from their doctors.

Mark cringed at the thought. He'd talked with his mom on the phone last night, but he didn't tell her about the high blood pressure. Since his father's death she'd been taking medicine for anxiety and depression, and he didn't want to upset her or his sister. It was his job to protect them, not cause them to worry.

The light on the iron started to flash, notifying him it was hot enough. He picked it up and began pressing the pants, a size bigger than the khaki pair he'd thrown on the floor. Tonight he would start training with Zoey.

He frowned when he thought of the adorable redhead who would witness his struggle to get back in shape. Part of him wanted to call the gym and cancel. Remembering his inability to resist temptation at the fast-food restaurant last night, he shook the desire away. Yes, he would probably humiliate himself in front of the beautiful woman, but he didn't have a choice. He needed help.

Chapter 4

I need help." Zoey stared at the bag that held the new skirt and shirt she'd bought from her favorite department store.

Her trip to the Concord Mall had started in innocence. She simply needed to get a new set of acrylic nails. She'd gone to the bank, withdrawn only the amount needed for the nail technician, then parked right in front of the shop. *The only problem is the nail place is right beside my favorite department store, and they were having such a good winter sale.* She pulled the new clothes out of the bag. *And I didn't have a new outfit for Christmas, and these were on sale for 25 percent off. Then with the additional 20 percent off for using my department store credit card. . .*

She flopped onto the couch, allowing the new clothes to fall onto the coffee table. "I promised myself I wouldn't put another penny on my credit cards." She picked up the new pair of dangling earrings. "At least I bought these with cash," she said in an attempt to comfort herself.

It didn't work.

Frustrated, she stood up and walked into the bathroom. She turned on the shower. A headache had wended its way up her neck and into the back of her head. Stress, no doubt.

She stepped into the shower, allowing the hot stream to soothe the stress in her neck and back. She was a mood shopper, a stress shopper, a binge shopper. Whatever it was called, Zoey knew she shopped for the way it made her feel, not because she needed the items.

"God, this isn't good. I'm not glorifying You when I spend money I don't have. Forgive me, Lord. Show me how to use restraint."

Zoey turned off the water, wrapped a towel around her, then stepped out of the tub. "Before I head to the gym, I'll have to make a quick stop at the mall to take back the outfit."

❧

Zoey stared at the large red-and-white SALE signs plastered on the windows of her favorite store in the mall. She watched as an ultra-thin, thirtyish woman walked out the glass door. Her outfit, a name-brand red-and-white getup that Zoey had drooled over many times before, was impeccable. The woman's long blond hair was cut in perfect choppy layers well past her shoulders. And that purse! Zoey bit her bottom lip. *I practically had to throw myself out of the store to keep myself from buying that purse earlier today.*

She glanced down at the bag containing her new Christmas outfit. Pulling out the green-and-white-patterned blouse, she caressed the silky material. *The purse would have matched perfectly with Zoey's outfit. But if I had to charge to get this outfit, then I don't need it.*

She imagined walking into the store and placing the newly purchased clothes on the counter. What would she tell the clerk when she asked why Zoey was returning the merchandise? Zoey gazed into her rearview mirror. "I have to return these items because I put them on my credit card, and I have a problem with spending too much on my credit card, and so my conscience is telling me I have to bring these back."

She growled as she flipped the mirror away from her reflection. Her heartbeat quickened as she envisioned shoppers waiting impatiently behind her as the clerk scanned the clothes. *What if she has to call a manager?*

Zoey shook her head. She hated to be the center of attention, a 180-degree turnaround from the way she had been in high school. Wearing a dark ensemble every day, she had thrived on the attention, negative or positive, she received from her clothes and actions. Since Micah's birth, so much had shifted in Zoey's mind, heart, and soul. Now, the only group attention she could handle was when she led an aerobic class of some sort. She exhaled a long breath as she tucked the blouse back in the bag. "I can't do it."

She shoved the key in the ignition then turned on the car. She pulled out of the parking space, heading toward the road. "It was only fifty-five dollars. I really like the outfit." She tapped the steering wheel. "I'll just have to pay it off. Lord, help me not to spend any more."

❧

Mark had avoided the workroom all day. Betty told him she'd put a sign-up sheet for their "biggest loser" contest on the counter. He wondered at the timing, believing most employees wouldn't be interested in joining a weight competition before the holidays. To his thinking, January seemed to be a better time. Nevertheless, several times throughout the day Betty had slipped into his office to let him know who'd signed up so far. She had talked with the night custodian about the contest, and even he'd stopped by a few hours ago to sign up. It was a good thing. Too many of the people he worked with were overweight. They needed to encourage each other to live a healthier lifestyle. Still, it bothered him to admit his weight gain.

He looked up at the clock. He had to be at the gym in less than an hour. *I might as well get in there and sign up.*

Mark pushed open the door and spied Kevin signing the sheet Betty had left out. Mark frowned. "What are you doing, Kevin?"

He turned around and scowled at Mark. "Signing up for the competition. Just like I said yesterday."

"But I thought you were kidding."

"Why would I be kidding?"

"Because you're thin. You don't need to lose any weight."

Kevin moved closer to Mark. He straightened his shoulders, peering up at Mark. "You just don't want me to sign up because you know I'll beat you."

Mark blew out a breath. His colleague was wacko. The competition he felt with Mark was absurd. It made no sense. Their jobs were equal as far as position and pay, and to Mark's knowledge, no one higher up was planning to retire, allowing one of them to move up. "You're challenging the wrong guy, Kev."

Kevin poked Mark's belly and smiled. "Really?"

Fury raced through Mark's veins. He had no idea what his colleague's problem was, but he'd just about had all he could take. If a guy had poked him like that a decade before, Mark would have punched him in the face. He grabbed the pen from Kevin's hand then walked to the sign-up sheet and quickly scrawled his signature. "I guess we'll have to wait and see what happens, little man."

Kevin huffed. "Real Christian-like," he mumbled as he walked out of the workroom.

Mark pounded the side of his fist on the countertop. Once again, he'd allowed his colleague to get under his skin. And once again, Kevin was right. Mark acted anything but Christlike. Mark knew Christ didn't want him to be a doormat, but he also knew that Kevin routinely tried to goad him; therefore, the correct response would have been simply to turn the other cheek. Mark growled as he walked out of the workroom and toward his office. *Forgive me yet again, Lord. You've worked on my pride more than anything else over the years. Obviously, I still have some growing to do.*

He grabbed his things, locked his office, and headed out the door. All the way to his car and all the way to the gym, Mark prayed that God would help him be a better witness to his colleague. Once at the gym, he picked up his gym bag and jumped out of the car. "Help me focus on losing weight for the right reasons, and not just to beat Kevin."

He pushed open the door and inhaled the mixture of sweat, metal, and rubber. Despite the embarrassment he felt that a beautiful, young, tiny woman would be his trainer, he looked forward to this workout. He was ready to feel better.

A familiar figure caught his eye. He turned to the right and saw Kevin walking on a treadmill. His heart seemed to plunge into his gut. *Isn't it bad enough that Zoey has to train me? Now I have to share a gym with Kevin.*

The smart-aleck comments he'd have to endure sped through his mind. The last thing he wanted to do was train anywhere near Kevin Fink. The urge to turn around nearly swallowed him whole. It seemed whenever he walked into this gym, he wanted nothing more than to walk back out.

"Hey, Mark."

He turned at the sound of Zoey's voice. Her hair was pulled up in two knots at the top of her head. The style made her look younger and even more adorable. "Hi, Zoey."

"You ready to get started?"

"Sure."

"Okay. Head to the lockers and get changed. Meet me at the pool."

Mark nodded. He glanced at Kevin as he walked toward the locker room. The guy had already left his treadmill and was walking toward the pool. "That doesn't surprise me," Mark mumbled to himself. "It's going to be a long hour."

After changing into his swimming trunks, Mark walked into the pool area. Zoey was already in the water. After a quick glance around, he was surprised he didn't see Kevin anywhere.

"Okay, Mark. Go ahead and get in the water."

Surprised at the excitement he felt at swimming a few laps, Mark jumped in the water beside Zoey. The cold rush stole his breath, but within moments his body adjusted and the water felt pleasant and refreshing.

Zoey led him through a few warm-up water exercises that he'd never seen before. He wondered if they'd actually do any good, but he'd chosen to pay to have a trainer, so he'd do what she said.

She ducked her head under the water then smoothed her hair away from her face. Her clear complexion glistened in the water, and Mark found himself wanting to touch her skin with the back of his hand.

"You ready to start swimming laps?"

He nodded and smiled as she grabbed the side of the pool. "Are you going to swim with me?"

"Sure." She frowned. "We're in this together. I'll encourage you every step, or lap, of the way."

Mark had to admit he liked the sound of that, and there was something about the way she said it that seemed personal, as if she wanted to get to know him. Forget it, White. You're in dreamland. The knockout redhead is not interested in you. "Okay. So how many laps are we doing?"

She bit her bottom lip, an adorable puzzled expression on her face. "I'm really not sure. I'd like to start swimming some so that I can get a feel for how much you should do to start out."

"Okay. Let's go."

Mark pushed off the side of the pool. They swam one lap, then another, then another. Soon his legs and arms burned at the exercise. But it felt good. Better than he expected, and he found himself enjoying each stroke.

Finally finished, Zoey hopped out of the pool and sat on the side. "That was terrific, Mark. You're in better shape than I thought. We're going to get that blood pressure down in no time."

Mark jumped out and sat beside her. "You know what, that did feel great. I should have joined years ago." He shook his head. "I don't know why I didn't."

"Well, you're here now." Zoey stood and wrung out her hair in the pool. "Let's get changed and head for the weights."

"All right." Mark walked into the locker room. Already he felt stronger and healthier. *Thank You, God. This is a good thing.*

❧

Zoey patted Mark's shoulder. "You did great. The first session is over."

She watched as he wiped perspiration from his face with a towel. He blew out a long breath then looked up at her from the weight bench. Zoey's stomach flipped when his deep brown eyes peered into hers. "It felt great, too."

He stood to his full height and Zoey found herself craning her neck to look him in the eye. "You'll probably be pretty sore tomorrow, but—"

"I know," Mark said, interrupting her. He pounded his chest and lifted his right eyebrow. "But I'm a man, and a real man can take it."

Zoey laughed at his macho Tarzan impersonation. She'd spent only a little time with Mark, but already she knew he wasn't a chauvinist. Though he'd mentioned them only a few times, she knew he cared deeply for his mother and sister, and he'd treated her with the utmost respect since the first moment they met. *Although I'm pretty sure he was taken aback at the idea of a hundred-pound woman being his trainer.*

"Do you happen to have any recipes for people with high blood pressure?" Mark's question broke Zoey from her thoughts. She huffed and shook her head. "Yes. I found some last night, but I left them at my apartment."

"That's okay." Mark wrapped the towel behind his neck. "I was just going to take a quick shower here then run over to the grocery." He patted his temple with his index finger. "I'll just have to shop with my brain and not with my stomach."

"The first thing you need to do is stay away from the inner aisles. Try to buy as much as you can along the walls. That's where you'll find your fresh veggies and fruits, lean meats, and low-fat dairy products. And make a list. Try to get everything you need today so that you don't have to go back for a week, and—"

"Hello, Mark. I'm surprised to see you here." Zoey turned at the unfamiliar voice. "What a pleasant surprise." The thin, light-haired man gazed up and down her body in a way that made her want to ball her fist and smash his fake smile into his face. She loathed it when men treated women as objects, and no doubt a scowl twisted her face.

"Care to introduce me to your friend?" The words slipped through his teeth like honey, and yet repulsion overwhelmed her when the guy reached for her hand. She glanced at Mark, noting his tense posture and set jaw.

"Then I'll introduce myself." His much-too-soft hand wrapped around Zoey's. "I'm Kevin Fink. And you are?"

Zoey cleared her throat. Something about this man sent red flags waving through her mind. Call it a hunch, a sixth sense, whatever. When she was a girl, her daddy told her to trust her instincts. Her instincts warned her to stay clear of this one. Still, she had to be cordial. Trying to keep her tone friendly, she said, "I'm Zoey Coyle. I don't believe I've seen you here before."

More than she really saw it, she felt Mark move slightly away from her. The air seemed to seep from his chest when she introduced herself to Kevin.

"I just joined today." Kevin stepped closer, invading her personal space. "Believe me, you would have seen me before." His gaze traced her body again. "I would have made sure of it."

Disgusted, Zoey took a step back. She crossed her arms in front of her chest. He would not talk to her like that. Sure, he hadn't actually said anything inappropriate, but his gazes needed to be looking elsewhere. She opened her mouth to let him have it.

"I'll see you Monday, Zoey."

Mark's words stopped her. She looked at him, unsure what his tone and expression meant. He seemed angry, hurt, and embarrassed—all wrapped up into one big emotion.

He turned away from her, and Zoey stepped closer to him. "I wondered if you'd like me to go shopping with you."

Mark gazed into her eyes, a gentle look on his face; then his expression hardened and he looked away. "I think I'll go by myself."

He lifted his hand, and for a brief moment Zoey thought he might touch her cheek. She sucked in her breath, surprised at how much she wanted to feel his hand against her face. He lowered his arm. "Try to remember the recipes on Monday."

She nodded, unable to say anything. She watched as he made his way to the locker room. Something about the man—his kindness, his sweetness, she couldn't quite put her finger on it—drew her, and she wanted to spend more time with him.

"So, Zoey. . ."

She turned to face Kevin. The smile that stretched across his face reminded her of a villain about to get his way.

"I know a terrific deli a few blocks away."

"Thanks for the offer, Kevin. But I think I'll have to pass."

"Are you sure? They have the best chicken salad in all of Wilmington."

"I'm sure."

Zoey walked away from Kevin before he could ask her again. She could tell the guy wasn't used to taking no for an answer. And he was a good-looking guy. A lot of girls would probably be thrilled to go out with him, but she'd learned a long time ago that she had to base her choice of a mate on more than just looks. She needed a man of godly character.

Her mind drifted to Mark. He'd left so quickly when Kevin approached them. She thought he'd want her to go with him to the store. Several times during the session, she'd felt sure he was interested in her. *But I guess not.*

Zoey walked into the locker room, opened her locker, and pulled out her things. She'd wait until she got home to take a shower. She hefted her bag over her shoulder. *It wouldn't be the first time I was wrong about how a guy felt about me. Micah's proof that I'm not always the best judge of a man's motives. Which is why from now on, I do it God's way.*

She made her way out of the gym and toward her car. Her phone vibrated and she pulled it out of her bag. Seeing Brittany's name on the screen, she sighed. "Now if I could just get Brittany to do that, too."

Chapter 5

Having showered and dressed at the gym, Mark pulled a comb from his bag and headed toward a mirror. He grimaced as he ran the prongs across the balding spot on top of his head. Logically, he knew most people didn't notice. He was a tall guy, and it was a small spot at the very top. But he knew it was there, and he hated it.

"Hey, buddy." Kevin's voice sounded from the other side of the room. Before Mark could respond, a towel snapped and he felt a sting against his hip.

Mark turned and grabbed the towel from Kevin's grip. "Watch out, Kev, or I'll have to pay you back."

"Go ahead." Kevin spread his arms and shuffled his feet. "If you can catch me."

Mark rolled his eyes and tossed the towel back at Kevin. "Maybe another time. I've got to get going."

Kevin moved closer, nudging Mark with his elbow. "Hot date?"

Mark thought of the text message he'd received from Maddy before he got in the shower, asking him to join her and their mother for dinner. If he got out of here quickly, he could spend about an hour with his mom and sister before he headed to Chris's for the first Boston Celtics game of the season. "Not exactly."

"Didn't think so." Kevin snorted, and Mark growled. Kevin rolled the towel then rested it on his shoulder. "But I do."

Mark tried to act uninterested, but his chest squeezed at the thought that Kevin Fink might have a date with Zoey. *I shouldn't have walked away. Why didn't I tell her she could get groceries with me?*

He inwardly berated himself for his thoughts. Something had changed in him over the last several years. He'd become a Christian, and he loved the Lord with all that was in him. He strived to be a good son, brother, church member, and employee. He always did the right things, said the right things, even tried to think the right things, but something was missing. Something—

Kevin's whistle interrupted Mark's thoughts. "That redheaded trainer of yours is hot."

Bile rose in Mark's throat. "Is that who your date is with?"

"I wish." Kevin snorted again. "Nah. I asked one of the chunky girls in the aerobics class out. She'll probably cost me a fortune to feed, but who knows, maybe I'll—"

Mark raised his hand before Kevin could finish the sentence. He didn't want to hear another word from Kevin's lips. "Sorry, Kevin. I've got to get out of here."

Kevin shrugged. "Whatever." He turned toward the shower. "Hey, if you see a plump, dark-haired girl out there. . ." He touched his eyelid. "She's wearing some seriously dark green makeup. Tell her I'll be right out."

"Sure thing." Mark walked out of the locker room. A woman fitting Kevin's description sat in a chair outside the door. Her eyes brightened and she sat up straighter when she saw him walk through the door, until she realized he wasn't Kevin and she looked away.

I definitely don't attract the ladies anymore. Why would I ever think an amazingly gorgeous woman like Zoey would give me the time of day?

Starting to head toward the door, he glanced back at the woman who waited for Kevin. His conscience ate at him, as he knew his colleague had no decent intentions toward her.

Knowing the woman might decline, he exhaled as he turned back toward her. "Hi. I'm Mark." He extended his hand.

She shook it. "Myra. It's nice to meet you."

"I was wondering if you'd care to join me for a bite to eat."

The woman's face reddened, yet a full smile bowed her lips. "I'm sorry. I've already made plans."

What do I do? Kevin's less than honorable intentions raced through Mark's mind. Myra seemed like a sweet woman, and she was much younger than Mark had first realized. She probably didn't have the experience to spot the snake disguised as a man. *I can't lie.*

Even as the thought flashed through his mind, the words slipped from his lips. "Well, you see, Kevin is a colleague of mine."

The woman leaned closer.

"And—and something has come up at home."

Myra's expression fell.

"With his mother. And he asked me to tell you—"

"But my ride has already left." Myra glanced up at the clock. "She was heading to work, and now—" She pulled her cell phone out of her purse. "I'm not sure—"

"Why don't you let me take you to dinner?"

Myra bit her bottom lip. She took several deep breaths, her gaze shifting from the clock to her cell phone. "Okay. What did you say your name was?"

"Mark. Mark White." Part of him wished she'd said no. Her willingness to allow a complete stranger to take her to dinner needled at him. Kevin would not have treated this young lady well. He'd have taken advantage of her naiveté.

Mark walked her to the door then opened it and motioned for her to go out first.

"Thanks, Mark." She smiled up at him, her expression entirely too trusting.

"No problem. So where would you like to go?"

❧

Zoey almost hit the car parked in front of her when she saw Mark walk out of the gym with another woman. It was true that Myra was sweet and kind, and Zoey admitted she was kind of cute, but Zoey had thought for sure that Mark was attracted to her. She gazed in the rearview mirror. *And I'm prettier and thinner and*—

She looked down and shook her head. *Forgive me for my superficial thinking, God.* She wanted so much not to worry about wearing the best clothes, sporting the cutest nails, getting the trendiest haircuts, working out for the greatest body. *It's like I'm not comfortable in my own skin. Ever since I got pregnant. . .*

Once upon a time, appearances were the last thing on Zoey's list of concerns. She didn't care how messy her hair was, how dingy her clothes looked. She bit the inside of her lip. Maybe her thinking wasn't exactly right. Maybe she'd always been worried about appearances, only back then she was obsessed with not looking good.

"What makes me think like this all the time, Lord?" she whispered as she carefully shifted her car in reverse and backed out of the parking space.

"I could blame it on the television or the Internet or magazines or books." Zoey tapped the top of the steering wheel. "I could say it's because appearances seem to be all men care about."

She turned down the road leading to her apartment. "But I know those things aren't the problem. Sure, they encourage the problem, but they're not the source." She parked the car, scooped up her bag, and walked toward the front door. "God, my value has to come from You, and You alone."

She rustled through her bag to find her keys. "Why I am always throwing the keys back in my bag after I park in front of the apartment, I'll never know."

Her mind drifted back to Mark. Prettier than Myra or not, Zoey inwardly admitted she'd wanted her new client to be interested in her. She wanted to get to know him better. She had a feeling, deep down in her gut, that he was a godly man. Not superficial. Not self-seeking. But a man of integrity.

Her fingers found her key chain, and she yanked the keys out of her bag then opened the door.

"Zoey!" Brittany's scream nearly ripped off the ceiling.

Zoey watched, horrified, as Neil moved away from her sister on the couch.

Brittany wiped her mouth with the back of her hand. The lights were off, but nothing appeared to have happened. Yet.

"Time to go home, Neil." Zoey strolled into the apartment. She dropped her keys on the end table then walked toward the kitchen.

"You can't tell my guest what to do."

"Sure I can. You haven't paid your part of the rent for the last two months."

"That's because—"

Zoey raised her hands. "The reasons don't matter. I'm paying for the apartment." She pointed to her chest. "I'm asking Neil to leave."

Neil huffed and rolled his eyes at Zoey. "Whatever." He peered down at Brittany. The scowl on his face raised goose bumps on Zoey's skin. "You can make it up to me later."

He waltzed to the door, slamming it behind him. Zoey sighed at the relief she felt that he was gone.

"Why did you do that?" Brittany jumped off the couch and moved toward Zoey.

Zoey's heart fell as she noted two small dime-sized marks on each of Brittany's cheeks. She'd seen them before when Neil had grabbed her face, cupping her chin and embedding his middle finger and his thumb into her cheeks. "Where'd you get those bruises, Brittany?"

"What bruises?"

"The ones on your cheeks." Zoey gently touched the places.

Brittany's expression fell and she raced to the bathroom. Zoey knew they were fresh because the skin was still pink. She knew Brittany was checking to see how bad they were. "Just stay out of my life, Zoey."

"I'm worried about you. Neil's getting worse, and you seem to have more places—"

"You're wrong. You have no idea how good Neil is to me. Look in the kitchen. He brings me flowers. Takes me nice places. He loves me. You just judge him all the time. You all do."

Zoey frowned. "Who's 'you all'?"

"Mom. Harold. Everyone."

Zoey followed her sister into the bathroom. She leaned against the bathroom wall as Brittany started the shower. "Brittany, we all love you. We want what's best for you, and we're worried—"

"Neil says you don't. He says I should quit school and move in with him. Let him take care of me."

Zoey knew Brittany tried to sound strong, but Zoey detected the hint of fear in her tone. Taking a deep breath, Zoey knew if she blew up, she'd lose her sister's willingness to at least argue with her about it. "I hope you won't. You've wanted to be a teacher for as long as I can remember."

Brittany let out a slow breath. She looked into the shower stall, but Zoey saw the lone tear that slipped down her cheek.

Praying God would guide her words and soften Brittany's heart, she touched her sister's arm. "And I want you to stay here with me. I'll miss you if you leave."

Brittany swiped the tear away from her cheek. "Just leave me alone, okay?"

A retort begged to slip from Zoey's lips, but her spirit nudged her to be quiet. "Okay." On an impulse, she wrapped her younger sister, who was a good five inches taller than her, in a tight hug. "I love you, Brittany."

Brittany groaned, but she didn't push Zoey away.

Please, God. Please draw Brittany back to You.

❧

Mark's conscience ate at him as he tried to take another bite of the chicken salad wrap he'd ordered. Myra sat across from him chattering about gossip from her office. Not only was he fighting himself about the lie he'd told, but he was also trying to think of a good way to veer the topic away from her work grapevine.

My motive was pure. Mark inwardly tried to persuade himself against the guilt he felt. Kevin might have taken advantage of her.

The truth nudged at his heart. A lie never solved a problem or really protected someone. Myra believed he was interested in her, but he wasn't.

Tell her the truth.

Mark forced the bite down his throat then took a long drink of his lemon water. "Myra, I need to tell you something."

She flattened the napkin on her lap. "Well, sure. I've been yakking the whole time." She reached over and patted his hand. "I'm enjoying your company."

Heat raced up Mark's neck, and he feared it spilled across his cheeks. If the slight smile she gave him was any indication, he felt fairly confident his blush was noticeable and that she misconstrued it as attraction instead of guilt.

He cleared his throat. "I wasn't exactly honest with you."

She cocked her head to one side and furrowed her brow. "About what?"

He scratched the stubble at his jawline. "About Kevin not being able to go out with you tonight."

A slight giggle slipped from her lips. "I know."

"You know?" Mark's heart seemed to shed half the pounds he was attempting to lose. Maybe Myra was smarter than he'd originally believed.

"I could tell you were fibbing about Kevin." She dabbed the corner of her mouth with her napkin then rested her elbows on the table and leaned closer to him. "I think it's really sweet that you wanted to go out with me so much. I'm really flattered."

Mark's heart sank. "It wasn't exactly like that."

She reached across the table and touched his hand. "It's okay. You don't have to be embarrassed."

Peering at her, he leaned back in his chair. "I'm sorry, Myra, but you're mistaken."

She frowned. "You mean you didn't want to go out with me?"

Slowly he shook his head. "You seem to be a really nice person, but no, I didn't want to go out with you as a date. We could be friends, but—"

She glared at him. "Then why didn't you just let me go out with Kevin?"

He swallowed. How could he say this without gossiping about his colleague? "He didn't have the best of intentions."

She squinted her eyes. "And you know this because. . ."

"Because he told me in the locker room."

She leaned back in her chair, studying him for several moments. "Let me get this straight. You acted like you were interested in me, convinced me to leave Kevin at the gym, because he didn't have the best of intentions. What were your intentions, Mark?"

"To protect you." *God, help me here. Show me what to say to convince her that I was trying to do the right thing.* Uncertainty filled him. Obviously, lying hadn't been the right thing.

"Why? You don't know me." She crossed her arms in front of her chest. "I suppose you thought since Kevin's a thin, athletic man, he wouldn't be interested in a fuller-figured woman."

"I never said that."

"But you thought it."

"No. I didn't think it, but—"

"But what?"

God, help. "But Kevin did."

"How do you know what Kevin thought?"

Mark shook his head. "No. It's what he said."

Fury washed over Myra's features. Finally, she understood that Kevin was the villain, not Mark.

"How dare you?" She pushed her chair away from the table. "How dare you say that to me?"

Puzzled, Mark stood and reached across the table to encourage her to sit down. "I was trying to help you, Myra. I was afraid you wouldn't see through his words and that he'd talk you into—"

"So not only am I fat, but I'm an idiot." Myra pushed his hand away. "Thanks for dinner, Mark. I hope I never see you again."

Before Mark could respond, she turned and walked toward the door. The waiter approached and handed him the ticket. "Man, never tell a woman she's heavy." He looked at Myra as she walked out the door. "She was kinda cute."

Heat rushed through Mark. "I didn't say she was heavy." He pulled out his debit card and handed it to the man. "Could you take care of this quickly? She doesn't have a ride home."

The man clicked his tongue. "Don't make that woman walk."

"I won't."

It seemed forever before the waiter returned with his card. Mark signed the bill then rushed outside. He didn't spy Myra anywhere. Wishing he'd gotten her number, he headed toward his car. Maybe she'd realized she didn't have a ride home and gone to stand beside his car.

A familiar sports car pulled up beside him. "Hey, buddy."

Mark peered into Kevin's vehicle. He noticed Myra sat beside him. "Listen, Myra."

"I think you've said enough for one night." Kevin's voice sounded firm, but Mark caught the hint of teasing in his tone. "My gorgeous date and I are going to catch a movie then maybe a little dessert."

Kevin winked and sped away. Mark's stomach turned. He'd missed having dinner with his mom and sister and going to the store. So much for trying to be a good Samaritan. He blew out his breath then opened his car door and slipped inside. A true good Samaritan would have handled the situation quite differently, with a whole lot more up-front honesty.

Mark drove to Chris's house. Bruce's car was already in the driveway. Normally, Mark couldn't wait to dig into the boneless wings and blue cheese dressing, nachos and salsa, and whatever delicious dessert Chris's wife came up with. She always had game night pity on Bruce and Mark since they were still bachelors. But tonight his stomach still turned at what had transpired with Myra and Kevin. And he couldn't seem to get his mind off Zoey.

"Hey, man." Chris opened the front door and high-fived Mark. He pointed toward the car. "Saw your headlights pulling into the drive. I was afraid you were going to be late. Tip-off is in fifteen minutes."

Mark took off his jacket and hung it on the coatrack. "Just running a little late."

"Where you been?" asked Bruce.

Mark walked into the great room, grabbed a soft drink off the table, then plopped onto the couch. Popping open the can, he figured he'd earned the high-calorie, high-sugar beverage. "I joined a gym and had my second workout tonight."

"No way." Bruce leaned forward on the recliner and reached for Mark's biceps. "It'll take awhile to tone those babies up."

"Ha-ha." He took a long swig of the soft drink. "I just figured—"

"Does it have something to do with your doctor visit?" asked Chris.

Mark looked at the half-empty can in his hand. "Doc did tell me my blood pressure's a bit high."

"Maybe you don't need to be drinking that." Chris went into the kitchen then came back with a water bottle. He handed it to Mark. Feeling like a scolded boy, Mark took the drink and focused on the television. He'd known Chris since he was thirteen years old. Chris was there for him when he broke his leg, when his dad died. Chris knew. . . Mark stared at the water bottle and scowled. Sometimes, Chris knew too much.

Chapter 6

Zoey tried to focus on the road and ignore her younger sister as Brittany huffed for what had to be the fiftieth time.

"I can't believe I let you talk me into this." Brittany growled and shifted in the passenger seat of Zoey's car.

"It's Cam's birthday, and Mom is fixing a big lunch for the whole family. Even Grandma and Grandpa are going to be there. You should be, too."

"I don't mind lunch, Zoey," Brittany grumbled. "I just don't want to go to church."

"It's an hour. You'll live."

"But we'll be back next week for Thanksgiving."

"You'll live."

Brittany didn't respond; she just continued to shuffle in her seat and growl intermittently. Zoey fumed over Brittany's self-centered attitude. If the activity didn't revolve around Neil, Brittany wanted nothing to do with it. Zoey couldn't believe that her sister, the one who'd spent all of high school enjoying basketball games, schoolwork, church events, and outings with friends, was now so wrapped up in her boyfriend that she couldn't focus, even for one afternoon, on something or someone else.

Brittany's cell phone beeped. Her sister read the incoming text and responded to it. Zoey watched as Brittany's expression fell and her body seemed to slump farther into the passenger seat.

"Was that Neil?"

Brittany didn't respond. Her gaze remained focused out the windshield.

Zoey's gut twisted in a knot. "He's mad, isn't he?"

Brittany pierced Zoey with an expression of fury. "What do you care?"

"I care about you, Brit." Zoey touched her younger sister's hand. "I hate seeing what he's doing to you."

Brittany didn't respond, and Zoey prayed her sister knew, deep down in her heart, that what Zoey said was true. The ride was silent, but Zoey's heart continued to plead for God's mercy toward her sister. *Please, God, show her.*

Brittany's cell phone beeped again, and again Brittany responded. With each mile, Zoey felt her sister's tension grow. Zoey's spirit groaned in intercessory prayer within her, and she continued her silent plea for help for her sister.

Finally at the church, she led Brittany into the sanctuary.

"Brittany. Zoey." Harold wrapped his arms around both of them, smashing them into each other. "I'm so happy you both made it."

Zoey patted his back. "I'm glad to be here. I've missed everyone."

Harold released his grip on Zoey but held tight to Brittany. He guided her away from the family. Zoey knew he would try to talk to Brittany. And though he never believed it, Harold always knew just what to say, or not to say, to help her and her sisters see things more clearly.

Candy grabbed Zoey in a hug. "I'm glad you came. For one afternoon I'll have someone older than three to talk to."

Zoey laughed as she squeezed her fifteen-year-old sister. "You're smitten with those twins and you know it."

Candy waved her hands in front of her. "I didn't say I don't love them. They're just exhausting. You'll see."

Zoey grinned when she saw her mom and twin sisters walk into the sanctuary. Candy leaned over and whispered, "That's the third time they've had to go to the bathroom since we got here. Fifteen minutes ago!"

Chuckling, Zoey walked toward her mom and scooped one of the girls into her arms. "How are you doing?" She touched the tip of Rebecca's nose. The twin giggled and shifted in Zoey's arms.

"I'm so glad you made it." Her mother wrapped her arms around Zoey. "You two live close enough that we should be able to see you once a week. It's been almost three. We want to see you more."

"I agree." Zoey hugged her mom then put Rebecca back on the ground and winked at Rachel. "Our schedules are so crazy."

Her mom waved her hand in the air. "I know. I know."

Zoey noted that her mom hadn't had a manicure in quite some time. Her hair seemed a little longer than Zoey knew she liked to wear it. Zoey clapped her hands. "You know what? We need to have Harold watch the twins one Saturday and you and Candy can drive up to Wilmington and we'll all get our nails done and our hair cut."

"That sounds like a lot of fun," Candy chimed in from several pews in front of them.

"We'll plan it over Thanksgiving break." Her mom motioned toward the front pews. "But I think it's time to get started. We need to have a seat."

"Where's Micah?"

Her mother smiled. "Cam and Sadie will be here. Grandma is with them. They'll come in right on time. Not a moment earlier."

Just as her mother said, Zoey didn't get to see her son until just before the service started. She knew she'd get to spend time with Micah after church. She peered down the pew, feeling such thankfulness to be sitting beside Harold, her mom, and all her sisters. In the row in front of them were her grandparents, Uncle Cam, Aunt Sadie, Ellie, and her precious Micah.

He's grown so much. Zoey longed to touch the back of his sandy-red hair. He looked like such a handsome fellow in his brown corduroy pants, blue button-down shirt, and blue and brown sweater vest. Sadie always dressed Micah in the most adorable clothes. He always looked clean. His hair was always trimmed. But beyond appearances, Zoey knew Sadie cared for her son as fervently as Zoey would have. In a matter of minutes, the singing and announcements would end and Micah and the other three- to five-year-old children would leave to go with their children's church leader.

"Can I have a pen, Mommy?" Micah's sweet voice echoed through the sanctuary while one of the deacons made announcements, causing a few of the couples around them to turn and look at him. They smiled, but Zoey watched as Cam whispered in Micah's ear. Probably telling him to be quiet.

Sadie handed a pen to the little guy, but Micah threw it down. "I no like that one."

This time Cam lifted Zoey's son onto his lap. She couldn't hear his words, but Zoey knew Cam was telling Micah he couldn't yell out during church.

Micah started to squeal, and Zoey reached into her purse, finding a blue and a red ink pen. She handed them over the pew toward Micah, but he was already angry and smacked them out of her hand.

"Okay, little man, we're going to talk in the foyer." Cam's voice was firm, and Micah's protests grew louder.

Zoey rummaged through her purse. Micah didn't need to get into trouble. In only a matter of moments, the music would begin and the congregation would sing with the music minister; Zoey was sure he'd quiet down then. She whispered to Cam, "I may have a purple one. Just a sec."

Cam peered at Zoey. "He can't be rewarded for throwing a fit."

"Purple pen. I want purple," her three-year-old screamed as Cam headed toward the door with the boy.

Zoey's heart ached. He was just a little boy. It was hard to sit still during church. She glanced at Brittany, who continued to text back and forth with Neil during the service. Even her nineteen-year-old sister wasn't behaving as she should. Zoey didn't want Micah to be in trouble. She twisted the strap of her purse. Maybe he would have sat still with her. She'd wanted to offer to hold him, but they'd come in a bit late.

Sadie reached over the pew and patted Zoey's hand. "He's okay," she whispered.

Zoey let out a breath, intellectually knowing that Micah was all right and that he couldn't throw a fit in church and that Cam had to take him into the foyer to quiet him. But her heart still hurt because her little boy had gotten into trouble. *I wouldn't want him to be rude and disrespectful, either.* She looked at Sadie and nodded, and the older woman winked before turning back in her seat.

Sadie had been a true gift from God. Having been through the pain of giving up a child for adoption, Sadie knew just what to say and do to ease Zoey's aching heart through the decision. After the death of Ellie's adoptive mom, Cam's first wife, God allowed Sadie a second chance at being Ellie's mom when she and Cam fell in love then married. *I won't be able to be Micah's mom, but I am able to be in his life, and I know Cam and Sadie are good, loving parents to him.*

She focused her attention back on the pastor. After the service, she would relish the afternoon with Micah and her family.

❧

Mark enjoyed the excitement in his young friend Tyler's voice as they approached Timothy's Riverfront Grille. Today Mark, his mom, and his sister would share lunch with a family they'd met during Maddy's cancer treatments. Afterward, they'd take a tour on the *Kalmar Nyckel*. Though he'd taken tours more times then he could count, Mark still enjoyed riding the historic boat. He found his anticipation swelling as he listened to the excitement in the ten-year-old's voice.

"What time do we set sail?" asked Tyler.

"Two o'clock." Mark smiled as he glanced at the boy in the rearview mirror.

"I can hardly wait." Tyler squirmed in his seat.

"You'll have to eat first," his mother responded from the seat beside him.

Sounding like they were still young teen girls, Maddy and her cancer-surviving friend, Trisha, giggled at some private joke from the backseat of Mark's mother's van. Mark never tired of the two girls' laughter, and every three or four months when the families took an outing together, Mark praised God anew that Maddy was healed.

"I'll eat, Mom," Tyler said. "We're almost there, aren't we?"

"Yep." Mark took one last turn then pulled into the parking lot of the restaurant. He turned off the vehicle and opened the door. "We're here."

"All right." Tyler jumped out of the van. He motioned for his sister and Maddy to get out. "Come on, girls. We've got to eat quick. What time did you say we set sail?"

Mark chuckled.

"We have two hours to eat, son. Let's enjoy our lunch first," Tyler's mom answered.

"Aah," Tyler whined, his expression drooping.

"How 'bout you ladies go get our table, and Tyler and I will walk over to the port for a few minutes," said Mark.

The boy's eyebrows lifted. "Could I, Mom?"

"I suppose," his mom responded. "But don't take long and don't drive Mark crazy."

"Okay." Tyler's face lit up; then he turned and raced toward the ship they'd ride that afternoon.

Mark followed quickly behind him, admitting he felt as anxious as his young friend. The cool November wind bit into his face, but Mark enjoyed the temperature, finding the harsh wind even more nostalgic as he and Tyler made their way toward the ship. He'd been no older than five the first time his dad took him for a ride on the *Kalmar Nyckel*. He loved the history of the ship, how it sailed to the New World from Sweden in 1638.

"Did you know that the people in Delaware's first permanent European settlement rode over on this ship?" Mark commented to Tyler.

Tyler looked up at Mark. "You tell me that every time we come."

Mark chuckled. "My dad used to tell me every time he brought me, too."

A stab of pain wrenched Mark's heart. Tyler was fatherless at the young age of ten. Not because of death, but because Trisha's illness had been too much for his dad, and he'd ditched his wife and two children. *What a great guy.* Mark inwardly fumed every time he thought of it. He missed his father fervently. Tyler had to deal with missing his dad as well as knowing the guy chose not to stay with them.

Mark tried to shake away the bitterness he felt toward the man he'd met only one time, and years ago at that. Each time he saw Tyler, he was reminded to pray for the boy's dad.

Mark focused on the mammoth ship before them. The hull was painted a light blue; the sails all hoisted high atop the foremast, main mast, and mizzen, awaiting the trip she'd make in only a couple of hours. Above the captain's quarters, an enormous American flag flew freely through the cool air. He noted the mermaids, castle, and fish intricately carved into the stern.

As a boy he'd envisioned sailing the ship as the captain, responsible for a whole crew of men. He dreamed of fighting off pirates and dangerous sea creatures. With his captain's hat placed firmly atop his head and his faithful plastic sword strapped against his waist, he would fight off the bad guys and critters who just happened to look a lot like his dad dressed up in blankets or paper or whatever they could find. And no matter how long Mark had wanted to, his dad would play with him.

He glanced at Tyler, wishing they didn't live over two hours away. *I'll be a better dad than Tyler's is.*

The thought brought a vision of Zoey to mind. Mark wondered if she wanted to have children. Not that he wanted to have children right now, but one day he would. And it was something he would need to look for in a prospective mate.

What am I thinking? He gazed down at his much-too-large midsection then remembered the balding spot atop his head. *I don't think my gorgeous trainer would consider me good date material. Even if she does have every quality I'm looking for: godly, kind, giving, pretty. I'm pretty sure I don't have all the qualities she's looking for.*

Mark cleared his throat and peered out over the river. He couldn't deny he'd love to take her with him on the ship, to share one of his favorite childhood memories with her.

He shook the thought away and focused on Tyler. "Have I ever bought you a captain's hat?"

Tyler's face fell. "Yeah, but Sammy sat on it and smashed it. The overgrown horse."

Mark laughed as he envisioned the enormous mastiff Tyler and his family owned. The dog was as sweet and docile as she could be, but she probably weighed every bit of one hundred forty pounds.

"Why don't I buy you another one?"

"Really?" Tyler looked up at Mark and straightened his shoulders. Excitement animated his features. "I'll be more careful this time. Won't put it on the couch. I'll keep it on my dresser."

"Sounds like a good deal to me." Mark patted the boy's shoulder. "We'll get it after we eat, but before the ship sets sail."

"All right." Tyler pumped his fist. "This is an awesome day."

Mark walked with Tyler toward the restaurant. A red-haired woman slipped into a building a few shops down the road. Thoughts of Zoey swirled through his mind anew. He thought of a red-haired urchin wearing a captain's hat and battling sea creatures. He shook his head. *I gotta think about something else.*

⁂

Zoey's heart flipped as her young son padded down the hallway with one sock on and one off. He rubbed his eyes in one quick motion as he made his way straight to Sadie. Tightness squeezed Zoey's chest when Sadie lifted him into her lap and nestled her nose against Micah's neck. "Did you have a good nap, Micah?"

He wrapped his pudgy arms around Sadie's neck as he nodded.

Much of the time Micah acted younger than the twins, even though he was over a month older. Zoey knew Cam and Sadie were having him tested for auditory and sensory development and other stuff that Zoey didn't understand. It pained her to think she could have somehow caused Micah to have some kind of brain malfunction, even if it were mild. Sadie assured her that his delay most likely had nothing to do with the pregnancy, but Zoey couldn't help but feel responsible. She had been so young when she got pregnant, and she had no idea if Micah's biological dad had used any kinds of drugs or. . .

"He is fearfully and wonderfully made."

Zoey inhaled a deep breath. *Thank You for the reminder, God. I can't worry about those things now.*

"I bet Zoey would like to play your memory game with you." Sadie looked at Zoey and smiled.

Zoey's chest swelled as her son jumped off Sadie's lap and raced toward the shelf that held the game. "Is he a bit young for it? I mean—is he ready?" Zoey asked her aunt.

Sadie nodded "Don't you worry, Zoey. That boy is smart as can be. Must be the genes."

Zoey couldn't help but grin. Anyone else would never fully understand the depth of pain involved in watching another woman be the mother to her biological child. But Sadie did, and she tried to make the relationship between Zoey and Micah easy and enjoyable. She wasn't threatened by Zoey and tried to include her. For that, Zoey would forever be grateful.

"Come here, Zoey." Micah grabbed her hand and guided her to an open spot in front of the television on the carpeted floor. He plopped down and pointed for her to sit beside him. After opening the box, he started to line the cards in rows, facedown. "Like this. You want to help?"

"Sure." Zoey joined her boy in forming a large square with the small cards. She glanced back at Sadie. "Are you sure he's old enough for this game?"

"Just play."

Zoey turned back toward Micah. "Okay. You go first."

She watched as Micah cocked his head to the left and then to the right. He selected a card in the far corner and turned it over. "The yellow duck," he squealed.

"You like the duck?"

Micah nodded, biting his lip with the entire row of his top teeth. He flipped over another card. It was a butterfly. He shrugged his shoulders. "No duck."

"No duck yet," Zoey replied. She selected one card then another. "No match for me, either."

They both took several more turns, and though neither had a match, Zoey smiled at the animation on Micah's face as the cards were turned. It was obvious which cards he liked the best, and Zoey loved watching his expressions.

"Duck!" Micah squealed when he turned over a card in the center of the square.

"Oh my." Zoey tapped her lip with her finger. "Where was the other one?"

She looked at the four corners. She knew it was in one of them, and if she could remember which, she'd give Micah a hint. This game was too hard for him.

"I remember, Zoey." His pudgy little fingers reached for the card in the upper left corner. He flipped it and laughed. "Duck!" He scooped the cards into his hands and placed them beneath his leg. He pointed to his chest, a full smile framing his face. "I get to go again."

"Yes, you do."

Zoey watched as Micah turned another card. "Choo-choo! The train is my favorite," he squealed as he twisted his little body back and forth in excitement.

Zoey scanned the back of the cards. They'd seen the match to that one as well, but it was more toward the center. She just couldn't quite remember where.

Micah grabbed a card and flipped it over. His giggle pierced the air. "Choo-choo!" He scooped up both cards and shoved them under his leg as well. Looking at Zoey, he raised his eyebrows as he pointed to his chest. "I get to go again."

Zoey sat stunned as Micah made two more matches before she had a chance to go again. She glanced over at Sadie, who shrugged her shoulders. "I told you. He's a pro."

Zoey flipped two cards again. No match for her, but before she got a chance to go again, Micah made two additional matches. She leaned over and rubbed Micah's head. "You're one smart boy."

Micah beamed as he stood up and pointed to his chest. "Smart boy." He settled back onto the carpet, being sure to push all his matches beneath his legs.

By the time the game ended, Micah had made every match but three sets, and Zoey was pretty sure he had let her take the butterfly set. He didn't seem to like those cards.

"Come color with me?" Micah grabbed Zoey's hand and led her toward the table.

Zoey's heart constricted when she looked at the clock. She'd have given anything to color with her son, but Brittany had to be at work in an hour, and it would take them at least forty-five minutes to get home.

She glanced at her younger sister, who surprisingly hadn't been hounding Zoey about the time. She looked back down at Micah and scooped him up into her arms. "I wish I could, buddy, but Brit's gotta go to work."

He puckered his lip, and Zoey thought her heart would shatter.

"It's okay, Micah." Sadie lifted him out of Zoey's arms. "Give Zoey a kiss. She'll be back to see you soon."

He leaned over and placed a slobbery kiss on Zoey's lips. She yearned to take him back into her arms, but she knew she couldn't. Brittany needed to go, and Zoey needed to get out of there before she caved to her emotions and grabbed the boy and ran off.

After saying good-bye to their family, she and Brittany began their silent drive back to Wilmington. Brittany had been unusually quiet at the house today, but she'd also been less aggravated and grouchy. Zoey could only hope that was a good thing.

She also noted Brittany didn't text Neil the whole way back in the car. That has to be a good thing, too. Wonder what Harold said to her at church.

After dropping Brittany off at work, Zoey headed to the apartment. It was almost six when she walked in the door. Plopping down on the couch, the silence of the room wrapped itself around her and she remembered how good it felt to spend time with Micah.

Sadie's right. He's so very smart. He's going to be okay. Zoey kicked off her tennis shoes and grabbed the remote control. She didn't want to watch television. She missed Micah. She missed being able to be his mother.

She wanted to talk with someone. To tell someone how she felt, that she needed a friend to listen.

Mark popped into her mind. She liked him. Really, really liked him. But for all she knew he was dating Myra. But maybe he wasn't. *And I really, really like him.*

She pulled her cell phone out of her front jeans pocket. His number was right there. With the touch of a button she could call him.

Why not? What would it hurt?

She pushed the button, and his phone began to ring. Zoey's heart raced. A shiver raced down her spine. *But what am I going to say? He doesn't know about Micah. What am I going to do. . .just tell him all about having a kid just out of high school?*

Embarrassment washed over Zoey. She couldn't talk to Mark. She didn't know him well enough. He would think she was crazy, and if he was dating Myra—what would he think about his physical trainer calling him, especially if he already had a girlfriend?

She started to push the END button when Mark's voice sounded over the phone. "Hello."

Panic took her breath. Zoey forced her mouth open. "Sorry, Mark. Didn't mean to call you."

Before he could respond, Zoey shut her phone. She fell back against the couch. *I'm such a wimp.*

Chapter 7

Mark spent the entire day thinking about Zoey's call the night before. He'd been tempted several times to call her back, dreaming up various excuses to do so: reminding her to e-mail some recipes, asking her to join him on a grocery store run as she'd already offered, inviting her to dinner. He shook his head at the last thought. He had to quit thinking of being interested in Zoey. The idea of her reciprocating those feelings was preposterous. It was complete nonsense. *What do I have to offer her?*

Your faith. Your loyalty. Your kindness. Your love.

"Hey, man." Kevin walked up behind him and tapped his shoulder. Mark pushed his thoughts away and looked at his colleague. "I enjoyed my date the other night. Myra's quite the sweet little piglet."

Mark seethed at his colleague's disrespectful attitude toward women.

Kevin patted his trim stomach. "See ya at the gym." He headed toward the door. "Hey, are you working with your trainer tonight?"

Mark tried not to spit the answer through gritted teeth. "Yes."

Kevin shuffled his eyebrows. "All right."

"I thought you were dating Myra."

"I can't help what that woman thinks. I never asked her to be my girlfriend."

Mark turned back toward his office. He couldn't say anything. If he did, the words wouldn't bring honor to God. And if Kevin had any kind of response to the words, Mark might not be able to keep his fists from answering back. *God, I want to pray for that man. I want to want to see him come to know You. But Lord, I can't stand him.*

His spirit nudged at his heart. *"You just keep bringing him before Me."*

Mark grabbed his keys off the desk and locked his office door. He waved to Betty. "See you tomorrow."

She scurried toward him. "It's been two weeks. So how much have you lost?"

"Seven pounds."

"Mark, that's wonderful. I've lost five. I joined an aerobics group at my church."

He twisted the keys between his fingers. "That's terrific, Betty. We're doing great."

274

He left the office and drove to the gym. Kevin was already there, and Mark could see him through the glass windows working out on a treadmill. Trying not to think about his colleague, Mark walked into the gym and headed toward the locker room. He had only five minutes before he was to meet Zoey. After leaving his stuff in his locker, he walked to the pool. Zoey was already swimming a lap toward him. The woman looked so graceful gliding through the water.

She saw him and pushed herself out of the pool in one motion. "Hey." The smile that bowed her lips nearly knocked him off his feet. It had only been two days since he'd seen her, but hearing her voice and seeing her smile validated how intensely he'd missed her.

"Hey."

"Sorry about that phone call." Zoey grabbed her hair and wrung out the water. "I didn't mean to call you."

"That's okay."

Mark's heart raced as she seemed to study him for several moments. She looked away from him, and Mark waited for her to tell him to get in the pool, but she didn't say a word. He walked toward the side.

"Wait." Zoey stopped him from jumping in. He looked over at her. She bit her bottom lip. "That's not true."

Mark frowned. "What's not true?"

"I did mean to call you." She shifted her weight from one foot to the other. "I needed someone to talk to, and—"

"You meant to call me?" Mark pointed to his chest. Zoey Coyle, his beautiful, sweet, wonderful trainer, had called him—on purpose?

"Yes." Zoey crossed her arms in front of her chest. "I mean, I shouldn't have. I saw you leave with Myra, and if you have a girlfriend—"

"Myra's not my girlfriend."

"Well, I offered to take you to the store; then I saw you leave with her, and. . ."

Mark almost fell over from what he was hearing. Was it possible Zoey could be interested in him? *What are you waiting for, Mark?* he chastised himself. "Would you like to go with me today?"

She shook her head. "I didn't mean to make you feel like you have to take me along to the store. . . ."

Mark placed his hand on hers. She looked up at him, and he drank in her chocolate brown eyes. Zoey was too beautiful for words. "I'd really like to go together."

"Okay."

A slight coloring of red made its way up her neck and to her cheeks. *She looks even more adorable.* The urge to trace her jaw to her lips nearly overwhelmed him. He wanted so much to kiss her.

She cleared her throat. "That doesn't mean I'm going easy on you tonight."

Mark smiled and tapped the end of her nose. "Of course not."

"Get in that pool."

Before he could respond, she pushed him in.

⌖

Zoey Coyle, I cannot believe you practically threw yourself at the guy's feet. Zoey inwardly berated herself for what had to be the hundredth time since she'd pushed Mark into the pool.

She studied her client as he swam the length of the pool. A year ago, maybe as recently as a month ago, Zoey never would have believed she'd be attracted to Mark. He was cute, but more in a teddy bear way, and his receding hair made him appear a few, if not several, years older than he was. Still, something about him drew her.

Mark swam beside her. Sucking in deep breaths and blowing out his mouth, he grinned at her. "Okay, slave driver, what else do you have for me tonight?"

A thrill sped down Zoey's spine at the sweetness of his smile. His eyes shone with a kindness that Zoey didn't see in many men. In many people, for that matter. Her thoughts drifted to Harold, her sweet, unassuming, yet God-fearing stepfather. Mark's gaze reminded Zoey of him. The realization made her heart thump faster.

She clapped her hands, forcing her mind to focus on her job. "I think I've worked you hard enough tonight."

"You think?" Mark clumsily lifted himself out of the water. He grabbed the towel from the chair beside her. "I'm not sure my legs will move tomorrow."

"Sure they will. It was just a couple more laps than last time."

"A couple more laps, she says."

Zoey laughed as Mark wiped off his face.

"So do you mind if we grab a bite to eat before we head over to the store? I'm starving."

Zoey felt her cheeks warm at the mention of going to the store with him. Why couldn't she just have fibbed and told him that she hadn't meant to call him? Sometimes she wished she could ignore the Holy Spirit's prodding toward honesty, uprightness—godliness. *You know that's not true, God. I'm so thankful for our daily relationship.* She glanced at Mark, taking in the expectant look on his face and feeling embarrassed once again at having practically forced him to take her grocery shopping. *Oh, but Spirit, I do wish I just simply wouldn't have dialed his number last night.*

She shook her head. "Look, Mark, I really didn't mean for you to feel obligated—"

Mark raised his hand. "I'll take that as you're willing to stop by the deli a few blocks over before we go. And while we're there, I'd like you to tell me a few other places I can eat at, because I'm afraid I'm going to turn into a low-calorie sub sandwich if I have to eat there too many more times."

Zoey laughed, appreciating his attempt to ease her embarrassment. "Okay. I must admit I am a bit hungry. Get changed and I'll meet you in front of the locker room."

Mark saluted her. "It's a date."

"Well, not. . ."

Mark raised his eyebrows as if to challenge her. "It's official. It's a date."

Zoey felt her jaw drop as Mark walked past her and toward the locker room. If any other man had told her she was going on a date with him, Zoey would have set him straight before he had a chance to utter another sound, but Mark's challenge wasn't about control. It was a way to ease her discomfort, and she liked that.

❧

Mark watched as Zoey took another bite of turkey sandwich. She swallowed then pointed at him. "Another thing I've found is that you don't want to completely give up on all the foods you love." She picked up her lemon water and took a quick drink. "Give yourself one day a week to eat a hamburger or enjoy a dessert. Just watch the portion and only allow one day. Take Harold, for instance: His favorite dessert is chocolate cake—"

"Who's Harold?" Enjoying his time with Zoey, Mark allowed the question to slip out before thinking it through. She must have noted the jealous tone, because she grinned.

"My stepdad."

"So your mom and dad are divorced?"

"No." A pained expression crossed Zoey's face, and Mark regretted his question. "My dad died. . .about seven years ago."

"I'm sorry. My dad died ten years ago. He had a stroke. I think I may have told you that."

She nodded. "My dad was in an accident."

Their conversation halted, and Mark watched as Zoey dug through her bag of baked chips. It was obvious she'd been close to her dad. He understood her pain. He wondered about her stepdad. What did she think of him? Did she have any siblings? Was she close to her family? He wanted to know more about her, to know her history and what she wanted from life. He touched the top of her hand. "Tell me about your family."

She smiled. "Well, I have four sisters."

Mark almost choked on a bite of steamed veggies. "Four!"

Zoey laughed as she handed him a napkin. "That's right. I'm the oldest. My nineteen-year-old sister, Brittany, and I share an apartment. My fifteen-year-old sister, Candy, is still at home with Mom and Harold and my three-year-old twin sisters, Rebecca and Rachel."

"That's a houseful. So the twins' dad is Harold?"

Zoey nodded. "At first I hated Harold, but I kinda went through a hard time. . . ." Zoey frowned and scrunched her nose and mouth as if she'd just sucked on a lemon. "But Harold was really good to me during that time—encouraged and helped me—and I learned to trust him." Her gaze met Mark's and his heart thumped in his chest. "He's my second dad, and I love him."

"That's great. Do you get to see your family a lot?"

"Not as much as I'd like. They live forty-five minutes away, and with work and school—it's hard. I really miss Micah—"

"Micah?" Mark frowned, trying to remember if Zoey said she had a brother in that mass of sisters.

"He's my. . ." She bit her bottom lip and looked away. "My cousin—sorta." She gazed back at him. Her eyes seemed to search his face to see if she could truly trust him. He wanted to tell her she could trust him with anything, but the hesitancy in her expression held him back. She opened her mouth, then shut it, then opened it again. "Tell me about your family."

"I have a sister, Maddy, who's twenty-one."

"Like me?" Zoey's expression brightened and she pointed to her chest.

Mark couldn't help but smile. He loved the bubbly side of her personality. "Yes. And then there's my mom. And that's it."

"Are you close to your family?"

"Very." Mark folded his hands together. "My sister battled and defeated leukemia when I was a senior in high school. The same year my dad died. I've always felt responsible for taking care of my mom and sister."

"Wow. That's amazing that she's a cancer survivor." She twirled her fork between her fingers. "I can't imagine how hard it was to go through your dad's death and all your sister was dealing with."

"If it hadn't been for God—"

"I knew it!" Zoey yelled and clapped her hands, then covered her mouth. She raised her eyebrows and ducked her head, scanning the room to see who'd heard her outburst. "Sorry," she mumbled as she moved her hand. "It's just that I just knew you were a Christian. It was obvious in the way you talk, in the way you carry yourself. . ."

"Really?"

"Absolutely."

Mark studied Zoey as she picked up her sandwich and took a bite. "I think that's the best compliment anyone has ever given me."

She swallowed. "Then I'm glad I said it."

"For the record, I thought you were a Christian, too."

She nodded. "Thank you. I've spent the last four years trying to build my relationship with God after spending most of my high school years trying to rip it apart."

Mark watched Zoey. She was beautiful. A man couldn't help but notice her walk into a room. But having spent some time with her, Mark realized she was more beautiful than he'd originally imagined. He'd never again just "notice" her. Her godly beauty went too deep for that. "Zoey, I'm glad you agreed to have dinner with me tonight."

She huffed, crossing her arms in front of her chest. "If I recall correctly, I wasn't given a choice."

Her tone was filled with jest, and Mark grinned. "Then I'll have to force you to a movie this weekend as well."

Her expression fell, and Mark's gut clenched. It was too much to ask. . . . *I knew she wasn't really interested in me.*

A verse from 1 Timothy wended its way into Mark's mind. "Physical training is of some value, but godliness has value for all things."

He sucked in his breath. Zoey hadn't accepted his offer to go to the movies, but he couldn't think about that. Not in the way he repeatedly had. Zoey's acceptance or rejection of his offer had nothing to do with his value as a person, as a man, as God's child. His value and worth came directly from the Father of the universe.

Mark needed to lose weight to be healthier. And of course he would have preferred to keep the thinning patch of hair on top of his head. But those things were superficial, having only some value. I suppose the value of the hair would be to keep my scalp from burning in the summer.

He bit back a chuckle at the thought. Sobering his thoughts, he knew his feelings of insecurity and inferiority due to his appearance were more than superficial; they were sinful. God cares more about my relationship with Him than He does about my semi-bald head and soft center.

He cleared his throat. "Of course, I won't force you to a movie, but I would love to take you to one."

Zoey's expression softened, and a full smile bowed her lips. Adorable dimples deepened in her cheeks. "I'd like that, but I'll be visiting my family for Thanksgiving."

"How about next weekend?"

Her eyebrows rose as she clapped her hands. "I've got an idea. Why don't you come over to my place first, and I'll fix you one of the dinner recipes I gave you."

"You gave me recipes?"

"Didn't I?" She smacked her forehead. "I forgot them in the car; then I spilled orange juice on them; then I forgot to make more copies." She shook her head. "Give me your e-mail address, and I'll send them to you."

"That would be great." Mark jotted down the address on the back of a napkin. His heart nearly burst with excitement. She had said yes.

Chapter 8

Mark scooped a second helping of sweet potato casserole toward his plate. Thanksgiving dinner could end up being the downfall of his diet. Or maybe it wasn't Thanksgiving dinner; maybe it was that his mother was such a wonderful cook. Praying for willpower, he dropped only half of the spoonful onto his plate.

"Aren't you going to eat more than that, son?"

Mark looked at his mother, whose eyebrows furrowed into a line of surprise. "Mom, I'm really trying to stay on my diet."

She squinted her eyes, her expression questioning. "Why are you so determined, even through the holidays, to stay on your diet?"

Mark shoved a forkful of his favorite dish into his mouth. He was going to have to tell his mom about his blood pressure. Over the past few weeks, she'd become more and more suspicious of his eating habits, and he simply couldn't lie to her.

"Well. . ." Mark looked across the table, noting how his friend Bruce, a bachelor, leaned close to Maddy and whispered something in her ear. A flash of protective adrenaline shot through him as he realized his younger friend had paid more attention to Maddy than usual.

"Bruce?"

His friend looked at him, and Mark could see the genuine care for his sister in Bruce's gaze. Mark glanced at his sister and noticed that her gaze seemed to be pleading him not to say anything that would embarrass her. He swallowed back the desire to pummel any man who tried to make a move on his sister. Bruce was a good Christian man, and Mark had to come to grips with the fact that Maddy had grown up. Mark himself was falling for a woman his sister's age.

"Don't try to change the subject." His mother's determined tone interrupted his thoughts.

He glanced back at his mom. The hesitant gleam in her eyes made his heart race. It had been so hard to see his mother's anxiety ebb and flow in horrendous highs and lows when he was a teen. He couldn't tell her. Not yet. "I'm forty pounds overweight, Mom."

He hadn't lied in the least bit. He just didn't share the full reason he was so interested in losing weight right now.

His mother studied him for a long moment then released a slow sigh. "I guess I'll just have to trust you to God. He's taking care of you."

Mark grinned then sneaked a quick peek at his sister and Bruce, who were wrapped up in their own conversation. "Yes. He's taking care of all of us."

❧

Zoey mixed the mashed potatoes she'd made with garlic and skim milk, instead of whole milk and butter. Admittedly, she loved the fatty mashed potatoes smothered in margarine that her grandma made. But these were much healthier and still quite tasty. After grabbing a pot holder, she pulled the lemon chicken out of the oven. Not only did it smell wonderful, but at only 150 calories per chicken breast, it would be doubly delicious.

"I can't believe I let you talk me into this," Brittany whined as she walked into the kitchen. "I endured three whole days of family togetherness last weekend; now I'm spending Friday night doing this." She smacked her hands against her thighs. Though pinned up on the sides, Brit's long brown hair flowed past her shoulders. Her sweater and jeans fit snugly against her tall, thin frame.

Zoey ignored Brittany's negative attitude. Zoey had enjoyed each moment with her family, especially with Micah. Much to her surprise, she'd been bubbling with excited anticipation all day about seeing Mark again. "You look really pretty, Brit." Zoey meant every word. Her sister was a beautiful young woman, despite the emptiness in her gaze. Today was the first time since she'd walked in on Brittany and Neil kissing that Zoey allowed him to come back to the apartment. A twinge of guilt sped up her spine because she hadn't told Mark that Brittany and her boyfriend would be joining them for dinner.

But Zoey didn't have a choice. Brittany was getting antsy to have Neil over, and Zoey didn't feel comfortable with it. When the idea to have him visit when Mark was there popped into Zoey's head, she just had to go with it. *Besides, Mark is a Christian, and he's my friend. If I need any help with Brittany and her boyfriend, he'll help me.*

She placed the pan of chicken on the stove. *Of course, I didn't really give him much of a choice, did I? Please, God, I pray nothing has to be said to Neil or Brittany tonight.*

Zoey shuddered at the thought. Brittany had become more withdrawn over the last few weeks. More secretive. She'd made fewer phone calls to their mom and hadn't answered Zoey's texts. Plus, she'd noticed a bruise on Brittany's arm a couple of days ago. A bruise that looked like someone had grabbed her arm and squeezed it. Brittany denied that Neil did it. She always denied it.

A long sigh slipped from Zoey's lips. *I've just got to keep praying.*

"How long is this dinner going to take?" Brittany whined as she grabbed the plates from the cupboard.

Zoey shrugged. "I don't know. I guess it depends on how much we enjoy each other's company."

"Great," Brittany huffed as she set the plates on the table then went back to the kitchen for silverware and napkins. "Shouldn't the guys be here by now?"

Zoey looked at the kitchen clock. "Yeah. They should. They're ten minutes late."

"Well, I hope they hurry. I'm starving."

❧

Mark berated himself as he opened his car door and headed toward Zoey's apartment. *I cannot believe I ate three pieces of that chocolate fudge.* Mrs. Adams was undoubtedly one of his favorite customers. Mid-eighties, white hair, twinkling eyes, ready smile. The woman looked as fragile as spun glass, but she loved to bring him treats. And her Christmas treats were simply too good to pass up. He growled as he trudged up the sidewalk. *How many calories are in a piece of fudge, anyway?* Mark raised his hand to knock on Zoey's door.

"Hey, are you lost?"

Mark turned at the unfamiliar voice. A hulking twentysomething guy stood behind him. A scowl marred his face, and he squinted his eyes. Widening his stance, the guy balled his fists against his thighs. "You're not here to see Brittany, are you?"

"Zoey's sister?"

"Yeah."

Fury seemed to spew from the overgrown hulk's ears. A primal urge to challenge the younger man swelled within Mark. He didn't appreciate the guy's accusatory tone or his stance. A retort made its way to Mark's lips as he fought the urge to ball up his own fists. Then recognition dawned on Mark. "Aren't you one of the linebackers for Wilmington?"

The guy raised one side of his mouth in a half smile, half smirk. "Yeah."

The sudden change of thought allowed Mark to bite back a nasty comment and attempt to cool the tension. Mark extended his hand. "Hey, I'm Mark White. I used to play football a few years back. Got hurt and couldn't use my scholarship."

The guy's countenance softened as he shook Mark's hand. "That stinks. What position did you play?"

"Quarterback."

"Name's Neil Thurman. So you're here to see Zoey?"

Mark fought back the urge to shake his head. Neil wasn't worried that Mark might be here to see Brittany. The guy just wanted to pick a fight. "I am."

"Good. Maybe you can knock some sense into that girl."

Mark frowned at the younger man. His tone wasn't in jest. He meant it.

Zoey's response when he said he would force her to the movies popped into his mind. Had Neil treated Brittany poorly? Mark crossed his arms in front of his chest. "A real man would never mistreat a woman."

Neil shook his head. "I didn't say mistreat her. I said knock some sense into her. There's a difference."

"So a guy should only hurt a woman when she deserves it?"

"That's right."

Mark took a step closer to Neil. "Wrong. A real man would never hurt a woman. A godly man would—"

"You have got to be kiddin' me." Neil pointed to his temple and twirled his index finger. "You're as crazy as Zoey." He swatted the air. "I'm not in the mood for this tonight. Tell Brittany I'll see her later."

Mark watched as Neil proceeded down the sidewalk and got back into his sports car. Without a second glance, he sped out of the parking area and onto the street. Mark shook away the twinge of guilt he felt at Brittany's boyfriend running off. No woman needed to deal with a man who thought so little of her. He'd never met Brittany, but she didn't need Neil Thurman in her life.

He turned to knock on the door when out of the corner of his eye he spotted a silver device on the ground. He picked it up. A cell phone. *Must be Neil's.* He shoved it into his coat pocket. He'd give it to Brittany once he got inside. He knocked on the door.

"Come on in." Zoey motioned him inside. Her apartment smelled like a mixture of lemons and cinnamon. Her warm smile lightened his mood. "Let me have your coat."

"Sure." Mark handed her his coat as he took in the varying light and dark chocolate colors of the room. Touches of deep green, as well as a small Christmas tree, accented the dark colors, and Mark found the room very soothing and comforting—the perfect place to relax and enjoy a football game or an afternoon nap.

"Did you happen to see Neil out there?" asked the tall, dark-haired woman he assumed to be Brittany.

"Uh—"

"Brittany, first meet the man!" Zoey exclaimed. She let out an exasperated sigh as she pointed at each of them. "Brittany, this is Mark White. Mark, my sister Brittany."

Mark extended his hand. "It's nice to meet you, Brittany."

"It's nice to meet you, too." Brittany blew out a long breath. "He's probably mad. Let's just go eat."

"Yes, I'm starved. Mark, I made lemon chicken and mashed potatoes, but these mashed potatoes are made with. . ."

Zoey's words started to jumble together as Mark thought of his encounter with Neil outside the door. *What do I do, God? Do I tell her?*

He thought of the guy's phone stashed in his coat pocket. Scanning the room, he frowned. Where had Zoey put his coat? He didn't see it anywhere. He looked back at Brittany. Her face was drawn in an exaggerated frown. *Lord, she doesn't need to mess with Neil Thurman. I don't know anything about her, but I do know she needs Your protection from men like him.*

Mark peered at Zoey. She flitted around the room, making sure plates and silverware were straight and the glasses had ice in them. He could tell by her body language that she was trying to get Brittany not to think about Neil. The interaction tore at Mark's heart, and he found himself wanting to help Zoey protect Brittany.

He thought of Myra and how angry she had been with Mark when he lied about Kevin. *This isn't a lie. I just haven't had a chance to disclose the information.*

But Brittany asked me point-blank if I'd seen Neil.

But then Zoey cut me off before I could answer.

Mark rubbed his temple to stop the battle inside his head.

"Here. Have a seat." Zoey pointed to a chair at the dining room table.

As he sat, Zoey and Brittany also took their seats. Zoey extended her hands and looked at him. "Will you say our blessing?"

Mark watched Brittany roll her eyes as she took Zoey's hand in her own. She huffed as she extended her free hand toward him. He forced a grin as he took the sisters' hands in his own. His prayer stuttered out as he still warred over how to tell Brittany that Neil had come and gone. The tension between the sisters was as thick as the bowl of mashed potatoes Zoey had made.

He finished with an "Amen," and Brittany pulled back her hand as if he'd smacked her. She slouched in her chair. "I just wish Neil would hurry up and get here."

"Well. . ."

Mark started to answer when Zoey nudged him with a large bowl. Her gaze begged him to comply with her request.

"Would you like some salad?"

"Sure."

Using the tongs, he heaped the lettuce-and-tomato salad onto his plate. "What kind of dressing do you have?"

"It's already in the salad. Try it. I think you'll like it."

An unfamiliar song sounded from another room. Mark looked up. Brittany had her phone in her hand. She hopped up from her seat. "That's Neil's ring tone!"

She turned and scowled at Zoey. "Why's it coming from your room?"

"What?" Zoey jumped up.

"Why is Neil's phone in your room?" Brittany squealed, tears filling her eyes.

"Ladies." Mark stood, trying to get their attention.

"Why would it be in my room? I don't want him in this apartment. Why would you let him in my room?" Zoey yelled back.

"Ladies," Mark tried again.

"I would never let him in your room," Brittany retorted.

Mark touched Zoey's arm. "Where is your room?"

Zoey peered at him. "What?"

"Neil's phone is in my coat pocket."

"What's it doing in your coat pocket?" Brittany swiped her eyes with the back of her hand.

Mark let out his breath. He watched as Zoey went to her room and brought his coat to him. "He dropped it, and I picked it up. I was going to give it to you when I walked in."

"But I asked you if you saw him outside. You said no."

Mark shook his head as he pulled the phone from his pocket and handed it to Brittany. "I didn't say no. I never had a chance to answer."

Brittany gripped the phone as she crossed her arms in front of her chest. "Well, where'd he go?"

Mark looked at Zoey. Her affection and fear for her younger sister were obvious. The intensity of her concern drew him even more to her. He would do whatever he had to do for the redhead who seemed to be capturing his heart. He gazed back at Brittany. "He left because I said I didn't appreciate him telling me that I should hit a woman to keep her in line."

Brittany squinted her eyes and shook her head. "He would never say that."

"Not those words. His words were that he hoped I could knock some sense into your sister."

"What?" Zoey placed her hand on her chest. "I knew it, Brittany. I knew he's been mistreating you."

Brittany turned her head and stared at the wall. "He meant that figuratively."

"Did he?" Mark reached out to touch Brittany's arm, but she flinched away from him. Her action sent a wave of nausea over him as he realized that Neil Thurman had made her afraid of a simple touch.

"You have no right. You don't even know me," Brittany wailed as she swiped a stream of tears from her eyes. She turned toward Zoey. "I want him to leave."

Mark turned to Zoey, whose expression revealed fear, uncertainty, sadness, and another emotion Mark couldn't quite decipher. He touched Zoey's hand. "Please call me if you need any help."

She barely nodded as Mark walked out the door. *God, help Neil Thurman. Guide him to Yourself. And guide Brittany away from him.*

Zoey spent most of the next week in prayer for her sister. She prayed in line at the grocery, while her clients lifted weights, as she walked from one class to another. During that time her feelings for Mark deepened. He'd been willing to stand up for her sister by telling her the truth, without sugarcoating it and without being unkind. It was a trait she'd seen and appreciated in Harold.

It had been a long day of classes. With finals only a week away, Zoey was overwhelmed by all the studying she had to do. *But right now I need a five-minute break.* She flopped into her desk chair and turned on her computer. Leaning back in her chair, she unlaced and pulled off her tennis shoes while it booted up. She'd see Mark tomorrow at training, but she couldn't help hoping he'd sent her an e-mail.

Finally ready, she opened her inbox. Just as she hoped, she had a message from Mark. She clicked the screen open with her mouse.

TWELVE POUNDS DOWN! screamed at her in bold green letters. She giggled as she scrolled down below the exclamatory message.

> *The hardest part was the beginning. But now that I have a routine, I think the weight will start coming off faster. Thanks for your help. Can't wait to see you tomorrow.*
>
> *Love,*
> *Mark*

Zoey felt a blush creep up her cheeks at the "Love, Mark" part. His first e-mail had simply said "Sincerely"; then it changed to "Yours truly." Now he signed his e-mails "Love." Deep down Zoey couldn't deny the thrill she felt each time he wrote it.

After a quick reply back to Mark, she scrolled farther down her e-mail. Most of the messages were from various stores encouraging her to be a part of the latest sale. With every amount of restraint she could conjure, she deleted one after the other until she got to an e-mail from her aunt Sadie. She opened it and read the brief message. *Enjoy some pics of Micah and Ellie.*

Clicking on the attachment, Zoey felt her heart practically melt at the sight of Micah in his black pants, red-and-black-plaid button-up sweater, and red Christmas tie. The little tyke looked like such a big boy sitting on a white block with his legs crossed and his hands in his lap. The next picture was of him and Ellie cheek to cheek, hugging each other. They looked nothing alike, Ellie with her dark hair and eyes and Micah with his red hair and light blue eyes, but the two of them were inseparable. As much like biological siblings as two kids could get. A mixture of envy and thankfulness swelled within her. She was happy for Cam and Sadie, that they could have a second child in Micah. Happy for Ellie, that she could have a brother. And yet she hated missing so much of Micah's life.

She turned on her printer. Only two weeks until Christmas, and she still hadn't bought the first present. She glanced at the calendar above her computer. Payday was four days away. She could wait four days to buy something for Micah.

She printed the pictures. One of him leaning against a block with his chin resting in his chubby little hand was especially adorable.

She turned to her computer to turn it off when she noticed an ad from one of her favorite children's clothing stores at the Concord Mall. Her heart raced at the message indicating only twenty-four hours left for the biggest sale of the season. If she bought something today, she'd be able to save an additional 20 percent. She bit the inside of her lip as she tapped her fingernails against each other. Blowing out a long breath, she clicked on the Web site. As long as she didn't spend too much, she could turn around and pay off the expense when she got paid.

Chapter 9

Another week passed and it was time for Mark to go back to the doctor. He closed the bank account files he'd been working on and shut down the computer. Planning to stop by to see his mom and Maddy before the appointment, he'd taken half the day off this time.

Part of him dreaded returning to see Dr. Carr, fearing the prognosis might be the same or worse. The other part of him knew he had worked hard to lose weight and eat less fatty foods, so he hoped the visit would be positive. The memory of the chocolate chip cookies he'd eaten yesterday made its way through his mind.

The holiday season, filled with delicious festive foods, had worn down his discipline at times. It was true he'd stayed away from fatty fried foods, but the candies and the desserts—mmm, they were too good to pass up.

Didn't Zoey say I could pick a day of the week to eat some of the foods I like? Of course, he hadn't exactly picked a single day. After all, the candies didn't show up just one day of the week. He pushed the thought away. He'd worked extra hard at the gym on the nights he'd splurged with a piece of candy or two. Now wasn't the time to worry about how much he had eaten. He grabbed his coat from the rack and put it on.

"Time for the doctor visit, huh?"

Mark turned at the sound of Betty's voice. He took in her multicolored Christmas sweater as well as the jingle bells dangling from her ears. Her ready smile warmed his heart, and Mark gave her a quick hug. "Yep. So how much weight have you lost?"

"Ten pounds."

"Betty, that's wonderful."

"I wonder who's winning."

Mark couldn't help but grin at the excited gleam in her eyes. "Well, Barb seems to be doing a good job of weighing everyone each week."

"Yes, and she's going to post this month's results tomorrow." She clasped her hands together and nudged him with her shoulder. "Then we'll know who is our biggest competition."

Mark laughed, and Betty punched his arm. "Hey, I want to win that treadmill."

"Me, too, Betty." He looked at his watch. "But I'd better go. I'm meeting my mom and sister for lunch."

"Okay. I'll see you tomorrow."

Mark left the bank and drove to his mom's house. It had been less than a week since he'd visited her, but he still felt a wave of nostalgia wash over him as he pulled into the driveway of the home of his youth. Mom had never gotten rid of the basketball hoop that he and his dad had played one-on-one with every weekend. The privacy fence still had the perfect circular hole his dad had cut in it for Mark to practice precision with his football throws. Unnoticeable to most people, even the white vinyl still contained the various dings that he and his sister had made while doing one activity or another.

He noticed one of the strands of Christmas lights had fallen underneath the bay window. Before going inside, he fixed the lights and adjusted the Nativity scene light set that must have been shifted by the wind. His mom still decorated the house for Christmas just as she had when he was a kid. He loved that. He relished the memories of past holidays he'd shared with his family, especially before his dad died.

Maddy opened the door and pounced into him, almost knocking him off his feet. "Hey, big brother."

"Hey to you, too, twinkle toes."

Maddy laughed and lifted her hands above her head, intertwined her fingers, then twirled in the snow. "Does that mean you're going to watch me do *The Nutcracker* this year?"

"Don't you make me every year?"

Mark's mom had taken Maddy to see *The Nutcracker* play when Maddy was just six. She loved it so much that every year, even the year when she was the sickest, his little sister performed the play for their family. It didn't matter that Maddy had never taken a ballet lesson or that she was one of the clumsiest people Mark had ever known. It didn't even matter that the whole thing was atrocious and downright embarrassing. She still performed for them.

"Come on." She grabbed his arm. "Mom's got the potato soup ready."

His stomach growled of its own volition at the mention of his mom's homemade potato soup. He'd never tasted better. He followed his sister into the house. The succulent aroma nearly made him dizzy. Knowing he had his appointment today, he'd had only a banana and a small glass of juice for breakfast.

"Hi, son." His mom grabbed him in a bear hug as he walked through the front door. "We live in the same city and it seems like forever since I've seen you."

"Mom, I just saw you both less than a week ago, and you know I've been working out three days a week."

Maddy grabbed the waist of his pants and pulled on it. "And losing weight, it looks like."

"Maddy." He swatted at her like he did when they were kids and she was pestering him for one thing or another.

"Still going to a gym. Still losing weight. What's all this about?" His mom pinched his cheek then stepped back, placed her hands on her hips, and stared at him. "Do you have a girlfriend?"

Mark felt heat rush up his neck. "What? No."

Maddy released the waist of his pants. "Tell the truth, big brother."

"I am telling the truth."

Maddy jumped in front of him and smashed his cheeks together with both of her hands. He swatted at her some more. Practically nose to nose, she squinted at him. "He doesn't have a girlfriend, Mom. But I think he likes someone."

"What?" Mark grabbed both of Maddy's wrists and gently pushed her away from him. "I came for lunch. Can't a man just visit his mom and sister without getting the third degree?"

His mother grabbed his hand and guided him to the table. She poured him a bowl of soup and set it on the table beside a ham sandwich. "So what's her name?"

"Mom, I said I didn't have a girlfriend."

"What's she look like?" Maddy sat beside him. She took a bite of ham sandwich and mumbled, "Where'd you meet her?"

Mark lowered his head. Dealing with these two women was impossible. He might as well not even try to keep his feelings for Zoey from them. "Her name is Zoey Coyle."

Maddy moved closer to him, and his mother slipped into the chair beside him. Maddy smiled. "What a cool name. How old is she?"

"Twenty-one."

"My age?" Maddy placed her hand on her chest.

"Isn't that a bit young?" asked his mother.

"I don't think so."

"Where'd you meet her?" asked Maddy.

"The gym."

"Is that why you joined the gym?" asked his mom.

"What does she look like?" asked Maddy.

Ignoring his mom's question, he replied, "Red hair, chocolate—I mean, brown eyes, small build."

"Oh, she sounds cute," said Maddy.

"Is she a Christian?" asked his mom.

"Yes."

"That's good." His mom leaned back in her chair. "Go ahead and eat, Mark. Your soup is getting cold."

Mark blew out a sigh of relief. For a few minutes anyway, the interrogation had ceased.

~

A thrill raced through Zoey when she picked up her ringing cell phone and saw Mark's name on the screen. With each passing day, she found herself more eager to see and spend time with him.

"I went to the doctor today."

The lilt in his voice assured her that the visit had gone well. "And?"

"Fifteen pounds! He's not taking me off medication yet, but he's not increasing the dose, either."

"That's terrific, Mark. I'm so happy for you."

"So what are you doing tonight?"

Zoey looked around her apartment at the dusty furniture, dirty hardwood floors, and pile of laundry trying to spew from the hall closet. "Nothing."

"Would you care to get dinner with me to celebrate? My treat, of course."

"Sure. What time?"

"Pick you up in an hour?"

Zoey looked down at her sweat-stained workout clothes. She forced her tone to stay light. "Sounds good."

Clicking off the phone, Zoey raced to the bathroom and started the shower. Was this a real date? Or was the invitation merely from a grateful client? If it was a date, what should she wear?

She jumped into the tub, allowing the warm water to soothe her tight muscles. *I do have that new red dress I bought for Christmas.* She shampooed and conditioned her hair and washed up in only a few minutes.

Should I wear my hair up or down? If Brittany was at the apartment, Zoey would let her help. It seemed like ages since Zoey had been on a real date. Of course, they were supposed to have gone to the movies after she fixed dinner the other night, but the Neil-and-Brittany saga had nixed that.

What is the matter with me? Zoey stopped and looked at herself in the mirror. She'd gone on several dates with some really great guys. She had no reason to be so worked up over a date with Mark.

"It's because I really like him." She whispered the truth aloud as she put on her makeup.

God, no matter how I feel about Mark, help me keep my mind focused on You.

She blow-dried and fixed her hair then slipped into the red dress. Her unease had settled and she determined to keep her mind and heart focused on God's will for her life. If Mark was part of God's will, then she would know.

The doorbell rang and she walked to the door. Taking a deep breath, she opened it and smiled at her date. Mark looked amazing in black pants, a deep green button-down shirt, and a matching tie.

"Wow." The single word spilled from his lips, and Zoey could tell he thought she looked good as well. "Zoey, you're too beautiful."

She furrowed her brow. "Too beautiful?"

"Why would you ever go out with a guy like me?"

Heat warmed her cheeks. "Because you're a terrific guy." She grabbed his perfectly straight tie and straightened it. "And you're not too bad-looking yourself."

He offered her his arm. "Are you ready?"

She slipped her hand into the crook of his elbow. "I sure am."

Zoey felt like a princess all the way to the restaurant. Rarely did she have an opportunity to wear a nice dress, and even more uncommon was the elation she felt at having such a wonderful man beside her. One who, to her pleasure, was obviously very smitten with her appearance.

She raised her eyebrows and gawked at Mark when he pulled up to the Concordville Inn. "Have you ever been here?"

"Several times. You?"

Zoey shook her head.

Mark parked the car then rested his hand on top of hers. "Then it's the perfect place for a celebration."

"How so? It's your celebration and you've been here many times."

He shrugged. "I already know the food is delicious, and I'll get to watch you enjoy your first experience."

Zoey drank in the ambience of the restaurant, the town's lights, and the clear, crisp night. "This will definitely be my splurge night."

Mark chuckled. "Mine, too."

He guided her into the restaurant and toward the hostess stand. He had to have planned this. He already had reservations. Her mind spun at the various reasons why he might have already planned this evening. *Did he plan to take someone else and the date fell through?*

Trying to push away her restless thoughts, she walked through the brick-framed arch and gazed around the dining room. The top half of the walls were painted a rich taupe and adorned with contemporary artwork and rectangular light fixtures. Beautiful wood crown molding traced the perimeter of the walls and even sectioned off the ceiling. Ceiling lights added an additional glow to the bright white tablecloths covering each table. Rich chocolate brown and dark terra-cotta cushions graced the mahogany-framed chairs and booths. Bright red cloth napkins, a table light, and a single red carnation graced each table. Zoey had never been to a place so fancy.

The waitress guided them to their seating, and Zoey sat back in the booth and gazed at her date. Feeling a bit apprehensive at the elaborateness of the celebration, she traced the fanned napkin with the tip of her finger. "Congratulations, Mark. We're over a fourth of the way there."

"Thanks to you."

Trying to calm her nerves, she smiled, mentally telling herself to enjoy the place—and Mark. "I've been glad to help. You've been an easy client."

"I've tried."

She picked up the menu, surprised at the many foods the restaurant offered. "So what's good?"

"My favorite is the filet mignon and crab cakes."

"Mmm. I love filet mignon."

Mark didn't respond, and Zoey looked up at him. His dark eyes seemed to deepen, and a chill raced through Zoey at his intense gaze. "That dress is absolutely beautiful on you."

Zoey crossed her arms, rubbing her hands against her biceps to ward away the goose bumps. "Thanks. I guess it's my little gift to myself."

"Really?"

The intensity in his eyes didn't waver, and Zoey started bouncing her leg. It had been a long time since she'd felt attractive to someone, and she didn't know what to do with the nervous energy it evoked in her. "Yeah. I paid off one of my credit cards, and to celebrate I bought this dress." She took a sip of water then pointed to the dress. " 'Course, now this is on the card, but that's it. Nothing else."

Mark's intensity shifted to a frown. A twinge of guilt raced up Zoey's spine. It didn't make much sense to pay off a credit card then put something else on it to celebrate. In fact, it sounded downright ludicrous, even to her own ears. She shouldn't have bought this dress. And the compulsivity! She'd bought it for no real or good reason.

Mark picked up his cloth napkin and placed it in his lap. "Would you like some help with your credit cards?"

A hot trail of defensiveness sped through her. Moments ago he'd gazed at her as if she were the main course, and now he was going to lecture her about money? The heat of embarrassment tinged her cheeks. She knew she needed better control of her spending, but that wasn't any of Mark's business. "Excuse me?"

He shrugged his shoulders. "You've helped me. I could help you."

Zoey pursed her lips and glared at him. "Did I ask for your help?"

"Why are you being so defensive?" He pointed to the dress. "It's obvious you shouldn't have bought that outfit."

She sucked in her breath. "I like this dress. I—I thought you did, too."

"Yes, it's fine, but is it worth having more debt on your credit card?" He reached across the table and grabbed her hand. "Zoey, I think you have a problem."

Zoey jerked her hand away from him. "How dare you?" Deep in her heart she knew he spoke the truth, but it wasn't his place to say such things to her. "I have a problem?" She pointed at herself then motioned toward him. "Let me ask you, Mark. How many times have you splurged already this week?"

"What?"

"You heard me. It's been six weeks. With the diet and exercise I have you on, you should have lost twenty pounds. So where are you cheating?"

Anger contorted his features, and he leaned toward her with gritted teeth. "I was offering to help you. I was not trying to challenge you."

"Were you? Were you really?"

"Mark, I cannot believe we ran into you here."

Zoey turned toward the thin sandy-haired woman beside them. Who was this? Was she his girlfriend, too? The man was just full of surprises tonight.

Mark turned toward the woman and gasped. "Maddy?"

"This has got to be Zoey," the young woman responded. She turned and motioned for an older woman to walk toward her.

"Mark!" the older woman exclaimed then placed her hand on her chest when she looked at Zoey. "And this must be Zoey."

A pained expression crossed Mark's face as he turned toward Zoey. The smile on his lips was obviously fake as he motioned toward the women. "Zoey, meet my mother and my sister."

Chapter 10

Mark wanted to crawl under the table when Maddy nudged Zoey and slipped into the booth beside her. His mother pushed him over as well. She extended her hand across the table. "Hi. I'm Sylvia. It's such a pleasure to meet you."

Zoey smiled. It was forced. Mark could see the daggers of anger her eyes shot at him. "I'm Zoey Coyle. It's nice to meet you."

"And I'm Maddy." His sister leaned closer to Zoey, wrapped her arm around Zoey's shoulder, and squeezed her.

Mark closed his eyes and shook his head. He loved his mother and sister, but the two of them were exasperating. They were busybodies—well, not exactly in a bad way most of the time. Most people thought they were easy to talk to and had the ability to make you feel better about yourself. And he knew they were intuitive, but at this moment he wished they would have taken all their wonderful qualities and sat on the other side of the room.

"Mom, sis, we've already ordered," Mark tried to explain, but his mother swatted away his words.

"Not a problem. We know what we want."

Maddy winked at Mark. "Maybe they want to eat alone, Mom."

Mark breathed a sigh of relief at his sister then glanced at Zoey. She bit the inside of her lip and glared at him. Before he could respond, his mother reached across the table and touched Zoey's hand. "Your dress is beautiful, dear."

Zoey cocked her head and blinked at Mark then smiled toward his mother. "Thank you, Sylvia. Mark and I were just discussing my dress."

Maddy shuffled her eyebrows. "I bet he thinks you look really pretty." Her tone was teasing, and Mark knew she was about to say something that would embarrass him. "It looks beautiful with your red hair. Mark mentioned—"

Mark interrupted her. "Maddy, didn't you say that you might want to sit somewhere else?"

"I think it would be a treat to eat with your mom and sister, Mark." Placing one elbow on the table, Zoey rested her chin on the top of her fist and glared at him. "They'll be nice, polite company."

Mark snarled at her while his mother and sister continued talking. The woman was incorrigible. Far too defensive. It was apparent she had a problem with using credit cards, and he only wanted to help her. He didn't want to get involved with a woman who couldn't control her spending. In his business, he'd seen many couples end up in financial ruin or even divorce court because one of the partners couldn't control his or her purchasing habits.

"He said you had a great shape." Maddy's comment broke him from his thoughts.

"I did not!" Mark stammered and looked at his sister.

Maddy rolled her eyes. "I didn't mean to make it sound like you were talking bad about her." She turned toward Zoey. "You know, like you're in shape. He said you all met at the gym."

"And you know," his mom chimed in, "the two of you looked absolutely adorable sitting across from each other."

Mark closed his eyes and shook his head. It would be better if he just ignored the conversation completely. There was no telling what his mom and sister would say next. There was no telling what they would tell Zoey he'd said, whether he'd said it or not.

I thought this would be a nice dinner between Zoey and me. It would have ended in a fight if Mom and Maddy hadn't shown up. Now it will most definitely end in embarrassment. God, this is a no-win situation.

※

It had been a week since the so-called celebratory dinner with Mark. Since then she'd finished her class finals. A little over a week until Christmas—then she could visit her family and see Micah again. *Before I blink my eyes I'll be starting my last semester of college.* The notion seemed surreal, and Zoey could hardly believe how fast the time had gone.

Zoey grabbed a bag of rice puffs and plopped onto the couch across from Brittany. "So what are your plans for tonight?"

Brittany shrugged. "I thought I was scheduled to work, but I got my weeks mixed up."

"Not going out with Neil?" Zoey tried to keep her tone light. Things seemed to have grown more tense between Brittany and her boyfriend, and the last few days Zoey thought Brittany acted less willing to accept Neil's treatment.

She shook her head. "He has to work."

Zoey popped a rice puff into her mouth. "It's just you and me tonight, then."

"You're not going out with Mark?"

Zoey chewed the snack slowly then swallowed. She thought of the nearly silent workout she'd guided Mark through the day before. He still seemed upset about her "splurging" comments, and in truth, she was still miffed at his accusations about her spending. Even if they were true. She scrunched her nose. "Don't think that will be happening for a while."

Brittany curled her legs underneath her and leaned back in her chair. "What happened?"

It was the first time in weeks Brittany seemed interested in something outside of Neil Thurman. Zoey clung to the hope that her sister was beginning to see that her world didn't need to revolve around one person. *Oh Jesus, may she yearn for You. Is this a step closer?*

Zoey placed the snack bag on the end table, scooped up a couch throw pillow, and tucked it under her arms and against her chest. "Well, we went to dinner the other night."

"When you wore your new red dress."

"Yeah." Zoey cocked her head. "You saw it? I thought you were asleep when I got home."

Brittany shrugged. "I was in my bedroom, and Neil and I had just had a fight, and I wasn't asleep. . . ." She gazed at the far wall then looked back at Zoey. "Anyway, tell me about your date. You looked really great, by the way."

"Thanks." Zoey leaned farther into the couch, enjoying this moment with her sister. It had been too long since the two of them spent time talking. "Well, we kind of got into an argument about splurging."

"Splurging?"

"Yeah. I thought he liked my dress, but when I told him I'd put it on my credit card. . ." Zoey felt her cheeks heat up. Admitting to her sister that she had a problem with her credit cards was more humbling than she'd imagined, and saying the words out loud made it seem even more real. "He offered to help me stop using them."

"And?"

"And it made me mad, and I told him I knew he'd been splurging on food and that was why he hadn't lost as much weight as I thought he should have."

"Zoey!"

Guilt wended its way through Zoey. "Well, he had splurged more than he should have, and I didn't ask for his help—"

"But you need it. How much have you spent on Christmas?"

Zoey inwardly groaned. She didn't even want to think about it. She tried so hard not to spend too much money, but then some enticing sale would pop up in her e-mail, or she'd walk into a department store with a little cash in her pocket, determined to spend only the cash, but then she'd see a deal she couldn't pass up and she'd purchase more than she intended. *God, this isn't good. This isn't good at all. What is ruling my life?*

"Well, it hasn't been Me lately."

The Spirit's nudging nearly forced Zoey to her knees. She had to do some serious soul-searching. She'd known for weeks, months even, that she had a problem with her spending, but saying the words aloud to her sister, who seemed to have much bigger problems—*Oh, sweet Jesus.*

Get the plank out of your own eye. The words she used to say and feel toward people who were quick to confront her during her teen years popped into her mind. It unnerved her that people would focus so quickly on her sins and not address their own. *Even if mine did need to be addressed.*

She looked at her sister. Brittany did need to get away from Neil, and Zoey would encourage her in every way possible to draw closer to her heavenly Father again. But Zoey had an issue she needed to take care of as well. Acknowledging her own failings, she nodded. "I do need help."

Zoey felt Brittany's stare for several minutes after she'd finally admitted aloud her credit card abuse. Brittany sat forward in her chair and grabbed Zoey's hand. "Can I pray for you?"

Taken aback by her sister's offer, she felt tears pool in her eyes. "Of course."

With their hands clasped together, Zoey sniffed back tears while her sister petitioned God on her behalf. The prayer was short and to the point, but it was sincere. Once she'd finished, Zoey wrapped her arms around Brittany's neck. "Thank you."

Brittany smiled. "As much praying as you've done for me in the last few weeks, it's the least I can do."

"How did you know I've been praying for you?"

Brittany giggled. "Sis, even when you're lying flat on the ground with your face smashed against the carpet, I can still make out my name."

Zoey chuckled and grabbed Brittany's arm. "Let's go grab a movie. Your treat."

"My treat?" Brittany pointed to herself.

"Yeah, I'm not using my credit card, and you still owe me money for rent."

"You got it." Brittany laughed. "Let me get my purse."

Within moments, Zoey was driving to the movie theater. Brittany turned the radio to a Christian station, and Zoey's heart nearly burst with excitement as they sang along with the music. Zoey pulled into the packed theater parking lot. She couldn't wipe the smile from her face as she walked with her sister toward the ticket booth. It had been too long since they'd enjoyed each other's company, and it was a welcome event.

Two couples stood in front of them in line. The biting December wind sent a chill through Zoey, but she couldn't deny she loved the two inches of snow on the ground. To her mind, it just made sense to have lots of snow for Christmas.

One of the couples moved into the theater, and out of the corner of Zoey's eye she noticed a familiar person. Glancing toward him, she gasped when she saw Neil with his arm draped around a small brunette. Zoey peered back at her sister to warn her, but Brittany's blanched expression was proof she had already seen her boyfriend.

"Let's go." Zoey looped her arm around Brittany's and turned her toward the car.

Neil looked over to them and scowled. He didn't even say a word to Brittany.

Zoey leaned toward her sister. "Did you two break up?"

"No."

"Oh." Zoey kept her tone low, attempting to keep her emotions in check. Surely her sister would not see her boyfriend out with another girl and still allow the guy to be her boyfriend. *Please, God, Brittany needs loose of Neil. She needs You.*

Zoey slipped into the driver's seat of her car as Brittany sat in the passenger's seat. Zoey turned the ignition, begging God to give her the right words to say.

Brittany touched Zoey's hand. "Don't worry anymore, sis. That was from God."

Zoey furrowed her eyebrows and looked at her sister. "What?"

Brittany swiped a tear from beneath her eye. "I've been asking God to help me know what to do about Neil. I'm miserable, but I just couldn't seem to break up with him. I needed help. It won't be so hard now."

As she said the last sentence, a dam of tears burst from her eyes, and Zoey leaned over and wrapped her arms around her little sister. "It still won't be easy, but He'll see you through. Trust Him."

Brittany sniffed and nodded. She sat up and buckled her seat belt. She looked at Zoey and smiled. "I know what I've got to do with my guy. What do you have to do with yours?"

Zoey scrunched her nose. "I suppose I know what I need to do with mine, too." She'd have to make a phone call when they got home.

❧

Mark lifted his hands in surrender. "I gotta have a water break, guys."

"Hurry up, old man." Bruce dribbled the basketball between his legs. "We only have the gym for another thirty minutes."

"Give the guy a break," Chris huffed as he made his way toward his duffel bag. He unzipped it and rustled through it. "Water. Gotta have water."

Bruce laughed. "I don't know why I hang out with a bunch of old guys."

Mark took a long swig from his water bottle then wiped his forehead with the back of his arm. "If I remember right, it was only a moment ago I swiped the ball right out of your hands."

Bruce huffed and grinned. "That was luck."

Mark's cell phone rang. He pulled it out of his bag and read Zoey's name on the screen. Part of him wanted to toss the phone into the bag and head back onto the court. The other part was eager to hear her voice. He couldn't believe how much he'd missed her. He nodded toward his friends. "Be back in a minute." He walked into the lobby before he answered. "Hello."

"Hi, Mark."

Pleasure washed over him simply at the sound of her voice. "Hi."

"Listen." She paused, and already Mark detected the hesitation in her tone. "I need to apologize."

"Zoey—"

"No, listen. I was mean, and I'm sorry, and I do need help, and—"

A vision of Zoey in the red dress raced through his mind. "That dress was amazing on you. I didn't mean to make you feel like I didn't think—"

"I know. Will you help me come up with a budget I can live with?"

The opportunity to see Zoey quickened his pulse. "How 'bout tonight? In an hour?"

Zoey laughed. "I can hardly wait."

❧

Zoey stared at the overwhelming pile of unwrapped Christmas presents on her bed. Even before she'd worked out a budget with Mark, the Spirit had nudged her to go through all the purchases she'd made. The nudging was confirmed when he suggested she take back as many items as she could.

"Whoa!" Brittany exclaimed. Her gaze traveled from the pile on the bed to the smaller pile on the floor. "Where did you even have room to stash all that stuff?"

Zoey shrugged. "I have no idea." She bit the inside of her lip. "I'm taking back all the stuff I bought on credit."

"Please tell me it's that pile." Brittany pointed to the items on the floor.

Zoey scrunched her nose and shook her head. She stared at all the gifts weighing down her bed. "I don't know how I'm going to do this. What will all those people think of me?"

"You're not going to worry about what other people think of you. You're going to do what God is guiding you to do; then you're going to listen to Him from here on out."

Zoey raised one eyebrow and turned to face her sister. She touched Brittany's forehead with the back of her hand. "Are you feeling well?"

Brittany giggled. "I know. I've not exactly been one to talk lately, but I'm changing my ways, and I'm going to help you change yours."

Zoey groaned as she watched her sister shove toys and clothes into various bags.

"Do you have all your receipts?"

"Of course. You know how proud I am of a good sale."

"Good." Brittany stood up and grabbed Zoey's hand. "Now go get me your credit cards, because you're not holding them in the store."

Zoey's heart lightened. "You're going to go with me?"

"Yes."

Zoey trudged into the living area and grabbed her credit cards out of the wallet in her purse. Thankfulness for her sister wrapped itself around her. She had no idea how she would make it through taking all those things back to the stores. Feeling very much like a five-year-old handing her mommy the toy that she wasn't old enough to play with, Zoey knew Brittany was right. Until she allowed God to have complete control of her spending habits, Zoey didn't need to hold on to her credit cards.

Give me a humble spirit, Lord. This is my weakness. You and I both know it. But Your scripture says Your power is made perfect in weakness. Help me to lean on You in this weakness that I may be strong.

❧

Zoey ran her fingers through her newly trimmed hair. She sat down and leaned back in the beauty shop chair beside her mother. Brittany, with her new short bob, sat down in an empty chair on the other side of their mom.

"You girls have no idea how much I needed this," Zoey's mom, Kelly, said as she handed a piece of aluminum foil up to her beautician. "I'm sorry you have to wait on me, but you girls don't have gray that has to be covered."

"We don't mind, Mom," Brittany said. She tilted her head as she looked at her reflection. "Do you really like my hair short?"

"It looks really good," said Kelly.

"It really does," added Zoey, "but then, you're beautiful. You'd look gorgeous if you buzzed it."

Brittany laughed. "I'm pretty sure I'd scare the guys off then."

"No, you wouldn't."

Kelly cleared her throat. "Still no Neil?"

Brittany bit her bottom lip. "No Neil."

"She's doing great," said Zoey. She wrapped her fingers around the arms of the vinyl chair, praying Brittany wouldn't become emotional. They'd had a wonderful afternoon. Zoey had really looked forward to their mother-daughters date, especially since they couldn't get three haircuts at the beauty parlor at the same time over Thanksgiving break.

"What about you?" Her mom focused her attention on Zoey.

"What about me?"

"Isn't there a guy—I believe you've mentioned him—"

"It's too bad Candy couldn't come with us. You'd think they wouldn't have practice so often during Christmas break."

Kelly shook her finger in the air, peering at Zoey through the mirror. "Don't try to change the subject, Zoey. What was the guy's name, Brittany?"

Zoey peeked at her sister. Her face was lit up brighter than the Christmas tree at the back of the shop.

"His name is Mark."

Her mom snapped her fingers. "Yes. That was it. What about him?"

Zoey blew out a breath. She twirled a strand of her hair between her fingers. What was Mark to her? She thought about him all the time. More than all the time. She even woke up thinking about him sometimes. At first she'd dismissed it as simply being interested in the well-being of one of her trainees, albeit one she really liked. Having dinner with him and feeling such fury when he offered her help had proven to her that her feelings toward him were definitely more than that of a trainer. She looked at her mom and shrugged. "I don't know, Mom."

Brittany huffed obnoxiously and rolled her eyes. "Puh-leaze, Zoey. Just admit you've fallen for him."

Hearing the words was like a smack in the face. Zoey blinked at the impact of them, realizing the depth of their truth. She gazed at her reflection, then at her mom. "Brittany's right. I've fallen for him."

Chapter 11

Mark hadn't seen Zoey in almost three weeks. He'd gotten the flu just before Christmas and was stuck in bed for several days. Then she'd gone to see her family for a week at Christmas. And as was the tradition every year, he took his mom and sister to northern New York to visit her sister and brother for the week of New Year's. Though he and Zoey weren't officially dating, he'd bought her a small present for Christmas that he'd wanted to give her. He couldn't help but admit that he'd hoped his New Year's kiss would come from her instead of his mother.

Can't change the past. I'm going to see her now. Mark looked at the small present sitting in the passenger's seat. The gift wasn't much, just a gift certificate to her favorite nail place and one to get her hair fixed. He figured he'd encourage her "no credit card" lifestyle and give her the money to do a few of the things he knew she enjoyed.

Parking the car, he placed the gift on the floor beneath the dashboard, hoping she'd agree to get a bite to eat with him after their workout session. His heart hammered in his chest as he made his way into the gym. He couldn't believe how much he'd missed her.

"Mark!" Zoey's squeal sounded from across the room. She raced toward him and wrapped her arms around his waist. "I'm so glad to see you."

Surprised and thrilled to feel Zoey's embrace, he placed his arms around her and pulled her closer. She fit perfectly in his embrace, her frame small yet strong. Though she'd obviously been at the gym for several hours, he could still smell a hint of her fruity shampoo. The whole gym could have shut down around them and he wouldn't have cared as long as Zoey stayed in his arms.

She broke away from him then punched his arm. "I've missed you so much."

Mark took in the two knotted ponytails at the top of her head, the style that made her appear younger than she already was. Her eyes gleamed with merriment and the deep dimples in her cheeks nearly screamed at him to lean down and kiss them. He fought off the urge and flicked one of the ponytails instead. "I've missed you, too."

She grabbed his waist. "You've lost some more weight."

He nodded. "My last weigh-in at work, I'd lost twenty-seven pounds."

She winked. "Talk about a hunk." She clamped her lips then released a long sigh. "I mean. . ."

Mark knew she must be as nervous about seeing him again as he was about seeing her. Zoey had a bubbly side, but this was a bit excessive—though he didn't mind. The notion of her missing him as much as he missed her filled his heart with hope. He wanted a relationship with Zoey. The time apart had proven to him that he wanted her in his life and wanted to get to know her better. He tried to ease her discomfort by putting his arm around her shoulder. "Getting the flu right before Christmas will sure help a guy to lose weight."

Zoey smiled. Her tone sobered as she looked toward the gym equipment. "Talking through e-mail is not as good as in person."

"I agree."

She guided him to a chair. "We have a few minutes before we need to start. Tell me about your holidays."

Mark told her about his Christmas and New Year's with his mom and sister. "I never apologized for them dropping in on us at the restaurant."

Zoey swatted the air. "Are you kidding? I think they're great." She twirled the string of her drawstring backpack. "I would love to meet them again."

Pleasure filled Mark. "I'd love that. So tell me about your Christmas."

Zoey's face brightened. "I've brought pictures." She opened her bag and pulled out an overstuffed package of photos. She pointed to each one, describing who the person was and what he or she was doing. Her cousin Micah was in almost every picture, and he couldn't count the number of pictures in which she was holding the boy.

"He looks a lot like you." Mark pointed to a picture of Micah opening one of his presents while he was sitting in Zoey's lap.

Zoey nodded. Her eyebrows rose. "Do you think so?" Her expression became unreadable, and Mark could tell she wanted to explain something to him.

"Hey, Mark, how were the holidays?"

Mark turned toward the sound of Kevin's voice. To his surprise, Kevin extended his hand. Mark shook it. "They were good. How about you?"

"Wonderful. I went to church with my parents."

Mark studied Kevin. Was there a change in his colleague? Though Mark spent most days wanting to pummel Kevin, he also deliberately tried to pray for the man. Mark knew without Christ his own ego ran a bit too big as well. "I'm really happy for you."

"Have we met?" Kevin offered his hand to Zoey. He nodded when she shook it. "Kevin Fink."

"I'm Zoey Coyle." She frowned and Mark knew she was trying to figure out Kevin as well. "I believe we have met."

Kevin lifted his hand. "Oh, I'm sorry."

Zeke called Zoey's name and she turned and nodded to him. Kevin grinned at Mark, shuffled his eyebrows, then winked. Fury boiled within Mark. *That little snake. He's trying to wind his way around Zoey.*

Mark felt his fists ball at his sides. He took long breaths to keep from punching the man in the face. *One one-thousand, two one-thousand.* In his "before Christ" days, Mark wasn't exactly known for his ability to keep his cool. Even now he found it hard to stay calm.

Zoey turned back around and looked at Mark. "We'd better get started." She turned to Kevin. "It was nice to meet you again."

Kevin smiled, a smile so vile that Mark envisioned his fist uniting with Kevin's mouth and his teeth crashing to the floor. "Nice to meet you, too."

Zoey guided Mark toward the pool. "Your friend is nicer than I remember."

"He's not my friend." Mark's words came out with more vehemence than he intended. He wasn't angry with Zoey. But the gall of that man!

"Maybe you should try to be friends with him. Sounds like he's seeking Christ."

Mark closed his eyes and bit his lip so hard he feared he'd drawn blood. *God, I do pray for Kevin, but right now I just pray You'll help me not to pulverize him.*

❧

Zoey let out a long breath. She was about to tell Mark about Micah when his friend or colleague or whoever the guy was walked up to them. She'd been so excited to see Mark. When she saw his car pull up in front of the gym, she thought she would literally jump out of her skin. She'd missed him more than she ever would have imagined possible.

She missed the way he raised one eyebrow at her whenever he was frustrated, the way he pursed his lips when he was lifting weights, even if the weights weren't too heavy. She missed the sound of his voice and the scent of his cologne. Never would she have believed she'd noticed so many things about him until she wasn't able to see, hear, and smell those things. She couldn't remember the last time she'd felt this way about a man, and in her quiet time, she knew God was pleased with her feelings for Mark.

Then Kevin interrupted their conversation. Ever since then, Mark was as grumpy and cantankerous as could be. He huffed when she asked him to do anything and growled at all her suggestions. She bent down to pick up a weight and handed it to him.

"I got it," he snapped.

Zoey placed her hands on her hips. "What is the matter with you?"

Mark scowled. "Nothing."

"Something is wrong, and I'd like to know what it is."

"Could we just train, please?"

"Fine." Zoey stepped back and allowed Mark to get his own weights. She didn't even tell him what he needed to do; after all, Mark White already knew everything.

She crossed her arms in front of her chest. No one could get under her skin as quickly as he could. It was like he had a magnetic force that drew the anger right out of her. The problem was he drew other emotions out as well.

A vision of Yoda fighting some nemesis in *Star Wars* popped into her mind. *The Force is with Mark.* She had always hated the movie when she was a kid, but it was one of her mom and dad's favorites. Something about it being a big deal when they were kids. It didn't matter; the memory brought a giggle to her lips, and Mark turned and glared at her.

She raised her arms in surrender. "I didn't do anything, Mark."

Mark looked away then back at her. "I know you didn't. I'm sorry, Zoey."

He stood and took her hand in his. Her heart raced and she wondered if he could feel her raging pulse through her fingertips. "I've been looking forward to seeing you all day, and I wondered—"

"Hey, is anyone using this machine?" Kevin walked up and pointed to the Universal.

Zoey looked at him and shook her head. She couldn't help but notice that Kevin was a really good-looking guy, and when he smiled, wow! The guy reminded her of a younger Brad Pitt. Not that the actor wasn't still drop-dead gorgeous.

Mark pulled his hand away from her and slumped back onto the bench. His anger was back. She realized it was geared toward Kevin, but she didn't understand why. The guy had acted like a real jerk the first time she met him, but he seemed different now. No one knew better than Zoey how much a person could change once God got hold of him or her.

She glanced at Mark. She'd wanted to tell him about Micah. It was important that he know about her past and how God had changed her. She wondered if he would still accept her. *He doesn't seem to be willing to give Kevin that chance, and he's known Kevin a lot longer than he's known me.*

The realization saddened her. Maybe all the pining she'd done for him while they were apart was in vain. Maybe she'd placed him on a pedestal without realizing it. She and Brittany had been such amazing encouragements to each other through her sister's breakup with Neil and Zoey's efforts to stop using credit cards. If she had been wrong about Mark, Zoey knew Brittany would be there to encourage her again.

"Hey, are you two dating?" Kevin's question interrupted her thoughts.

She looked at Mark. He snarled and stared at Kevin. Zoey waited for Mark to respond with an affirmative, or at least to say that he liked her and wanted to get to know her better. But he didn't. He just sat there, his gaze practically shooting fire at Kevin. If Kevin's question made Mark so mad, why didn't he respond?

The hurt she felt gave way to frustration. She looked at Kevin. "No. We're not dating."

"Hey, then, if it's all right with you, man"—Kevin glanced at Mark then looked back at her—"would you like to catch a bite to eat when you get off work?"

Zoey peered at Mark, wishing he would look at her, wishing he would see the hurt he'd caused her by not saying that they were thinking about dating or that he cared about her or something. But he never looked up. He simply stared at the dumbbell at his feet. Zoey peeked at Kevin. "Sure. That would be great."

❧

Mark could not believe Zoey agreed to get something to eat with Kevin. It's just proof that women are blind.

Or maybe it's proof that you need to step up and tell her how you really feel.

He smacked the top of the steering wheel. He was a wimp for not telling Zoey how much she meant to him. Now he sat in his car in the back of a parking lot watching her and one of the lowest men he knew eat dinner at their favorite deli.

Kevin was evidently telling her some funny story because he was flapping his arms like a goofy bird. Mark could barely see her smile, but he couldn't decipher if she was having a good time. *Maybe if I parked a little closer I could see better.* He shook his head. *No. Then they might see me.*

The absurdity of his thought smacked him in the face, and he rubbed his temples. "What am I doing here?" he whispered. "Am I some kind of crazy stalker?"

He turned the ignition and drove out of the parking lot. He made his way to his house then went inside. Walking into his bathroom, he turned on the cold water and splashed his face. He grabbed the towel from the rack and wiped off. Peering at his reflection, he whispered, "God, this is crazy."

"Yes, it is. Your value comes from Me. Not from what you look like, what you used to look like, or what you'll look like in the future."

Humbled by the Spirit, Mark sat in his recliner and picked up his Bible. He turned to the scripture in 1 Timothy that God had shown him not too many weeks before. "For physical training is of some value, but godliness has value for all things"—he said the words aloud as a prayer to God and an audible reminder to himself—"holding promise for both the present life and the life to come."

Mark shut his Bible and quoted the verse repeatedly, aloud and in his mind. He drank in the meaning, allowing God to remind him of his worth through Christ and nothing else. After asking God to forgive him for his behavior toward Zoey, he went to his room and turned on his computer. He knew he couldn't say all he needed to say through e-mail, but he could start with an apology.

His cell phone rang. He looked at the caller ID. It was his mom. "Hey, Mom." He tried to sound cheerful even though he'd wanted Zoey to be the one calling him.

"Hi, Mark. I've been thinking a lot about you and Zoey, and I was wondering if you'd be willing to invite her over Friday night for snacks and board games."

Mark grinned. His mom and sister loved board games. Something in him told him that Zoey would as well. And this would give him the perfect excuse to ask her out again. "Mom, I think that's a great idea."

"Terrific."

Mark could hear Maddy's whoops in the background. He was sure his sister was either on the other line or listening through his mother's phone.

"Okay. Unless I hear from you, we'll expect you at eight."

"Sounds good." Mark shut his phone then opened a new message window on his computer.

Zoey was already logged on. Excitement welled inside him. That meant she and Kevin hadn't stayed out very long at all. As quickly as his fingers would move, he typed an apology message to her. He kept it general, because he wanted to tell her how he really felt to her face.

He waited several minutes, but though she still appeared to be logged on, she didn't reply. Maybe she'd just stepped away from her computer or forgotten to log off.

Knowing she was still mad at him, and that she had every right to be, he went ahead and asked her to dinner and to his mom's house on Friday. *Maybe that will show her I'm truly sorry.*

Several minutes passed. Still no response. *It's okay.* Mark logged off the computer and shut it down. *I'll see if she responds by morning. If not, I'll give her a call. Lord, I pray I didn't wait too long.*

Chapter 12

Zoey had just about had all she could take of Kevin Fink. The first time she met him she had thought he was a jerk, but then at the gym that afternoon, he'd seemed so nice. He'd even acted like he was interested in her faith. Now, however, his true self seemed to be making an appearance. He shared yet another crude joke, and she had to excuse herself from the table.

She headed to the back of the deli and into the restroom. After locking herself inside, she pulled her phone from her pocket. "That's funny. I have three missed calls from Brittany. I didn't even feel my phone vibrate."

She pushed the number and turned toward the mirror. Her hair was a wreck after a full day of work. She was tired and ready to go home. She never would have dreamed Kevin would want to stay at the deli this long.

"Zoey, it's about time you called," Brittany's voice sounded over the line.

"Sorry 'bout that. I didn't know you called. Listen, I need your help."

Zoey tilted her head and rested the phone between her ear and shoulder. She scoured through her purse for a brush or comb. She had no intention of trying to impress Kevin, but she didn't want the whole world to have to continue to look at the rat's nest on top of her head. After finding a hand-sized brush, she pulled out one ponytail then the other.

"First, I gotta tell you something. I've been using your computer because mine's not working right, and I forgot to log off your name—"

"Brittany, I told you not to do that. People think I'm online when I'm not." She worked the brush through her tangles.

"I know. Mark's instant-messaged you twice."

"What?" Zoey dropped the brush in the sink and grabbed the phone with her hand. "What did he say?"

"He wrote some big long apology about the way he acted at the gym. He said something about some guy Kevin and how he'd prayed for him for years, and he didn't want you to get wrapped up with him."

Zoey huffed. "I figured that out on my own."

"He said he needs to talk to you in person."

"Well, did you respond?"

"No. What was I supposed to say? I felt horrible reading him spilling his guts out on the computer."

Zoey tapped her fingernails against the sink. "Well, why didn't you just log off?"

"I was trying, but I'd saved my paper to your computer and I couldn't get the printer to work fast enough. He asked you to his mom's house for a game night, too. Do you want me to respond now?"

"No." Zoey stared at her reflection in the mirror. An idea popped into her head. "I'm going to run over to his house."

"You've been to his house?"

"No. But I know his address from the gym."

"Hey, did you call me for something?"

"I'll tell you later. Bye, sis." Zoey shut the phone and put it back in her pocket. She finished brushing her hair and put it up in a single ponytail. Rummaging through her purse, she found a tube of lip gloss, mascara, and some blush. She wet and dried her face then applied the makeup she had with her. Satisfied with her appearance, she walked out of the bathroom.

No surprise to her, Kevin had scooted his chair beside an attractive woman who sat at the table adjacent to theirs. When he saw her, he smiled and moved his chair back in one swift move. "I was beginning to wonder if you fell in." He spread his arms wide. "But I can see you were just freshening up for me."

Zoey bit back a growl. "Thanks for the sandwich, Kevin, but I have to go."

"But you didn't finish your food."

"I'm sorry."

She'd reached the door when her conscience got the better of her. She turned to apologize for her curt behavior, but Kevin had already moved beside the woman at the other table. Zoey almost laughed out loud. *Wow! Now I know why Mark got so upset each time Kevin talked to us.*

She walked out the door and slid into her car. Turning the ignition, she glanced at the clock. It was only eight. Not too late to visit Mark. She knew just where he lived since she hadn't been able to resist driving by his house one time while he was gone to New York with his mom and sister.

God, I want to be honest with him about the way I feel, about Micah. He's someone I'd be willing to take home to meet Mom and Harold and Micah. In fact, that would be a great idea.

She pulled into the driveway behind his car. Fear wrapped around her heart as she looked at the two-story town house. She gripped the car door handle. *Maybe I shouldn't be here. He's not expecting me, probably doesn't want to see me.*

But Brittany said he wrote a long apology message.

Mustering all the courage she could find, she stepped out of the car and walked to the front door. She stood there several moments before balling her hand into a fist, ready to knock on the door. *Oh boy. Oh boy. I don't think I can do this.*

She couldn't just stand there all night. What would his neighbors think? She clutched her fist with her other hand. It was cold outside, colder than it had been in days, and already her nose and cheeks felt the effect of the night wind. She should have worn her mittens and put on some earmuffs, especially if she was going to stand outside in the elements all evening. Taking another deep breath, she balled her fist again to knock.

The door opened, and Zoey squealed and jumped back. Mark gasped then pulled the door open all the way. "Zoey? What are you doing here?"

Zoey flattened her palm against her speeding heart. She took several breaths to ensure she hadn't just had a heart attack. "I wanted to talk with you."

He motioned her inside. "Come on in. You look like you're freezing to death. How long have you been out there?"

"Too long."

"Let me have your coat." Zoey inhaled the scent of Mark's home. It didn't smell like candles or even his cologne. It had more of a woodsy scent. As she scanned the room, taking in the deep green and brown colors of his furnishings, she was surprised at the similarity of their decorating tastes. On the far end table she spied a reed diffuser. *Sandalwood. That's what the smell is.*

"Come on, Zoey." He gently grabbed her arm and led her to an oversized chair. "Have a seat. Would you like a cup of coffee?"

Zoey nodded. "Actually, I think I would."

"Okay. I'll be right back."

Zoey stared at Mark's oversized flat-screen television as well as the Wii game station beneath it. She never would have figured Mark to be a Wii guy. But why wouldn't he be? The few times she'd had the opportunity to play one of the games, she'd really enjoyed it. Even if she was terrible.

"Do you like anything in your coffee?" Mark called from the kitchen.

"Just cream. Thanks."

Mark walked into the living room and handed her the coffee. He placed his cup on the end table and sat in the chair across from her. He clasped his hands in front of him. He seemed as nervous as she felt. "So you read my messages?" His voice was low and hesitant.

"Actually, no." She placed her coffee on the table beside her. "Brittany was on my computer, and I was still with Kevin."

"Oh." He nodded, and Zoey noticed a bright red streak cover his neck. He cleared his throat. "Well, what I said—"

"Kevin's not a very nice guy."

Mark shook his head. "I'm afraid he's not."

"You didn't know how to warn me."

"I didn't."

Zoey leaned forward in the chair. "What I need to know is why you would want to warn me. Is it just because we're friends?"

Mark shifted in his chair as he shook his head. "No. It's not."

Zoey moved closer to the edge of her seat. "Does that mean you. . ." How did she say it without sounding like she was fifteen again? *Oh, who cares? Just be honest, Zoey.* "You like me?"

Mark got up and walked toward the bookcase beside his television. He fingered the tops of several books. "Look at me, Zoey. I'm six years older than you. I've still got some weight to lose."

"Barely, and why would that matter?"

"I'm even getting a bald spot on the top of my head."

Zoey scrunched up her nose, inwardly giggling at the thought. "You are?"

He turned around and walked to her. Taking her hands in his, he guided her to her feet. Her heart sped up at the look in his eye. The intensity she remembered from the inn had returned to his gaze, sending chills up and down her arms. "Zoey, I'm absolutely crazy about you."

"Really?"

He released her hands and wiped his face with the palm of his hand. "The three weeks I couldn't see you were the longest weeks of my life. I thought I was going nuts. Every time I saw a red-haired woman I thought of you. I watched her until I knew she wasn't you."

A giggle swelled within her throat until she couldn't contain it any longer. "I'm crazy about you, too."

Before she could utter another word, Mark wrapped his arms around her and pressed his lips against her forehead. She hugged him around his waist. "It's been a long time since I felt this way."

"Me, too."

Mark held her for several moments. Zoey relished his scent, wondering if he would cup her chin and kiss her lips. She wanted him to, but she enjoyed the warmth of his embrace as well.

He kissed the top of her head again. "Did Brittany tell you about my mom inviting us to play board games on Friday?"

Zoey nodded. "I can't wait."

Mark released her. He touched the side of her cheek with the back of his finger. "How could a woman as beautiful as you give me a second glance?"

She bit the inside of her lip. His sweet tone and gentle touch overwhelmed her. Even more, the fact that he loved her Jesus and wanted to serve Him thrilled her to the core of her being. God was blessing her despite the mistakes she'd made in the past.

I need to tell him about Micah. Her stomach twisted with fear that he would be upset and reject her when she told him the truth. Not only was she not a virgin, but she'd also carried and birthed a child and given that child up for adoption. But she had to tell him. She'd have to face whatever response he had. "Mark—"

"Zoey, have you ever played a Wii?"

Zoey glanced up at Mark. The challenging glint in his eye made her smile. "Only a few times. I'm not very good."

"My mom bought this for me for Christmas, and I'm addicted to it." He patted his belly. "It's good for the weight loss, too." He held a control out to her. "Wanna try?"

Zoey laughed out loud at the childish expression on Mark's face. She could tell him about Micah on Friday. For now, she was going to learn how to play a Wii.

⁓

Mark couldn't mask his happiness as he walked into the bank the following morning. He didn't even want to hide it. Each day it seemed his pants fit looser. Today, he'd had to tighten his belt another notch. And tonight he'd see Zoey again at the gym, and probably enjoy dinner with her afterward. Life simply couldn't get any better.

He walked into his office, sat in his leather chair, then turned on the computer. Waiting for the system to boot, he arranged his phone messages in order of importance. He glanced at the calendar. He could hardly believe January was half over. Turning toward his computer, he clicked on his e-mail. He opened a message from Kevin gloating about what a great time he'd had with Zoey.

Frustrated, he pushed away from his computer and leaned back in the chair. *If anyone could make his blood pressure rise, Kevin Fink could. He's starting in on me awfully early. He's not usually even here yet.* Mark stood and paced in front of his desk. *I know good and well he didn't have a blast with Zoey, because she spent most of the evening with me.*

The man seemed to thrive on getting under Mark's skin. It was like his mission in life. Angry retorts buzzed through his mind. Normally Mark tried to count down from the fury, but this morning he'd had it. There comes a time when a man just needs to speak his mind.

Mark sat back down at his desk. In a matter of moments, he wrote a reply calling Kevin out on his little exaggeration. But Mark's frustration didn't stop there. He continued to type another five lines or so explaining that he was no longer going to take Kevin's manipulative actions. Not wanting the chance to calm down and change his mind, Mark sent the e-mail without reading over what he'd written.

I don't even care if it's full of typos or if the sentences don't make complete sense. Enough is enough.

With a huff, Mark stood again. This time he walked out of his office and headed to the coffeepot. Pouring a small cup, he peered into Kevin's office. The lights weren't on. What did the man do? Send the e-mail from his house? What is it about me that makes him feel so threatened?

He headed back to his office. He was done messing with Kevin. Praying for the man for the past five years hadn't changed him at all. If he said anything else today, Mark planned to put him in his place.

The front door opened and Betty walked inside. She saw Mark and started to cry. Mark walked forward and put his arm around her shoulder. "Betty, what's wrong?"

"Oh Mark, it's awful," she wailed.

Mark guided her to a cushiony chair in the lobby. He pulled a tissue from the box on the counter and handed it to his manager. "Betty, what is it?"

"There's been an accident."

"What kind of accident?"

Betty dabbed her eyes then blew her nose. "A car accident. And Kevin—" Her chest heaved and more tears rolled down her cheeks.

His heart sunk as a feeling of doom washed over him. "What about Kevin?"

"He's dead."

⁂

Two days later Mark sat in a metal folding chair staring at a casket draped with an arrangement of blue and white flowers. Zoey sat beside him, listening to the preacher talk about Kevin's life. It was a generic eulogy—one he knew his own pastor struggled through when the person who'd passed away didn't know Christ as his or her Savior. He glanced around the room filled with Kevin's family, their colleagues, and several of the bank's patrons before focusing on the casket again. Someone near him murmured, "Such a senseless tragedy."

Mark felt empty, like someone had taken out his insides and hidden them from him. He and Betty had been given the task of going through Kevin's files and e-mails. The last message he sent Kevin stuck in his mind. The anger Mark had felt at that moment had been pointless. It would not have changed Kevin's behavior and attitude, but it did change Mark—for the worse.

Zoey squeezed his hand and peered up at him. "Are you okay?"

Mark inhaled. "I will be. You know I've spent five years praying for him."

"I know."

Mark looked down at their intertwined hands. "Didn't do much good, did it?"

"Of course it did. It did you good." She squeezed his hand. "You can't control others' responses."

God, I should have controlled my response. I was so angry with him. Sure, I prayed for him, but how many times did I respond to his comments too sharply and too quickly? How many.times did he see more of the fleshly Mark White and less of You?

Guilt ate away at him as memory after memory of retorts flooded his mind. He wished he could take them all back, that he could have been a better witness to Kevin.

The preacher finished the eulogy and Mark took his place as a pallbearer with a couple of his other colleagues and a few of Kevin's friends from college. They waited as Kevin's father and mother said their last good-byes. Mark knew Kevin's father's pale expression and mother's tearstained face would haunt him for the next several months. The whole thing still seemed surreal—until the casket was closed and Mark lifted his portion of the weight. It was heavier than he thought.

God. The silent plea slipped through his mind. He remembered his father's death and burial. The pain attacked him afresh and piled onto the guilt he felt over Kevin. His dad had been a good man. Mark had nothing to regret in terms of his relationship with his father.

But with Kevin? Even though the man was dead, Mark still didn't like him. What did that make him? How could he have genuinely prayed for a man he didn't like? *Maybe I never did pray for him from my heart, Lord. Were my petitions shallow? Did I really want him to change, to come to know You, or was I just uttering words in my mind because I knew I should?*

Kevin's behavior toward women practically mirrored the way Mark treated girls when he was a teen. Mark had been selfish and egotistical. The memories embarrassed and saddened him. When he watched Kevin's actions, he felt as if his own sins were being rehashed and shoved in his face anew. *Did he ever have the opportunity to see You in me, or was I still so self-absorbed, stewing over how his actions made me feel, that I couldn't see clearly to be a living testimony? Was I just worried about me? Did I really want him to change?*

"You did."

Mark pushed away the Spirit's nudging. He should have been a better witness. The grave site, the burial, the rest of the funeral all passed in a blur. With the last song sung and the last prayer uttered, family and friends made their way to their vehicles, but Mark stood back watching Kevin's parents. His mother, almost too weak to stand, clung to his father's arm and shoulder. The man stood stoically, obviously trying to be strong for his wife, but Mark could see that his jaw was shaking and that at any moment tears would flow freely down the older man's cheeks.

Mark remembered how hard it had been to bury his father. How awful would it be to bury a child? He couldn't fathom it. Zoey walked up beside him and looped her arm around his. "I'm sorry, Mark."

Mark couldn't look at her. The guilt he felt gnawed at him. "Don't feel sorry for me. I didn't even like him."

"That's not true." Her gaze penetrated him. "If you didn't like him, then why do you feel so sad?"

"Because I should have liked him."

"No, Mark. You did care about Kevin. You prayed for him. You didn't have to be his best friend. You shouldn't feel all this guilt."

He peered into her face and pointed to his chest. "God placed me in his life. I should have been a better witness. If I had been more patient, maybe he would have accepted Christ."

Zoey furrowed her brow. "So now you're God?" She crossed her arms. "That's an awfully arrogant statement, Mark."

Mark blinked and shook his head. He motioned toward the grave site. "A man I should have treated better is dead." He pointed to himself again. "I'm saying with my mouth, and feeling with my heart, that I should have been a better witness to him." He squinted at her. "And that makes me arrogant? Explain how."

Zoey reached up and touched his cheek. Tenderness shone from her dark eyes. "No. Your believing you were in control of Kevin's choices makes your thinking arrogant. Each person has to choose Christ individually."

"But I should have been a better witness."

"Mark, we all sin and fall short of the glory of God. That means Christians, too."

Zoey's teeth chattered the last few words. Though he couldn't feel anything, he knew it was cold and they'd been standing outside a long time. He put his arm around her and guided her toward the car. In his mind, he knew she was right. But the thought of a man dying lost, without having accepted Christ—Mark shuddered. He'd spend the rest of his life telling everyone he knew about Jesus.

Chapter 13

Zoey walked into her favorite nail salon. Greeting her technician, she sat down and allowed Kim to start filing down her much-too-long nails. "Do you want a design today?" Kim asked.

Zoey grinned. "You know I do." She pointed to the fourth flower design on the pallet. "I want this one, only just on my ring fingers."

"Okay." Kim went back to work, applying the acrylic then filing the thickness and the tips of the nails until they were the length and shape Zoey wanted. Having spent most of her growing-up years biting her nails down to the nub, Zoey was always thrilled to see her nails neatly manicured and sporting a cool design. She looked at the painted white flower with streaks of pink through the petals and the hot pink gem on both her ring fingers. "Kim, I think this is my favorite design yet."

Kim smiled and pulled a nail tip out of the drawer behind her station. "I'm working on another design."

Zoey oohed over the yellow, pink, and orange lines that framed the edges of the nail. "I may have to try that next time."

Once finished, Zoey pulled the gift certificate Mark had given her as a late Christmas gift from her purse. At first, she had been furious with him for suggesting she needed to curb her spending, but once she admitted to herself, her sister, and Mark that he was right, she'd been striving diligently to live within her means. *And this gift allowed me to pay more than the minimum due on my credit card bill this month.*

She smiled at how good it felt to pay down her bills instead of adding to them. Mark had offered to assist her in writing up a budget, but with the holidays and Kevin's death, they'd never gotten around to it. *I think I'm doing pretty well though. I've cut up all the department store cards I had and kept only one major card for emergencies. And it's frozen in a cube of ice in the freezer.*

Waving good-bye to Kim, Zoey walked out of the shop and into the mall area. The windows of one of her favorite department stores were plastered with post-holiday sale signs. The urge to stop by for a quick look niggled at her gut. She thought of how that particular store allowed its customers to purchase even without the credit card on hand; she simply had to punch her social security number into the machine. *I have to stay strong. There is nothing I need in there.*

She turned her head and walked toward the mall's exit. *What I do need is to find a nail salon that's not in the center of the mall.*

She raised her eyebrows at the thought. It wasn't such a bad idea. It would keep her from being so tempted. As she pondered the possibility, she realized a lot of her shopping sprees happened right after trips to get her nails done.

She really liked Kim, but if the temptation was too great, she was willing to find another place. *Or I could just stop getting my nails done.* She looked down at her pink and white tips and the small white flowers painted on her ring fingernails. *Nah. As long as I can fit it in the budget, I love getting my nails done.*

Tightening her coat around her, she headed to her car. *What I should do is just cancel those cards; then I won't have an account in the stores' systems when I go to get my nails done.* Pleased with the idea, she slipped inside her car and drove toward the bank. She was meeting Mark for lunch. Afterward, she had an interview at the hospital. She wouldn't be able to start in an official dietician position until she graduated in four months, but she could work as a dietary aide. The opportunity to spend a few months getting to know the environment of her job thrilled her, and she prayed the interview would go well.

She pulled into the bank's parking lot and picked up the small paperweight she'd found at the bookstore. There was nothing fancy about it, just brown with black letters engraved on it. But Mark had struggled the last few days since Kevin's funeral, and she knew he needed the message on it: "My peace I give you."

The fact that she'd purchased it for 50 percent off and with the miscellaneous cash she'd allowed herself for this pay period made the gift even better. She hadn't felt the freedom of not purchasing every small item she wanted in a long time. And she loved it.

She pushed open the bank's front door as an older lady was walking out of an office on her left. The woman smiled. "You must be Zoey."

Taken aback, Zoey frowned. "I am."

The woman pointed to Zoey's head. "It's that beautiful red hair, dear. Mark loves it." She extended her hand. "I'm Betty Grimes, the bank manager."

Pleasure coursed through her at the thought that Mark had mentioned her to his manager. He'd talked about the kind lady he worked for, and she was thrilled he'd shared their budding relationship with her. Zoey pulled off her mittens and shook Betty's hand. "It's a pleasure to meet you."

She pointed toward a door on her right. "Mark's in his office. I know he'll be glad to see you."

Zoey could see through the glass walls that he didn't have a customer with him. His back was turned and he hadn't seen her yet, so she slowly pushed the door all the way open. "Hey, Mark."

He turned to face her. His eyebrows rose and his lips bowed into one of the biggest smiles she'd seen. "I'm glad you're here." He stood and walked to her, embracing her in a teddy bear hug. Her feelings for him seemed to be growing faster than in any other relationship she'd had, and yet he still hadn't kissed her. With each hug, each handhold, she longed for him to touch his lips to hers. *It hasn't been that long. We've only known each other a few months, only considered officially dating a week ago.*

But it seemed longer to her. She already felt connected with him, already felt confirmed that he was God's choice for her. She'd done the "dating thing" all wrong in the past, following her will and wants instead of God's plan for her. Now she didn't want to play games. She was nearing graduation, about to get a job in her field, and she wanted to settle down with the right man. With Mark.

Whoa, that's some heavy thinking, she inwardly chastised herself. *Don't shift the impulsivity from shopping to marriage.* The thought caused Zoey to pause. She'd never realized how quick she was to grab at things, but it was as true as God's Word. Taking a deep breath, she allowed herself to enjoy Mark's hug.

She released him and pulled her small gift from her coat pocket. "I got you a little something."

He raised his eyebrows.

"With cash."

He laughed and took the gift from her hand.

"It's just a little reminder that God wants you to have peace." She took it back from him and set it on a stack of papers. "It's a paperweight."

"Thanks, Zoey." He grabbed her arms. "Let me introduce you to Betty."

"We've already met. She likes my hair."

A blush traipsed up his neck and along his jaw. Deciding to goad him a bit, she grinned. "She mentioned you like it, too."

He reached up and twirled a small strand that had fallen at her shoulder between his fingers. "I really do like it."

The intensity of those chocolate brown eyes was back, and again she wished the man would just lean down and kiss her already. She could make the first move. *But I don't want to; I want him to do it.*

Trying not to let out a long sigh or pass out under his gaze, Zoey fought to read what he was thinking. He bit the bottom of his lip when his gaze moved from her eyes to her mouth. *He's going to do it.*

She closed her eyes, awaiting his touch. Instead, she felt a gentle pressure at her forehead. She opened her eyes to see he'd turned away from her. He picked his keys up off the desk. "Are you ready?"

Warmth flooded Zoey's cheeks. She'd practically thrown her kiss at him and he didn't take it. Exasperated, she shoved her hands in her coat pockets and pulled out her mittens. "Sure. Let's go."

Mark watched Zoey as she shoved a forkful of salad into her mouth. He'd come so close to kissing her. He believed she'd wanted him to as well. But he didn't want to move too fast, didn't want to mess up.

He felt weak since Kevin's death. Raw and tender. God was drawing him closer, and Mark had spent more time in scripture over the last few days than he had in months. Physically, he longed to hold Zoey, to claim her lips against his, but his mind knew he'd gone too far in the past, and though it had been years, he didn't want to make the same mistake with Zoey.

At some point he would tell her what he was like before he accepted Christ into his life. He had been every bit as cocky as Kevin, maybe more so. It was the reason Mark prayed for the man daily and also why he had gotten so angry with his colleague. Mark read Kevin's actions and knew his intentions like he read the label of a cereal box and knew what was inside.

Guilt tried to wend its way back into Mark's heart. *My peace I give you.* The words on the paperweight Zoey had given him slipped into his mind. He breathed the meaning into his heart, allowing it to set up in his mind. *God, You want me to have peace about Kevin. I wasn't a perfect witness, wasn't even a good witness sometimes. But I wanted to be.*

He thought of the scripture where Paul admitted struggling with doing what he didn't want to do and not doing what he should do. The first time Mark had read it, he'd scratched his head in confusion. Now he understood Paul's inner dilemma to the depths of his being.

Mark focused on Zoey. She looked professional and yet so pretty in her dark navy skirt and jacket and baby blue silk blouse. A single strand of pearls hung from her neck, and two small pearls dropped from gold spheres in her earlobes. Her long red hair was pulled up on the sides with a matching clip. Light pink lipstick covered her lips, making him yearn once again to claim them against his own. "Have I mentioned that you look beautiful?"

"No." Zoey took a sip of her drink. "But I needed to hear that. Thanks."

"Nervous?"

"Very." She traced her fingers along the side of the plate. "I've wanted a job like this since I decided my major a couple of years ago."

"You want to pray about it?"

She nodded. "I would love that. I can't believe I didn't think of it before. The Bible tells us when two or more are gathered, He hears and answers our prayers."

She reached across the table and grabbed his hand. He twisted it around so that he could caress her palm with his thumb. Her hand was soft and felt perfect in his grasp.

He bowed his head, thanking God for Zoey and her faith in Him and her desire to be in His will. "Calm her nerves, Lord," he prayed. "Guide her through the interview, and if this is the place You have for her to work, may she find favor in the eyes of her interviewers."

He hesitated, feeling the Spirit's nudging to pray for them as a couple. For a moment he worried he would chase her off with the prayer, but his desire to stay in line with God's guidance took over and he continued, "Lord, in the past I've prayed for the woman You have for me. . . ."

He heard Zoey suck in her breath, and she wrapped her hands around his thumbs. He went on, "I care a lot about Zoey. I know You've placed her in my life. May You guide our relationship. May we follow Your lead. Amen."

Mark lifted his head and peeked up at Zoey. She stared at him with just a hint of tears pooling in her eyes. "Thanks, Mark."

❧

As Zoey waited for her interview to begin, she mulled Mark's prayer over in her mind. He was waiting to kiss her. She could hear it in his tone when he prayed and see it in his eyes once he'd finished. She decided she was okay with that. In fact, she felt respected and lifted up by his desire to put God first in their relationship. It was something she believed. A man and woman could know true, complete unity only with God as the center, but to hear the man she was falling for say it aloud—well, it nearly took her breath away and made her fall a little deeper for him.

Trying to focus on the interview, she looked around the small human resources office. Though clean and orderly, the rust- and blue-colored furnishings and light taupe walls were in desperate need of updating. The position she sought was with the oldest hospital in the Wilmington area, which didn't bother her at all. The furnishings may have been a bit on the ancient side, but the patient care was known throughout the city.

Her heartbeat quickened at the thought of working one-on-one with a young mother concerning her child's diet or with an older man who'd been recently diagnosed with a medical condition. She yearned to help others with their nutritional needs. Sometimes the smallest change in diet made the biggest difference in a person's physical well-being.

The director's office door opened and a small, balding, sixtyish man stepped out. "Are you Zoey Coyle?"

His voice sounded very much like Mickey Mouse's; he even crinkled his nose when he spoke. Zoey had to take deep breaths so that a nervous giggle wouldn't slip out. "I am."

"Come in."

He motioned her inside, and she stood and followed him into the room.

A tall, thin, middle-aged black woman stood and shook her hand. "Hello, I'm Vera Jeffries."

Zoey learned she was the director of food services. She then met a doctor and the administrator of the hospital. They quizzed her with one question after another, but Zoey found herself focusing on the woman who would be her direct authority. The lady's expressions were firm but kind, and Zoey couldn't help but believe the woman would be terrific to work for.

"I have one last question." Ms. Jeffries leaned forward in her seat. "What made you decide to become a dietician?"

Zoey hesitated. How did she explain without telling more than she wanted? Her initial yearning to learn about foods and how they could and should be used to help the body came after Micah was born. Her poor boy struggled each time he ate, pushing his little legs against his belly as he cried out in pain. He'd drink formula and then spit up; then he'd cry; then he'd spit up some more.

It took several weeks of switching formulas, trying them for a few days, then switching again until they finally learned he was not only lactose intolerant, but also allergic to soy. Cam and Sadie had to buy a special formula for her son, and his belly settled down as soon as the other formulas were out of his system. He was the first living proof she'd witnessed of the smallest of dietary changes making the biggest difference in a person's life. Micah went from hurting and crying to resting and cooing.

Not too long after his birth, she'd also had the opportunity to go on a mission trip to South America. The plight of one family in particular would remain etched in her mind for the rest of her life. The day her group arrived, a young woman buried her infant daughter. Bacteria from unclean water and unsanitary conditions had permeated the baby's body until she didn't have the strength to fight back. It had been the most heart-wrenching experience—especially after having just given birth to Micah—that Zoey had ever witnessed. After that, she became a sponsor of that family.

The memory made her shudder. They weren't the only ones living in deprived conditions. When she saw how sick the people were due to bad water and limited food supplies, something in her just clicked and she knew she wanted to help people eat better.

Weighing her words, she looked at Ms. Jeffries then at the other interviewers. "The first time I knew I wanted to work as a dietician was when. . ." She paused. How should she describe Micah without saying he was her son? *God, I won't lie, but I don't feel it's necessary to share everything, either.* She cleared her throat.

"When a baby was born into our family not only lactose intolerant but also allergic to soy. The baby experienced several weeks of pain before his parents and the doctor were able to diagnose what was wrong." She shook away the memory, feeling it more deeply than someone who wasn't intimately connected to Micah. "It was a hard thing to observe."

Ms. Jeffries nodded. "That poor baby. It happens more often than you'd think, and it just takes time to figure out what will work best for their little digestive systems."

Zoey nodded. "Second was when I went on a mission trip."

The woman sat back in her chair. "Tell us about that."

As she began to share, Ms. Jeffries nodded in a way that let Zoey know she knew exactly what Zoey was talking about. She continued to share until the woman finally told them she'd spent ten years with her missionary parents in Africa. It was where she'd developed the desire to go into dietetics. Zoey's heart warmed as she felt a kindred spirit with the woman. When it was time to leave, Ms. Jeffries grabbed her hand. "I'll be in touch soon."

Zoey nodded. *God, I believe You led me to this place.*

Chapter 14

Mark eyed the chocolate chip cookies one of the customers had dropped off at the bank in celebration of Valentine's Day. It was Friday, his splurge day this week, but he and Zoey were planning to have dinner then stop by his mom's house. Their original board game night had been pushed back a couple of weeks because of Kevin's funeral and because Mark simply hadn't felt up to it. But God had remained faithful during this time, and Mark didn't want to disappoint his mom and sister by not being able to eat the goodies they'd inevitably fix for the occasion.

You don't need one, Mark.

He tried to look away, but it was like the treat had some kind of magnetic draw. His stomach growled for no reason. He knew he wasn't hungry; he'd had lunch only an hour ago. His feet seemed to move of their own accord toward the coffeepot and the counter that held the homemade goodies.

I'm like an addict drawn to my drug. I'm not even hungry, but I want one so bad.

He forced himself to look away. He thought of the fight he and Zoey had weeks ago when he confronted her about her excessive credit card use and she accused him of splurging a little more than he should.

And she was right, God. Mark urged his feet toward the restroom. He peered at his reflection in the mirror above the sink. *I've lost thirty-five pounds. My blood pressure is under control, and Dr. Carr is thinking of taking me off medication on a trial basis.*

Though they weren't dirty, he washed and dried his hands. The image of the plate of cookies popped into his mind. Knowing who baked them made the temptation even worse, because she made the best cookies in the world. *This is ridiculous. What's one cookie going to hurt?*

He rushed out of the bathroom and toward the counter. His cell phone vibrated in his pocket. He pulled it out. *Zoey.* He grinned as he flipped open the phone. "Hey."

"Hi. How's your day going?"

"Trying to keep myself from devouring a plate of homemade cookies."

"Don't do it." Zoey's voice sounded urgent. "Splurge night is tonight, and you've been doing so good. Think about it. I haven't spent any money on credit cards, and you haven't cheated with foods."

Mark laughed as he pivoted and walked away from the cookies and back toward his office. "I think God encouraged you to call right now."

"Probably so." Zoey popped her tongue. "Guess what else God did?"

Mark plopped down in his leather chair and leaned as far back as it would allow. "I don't know. What?"

"Got me that job at the hospital."

Mark leaned forward and smacked the top of his desk. "Zoey, that's wonderful. You had a feeling you'd get it."

"I really did." She must have opened the door because he heard the dinging of her car. "I'm heading into the gym. I'll see you later. No cookies."

Though she couldn't see him, he saluted the phone. "You got it." Shoving it back in his pocket, he turned toward his computer and started working on a loan he needed to finish before he left for the day.

God, I think You did have Zoey call me at that exact moment. He looked up at the ceiling, marveling that God was involved in the small and big things of his life. *Thanks.*

⁓

Zoey could hardly wait to visit Mark's mom and sister. The one time she'd met them, she could tell they'd be a lot of fun to be around. There was also no guessing what they'd tell her about Mark, and she thought that would be pretty funny, too.

Mark stopped in front of his mom's front door and waved his arms in front of her. "Whatever they say—"

Zoey laughed. "It will be fine."

Mark smacked his hands against his thighs. "Yeah. It will be fine for you. There's no telling what they'll say about me."

She shuffled her eyebrows. "I can't wait to know all your dark, sordid secrets."

Mark shook his head and rolled his eyes as he unlocked his mom's door then pushed it open. "Mom, we're here."

Before Zoey could fully step through the door, she was attacked by a younger, female version of Mark. The woman yanked off Zoey's mittens while an older woman pulled off her coat. "We're so glad you could come," his mom said.

"We're going to have the best time," Maddy added. "Mom and I have put every game we own out on the table. Tonight you get to pick." She clapped her hands together, a motion that took Zoey's thoughts back to seventh grade.

Zoey smiled, knowing the night would be carefree and entertaining. "Terrific. You all wouldn't happen to have Scattergories?"

"She's a word-game girl." Mark's mom, Sylvia, patted Maddy's forearm.

"We have it," Maddy answered.

"Oh no," Mark whined. "Not another woman to kick my behind at word games."

Zoey giggled as she followed Sylvia and Maddy to the dining area. Games of every size and shape were piled on one side, while several plates of veggies, fruits, sandwiches, crackers, and dips covered the other side. Zoey pointed at the food. "The food looks delicious. I won't have to eat for a week."

"Wait until you try Mom's homemade cheese dip." Mark grabbed a cracker, scooped a helping of the creamy cheese onto it, then popped it in his mouth. "Mmm. This is why I'm glad I skipped the cookies."

Sylvia moved the games onto the floor then set up Scattergories while Maddy, Mark, and Zoey filled their plates with snacks. "How many pounds have you lost, son?"

"The last time I weighed, it was thirty-five pounds. My goal is forty, and my last weigh-in is a month from Monday. For the bank competition, anyway."

"You look great, big brother." Maddy smacked at Mark's belly. "Feel them tight abs."

Mark pushed her away. "Don't feel them too hard, or I'll throw up on you."

Zoey chuckled as she sat down in one of the four chairs around the square table. She looked around the room. Most of the furnishings were older, but the house was clean and smelled like freshly baked brownies. Tonight would definitely be splurge night.

She grabbed a pen from the stack in the center of the table and doodled on the notepad to be sure it had ink in it. Maddy sat across from her. She tapped her pen against the wood. "So you're graduating this year?"

"Yeah. I just found out I got a job at the hospital where I applied, too."

Sylvia sat on her left. "That's great."

"That is exciting!" Maddy exclaimed. "What kind of job?"

"I'm going to be a dietician."

Mark added, "And she's going to be a great one." He pointed at his belly. "Look what a super job she's done on me."

Maddy rolled her eyes then winked at Zoey. "But he's not yet strong enough to take a little tummy tap from his baby sister."

"Tummy tap?" he bellowed. "You almost made me hurl all over the place. I hope you don't tummy tap Bruce like that."

Maddy crinkled her nose. "Bruce?"

"Bruce?" His mother added and gawked at Maddy.

Maddy shook her head. "Bruce and I are just friends." She looked at her mother. "I mean it. We really are."

Mark frowned. "Really? But I thought. . ."

Noting the tension that was quickly thickening in the room, Zoey chuckled and changed the subject. "Mark's been doing a good job. No cheating for a while now."

Mark's demeanor loosened, and he looked at Maddy and stuck out his tongue. She did the same.

"Would you two stop it?" Sylvia swatted at both of them.

Maddy raked her fingers through her long, sandy-colored hair then tied it up in a ponytail with the band she had around her wrist. Her small, fair features and bubbly personality made her seem years younger than Zoey. "I'm a year behind due to the leukemia. But you know," Maddy continued, "I wouldn't change it. I learned so much about my faith and about myself during that time."

She glanced at Mark, and Zoey knew that though she looked young, she'd physically experienced more than most people twice her age. With that experience came wisdom.

"I've learned to enjoy each moment. To be honest and up front." Maddy smiled and shrugged her shoulders as she turned her attention back toward Zoey. "To just be who I am."

"I'll toast to that." Sylvia lifted her soft drink toward the center of the table. Zoey laughed as she lifted hers and clinked cans with Mark's mom then Maddy.

When she reached for Mark's can, his gaze captured hers. He mouthed, "I need to talk to you later."

She nodded then placed her drink back on the table. Maddy's words weighed on Zoey's heart. She still hadn't told Mark about Micah. It wasn't fair to keep such a thing from the person she was falling in love with. *What if he already knows about Micah? What if he figured it out when I was showing him those pictures? Maybe he wants to talk to me because I haven't told him the full truth about myself.*

She tried to focus on the game when Sylvia rolled the letter dice and started the timer. Normally she was an excellent word-game player. But she couldn't stop thinking of how she should have been honest with Mark a week or more ago. Game after game she lost to Sylvia, then Maddy, then Maddy again, then Sylvia.

After a couple of hours, Mark threw down his notepad. "Ladies, I think you've beat me enough tonight."

Zoey scrunched her nose. "Me, too." She dropped her pen on the table. "I used to do better than that."

Reaching across the table, Maddy high-fived her mom. "Or maybe Mom and I are just that good."

Zoey lifted her index finger in the air. "Touché. You and Sylvia are definitely good."

Mark stood up and piled the women's plates on top of his. "I'll get the dishes."

Sylvia gingerly set a mug on top of his pile. "You're frootin' tootin' you will."

Zoey lifted her eyebrows, and Maddy leaned across the table. "It's the only slang term my mom uses. We have no idea where she came up with it. It's like a cross between the sound of a train and a bowl of Froot Loops."

Zoey laughed out loud, and Mark shook his head and motioned for her to join him in the kitchen. She picked up the empty soda cans. "I'll help Mark."

"Okay," Sylvia said. "We'll put away the games."

Zoey rinsed the cans then tossed them into the recycling bin while Mark rinsed off the dishes. She pulled a dishrag off a cabinet handle. "Your mom and sister are hilarious."

"Just a barrel of laughs."

"No, I mean it."

Mark turned off the water and wiped his hands on a towel. "Maddy did touch on something that I want to talk to you about." Mark folded his arms in front of his chest and leaned against the counter. "I want to kiss you, Zoey."

Warmth filled Zoey's cheeks, and her heart sped up. *Finally! God, I'm so ready for him to just kiss me already.*

"But I'm not going to."

The excitement streaming through her heart plunged to her feet and right out of her manicured toenails. "Okay."

"Not yet anyway." He turned away from her then looked up at the ceiling. "The truth is, I didn't know Christ in high school. I was a highly sought-after quarterback with a big ego, and I didn't always treat girls as I should have."

Zoey watched as Mark wrung his hands together. She reached for his hand. "Mark, we've all made mistakes."

He shook his head and pulled away. "No. I mean, yes, but. . ." He turned to face her. "Zoey, the things that made me sick about Kevin were just as true about me. I used girls for my own satisfaction and nothing else. I didn't care how they felt or what they wanted, just how they made me feel. That's why I couldn't stand for Kevin to be around you. I knew what he was thinking, what he wanted to do."

Surprised, Zoey sucked in the forwardness of his confession. Sudden jealousy slithered through her as she wondered about his high school years. Then her own mistakes flashed to the front of her mind. She needed to tell him about Micah, to let him know that she had made bad choices, that she had been selfish, only thinking of herself. That she had needed God's forgiveness and mercy just as much as he had. "Mark—"

"Listen." He captured a lock of her hair between his fingers. "When I became a Christian, I vowed never to act like that again, and I haven't. Then I met you, and you've set my emotions to spinning." He bent down and gently kissed the strand of hair. "And I won't disrespect you like that. I care about you. A lot."

Love filled her heart for the overgrown man. If he asked her to marry him that instant, she'd pack her bags and head to the church. But she had to be honest with him as well. "Mark, I need to tell you something."

He moved closer to her. "What?"

She gazed into his deep chocolate eyes. The love he felt for her was evident in those dark pools. She didn't want to do or say anything to hurt him or to make him care for her less. *Dear Jesus, help me be honest.*

Irrational fear raced through her, and a vision of Micah's dad running off when she told him she was pregnant passed through her mind. She didn't want to lose Mark. *But I have to tell him.*

"Mark, I. . ."

The words wouldn't come. They stuck to the back of her throat.

"What?"

She looked at him, mentally begging him not to run off as Micah's dad had. She blew out a breath. She couldn't say it. Not now. "Would you be willing to visit my parents next weekend?"

His face brightened, and he kissed her forehead. "Absolutely."

Chapter 15

Mark walked into the bank. He shrugged out of his coat and hung it on the rack. Though spring officially started in a week, April and May would pass before Wilmington warmed up to his liking. Twenty weeks. Their officewide competition had been going on for twenty weeks. At times it felt much longer, and yet the time had flown by. Anxious to find out the results of the "biggest loser" contest, he was the first in the office. He made his way to the counter, pulled out a coffee filter and coffee, and started the brew. *It doesn't matter to me if I win; I just want to know if I lost forty pounds.*

He walked back to the conference room. Someone had left the light on. He flicked off the light and a squeal and commotion sounded from inside the room.

What in the world? He turned the light back on and walked inside. His manager sat on the floor covered in balloons. "Betty? Are you all right? I didn't know you were in here."

"I'm okay." Betty laughed as she stood to her feet and placed a pair of scissors on the table. "I'm just glad I didn't stab myself." She pointed to the split bag tied to the ceiling light. "I figured we'd pull the string and drop a bunch of balloons on the winner. I was trying to make the string a bit shorter when you turned out the lights. I stabbed the bag, and the balloons and I went tumbling down."

A vision of Betty plunging the knife in her stomach popped into his mind and he shook away the horrible image. "I didn't think anyone was here. I didn't see your car outside."

"It's broken down. My husband had to drop me off this morning." She motioned toward the door. "Now go get me another trash bag from under the coffeepot and help me get these balloons in it. Remember, we weigh in at eight o'clock sharp."

Mark looked at his watch. It was 7:30. They didn't have much time to fill a bag with balloons and tie it to the ceiling as well as get the bank ready to be opened, but Betty had been so excited about the contest that Mark didn't have the heart to disappoint her.

Together they shoved the balloons into the bag. She tied it while he attached it to the light so that the string could be pulled and the balloons would

331

fall. With only a few minutes before business hours, they raced around getting computers, money, and other office equipment ready for the day.

He watched Betty happily scramble around the bank. She was as excited as he had ever seen her. Though he still wanted to make his goal, he sincerely hoped Betty was the overall victor.

Within moments the office buzzed with workers, ten of whom were participating in the competition. Betty clapped her hands. "Are we ready for weigh-in?"

"We sure are," the night custodian said. Mark noticed he'd lost a good amount of weight as well.

Barb called them up one at a time. Because several of the employees didn't want their actual weight told to the entire office, Barb wrote down their weight then used a calculator to figure out who'd lost the greatest percentage.

After several long, agonizing minutes, she lifted a piece of paper in her hand. "I have the results right here." Grinning from ear to ear, she pointed at each one who had participated. "One of you will take home this lovely treadmill." She motioned to the already-assembled machine that had been donated by a local department store.

Betty twisted in her spot. "Oh Barb, hurry up already."

Barb took a deep breath. "Okay, the winner is. . ." She pointed to the piece of paper. "And by the way, this person lost ten pounds more than his or her goal. I have been so proud of this person and his or her efforts to not only win the prize, but also get back into shape. I—"

"Barb," Betty whined.

The woman huffed then turned an exaggerated smile toward Mark's office manager. "The winner is Betty Grimes."

Betty's face lit up like Maddy's had when their dad purchased her first cell phone. Excitement for his manager welled within him. She'd worked hard and had wanted to win so badly. Mark waited until she stood next to Barb; he pulled the string, allowing the balloons to fall on top of her for the second time that morning.

He walked to her and wrapped her in a hug. "I'm so happy for you, Betty."

"I can't believe it, Mark." She pressed her palm against her cheek. "And I feel so much better with less weight. What was your final total?"

"I'm getting ready to find out." Mark turned to Barb. "What was my final weight?"

She flipped through the cards until she reached his. "Two hundred thirty-seven."

"Two hundred thirty-seven?"

Barb smiled and nudged him with her elbow. "Good job, Mark."

Two hundred thirty-seven! His goal had been two hundred forty. He'd lost a total of forty-three pounds. *Thank You, Jesus.* He pulled his phone out of his front pocket. He couldn't wait to tell Zoey.

❧

Zoey followed her sister into the church's gymnasium. She'd never attended this particular church, and she was overwhelmed at the size of it. Brittany walked past the basketball court, up the stairs, and past several classrooms until she finally stopped in front of a door. Brittany pushed a lock of hair behind her ear. "I'm really glad you agreed to come with me tonight."

"Of course. Why wouldn't I?"

"Well, I kind of have an ulterior motive." Brittany pulled the lock back out from behind her ear and shoved it into her mouth.

Zoey put her hands on her hips, recognizing her sister's nervous gesture. "Brittany. What are you up to?"

"Well. . ." Brittany pulled the hair out of her mouth and twirled it between her fingers. "There's this guy."

Zoey's mouth dropped. "You're kidding me."

Brittany dropped the hair and lifted both palms toward Zoey. "Listen. This guy is a Christian. It's obvious. You'll be able to tell right away. And, well. . ." She bounced on the balls of her feet.

"Well?"

"Well, I think he's going to ask me out, and I'm nervous about it, and I don't know what to say, and if he does, I want you to be with me." Brittany blew the words out in one breath.

Overwhelmed with thanksgiving, Zoey wrapped her arms around her sister. The Brittany she knew—the carefree, funny, even dramatic sister she'd grown up with—was returning. Zoey had feared Neil had squelched her sister's sweet spirit. *Why did I fear, Lord? You are greater than Neil Thurman.* "Of course I'll be here for you. Do you need me to get out my sister radar?"

Brittany laughed. "I'm telling you, Zoey, you'll like this one."

"Okay, then lead the way."

Brittany pushed her hair behind her shoulders then flattened the bright pink button-down shirt against her jeans. Whoever the mystery guy was, Zoey had no doubt that he had noticed her tall and beautiful sister.

Brittany opened the door. The chairs were set up in a semicircle. Zoey followed Brittany to two empty ones. As they sat down, Zoey scanned the room for possible beaus for Brittany. Several guys were sitting around the circle, but all of them seemed to be with a girl. A few minutes passed and more college students walked in, but she still couldn't pick out anyone whom Brittany might be interested in dating.

She leaned toward her sister. "Maybe he's not coming."

"He'll be here."

Zoey looked at her watch. It was almost time to start. The leader would be walking in at any minute. The door opened and a tall, thin man walked inside. He looked familiar, as if she knew him from somewhere, but Zoey couldn't quite put her finger on it. He looked at Zoey and recognition passed across his features. He pointed at her. "Zoey Coyle?"

She pursed her lips. "I know I know you, but I just can't place—"

He pointed to himself. "Logan Huff. I was in your mom's senior English class with you—for a while anyway." He grabbed her hand and shook it. "How are you doing? How's your mom?"

"Great. I'm great. She's great." She pointed to her little sister, who stood a good five inches taller than Zoey. "Did you know she was my sister?"

Logan glanced at Brittany. Crimson budded on his cheeks, but he didn't take his eyes from her. "Brittany, I didn't realize Ms. Coyle—I mean, Ms. Smith—was your mom."

Brittany clasped her hands together and rocked back on her heels. "Well, she was both that year, huh?"

Zoey tried to place Logan. Her senior year had been crazy with her mom getting married, then Zoey finding out she was pregnant and deciding to finish the year as a homeschooler. A memory of a tall, gangly guy who liked to hang around his mom's desk, talking to her all the time, paraded into her mind.

She snapped her fingers. "I remember you. You led the prayer group at school." She frowned. It was funny how she just suddenly remembered that. Her mom had encouraged her repeatedly to try it out, constantly telling her what a nice guy Logan Huff was.

"Yes, I did. I'll be graduating this May; then I'm going to start at seminary in the fall."

Zoey smiled. "That's wonderful. I graduate this May, too. I'm going to be a dietician. In fact, I just got a job."

"Good for you." Logan looked at the clock on the wall, then back at Zoey and Brittany. His gaze seemed to linger a bit longer on Brittany, and Zoey's heart warmed at the idea of he and Brittany getting to know each other better. She knew her mom would be thrilled, too.

"We've got to get started, but would you two like to go for a coffee after the study"—he gazed at Brittany again—"to catch up?"

Zoey's heart nearly burst with excitement for her sister. "I think we'd love that."

Both of them sat down, and Brittany leaned close to Zoey. Her voice was giddy as she whispered, "I told you you would like him."

Chapter 16

Mark peered out the windshield. He couldn't help but enjoy the serenity of the nature around him. He reached over and took Zoey's hand in his. She seemed more nervous than he did about his meeting her family. If her family was as crazy as his, he understood her concern. He squeezed her hand. "You know I'm going to love your family."

"Mmm-hmm."

Focusing on his surroundings, he noticed the land looked like snow-covered ocean waves, rolling high and low on each side. Large bare trees covered much of the ground without cluttering it. Occasionally they passed a large pond. Though frozen, the water brought back vivid memories of fishing with his dad.

Zoey pointed ahead. "There's Cam and Sadie's house." Mark spotted a stone house with a room built onto the side. The exterior walls of the room were made of nothing but windows. Several bushes and small trees lined the front of the house. He could imagine how beautiful the place looked in the spring when everything budded to life.

"You've got to be a little nervous." Zoey's voice was little more than a whisper, and her gaze stayed focused on the house ahead.

"A little, but not really. I'm excited to meet your family."

He'd known Zoey almost five months. They'd been dating for only two, but already Mark felt confident she was the woman he'd ask to be his wife. So many people he knew dated for a year or more before they got engaged, and normally he thought that was a good idea. But with Zoey, he was ready.

He pulled into the driveway, glancing at Zoey as he took the keys from the ignition. Her face had paled several shades. He couldn't imagine why she was so anxious about his meeting her family.

"Mom and Harold aren't here yet."

"That's okay. You can introduce me to your aunt and uncle, and don't you have a couple of cousins?"

She nodded, never looking at him. "Ellie and. . .Micah."

Mark snapped his fingers. "Yeah. He's the one with red hair like yours."

Zoey nodded. She clasped and unclasped her hands then picked at the skin on the side of her thumb. "I need to tell you something. I was going to tell you later, but maybe now is as good a time as any—"

"Zoey!" A small red-haired boy opened the front door and traipsed down the steps as fast as his little feet would take him. He didn't have a coat on.

A dark-haired woman raced out the front door behind him. "Micah, get back in here. Zoey will be in the house in just a minute."

Zoey swung open the door and scooped the boy in her arms before the dark-haired woman could catch him. "Hey, my little man."

Zoey kissed Micah's nose and cuddled him close to her. The resemblance between the cousins was uncanny. She tickled his chin and the little guy laughed, showing deep dimples in his cheeks, just like Zoey's.

"Let's get you inside, Micah." Zoey motioned for Mark to follow her.

He stepped out of the car and the dark-haired woman shook his hand. "Hi. I'm Sadie. It's a pleasure to meet you."

"Mark. I'm happy to meet you, too."

He followed Zoey's aunt into the house and was introduced to her uncle Cam and cousin Ellie. "Sadie, your daughter looks just like you." He walked to Zoey, who still held Micah, and rubbed the boy's hair. "So where'd you get your hair, little guy?"

Ellie laughed. "From Zoey, of course."

The room grew silent, and Mark watched as Cam, Sadie, and Zoey looked hesitantly at one another.

Ellie scratched her head then turned toward her mother. "I'm going to go put my special babies up before Rachel and Rebecca get here."

Cam chuckled. "Good idea."

Mark looked at Zoey and lifted his eyebrows. "Your little sisters, right?"

Zoey nodded. "God blessed Mom and Harold with beautiful little rascals."

Mark studied Zoey and Micah. She cared for this little cousin. A lot. Her attention almost never diverted to Ellie. Not that Zoey was unkind to the girl, but she simply didn't put Micah down. He seemed every bit as smitten with her. She held him tight as she plopped onto the couch. Mark sat beside her and Micah. "Was there something you were going to tell me, Zoey?"

She patted Micah's hair back and kissed his forehead. "Yes. As you can see, I'm pretty close to Micah—"

"We're here!" The front door slammed open and a small blond child walked into the room. A matching girl followed, only her hair seemed crooked on one side.

A frazzled yet attractive older version of Zoey, only with darker hair, walked behind the girls carrying a plate covered with aluminum foil. "Rachel, use your inside voice."

A large, gray-haired man followed behind her holding two more dishes, and another girl, this one a teenager, followed behind him.

Zoey sighed when she looked back at Mark. "That's my family."

A loud guffaw echoed through the room as Zoey's uncle Cam rubbed the head of the child whose hair was crooked. He looked at Harold. "Rachel get ahold of the scissors?"

Zoey's mom groaned. "Yes. Just before we left." She turned toward Mark and Zoey. "You must be Mark."

Mark stood and shook hands with Zoey's mother, Kelly, her stepfather, Harold, and her younger sister Candy. He tried to talk to the twin girls, but they didn't stay in one place long enough.

Her mother frowned. "Didn't Brittany come with you?"

Mark watched as Zoey's face lit up. She smiled so big he thought her dimples would disappear inside her cheeks. "She's coming on her own." Zoey rolled back on her heels. "With a date."

"It better not be Neil." Her stepfather folded his arms in front of his chest. The man was every bit as big as Mark, and Mark believed if he were Neil, he wouldn't want to mess with him. Linebacker for Wilmington or not. "I'll not have that boy step foot—"

"I agree," Cam added.

Zoey shook her head. "No, it's not Neil. It's a surprise."

Mark looked at Zoey. She hadn't told him that Brittany was dating someone. He was glad to hear it wasn't Neil. He also noticed Zoey still hadn't put Micah down. She'd hugged her mom, her stepdad, and all her sisters with Micah planted firmly on her hip.

"Surprise!"

Mark looked toward the door as yet another person headed inside the house. He wasn't used to this much family. Even when they visited his mom's siblings for a Christmas celebration, there were fewer people.

Her mom covered her mouth then spread her arms wide. "Logan Huff, I haven't seen you in years." She wrapped her arms around the tall, thin guy.

When Brittany followed behind, Mark realized this guy must be her date, and he must have been someone already approved by the family.

Zoey grabbed his shirt and pulled him close to her. "We still need to talk. After dinner, okay?"

Mark nodded. He had a feeling he knew what she was going to say.

❦

"You still haven't told him about Micah?"

Zoey stopped cutting the chocolate cake Sadie had made for dessert and looked at Brittany. "I haven't." She placed the knife on the counter and licked her fingertips. "It's not like I haven't tried. It seems like one thing or another happens and I don't get to tell him."

"If your feelings are as strong as I think they are," her mom said as she took small plates out of the cabinet and placed them on the counter, "then you need to tell him."

"I know it's scary." Sadie took the milk out of the refrigerator, shut the door, then put her arm around Zoey's shoulder and said, "But you gotta do it."

Tears swelled in Zoey's eyes. "What if he runs?"

Kelly huffed. "He won't run."

"Jamie did." For weeks, since she'd realized how much she cared for Mark, Zoey had been haunted by the expression on Micah's biological dad's face when she told him she was pregnant. As if it happened yesterday, she could still see him turn around and walk away.

"Micah is part of who you are." Sadie cupped Zoey's chin with her thumb and finger and stared into her eyes. "I know you wouldn't change that."

"Not even for a minute."

"Then go." Sadie released her chin and pointed toward the living room where Mark, Cam, Logan, and Harold were watching a basketball game.

Brittany giggled when a buzzer sounded from the television. "See, it's even halftime."

Kelly handed her two plates of chocolate cake. "And here's some dessert. You're all set."

"I think I'll wait on the dessert, Mom. But thanks." She exhaled a long breath and flattened her sweater against her jeans. "Okay, I'm going."

Zoey walked into the foyer and grabbed their coats off the rack then walked to the living area. "Hey, Mark, would you care to talk with me a minute?"

Mark's expression seemed so serious when he looked up at her. He smiled, but it was forced, and she feared what he would say when she told him the truth.

She pointed to the back door. "We could sit by the pond. It's frozen, but—"

Cam interrupted her. "Personally, it's my favorite spot."

"Sounds good." Mark took his coat from Zoey's grip and put it on. He opened the back door, allowing her to walk outside first.

They walked the thirty or so steps in silence until they reached her uncle's favorite bench. She sat down and he sat beside her. She watched as he clasped his hands then rubbed them together. "I suppose this is when you're going to tell me Micah is your son."

She sucked in her breath and looked up at him. "You knew?"

He shrugged. "Zoey, a person would have to be blind not to see how much the two of you look alike. And it's obvious he holds a very special place in your heart."

Zoey looked at her hands. She rubbed her finger against the pink gem on the nail tip of her ring finger. "I was scared to tell you. I was so young. So stupid. I didn't know what you would think of me."

"How old were you when you had him?"

"Eighteen. Barely. I got pregnant during my senior year of high school." She peered into Mark's eyes, praying she would still see love in those pools. "I made a lot of mistakes in high school, too. I guess the difference between you and me is that you weren't a Christian. I was. I was just fighting God with everything that was in me."

"Why?"

"My dad's death." She leaned back on the bench and stared at the frozen pond. "I didn't understand why God would take my dad."

"Do you know now?"

"No. I don't." Zoey gazed up at the clear, crisp sky. "But I know God is sovereign, even when I don't understand. I can trust Him."

She laughed as her own words smacked her in the face. She'd been so afraid Mark wouldn't want anything to do with her once he found out about Micah. God already knew how Mark would respond, and whatever happened, He was sovereign.

"What's so funny?"

Zoey looked at the confused expression on Mark's face. "I haven't told you because I've been so scared you'd run. Yet again, I wasn't trusting God."

Mark stared at her for several moments until her heart felt as if it were sinking into her stomach. "Are you gonna run?"

"I admit when we first walked in and I noticed how he clung to you and how you just wouldn't put him down—well, I started to figure that you were more than cousins. In my head I started doing the math."

He shifted his focus to the frozen pond, and Zoey thought her heart would freeze with fear. He looked back at her. "You were very young."

She bit her bottom lip and exhaled slowly. "I was barely out of high school when he was born."

"I'm surprised—and at first, I was a little hurt, confused about why you didn't tell me, taken aback that you've actually carried a baby for nine months—"

"Are you going to run?"

He touched her cheek with the back of his hand. A shiver traveled up her spine at his cold touch. "Why would I run from the woman I love?"

Zoey bit her bottom lip. "You love me?"

"Completely. God has restored both of us." Mark leaned closer to her. He cupped her chin and lifted her face. Before she could respond, Mark gently touched his lips to hers.

Surprised, she drew in a breath. Then he pressed his lips against hers again, this time with more urgency. She ran her fingers through his hair, realizing she'd never enjoyed a kiss more than she did at that moment.

When he finally released her, she blinked several times. "I thought you weren't going to kiss me."

The intensity she yearned to see returned to his deep chocolate eyes. "Zoey Coyle, I'm going to marry you."

"You are?"

"I am." He stood up then grabbed her hand until she stood facing him. "Is that okay with you?"

She nodded, "Uh-huh." She touched his lips with her fingertip. "Would you like to kiss me again?"

Mark laughed. "Once you tell me you love me."

Zoey rose to her tiptoes and threw her arms around his neck, squeezing him as tightly as she could. "I love you."

"That sounds good."

He bent his head down and captured her lips again. Zoey felt as if the heavens applauded and God sat on His throne nodding His approval. She'd prayed for the man God would give her, and He'd sent Mark. *Thank You, Jesus.*

Chapter 17

Mark peered in the mirror and tried to adjust his boutonniere. He hadn't been convinced about the Independence Day theme when Zoey first mentioned it, but the more she spoke of freedom from debt, freedom from food, and freedom from past mistakes, the more he realized he wanted to begin their marriage acknowledging those things while they freely pledged their lives together before God and their families.

"Are you ready?"

Mark turned at the sound of his sister's voice. His heart ached at her sunken cheeks and frail frame. The red bridesmaid dress hung from her shoulders like it would on a clothes hanger. Not even a week after he'd asked Zoey to marry him, Maddy discovered the cancer had returned. This time with a vengeance.

He made his way to his sister and gently wrapped his arms around her. "You look beautiful, Maddy."

"Thanks, big brother." Tears filled her eyes as she wrapped her bony arms around him. "I praise God He allowed me to see this day."

He fought the knot in the back of his throat as he tried to keep his own tears from falling.

Maddy pulled away from him. "Don't be sad, Mark. Please don't be sad." She adjusted his tie and smoothed the lapels of his tuxedo. "God has a purpose for all things, and I'm ready to see Jesus."

"But we're not ready."

"You have to be. It's His sovereign will."

Mark looked up at the ceiling as he remembered the night Zoey had told him about Micah. She'd fought God all through high school after her father's death, making several bad choices, until she finally accepted that God was sovereign.

He kissed the top of Maddy's head. "I know, sis."

She patted his chest. "Now, we will have no more of this sad stuff. This is the happiest day of your life." She smiled. "And I've seen your bride. She's beautiful."

Mark's heart swelled at the thought of seeing Zoey in her wedding gown. She wouldn't tell him anything about it, except that she'd chosen to wear white. Pure white. As a symbol that God had cleansed her and made her pure again. He couldn't have agreed more. He looked at his watch. "I'd better get out there."

Maddy hugged him one last time. "That's what I came for, to get you."

Mark walked into the sanctuary and stood beside his groomsmen. Logan leaned over and nudged his arm. "Are you ready?"

Mark straightened his jacket. "More ready than I've ever been in my life."

Though he knew it was a matter of minutes before his bride would be walking down the aisle to him, it seemed to take hours. He looked out at the crowd, spying several of his family and friends, as well as several people he'd never seen before in his life. Betty caught his eye and waved. He smiled and waved back at her.

The expectant gazes from the audience started to make him feel queasy, so he focused on the flowers and ribbons that Zoey and her mom, aunt, and sisters had arranged. Red and white were the predominant colors with just a smattering of blue. No one would guess the independence theme unless told. He liked that.

Even more so, he liked the way the white and the red ribbons blended together. It was by Christ's blood that they were made pure and white as snow, and that was the ultimate freedom.

Mark jumped when the music started. His heart raced and his chest tightened. At that moment, God's blessing and mercy overwhelmed him. He couldn't wait to take Zoey's hands and promise to love and cherish her for the rest of his life.

The sanctuary doors opened, and Zoey's cousin and junior bridesmaid, Ellie, walked down the aisle. Mark smiled at her and prayed to be patient as Zoey's sister Candy followed, then his sister, Maddy, then Zoey's aunt Sadie, and finally her maid of honor, Brittany. It felt like the entire city was going to walk down the aisle before his bride.

He sucked in his breath. If he remembered the rehearsal right, Zoey was next. Instead her twin sisters and Micah appeared in the door. Rachel nudged Rebecca, and Rebecca frowned and tried to shove Rachel. Rachel turned around and yelled, "Dad, Rebecca won't go."

Micah shrugged then walked dutifully down the aisle and took his place beside his father.

The audience chuckled as the girls continued to stand at the entrance until Harold appeared. He leaned over and whispered something to both girls. The twins intertwined fingers and stepped into the aisle at the same time. Mark couldn't help but smile as the girls sang, "Left, right, left, right," as they made their way to the front. Once they reached Mark, Rachel turned and hollered, "Dad, do we stop now?"

Mark leaned over. "You did good, girls."

Candy grabbed their hands and pulled them over to the side, and Rachel and Rebecca straightened their shoulders and grinned at the audience.

Mark sneaked a peek at Zoey's mom, Kelly, in the front row. Her hand covered her mouth, and her face blazed crimson.

The wedding march started, and Mark focused on the entrance again. The ushers closed the doors, and when they opened them again, his bride stood there on the arm of her stepdad.

Layers of lace and sparkles hugged her tiny frame to perfection. The mass of material at her feet glistened in the light. A veil covered her face, and Mark could hardly wait for her to reach him so he could peer into her beautiful eyes.

Finally, she stood just feet from him, and it took all his willpower not to grab her into his arms. The pastor spoke, but Mark didn't hear what he said.

Harold's voice boomed, "Her mother and I do." Then Harold lifted her veil and kissed her cheek.

Mark was speechless. Frozen in place. Zoey Coyle was about to become his wife. How he loved this woman. He blinked, and Logan nudged him forward.

He feared his heart would burst from his chest as he took her hand in his. "I love you," he whispered as they moved closer to the pastor.

"I love you, too."

❧

Zoey didn't know how a person could feel more blessed. The man she loved stood beside her, holding her hand, about to vow to spend the rest of his life with her. *God, You are too good to me.*

She looked into his eyes as the pastor asked Mark if he promised to love her, to cherish her, to honor her. The "I do" that slipped from his lips warmed her from the tip of her head to the soles of her feet.

When it was her turn to make the same promise, she prayed he could see to the depth of her soul how much she meant her answer. She loved him completely, but it was more than a feeling. It was a commitment. She looked forward to the opportunity to choose to love Mark day in and day out for the rest of their lives.

The pastor's voice rang out through the sanctuary again. "By the power vested in me and the State of Delaware, I now pronounce you husband and wife. You may kiss your bride."

Zoey's heart raced as Mark placed his hand against her cheek. "I love you, Zoey White."

She relished the sound of his last name alongside her first. "I love you, too."

She closed her eyes as he gently pressed his lips to hers then released her. She opened her eyes and looked at him. A smiled edged its way up her lips. "That's not good enough, Mr. White."

She wrapped her arms around his neck and pulled his lips back to hers. "You're my husband," she mouthed against his lips. "You can really kiss me now."

He chuckled as he squeezed her closer to him, kissing her with a mixture of gentleness and firmness. After several moments, he finally released her.

She blew out a long breath. "You can kiss me like that anytime you'd like, Mr. White."

"You promise?"

Before she could answer affirmatively, he pressed his lips to hers yet again. She'd never felt more blessed.

Epilogue

Mark set up a second card table in the living room. In a matter of minutes, almost the entire family would arrive to finish setting up for Kelly's surprise fiftieth birthday party. Mark hadn't been convinced it was the best of ideas with Zoey having just delivered their daughter four weeks ago, but everyone had outvoted him.

His five-year-old son, Tim, jerked on his shirt. "Dad, I put the napkins on the table like you said. What else can I do?"

Mark patted Zoey's father's namesake on the top of his carrot-colored head. "Go check on your brother."

"Okay."

"He was in my room the last I checked." Mark cringed at the thought of three-year-old Sam, his father's namesake, trying to play preschool games on the computer.

Mark walked into the kitchen, wending his way between Brittany, Sadie, and his mother until he finally reached Zoey. "What can I do to help now?"

She handed him their newest addition. "Take Maddy for me."

Mark walked into the living room and gently sat down in the recliner. He watched his sleeping infant. Their third child and first girl had been given his sister's name. Her full head of sandy-colored hair, just like Maddy's, felt like a small kiss from God.

Only three months after their wedding, his sister passed away. He'd never felt such sorrow. Not when his colleague Kevin died. Not when his dad died. He and Maddy had been close, even as children, long before she became sick. But God saw him through the pain. He used Zoey to help. Now in His immeasurable goodness, God had given him a little sandy-haired girl. He lifted her tiny face to his lips and pressed a soft kiss on her cheek.

"When are you going to let Uncle Logan hold her?" Mark's tall, thin brother-in-law stood over him. "You know I need the practice."

Mark chuckled. "Okay." He stood and placed Maddy in Logan's arms.

"You look wonderful, honey." A seven-months-pregnant Brittany walked up beside Logan and caressed Maddy's leg. "You'll make a terrific daddy."

"Where's my granddaughter?" His mother, Sylvia, walked into the room. He'd been so worried about her when Maddy died. His father's death had triggered depression and panic attacks in his mother, and she did struggle again after Maddy's death. Until Zoey had her first grandchild. It was as if God used Tim to lift his mother out of despair and show her she still had purpose in life. Now she watched the children so that Zoey could continue doing the dietician job she loved. His mother kissed the top of Maddy's head. She winked at Logan. "Looks like she's in good hands. I'll go find the boys."

Zoey walked into the room. "Mark, do you know where my cell phone is? I can't find it, and Candy and Brad aren't here yet, and I need to tell them where to park so Mom doesn't see their car. . . ."

Mark wrapped his arms around Zoey and kissed her lips. "Calm down." She bit the inside of her mouth and squinted at him. "Remember, you promised I could kiss you anytime I wanted."

A smile bowed her lips. "I remember."

He patted his pocket. "I'll call your sister and her fiancé on my cell phone."

"Okay." She turned and disappeared back into the kitchen.

Fifteen-year-old Ellie walked up to him. The teen was beautiful with her long, flowing brown hair and deep brown eyes. Mark knew Cam had a hard time keeping the high school boys away. "Do you care if the twins and Micah and I set up a board game in the basement?"

Mark shook his head. "Don't mind at all. Just be ready to come back upstairs when Kelly gets here."

Mark watched as Micah, the lone boy, followed Ellie and the twins to the basement. Micah could have easily been his own son. He looked so much like Tim and Sam, who favored their mother. And Mark did have a soft spot for his wife's first biological child. But he was also happy for Cam to have a son. After adopting three girls—ages three, four, and five—from Romania, as well as already having Ellie, Cam needed at least one other guy in the house.

"Candy's here," Sadie yelled from the other room.

Mark cringed. He'd forgotten to call her when Ellie asked about going to the basement.

"Don't worry, Zoey"—Mark could hear Candy's voice from the other room—"we parked around the corner. We got a flat and Brad had to change it, and. . ."

Mark's phone vibrated in his front pocket. He pulled it out and read the name on the front. "Everyone be quiet," he hollered. "It's Harold."

Silence wrapped the packed house as Mark clicked his phone on. Harold's hushed voice sounded over the line. "I didn't have to trick her. She asked me to stop by your house so she can see the baby. We'll be there in ten minutes."

"Who are you talking to?" Mark grinned as he heard Kelly's voice in the background.

"It's Mark." Harold's answer was muffled. "I'm telling him we're stopping by." He spoke back into the phone. "Ten minutes."

Mark clicked the phone off. "They'll be here in ten minutes."

The room flew into action as Cam called downstairs to get the kids. Mark's mother came out of one of the back bedrooms with the younger boys. Sadie and Cam, Candy and Brad, Brittany and Logan, and Kelly's parents all gathered together in the living area.

Zoey peeked out the front blinds. "I see them. Everyone ready?" She put her finger to her lips. "Quiet as a mouse until I open the door."

The doorbell rang, and Zoey opened the door. Choruses of "Surprise!" rang out through the room until Maddy squealed in protest.

Tears filled Kelly's eyes as she walked into the room and hugged each member of her family. Harold approached Mark and shook his hand. "We got her good."

Mark laughed as Harold made his way to Kelly, who was already holding and soothing Maddy. Mark watched the hustle and bustle of his family. Children romped everywhere. Adults talked and laughed. The noise was deafening. And he loved it.

When he'd met Zoey, his only concern was to lose enough weight that he wouldn't have to take blood pressure medicine, that he would be healthy. Eight years had passed since he met his wife, and he'd kept the weight off and still didn't need the medication.

But he'd gained more than he'd ever lost. He gained more extended family than he ever would have dreamed. He gained a wife and three beautiful children.

He sucked in a long breath. *God, when I walked into that gym, all I cared about was losing, but You had other plans. I did lose, but I also gained.*

I gained love.

A Letter to Our Readers

Dear Readers:

In order that we might better contribute to your reading enjoyment, we would appreciate you taking a few minutes to respond to the following questions. When completed, please return to the following: Fiction Editor, Barbour Publishing, Inc., P.O. Box 719, Uhrichsville, OH 44683.

1. Did you enjoy reading *Delaware Weddings* by Jennifer Johnson?
   ❑ Very much. I would like to see more books like this.
   ❑ Moderately—I would have enjoyed it more if _____
   _____
   _____

2. What influenced your decision to purchase this book?
   (Check those that apply.)
   ❑ Cover   ❑ Back cover copy   ❑ Title   ❑ Price
   ❑ Friends   ❑ Publicity   ❑ Other

3. Which story was your favorite?
   ❑ *Finding Home*   ❑ *For Better or Worse*
   ❑ *Gaining Love*

4. Please check your age range:
   ❑ Under 18   ❑ 18–24   ❑ 25–34
   ❑ 35–45   ❑ 46–55   ❑ Over 55

5. How many hours per week do you read? _____

Name _____

Occupation _____

Address _____

City_____ State _____ Zip _____

E-mail _____

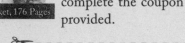